The Boy Who Sneaks In My Bedroom Window

Kirsty Moseley

Acknowledgements

I would like to say a huge thanks to the people who encouraged me to get here in the first place - the wonderful people that use Wattpad. Thanks to those people who have supported me with my writing for the last couple of years and gave me have the confidence to get to this point. Without your feedback and encouragement, my writing would be stuck inside a USB card getting dusty at the back of the drawer, never to see the light of day. So this book is dedicated to you awesome people who have followed me there.

However, the most thanks must go to my husband, Lee, who is always there when I need him and without which I would have never have started writing in the first place. Also, to my lovely family, who have only just found out that I've been writing stories, but as soon as they did have supported me wholeheartedly.

And thanks to you for reading this book, I hope you enjoy it.

Chapter 1

I sat on the kitchen counter, watching my mom make pasta bake; she was panicking slightly and kept glancing at the clock every couple of minutes. I knew why she did this, my dad was due home in exactly sixteen minutes and he liked dinner to be on the table as soon as he got in.

Jake wandered in, playing with his Spider-Man figures. "Mom, can I go play at Liam's?" he asked, giving her the puppy dog look.

She glanced at the clock again and shook her head quickly. "Not right now, Jakey. Dinner won't be long and we need to eat as a family." She flinched slightly as she spoke.

Jake's face fell, but he nodded and came to sit next to me. I immediately snatched the little man out of his hands and laughed as he gasped and snatched it back, smiling and rolling his eyes at me. He was a cute kid, with blond hair and grey eyes with brown flecks in them. He was my big brother, and as big brothers went, he was the best. He always looked after me at home and at school, made sure no one picked on me. The only one allowed to pick on me, as far as he was concerned, was him, and to a lesser extent his best friend Liam, who happened to live next door.

"So, Ambs, you need help with your homework?" he asked, nudging his shoulder into mine. Jake was ten, and was two years older than me, so he always helped with my school work

"Nope. I didn't get any." I smiled, swinging my legs as they dangled off of the counter.

"OK, kids, go set the table for me. You know how. Exactly right, OK?" Mom asked, sprinkling cheese on the pasta and putting it into the oven. Jake and I jumped down from the counter and grabbed the stuff, heading to the dining room.

My dad was very particular about everything, if everything wasn't exactly right, he got angry and no one ever wanted that. My mom always said that my dad had a stressful job. He always got easily annoyed if we did anything wrong. If you had heard of that saying *'Children should be seen and not heard',* well, my dad took that to another extreme. Instead, he liked *'Children shouldn't be seen or heard'*. At five thirty everyday he would come home, we would eat dinner straight away, and then Jake and I would be sent to our bedrooms, where we played quietly until seven thirty when we would have to go to bed.

I hated this time every day. Everything was fine until he came home, and then we all changed. Jake always went quiet and didn't smile. My mom got this look on her face, like fear or worry, and she would start rushing around plumping up the cushions on the sofa. I always just stood there and silently wished I could hide in my room and never come out.

Jake and I set the table quietly, and then sat down in silence, waiting for the click of the door to signal that he was home. I could feel my stomach fluttering, my hands starting to sweat as I prayed in my head that he'd had a good day and he would be normal tonight.

Sometimes, he would be in a *really* good mood and would hug and kiss me. Telling me what a special little girl I was, and how much he loved me. That was usually on a Sunday. My mom and Jake would go to hockey practice and I would be left home with my father. Those Sundays were the worst, but I didn't ever tell anyone about those times, or how he touched me and told me how pretty I was. I hated those days, and wished the weekends would never come. I would much rather it be a school day when we would only see him for dinnertime. I definitely preferred it when he looked at me with the angry eyes, than when he looks at me with the soft eyes. I don't like that at all, it made me feel uncomfortable, it always made my hands shake. Thankfully though, today was only Monday so I had almost a week before I would have to worry about that again.

A couple of minutes later he walked in. Jake shot me a look that told me to behave and he held my hand under the table. My father had blond hair, the same colour as Jake's. He had brown eyes, and was always frowning.

"Hello, kids," he said in his loud deep voice. A shudder tickled down my spine as he spoke. He set his briefcase on the side and took his seat at the head of the table. I tried not to show any reaction to him; actually, I tried not to move at all. It always seemed to be me that got everyone in trouble or that did something wrong. It always seemed to be me that made things worse for everyone. It never used to be like this, I used to be daddy's little girl, but since he started his job, three years ago, he changed. Our relationship with him changed completely. He still favoured me over Jake, but when he came home from work, it was like he wanted to pretend like Jake and I weren't there. The way he looked at Jake sometimes was like he was wishing he didn't exist, it made my stomach hurt to see him look at my brother like that.

"Hello, Dad," we both replied at the same time. Just then my mom came in carrying the pasta and a plate of garlic bread.

"This looks nice, Margaret," he said, giving her a smile. We all started eating in silence and I tried not to shift on my seat uncomfortably. "So, how was school, Jake?" he asked my brother.

Jake looked up nervously. "It was good, thank you. I tried out for the ice hockey team and Liam and I were," he started, but my father nodded, not listening.

"That's great, son," he interjected. "What about you, Amber?" he asked, turning his gaze on me.

Oh God! OK, be polite, don't ramble. "Good, thank you," I replied quietly.

"Speak up child!" he shouted.

I flinched at his tone, wondering if he was going to hit me, or maybe send me to bed with no dinner. "It was good, thank you," I repeated a little louder.

He frowned at me and then turned to my mom who was nervously wringing her hands together. "So, Margaret, what have you been doing today?" he asked, eating his food.

"Well, I went to the supermarket and I got that shampoo that you like, and then I did some ironing," my mom answered quickly. It sounded like a prepared answer, she always did that, had her answers ready so that she wouldn't say anything inappropriate to make him mad.

I reached out my hand for my drink, but I wasn't watching properly and knocked it over, spilling the contents over the table. Everyone's eyes snapped to my father, who jumped up from his chair. "Shit! Amber, you stupid little bitch!" he growled, grabbing the top of my arm and pulling me roughly from the table. Suddenly my back hit the wall, pain shot down my back and I bit my lip to stop from crying. Crying made it worse, he hated crying, he said only weak people cried. I saw him draw back his hand; he was going to hit me. I held my breath waiting for the blow, knowing that there was nothing I could do but take it, the same as always.

My brother jumped from his chair and threw himself at me, wrapping his arms around me tightly, covering me. His was back to

3

our father as he protected me. "Get the hell off of her, Jake! She needs to learn to be more careful!" my father shouted, grabbing hold of Jake by his clothes and throwing him to the floor. He slapped me across the face, sending me to the floor, then he turned to Jake and kicked him in the leg, making him moan. "You don't ever get in my way again, you little shit!" he shouted at Jake, while he was curled into a ball on the floor.

Silent tears were flowing down my face. I couldn't stand to see him hurt my brother; he was only trying to protect me. Jake always did that. Whenever I got into trouble, he would provoke my father so that he would take it out on him instead.

My father picked up his plate and drink and stormed into the lounge to finish his food, muttering something about us being 'the worst kids in the world' and 'how the hell did he get stuck with this life'.

I crawled over to my brother and wrapped my arms around him tightly, clinging to him as if my life depended on it. He groaned and pushed himself up to sitting, hugging me back, rubbing his hand across my stinging cheek, hissing through his teeth.

"I'm so sorry, Jake. I'm so sorry," I mumbled quietly, crying onto his shoulder.

He shook his head. "It's alright, Ambs. It's not your fault," he croaked, giving me a small smile and trying to get to his feet, groaning. I jumped to my feet and helped him up. I could hear movement so I glanced up to see that my mother was frantically clearing the table.

"Take your dinner to your rooms and eat, OK?" she instructed, kissing us both on the cheek. She needed to go to my father and do damage control, he would be in a temper in there from my mistake and she needed to calm him down before anything else happened. "I'll see you tomorrow morning. I love you both. Please be quiet, and whatever happens, stay in your rooms," she ordered, quickly kissing us again and handing us our half eaten dinners, before pushing us towards the back hallway.

We had a nice house, four bedrooms and it was all on one level. My father earned good money so we lived in a nice area, but I would rather the house was smaller so he wouldn't have to work in his job. Maybe then he would be like the old dad, taking us to the park and buying me toys and candy. Jake came to my room and we ate in silence, sitting on the floor near my bed. He held my hand tightly when we heard my father shouting at my mother from the lounge, something smashed, and I winced. This was entirely my

4

fault.

I started to sob so Jake wrapped his arm around my shoulder, squeezing gently. He always seemed so much older than me; he was so much more mature than I was. "It's OK. Everything's OK, Ambs. Don't worry," he cooed, stroking my hair. Once I had calmed down, and the shouting had stopped, we played snap cards for a little while.

When we were in the middle of the game, we heard stomping coming up the hallway, Jake stiffened as the footsteps went past my door. They didn't stop though, thank God. I let out the breath I didn't realise I was holding and looked at Jake, who smiled a small smile. "I'd better go to my room, it's after seven," he said looking at my alarm clock. "Lock your door. I'll see you in the morning," he said with a wink. He left the room and I watched him creep across the hall to his room, he turned back to me. "Lock your door, Ambs," he whispered, waiting there, watching me.

I shut my door and locked it quickly as he told me to. Putting my ear to the wood, I listened to make sure that Jake did the same to his. I ran back over to my bed and threw myself on it, crying silently. I couldn't stop, I was sobbing and sobbing. I had been stupid tonight and I got my brother hurt again! And probably my mother too, by the sound of the noises from the lounge.

Suddenly, there was a scratching, tapping noise on my window. I snapped my eyes up to see Liam outside, looking at me sadly. I got up and ran to the window unlocked it and slid it up quietly wondering what on earth he was doing here. Shouldn't he be at home?

"Liam, what are you doing here? You need to go, now!" I whisper yelled at him, shaking my head fiercely. But the stupid boy just climbed into my room through the window, closing it silently behind him.

I held my breath, looking at my door with wide eyes. If my father caught him here he would go crazy, he didn't like Liam to come over and play at our house, he always said he was too noisy. "Liam, get out!" I whispered, desperately trying to push him back towards the window. I winced, wondering what my dad would do if he had heard my window open and knew that Liam was here. Liam didn't budge; he just wrapped his arms around me tightly, and pulled me against his chest. I tried to push him away but he just held me tighter.

"It's OK," he whispered, stroking my hair. I started to cry again into his chest; thoughts of Jake being hurt earlier flooded my brain.

5

Liam was tall for his age; he was ten, the same as Jake. They were best friends, and had been since we moved in four years ago. He had chocolate brown hair, which he usually spiked up with too much gel, and light blue eyes that were like windows to his soul. When Liam looked at you it made you feel like you could fly. He was very cute; all my friends had crushes on him for some reason. Liam and I didn't get on at all though. He teased me all the time, he trips me, pulls my hair, and he has this annoying habit of calling me Angel for some reason, he's called me it since the moment he met me and it really makes me mad.

What on earth was he doing here now? And why was he hugging me? Maybe he thought this was Jake's room, maybe he went to the wrong window – but that couldn't be right, because Jake's room was on the other side of the hallway, his window faced onto the backyard.

I pulled back to look at him. For some reason he looked so sad; he had tears in his eyes as he just continued to hold me. He knew about my father, Jake had been covered in bruises once and had blurted out the truth to him. Jake and I had both begged him not to say anything though, and he never has.

"What are you doing here, Liam?" I whispered, wiping my face, but the tears continued to fall.

He pulled me onto the bed, rocking me gently, just like Jake always did when I cried. I looked at his chest and realised he was in Power Rangers shorts and t-shirt. I frowned, a little confused as to why he would be wearing that, it was freezing outside. Then it dawned on me that he was wearing his pyjamas. I looked at the clock to see it was almost half past eight. I'd been crying for over an hour.

"I saw you through the window. I just wanted to come and make sure you were alright," he whispered back, still hugging me tightly.

I looked back at the window. Liam's room was directly opposite mine and I could see into his room, which meant that he could see into mine. I bit my lip, oh God he'd seen me crying, I must look so weak to him. The only people I ever cried in front of were my mother and Jake.

"I'm OK. You need to go," I whispered, pushing him again, trying to get him off of my bed.

He just shook his head. "I'm not leaving until you stop crying," he stated, pulling me down so that we were now laying on my bed, facing each other. He had his arms wrapped around me so tightly

6

that I couldn't even squirm away. I felt safe and warm. I scooted even closer to him, pressing my whole body into his and sobbed on his chest.

I woke in the morning, still tightly wrapped in his arms; I gasped and looked at the clock 6:20 a.m. "Liam!" I whispered, shaking him.
— "Ahh, what, Mom?" he asked with his eyes shut.
"Shhhh!" I hissed, quickly covering his mouth before he spoke again. I can't believe we fell asleep, this is so bad.
His eyes snapped open and he looked at me, shocked, then looked around my room. "Oh no, did I fall asleep?" he whispered, sitting up and rubbing his hand through his hair, which was sticking up everywhere but actually looked better than when he has all that yucky gel in it.
"You need to go home, Liam. Quick!" I hissed, pushing him towards the window. He opened it and started to climb out but I grabbed his hand making him stop. He looked up at me a confused expression on his face. "Thanks," I whispered, smiling gratefully at him. I really needed that hug last night, that was probably the nicest thing Liam had ever done for me.
He smiled back. "You're welcome, Angel," he replied, smiling and climbing out.
I watched as he went through the hole in the fence and climbed back into his own window. He closed it and waved at me, I waved back and then went to go get dressed. The thought of Liam sneaking over here and being in the house when he wasn't allowed, made my stomach hurt. We were so lucky not to have gotten caught. I dreaded to think what would have happened if his parents had gone into his room in the night and saw his bed empty, or what would have happened if I hadn't have woken up early. I shuddered at the thought of what my father would do if he had walked in here to find Liam in the house at night-time.

Chapter 2

~ 8 years later ~

I woke to the familiar sensation of being crushed; I wriggled, pushing my shoulder backwards. Liam shifted his weight off of me slightly. He was spooning me from behind, breathing deeply into the back of my hair. His heavy arm was draped over me, pinning my arms to my chest, he was holding my hand tightly, our fingers interlaced, his leg was slung casually over mine. I could feel the usual 'morning glory' pushing against the small of my back.

I quickly silenced my phone alarm and elbowed him in the stomach. "Six o'clock," I mumbled sleepily, closing my eyes.

"Ten more minutes, Angel. I'm still tired," he murmured, pulling me tighter to his chest.

"Nope, no ten more minutes. Last time it turned into another hour, and Jake nearly caught you in here," I mumbled, elbowing him in the stomach again.

He moved his arm and pinned my hands down to the bed near my head, in a praying position. "Just ten more minutes, Angel," he whined. I sighed and closed my eyes again. There was no arguing with him when he was like this, I just didn't have the energy this time of the morning to get into a fight with him. We both drifted back to sleep, instantly.

"Amber, you had better already be up!" my brother shouted, banging on the door. I jerked up and so did Liam, it was almost half past seven.

"Er…. yeah I'm up already, Jake," I shouted back, glancing at Liam who was rubbing his face, looking a bit dazed.

"Good. I'm going to have breakfast. Hurry up will you. Liam's driving today so be ready to leave in thirty minutes," Jake called through the door, before stomping off down the hall.

"Jeez, Angel, why didn't you wake me up?" Liam accused, frowning.

I looked at him warningly and gave him my best death glare. "I did, you jerk! You said *ten more minutes* then pinned me to the bed to stop me from elbowing you!" I growled sarcastically, doing a bad impression of his voice.

He chuckled and pushed me back down on the bed, pinning my hands above my head and rolling on top of me. "Pinned you to the bed? Were you dreaming about me again, Angel? I could make that dream come true for you," he mocked, with his face inches from mine.

"Yeah, you wish! Now get the hell off me, Liam, and go get ready. You're driving today, apparently," I hissed, nodding to the window. He sighed and pushed himself off me, pulling on his jeans and t-shirt. He climbed out of the window, silently, sliding it back down after him. I walked over and locked it before heading in for the quickest shower ever.

Exactly twenty-six minutes later, I trudged into the kitchen with a frown, Liam was there leaning casually against the counter, eating *my* cereal. Damn it, every morning! His brown hair was messy in his usual *just got out of bed* look, which to be honest he did get out of bed and it looked just like that. All he ever did was run his hands through it a few times and add a bit of wax.

He looked the same as he did every morning, like a freaking supermodel. He wore low slung ripped jeans that showed his boxers a little, and always made the girls swoon. Today he wore a white t-shirt that showed off his perfect sculpted body, and an orange and grey checked short sleeve shirt over it, which he wore completely unbuttoned. His blue eyes were glittering with amusement as he looked at me.

"Running late this morning, Angel?" he asked with a smirk.

I gave him a drop dead look, making him chuckle. "Shut up, Liam! Why the hell are you eating *my* cereal again? Don't you have any food at home?" I asked, snatching the bowl from his hands and eating the contents. He just watched me with an amused smile.

Jake threw me a juice box. "You do look a little harassed this morning, Ambs. Everything OK?" he asked, looking at me a little concerned.

I glared at Liam again as he started to laugh. Of course I looked harassed, I had half an hour to get showered and dressed.

9

"Slept in," I muttered with a defeated sigh.

Jake had no idea that Liam slept in my room with me every night, if he did he would go crazy. Jake was very protective of me, he always had been, but he had gotten worse since my dad had left when I was thirteen. Well, I say *left*, but in reality Jake and Liam came home early from hockey one day to see that my father had beaten me senseless, and was trying to rape me. Jake had finally snapped, and he and Liam had beaten the crap out of him, almost killing him in the process. They had thrown him out of the house and told him that if he ever came back, they would kill him. He never came back though, that was three years ago.

A little while after that, my mom got a job with a huge electronics firm, she was the PA to the director and so she travelled a lot. She was gone twice as much as she was here, so we only saw her for about one week a month, if that. Jake was my only supervision, although at times it was more like I was the one taking care of him.

Liam was also very protective of me, but we still didn't get on - even though he had literally spent every single night wrapped around me in my bed for the last eight years. He had snuck back into my room the following night after seeing me crying again and we had ended up falling asleep again. After two weeks it had just became a regular thing. It wasn't something that we ever talked about, I just left my window unlocked and he let himself in once his parents had checked in on him to make sure he was asleep. We had never once been caught in eight years. We'd come close a couple of times though. A couple of years ago, Liam's mom had found his bed empty, but he took the hit and lied, saying he'd snuck out to a party and stayed at a friend's. No one suspected he was next door with me.

He still teased me like crazy and annoyed the life out of me just as much as he did when we were kids, but I always knew he would be there for me if I needed him. It was like he had a split personality. By day he would annoy me, making me crazy and angry all the time, and by night he would be the sweetest boy in the world and would cuddle me, making me feel safe and secure.

"You're looking hot today, Angel," Liam stated, with his trademark smirk, looking me up and down slowly, making me squirm.

Yeah, right! My brown hair was still damp because I didn't have time to dry it because of his stupid 'ten more minutes' so I had pulled it back into a messy bun. I had thrown on my dark blue skinny jeans and red V-neck top and pulled a black hoodie and black converse. I had added the bare minimum make up, as usual, just a little mascara to make my grey-green eyes stand out, and some clear lip gloss. I did not look hot. Freaking asshole! I gave him the finger and walked out to his car. Leaning against it, angrily, waiting for them to grace me with their presence.

The drive to school was the same as usual, they sat in the front talking about football and parties, and I sat in the back listening to my iPod, trying to ignore Liam smirking at me in the mirror. We pulled in to the school and the car was immediately swamped by people, the same as every morning. Liam and Jake were considered 'hot players' at our school. They were seniors and every girl's dream, the boys wanted to be friends with them, and the girls wanted to sleep with them.

Liam laughed as I cringed getting out of the car, trying to avoid the horde of skanks that banged into me because they were trying to throw themselves at him. One girl elbowed me on purpose. I looked at her in her tiny skirt that looked more like a belt and her top that showed her stomach, and grimaced. Jeez, she is such a ho!

"Holy crap, Jessica, did you know you left your skirt at home?" I asked with mock horror.

She scowled at me and I heard Liam and Jake laugh. "Whatev's, you do know that the emo look doesn't work for you, right?" she spat back.

I just laughed and walked off. It was usual for Jessica and I to have these sort of comments for each other. She had dated Liam for a little while, well, if by dating you mean having sex a few times, and then getting dropped. She still wasn't over it and wanted him back, much to his disgust.

"That wasn't nice, Angel." Liam laughed, as he caught up with me and threw an arm around my shoulder. He bent his head close to mine. "Sorry about this morning," he breathed in my ear, sending shivers down my spine. I elbowed him in the ribs making him chuckle and pull back. "And ignore Jessica, I think you rock the emo look," he added, with a flirty wink.

Jake slapped him on the back of the head. "Dude, that's my little sister!" he scolded angrily, pulling him off me. Liam just laughed and winked at me again, making me roll my eyes. Liam pulled away and walked straight up to what looked like his newest lay. He smiled at her seductively and she blushed as he immediately started flirting with her.

I found my friends who were practically eye shagging Jake and Liam with dreamy expressions. "Hey, Kate, Sean, Sarah," I chirped as I walked up to them.

"Hey, Ambs, did you ride in with hot piece of ass one and two again today?" Kate asked, staring after my brother as he walked off.

I laughed and shook my head. "Nope, just plain old Jake and Liam same as usual."

Kate sighed. "How the hell can you be unaffected by how freaking hot they are? I mean, you're so lucky to live with Jake! I would love to watch his hot ass walk around all day," she purred, fanning her face.

I pretended to gag. "Kate, that's my brother and his asshole friend! How on earth can you get past the man-whore behaviour? Both of them are jerks." I shrugged. I didn't get why, but every single girl in this school was in love with them. Jake was a great person, but he treated girls like objects, and Liam, well Liam was just an all-round jerk.

"They are the two best players on the hockey team and look like sex gods, and I wish I could *get past it*," she said suggestively, waggling her eyebrows with a grin, making me laugh. She hooked her arm through mine and pulled me towards our first class.

School was good, as usual; I was quite popular due to the fact that my brother and his best friend were the most wanted boys there. They looked after me of sorts, which basically meant that they warned all the guys to stay away from me, which actually suited me fine because I didn't want to date. Most of the girls wanted to be my friends so that they could get closer to my brother. The girlfriend wannabe's were pretty easy to see through though, mostly you could tell if they wanted an introduction, by what kind of clothes they were wearing - if they weren't wearing much then they were after my brother or Liam.

I loved my classes, I was quite popular amongst the teachers too because my grades never went below a B. I always did my homework, and was never tardy; I prided myself on it, though I wasn't a nerd. At lunchtime I was sat with my friends when I heard the usual whispers and giggles. Girls started checking their hair and fixing their make-up so I knew that my brother and his friends were arriving in the canteen. I sighed as Kate and Sarah started lusting over them as usual.

"Oh yay, hot piece of ass number one is coming over!" Sarah giggled, elbowing Kate in the ribs.

I rolled my eyes as a hand shot out from behind me stealing a handful of my fries. "Hey, Angel," Liam breathed down my neck.

I slapped his hand as he went to steal some more. "Liam, for goodness sake! Go buy your own food, you tight ass," I ranted, annoyed.

He laughed. "Oh you know you want to share with me," he replied, plopping down next to me on the bench, shoving me over with his hip.

"Liam, what do you want?" I asked with a sigh, moving my plate away from him.

He threw his arm around my shoulder. "I just wanted to visit with my girl. I know you've been missing me not seeing me all morning, and all," he said cockily.

My friends all sighed and stared at him longingly. "Will you get your man-whore arm off me, Liam, for goodness sake; I don't want to catch anything!" I scolded, shrugging him off.

He chuckled again. "Don't be like that, Angel. I just wanted to let you know I'll be driving you home today. Your brother has a date, so…." he trailed off, smirking at me.

Great, just great! He was driving me home. Fantastic. He always made the drive home as long as possible just to annoy the life out of me. Then, he insisted on waiting at my house until my brother came home, which meant that I had to cook for him too. Damn it, he is so annoying!

"That's great, Liam. Run along now, I'm sure you have some more STD's to spread around," I said, waving my hand in a buzz off gesture.

He laughed and kissed me on the cheek as he stood up. "Pretend all you want, Angel, we both know you'll be wanting me to sleep with you tonight." He winked at me slyly, giving what he said a double meaning, and I prayed no one else picked up on it.

"Of course I will, Liam, because I'm *so* in love with you." I sighed, rolling my eyes and rubbing my cheek where he kissed me.

"I love you, too." He smirked at me as he walked off to the same girl from this morning. He slipped his arm around her shoulder, his dirty, slutty lips lowered onto hers. I frowned and looked away back to my friends when he started making out with her in the middle of the canteen.

Kate and Sarah and half the girls in the canteen were staring after him lustfully. "Jeez, that guy is so freaking annoying! Why couldn't my brother choose a nice best friend, someone who isn't an arrogant, self-obsessed, asshole?" I ranted, throwing my hands up.

"Oh stop whining! Liam James just had his arm round you and kissed you on the cheek, I would give anything for those sweet lips to be on me," Sarah said dreamily, making me laugh.

13

"Whatever. Come on, let's get to our next class," I suggested as we picked up our trays and headed out.

After school I reluctantly made my way to the parking lot, where a smirking Liam was leaning against his car waiting for me. "Hey, beautiful." He winked at me flirtily and opened my door for me.

"Hello, Liam." I climbed into his car, already annoyed with his flirty ass, if Jake was here he would have slapped him for that one.

He climbed in next to me. "So then, Angel, I just need to stop by the store on the way back." He put the car into drive and pulled out of the parking lot.

"Great," I mumbled. I decided to look out of my window and ignore him; I was still annoyed with him for the whole *'ten more minutes'* thing this morning.

He pulled into the parking lot of the store a few minutes later. "Come on, Angel," he said, getting out. I just sat there and crossed my arms over my chest refusing to leave the car. He walked around the car and opened my door for me. "Come on, Angel," he repeated, holding his hand out for me.

"It doesn't take two of us to go in, Liam. I'll wait here," I countered. He reached into the car and picked me up easily, slinging me over his shoulder, laughing. He kicked the door shut and started walking towards the store. "Put me the hell down, asshole!" I shouted, slapping on his back.

He just laughed at my meager attempts to get down, and continued walking. Once we were in the store he finally set me on my feet. I looked around, embarrassed, checking to see if anyone saw that, but it appeared that they didn't. He reached out his hand and tucked some of my loose hair behind my ear, his fingers lingering on my cheek.

I slapped his hand away from my face and gave him and looked at him angrily. "That was so embarrassing!" I hissed.

"What's the problem? Most girls would love for me to do that to them," he replied, shrugging and walking off towards the magazines.

I stomped my foot, then blushed because I had just stomped like a child; thankfully Liam wasn't watching otherwise I would never hear the end of it. He grabbed a sports magazine and a bar of chocolate and stalked off towards the counter to pay.

I was happily flicking through Teen Vogue when two boys walked over to me. I stiffened. "Well hello there," one of them purred. I nodded in acknowledgement, and put the magazine back, walking off quickly to find Liam.

14

"Hey, where you going?" the other guy asked, grabbing my hand.

My heart started to race as I looked around, frantically. "I'm looking for my boyfriend," I lied, trying to sound confident.

"Boyfriend? I don't see a boyfriend," the other guy said, sneering at me. "How about we go somewhere and get to know each other better?" the boy who was holding my hand offered, pulling me towards him slightly.

I felt sick. Oh God, Liam, help me please! I know I'm pathetic but I just hate confrontation and I hate people touching me, especially people I don't know.

"Hey, Angel," Liam said, slinging his arm around my shoulder and glaring at the two guys who immediately dropped my hand and took a step back. I moved closer to Liam's side and pressed into him so hard that it actually hurt. "I hope you guys weren't hitting on my girl," he said casually, but I could hear the anger in the tone of his voice. Liam has always been protective of me; one time a boy pushed me over into a puddle when I was seven, and Liam went straight round to the boy's house and punched him in the face.

"No way, man. We were just talking, that's all," the guy lied, holding up his hands innocently.

"That's good. Come on then, Angel, let's get you home," Liam said, guiding me towards the door. Once we were outside, he turned to look at me. "You OK?" he asked, looking at me concerned. I was OK; my heart had stopped trying to break out of my chest as soon as I heard his voice.

I nodded and smiled at him gratefully. "Thanks," I muttered. He opened the car door and waited for me to climb in, before going around to his side again. Once he was in he tossed something into my lap, I looked down it was a bar of my favourite chocolate, I couldn't help but smile. "Thanks, Liam." He was always doing sweet things like buying me candy, it was just a shame he was such a man-whore jerk, otherwise he would probably be a nice guy.

When I got to my house, I went straight to work making a lasagne for dinner. Liam hovered around the kitchen behind me, making me feel violated as he stared at my body. "For goodness sake, Liam, my eyes are up here!" I cried angrily, pointing to my face.

He laughed. "Wow, you really are in a bad mood with me today, huh?" he teased, smirking.

"Yeah I am. I can't believe you this morning. I hate rushing around; I've looked and felt like shit all day," I cried acidly.

"I think you've looked hot all day," he countered, shrugging.

15

"Ugh, can you just stop talking to me? I'm not in the mood." I threw the food in the oven and started to chop up some salad.

"Fine, whatever." He shrugged again and came to stand next to me, helping me chop up the salad stuff. He was standing so close to me that I could feel the heat radiating from his body to mine, it was strangely calming.

"I'm gonna go start my homework. That lasagne will be done in half an hour; I suppose you're staying for dinner," I stated. It wasn't a question, I knew he would. I'm not sure whether Jake asked him to stay with me when he was out, but Liam always did anyway.

"Sure, seeing as you asked me so nicely." He smirked.

"I wasn't asking," I growled sarcastically as I turned to walk off.

He grabbed my hand and stepped closer to me, he was so close my chest was touching his, I could feel his breath blowing across my face. "Angel, I'm sorry about this morning, I am. Please stop being all bitchy to me, it doesn't suit you," he said quietly.

I took a deep breath and sighed. "OK, yeah, I'm sorry too. I guess I have been a bitch to you," I admitted, trying to look away from his beautiful sky blue eyes that felt like they were seeing my soul.

"So, am I forgiven?" he asked, smiling.

I liked this Liam, he was the one that looked after me, he was different when we were on our own. He gave me his adorable puppy dog face that I just couldn't say no to, and I felt my will to hate him crumble.

I laughed and rolled my eyes. "Whatever. I'm going to do my homework before dinner." I pulled out of his hold and walked away quickly.

That felt weird being close to him like that, I could still feel the tingles of electricity flowing through my hand where he had held it, I could still smell his sweet breath that had blown across my face. I had no idea what this weird atmosphere was in the kitchen; it was all just too confusing. I shook my head and pulled out my calculus homework, making a start on it at least.

After we had eaten dinner in silence, I finished my homework. It was only eight thirty so Liam decided to put on a movie. He put on The Final Destination and we sat on the couch watching it. I felt a little uncomfortable for some reason but I couldn't work out why. I was just sitting there the same as usual, but something felt off. I kept sneaking little glances in his direction; he was sitting there watching the movie, one leg folded over the other, his arm casually slung over the back of my chair.

Neither of us moved until the movie finished. I stifled a yawn. "I think I'm gonna go to bed, Liam, I'm pretty tired," I murmured, getting up and stretching like a cat. When I looked back to him, I noticed that he was watching me intently. I cleared my throat because he was still staring at me with a strange expression on his face.

"Oh right, yeah OK. I'll just shoot home then and I'll be back in like thirty minutes," he said, standing up to leave.

I followed him out and locked the door behind him, a little puzzled. Why was everything so tense and strange between us tonight? It's was probably just because I was so pissed off at him this morning it's made things a little awkward.

I changed quickly into a tank top and shorts, brushed my teeth and hair, then slipped into my bed. The bed felt cold and too big, just like it did every night. After about twenty minutes or so, I heard my window slide open and then closed again. Clothes dropped to the floor and then the bed dipped behind me.

"Hey, you asleep?" he whispered.

"No, not yet," I mumbled.

I lifted my head so he could put one of his arms under my neck. He pressed his chest right up against my back and wrapped his other arm around me, throwing his leg over mine. I heard him sigh as I wriggled to get closer to him, I loved Liam sleeping in with me, the bed didn't feel right without him there.

"What's wrong?" I asked, pulling his arms tighter around me and pressing my face into his arm, smelling his beautiful scent that was like nothing else in the world.

"Nothing, Angel. I'm just tired, that's all," he mumbled against the back of my head, pressing his lips into my hair.

"OK. Goodnight, Liam," I whispered, kissing his arm.

"Goodnight, Angel," he replied, kissing the back of my head.

Chapter 3

I woke at six o'clock as usual to my alarm going off; I silenced it and tried, unsuccessfully, to move away from Liam. I had my head on his chest and my leg draped over his crotch, which as usual, was already full of the 'morning glory' that happened to all boys. He had his hand on my knee, pinning my leg there, and his other arm wrapped tightly around my waist. As I tried to move, he tightened his hold, mumbling something in his sleep about not wanting to go to college anymore.

I moved my arm and tapped his stomach. "Six o'clock," I mumbled, tapping him again when he didn't open his eyes.

He groaned and tightened his grip, pulling me so that I was completely on top of him. I could feel his erection pressing between my legs. I gasped at the feel of it, it was strange but it actually felt nice. What the hell is wrong with me? This is Liam for goodness sake! I tried to wriggle free, but it just made us rub together in places that I would rather not think about my brother's man-whore of a best friend touching. My body started to tingle and I couldn't help the little moan that escaped from my lips. Oh my God, that actually feels nice!

"Liam!" I whisper yelled at him.

He snapped his eyes open and looked at me, shocked. His expression quickly changed to his trademark smirk, which I wanted to slap right off of his face. "Well good morning, Angel. Wow, this is a first," he purred, raising his eyebrows, his smile amused.

"Will you let go of me for goodness sake?" I whisper yelled at him. He raised his hands in a *I surrender* fashion and I quickly rolled off him. "It's six," I grumbled, frowning.

He rolled onto his side to look at me. "OK. Don't be mad at me all day today, please. I didn't know I did that, I'm sorry, Angel, OK?" he whispered, kissing my forehead before quickly climbing out of the

18

bed and throwing on his clothes.

"OK, whatever," I mumbled, settling into his warm spot in the bed where he had been laying.

"I'll see you later." He shot me a wink before climbing out of my window. Rolling over, I buried my face into his pillow, I could still smell him and it made me feel safe and calm. I drifted back to peaceful sleep for another hour.

After getting dressed more peacefully than yesterday, I stuck in my iPod and was happily dancing down the hallway when I spotted him eating my cereal *again.* Every freaking day! I sighed and stole the bowl out of his hands.

"Damn it, Liam, there's like four other cereals in the cupboard and you only eat mine! Why? Do you do it just to piss me off?" I asked, frowning, as I started munching on my breakfast.

"Good morning to you too, Angel," he said politely, with an amused smile on his face.

"Right, hi." I plopped down and eating my cereal as Jake came into the kitchen.

"Hey, guys, you nearly ready to go?" Jake asked, throwing us each a juice box as usual. We both nodded and headed to Liam's car.

As I got to school, Sean grabbed me and pulled me off for a talk. "What's up?" I asked, concerned. He actually looked a little frantic; his hair was all messy, it looked as if he had been pulling on it or running his hands through it a lot, his eyes were tight with stress.

"I forgot it's Terri's birthday tomorrow, and I have no idea what to get her!" he cried desperately, running his hands through his hair roughly, confirming my earlier suspicions about the style.

"Calm down, you've still got time. Now, what sort of thing does she like?" I asked, thinking about Terri and all the things I knew about her.

"I wanted to get her something she could keep, but I don't know what…." He closed his eyes, obviously panicking.

"Sean, calm down. How about some pretty earrings? She likes studs, right? You could also get her a new jewellery box or something to put them in," I suggested.

His face brightened. "Yeah! She has this like old crappy jewellery box at the moment. That's a great idea! Oh God thank you, Amber. I owe you big time! I'm gonna skip this morning so I can go get it," he said, smiling excitedly and running off, shouting bye over his shoulder. I walked back to the school and noticed that there was hardly anyone around.

Holy crap, am I late? I started to run down the hallway; I could see Liam and a couple of his friends walking towards me.

"Slow down, Angel, you'll fall," Liam shouted, smirking at me as I half ran, half walked towards him. As I passed him, he stuck his foot out tripping me up, but before I hit the floor he wrapped his arms tightly around my waist, and pulled me upright. "Jeez, Angel, I know I'm hot, but you don't need to fall at my feet," he teased, making all his friends laugh. I slapped him hard on the chest, glaring at him. "Oh I like it a bit rough, Angel, you know that," he said, smiling wickedly. He still hadn't let go of my waist, he stepped forward and pressed his body against mine, his hands slipped down to my ass. "Mmm nice," he purred in my ear.

I hated being touched; it brought back memories of my Father. I gasped, and before I could even think about what I was doing, I jerked my leg up and kneed him in the balls. He grunted and let go quickly, bending in half and clutching his groin.

"Keep your fucking hands off me!" I shouted, trying not to cry. I was struggling to breathe and my hands were shaking.

I turned to run away but he grabbed my hand and pulled me back to him. "Angel, I was only joking around, you know I'd never hurt you," he moaned. His voice cracked, it sounded like he was in pain.

He looked straight into my eyes; I could see the honesty in his deep blue watery eyes. He pulled me into a hug and put his lips to my neck, just where it joined my shoulder and breathed deeply through his nose, sending his hot breath blowing down my neck and back. This is what he always did to calm me down, when I would sob on his shoulder; this was the only thing that seemed to work. I could feel his heart beating fast against my chest, so I focused on matching my breathing to the pace of his. I breathed in his smell until I had calmed myself down. I pulled back and he was just looking at me, sorrow clear across his face.

"I'm sorry. I shouldn't have done that, Angel, I didn't think," he said apologetically.

I nodded and sniffed, wiping my face on my sleeve. "I'm sorry too. Did I hurt you?" I asked, wincing at the thought of how hard I had kneed him.

He shrugged. "I'm OK, it was my fault," he replied, bending to look into my eyes again. I looked away quickly, feeling uncomfortable. I had a feeling that when Liam looked into my eyes, he could see the real me, the one I tried to hide from everyone, the scared little girl that doesn't like people to touch her because it brought back memories of those Sundays and my father leading me over to the couch, guiding me to sit on his lap. When people touched me, even girls, my heart went into overdrive and I always start to feel sick. The only exceptions to this are my mom, Jake and Liam. This was the exact reason that I didn't date. The thought of someone touching me or kissing me, made my skin crawl.

I looked away from him and noticed that he had a big wet patch on his shoulder where I had been crying. I wiped it, frowning. "I ruined your shirt."

"I've got others, Angel, don't worry," he replied with an easy smile, it wasn't a smirk that he gave other people, it was a genuine smile, the ones I usually only get at night or when no one was around.

I looked around and realised we were alone in the hallway; I gasped in shock. "Where?" I muttered, looking up and down the hallway desperately.

"They went to class," he answered. "Come on, there's no point going in late, so let's go get a drink or something." He pulled me by the hand to the parking lot, towards his car.

"Liam, what? I can't skip class!" I cried, glancing around quickly to see if anyone noticed two students just waltzing out of the school.

He laughed. "Come on, Angel, one class won't hurt. You're already ten minutes late for it anyway." He opened the passenger door and gestured for me to get in.

I sighed and reluctantly climbed in. I didn't really mind spending time with Liam but it just depended which Liam would be here with me, the night or the day one. Night Liam was considerate, loving and thoughtful. Day Liam was a flirt, slut and a jerk. However, both night and day Liam's made me feel safe and protected. I turned to look at him while he was driving; he had a small smile on his face.

"What's up with you?" I asked, a bit concerned this was going to turn into some sort of joke that would end badly for me or embarrass me.

"What do you mean? I can't be happy that we're spending some time together?" he asked, giving me a flirty wink. I rolled my eyes and groaned. Great, an hour with daytime Liam is my worst nightmare.

I wasn't paying attention to where we were going so I was surprised when we pulled into the parking lot for the ice rink. He grinned and got out; I followed him with a frown. "What are we doing here?" I asked as he grabbed my hand and pulled me inside. Maybe they had a good café inside or something, that was the only reason I could think of for him to bring me here.

He ignored my question. "Hi, two please," he said to the lady behind the counter, handing over the money. I gasped; we were actually going to skate? I'd been skating a few times in my life but I was completely terrible at it.

"You need skate hire?" the lady asked with a friendly grin while her eyes roamed over Liam's body discreetly.

"Yeah, an eleven and a five please," he replied, winking at me. I frowned as he spoke, wondering how on earth he knew my shoe size.

She passed him two sets of skates and he grinned again, grabbing my hand and dragging me to the benches. I noticed that the lady didn't stop watching Liam as he walked away, and she actually licked her lips at his ass. I laughed and rolled my eyes at her, which made her blush and look away.

"What's so funny?" Liam asked, looking at me weirdly.

"You've got another fan," I stated, nodding my head towards the woman. "You just can't help yourself, can you?" I teased with a small smile.

"Don't worry, I'm not interested in her," he replied, looking at me as if trying to tell me something.

"Worried? Liam, I wasn't worried," I scoffed, as I rolled my eyes.

We changed into our skates and walked towards the ice. There was no one else on there, probably because it was only just after nine in the morning. "Why are we doing this? You know I can't skate." I winced, looking at the ice, starting to panic.

He laughed and pulled me onto the ice. "I know, I remember. Don't worry, I'll help you." Liam and my brother played Ice hockey for the school; Jake was the goal keeper and Liam the striker. They had both been skating for years, but I had never been able to do it. I loved to watch people skate and always wished I could learn, but I literally couldn't stand up. He grabbed both of my hands as I slipped and slid all over the place. He was skating backwards, facing me. "You're bending your ankles in slightly, Angel. Try to keep them straight, that's why you have no control," he said, looking at my feet.

I stood straighter and felt my feet slide out from under me; instantly, he grabbed me around the waist and leant backwards so that we both fell and I landed on top of him, his body breaking my fall. He chuckled under me; I pushed myself up to my knees so I was straddling him, then sat down next to him. I couldn't stand up so I

22

waited for him to get up first.

"OK, attempt number two." He smiled, pulling me to my feet easily. "Stand up straight and keep your feet still, I'll pull you around until you can get your balance." He kicked at my skates gently, nudging them to get them closer together as he gripped my hands tightly.

I managed to stay on my feet for a while before losing my balance. Again, he grabbed me around the waist and leant back so that I fell on top of him. "Why do you keep doing that?" I asked, pushing myself into a sitting position again. I could feel the ice starting to wet the back of my jeans, making me shiver.

"Doing what?" he asked, looking at me with a confused expression.

"Every time I start to fall, you make yourself fall backwards so I land on top of you. You're going to hurt yourself," I explained, frowning.

He shrugged. "Rather me than you," he mumbled under his breath, pulling me to my feet again. I just stared at him, shocked. Did he just say that? Maybe I heard him wrong. "You're getting better; you lasted at least a minute that last time," he teased with his trademark smirk.

OK, that's more like the Liam I know, I just heard him wrong that's all. "Ha ha. Well a minute is good for me. You know I can't do this," I grumbled, instantly falling again. He managed to just hold me up this time by grabbing my hips, pressing our bodies together and lifting me up off the ice so I could get my footing back from scratch. I felt my heart start to beat faster, but it wasn't because of the usual fear of someone touching me, it was something else that I couldn't understand. I blushed and looked away as he set me back on my feet.

"Why are you blushing?" he asked, frowning at me but looking amused at the same time.

"I'm not. It's just cold, that's all. My ass is frozen I think." I turned my hips to show him my wet jeans, rubbing my ass to try and get some of the cold away. I heard him pull in a deep breath and let it out as a sigh. I looked back up to see he was frowning with his eyes closed; it looked like he was in pain or something. "You OK?" I asked, still rubbing my behind. He nodded and shrugged out of his shirt, standing there in his low slung jeans and tight t-shirt that showed off his muscles underneath. He put his shirt around my waist and tied it into a knot at the front. "What are you doing? You'll get cold," I scolded, as I tried to untie the knot he'd made.

23

"Don't worry, I'll be fine. Next time I'll bring a spare sweater for your very fine ass," he replied, grabbing my hands and starting to pull me along again.

Next time? What does he mean, *next time*? Not that I'm not having a nice time, but being here with Liam, it was strange, it felt weird. Well, that wasn't strictly true; it actually felt *good,* which was what felt weird.

"That's it! You're getting it," he cooed - which of course made me lose my balance again. I pushed myself up off of him for the third time, laughing hysterically. OK, this really was fun, and it didn't hurt. Usually, when I had come skating with Jake and he had tried to teach me, he just let me fall on my butt all the time. Within about thirty minutes I was usually so bruised and sore that I just gave up. "See, now you're having fun." Liam laughed, brushing the ice crystals off of his back and grabbing me again. We managed to skate all the way round three times before I fell. I really was getting better.

After what seemed like forever, the rink was starting to get busier and my stomach was growling. I was falling less and less often, but I was still holding his hands in the death grip. "What's the time?" I asked casually as we stopped by the side of the rink. First period must be nearly over now, surely.

He pulled his cellphone out of his pocket and sucked in air through his pearly white teeth, making a hissing sound. OK, that didn't sound good, maybe we'd missed second period too.....

"Er Angel, school's gonna be over in an hour," he said, wincing.

"WHAT?" I almost screamed, making him flinch and causing me to lose my balance. He grabbed hold of me and slammed me into the plastic side of the rink to keep me up, his body pressed into me, his face inches from mine. My heart started to speed up again. He didn't move. He just stood there looking at me, staring into my eyes until I started to feel a little light-headed. Suddenly, I realised it was because I wasn't breathing, so I sucked in a ragged breath, which seemed to snap him out of it.

He pulled back but left his hands on my waist, holding me up. "We'd better get going. If your brother finds out I've been with you all day he'll cut my balls off," he said with mock horror, making me laugh.

Instead of holding my hands to help me to the side, he just continued to hold my waist, skating backwards as he pulled me along. I didn't really know what to do with my hands so I put them on his shoulders. As I started to fall again he bent down and scooped me into his arms, gripping one of his forearms firmly under my ass, and forced my thighs around his waist with the other hand as if I weighed nothing at all. He turned on the spot and skated forwards, fast. It was actually quite scary. I held my breath and threw my arms around his neck, pressing myself to him as tight as I could, probably choking the life out of him but he didn't complain. Instead of getting off of the exit like I was expecting, he skated around the whole rink again, before finally walking off of the ice and plopping me on the bench.

What the hell was that about? "Why'd you do that?" I asked, feeling a little uncomfortable that I just had my whole body completely wrapped around him. I don't know why I felt uncomfortable about it though, he wrapped his body round mine every night.

"Do what, Angel?" he asked, looking confused.

I pointed to the ice. "Skate around again. Why didn't you just get off at the exit? You skated past it," I explained, frowning, but smiling at the same time, this boy really is weird!

He looked slightly uncomfortable but then re-arranged his expression into his usual *'make all the girls melt'* smirk. "You slowed me down the whole time; I just wanted one lap where I could skate forwards, that's all." He shrugged.

Right, now I feel slightly guilty that I didn't let him have any fun, he had to baby me the whole time. "Liam, you go on and skate some. I'll sit here, it's fine. You should get to have some fun too," I suggested, giving him a half smile.

He grinned. "I had a lot of fun." His expression looked completely honest; he quickly stood up and went to get our shoes.

On the way back to school he pulled into the McDonalds drive thru. "Hi, can I help you?" the speaker asked.

"Er yeah, can I get a big mac meal with a coke, and a quarter pounder with cheese meal with a strawberry milkshake. Do you still do those cheese melt things?" Liam asked.

"Yeah we do," the speaker crackled.

He grinned. "Great, a pack of those too then please." I just stared at him, a little dumbfounded; he had just ordered my food and knew exactly what I would want. He turned back to me and frowned. "What are you looking at me like that for? Did I get it wrong?" he asked, looking slightly concerned and unrolling his window again, ready to change the order.

I shook my head, looking at him in amazement. "How did you

know what I have?"

He just laughed and looked at me like I'd said something stupid. "You always have the same, Angel. And you love those disgusting cheese things too but they don't do them all the time so...." he trailed off shrugged and pulled the car up to the next window.

OK, now he is starting to freak me out. First he knew my shoe size, now he knows what I order at McDonalds? I mean, I know I've probably been here with him and Jake a thousand times, but even Jake doesn't know what I order and he's my brother for goodness sake. Liam just laughed at me again and pulled the car into a space so we could eat.

He was chatting openly about some concert that he wanted to go and see and some movie that he saw last week about zombies that he said would have scared the life out of me. I was surprised how easy it was to talk to him; I'd never spent much time with him on my own before. He was usually always with Jake or a load of the boys, or had some skank draped all over him, or we were asleep. He was actually a really nice and funny guy. I couldn't help but wonder why he hides his awesome personality behind the man-whore, male chauvinistic pig attitude; he should be like this more often.

"Can I ask you something, Angel?" he asked, looking at me seriously. I nodded and finished the rest of my milkshake. "Don't you trust me? How could you think I would hurt you earlier at school? I've had plenty of opportunities to touch you or force you into something over the last eight years, haven't I? Why would you think I would hurt you?" he asked, looking really sad.

I dragged in a deep breath. "You just took me by surprise that's all; I do trust you, Liam, honestly. I know you wouldn't hurt me, it's just hard for me, I don't like people touching me." I frowned not really wanting to talk about it. No one ever pushed me for details of what used to go on with my father. I had refused to go to therapy after he left, my mom and Jake had tried to talk me into it, but I just didn't want anyone to know. I was ashamed of it and what he used to make me do. No one ever forced me to talk about it though, and I loved them even more for it.

Liam took my hand. "I know you don't, but I would never hurt you, I need you to know that," he said, rubbing circles in the back of my hand. He still looked really hurt and upset, I wanted to make him feel better but I didn't know how.

The only thing I could do was tell him the truth. "Liam, when people touch me my heart beats too fast and I start to feel sick and a little dizzy. It's not something I have control over. The only people that it doesn't happen with are my mom, Jake and you. I'm sorry if I upset you, but I can't help it. I do trust you, honestly."

This seemed to make him feel better and his face brightened. "OK good. Come on then, let's get back before your brother has the attack dogs out waiting to rip my throat out," he suggested, chuckling. I settled back into my seat as he drove us back to school. We pulled into the school parking lot five minutes before the final bell. "Er, Angel, it's probably best not to mention today to your brother. I'm not supposed to hang out with you," he said with a shrug.

Not supposed to hang out with me. What does that mean? "Why aren't you?" I asked, confused.

He looked me in the eyes again, making my heart speed up a fraction. "Jake said so. And on account of me being a *'disgusting man-whore'* as you so often put it. Apparently, I just want to tap your very fine ass," he said with a smirk. "Which I would be more than happy to do, if you want. You know, as payment for the skating lesson," he teased, winking at me.

I gasped. I had just spent the whole day with this boy and had a nice time and he can ruin the whole thing in one freaking sentence. "You really are a pig sometimes, you know that?" I growled as I stepped out of the car and slammed his door. I stomped off in the direction of the math building which is where I should be, at least I can make it look like I've been there if I walk from the right direction.

I saw Jake walking towards the car so I gave him a few minutes before I made my way up and got in the back like nothing had happened. "Hey, Ambs, you have a good day?" Jake asked as I got in the car.

"Actually yeah I did, right up until the very end when some slut hit on me," I answered with a shrug. Jake immediately slapped Liam around the back of the head.

"Ouch, shit, what was that for?" Liam asked, rubbing his head.

"For hitting on my little sister." Jake shrugged.

"How did you know it was me?" Liam whined. I giggled as Liam shot me a dirty look and pulled out my iPod.

"Ambs, seeing as its Friday......" Jake said, trailing off.

I groaned, knowing instantly what this was about. His weekly tradition. "No! No parties! Come on, Jake, seriously? Does it have to be at our house *every* week? There isn't even a game tonight! It's supposed to be an *after game* party. I mean, can't someone else have it for a week so I don't have to clear up after your drunken idiot

27

friends?" I asked, glaring at Liam again.

"Hey don't bring me into this; I always help to clear up!" Liam cried defensively.

I sighed, feeling defeated. My brother had a party at ours every Friday night because we had no parental supervision so it was easiest to have it at ours. I don't know why I bothered whining about it, it happened regardless of whether I liked it or not. I turned my iPod up to drown out the boys taking about girls they were going to screw, and looked out of the window. I could see Liam trying to make eye contact with me in the mirror but I just ignored him and pretended to be completely lost in song.

Chapter 4

After dinner Jake and Liam went out and got some drink for the party as usual. So I took the opportunity and had a nice long bath, making myself feel relaxed and refreshed. I groaned at the thought of another party. They didn't get too wild or anything like that, but they would last until two or three in the morning. On top of lack of sleep, there would always be a huge mess to clean up in the morning, both inside and out.

I sighed and wrapped myself in a towel. As I stepped out of the bathroom I walked straight into Liam. His hands shot out to steady me, grabbing my waist so I didn't fall over. I clutched the towel tighter around myself as I tried to calm my shocked heart.

"Wow, I like the outfit," he teased, looking me up and down, slowly. I slapped his hands away and stormed into my bedroom, slamming the door behind me.

As soon as the door closed, he knocked. "What, Liam?" I asked angrily, through the door.

"Angel, open the door please," he requested, trying the handle.

"Liam, will you just go away? Seriously, I'm not dressed!" I frowned and stomped my foot, then immediately blushed and thanked God that he was outside the door, so he hadn't seen that.

"Angel, please?" he begged.

I sighed; I hated it when he used that voice. That was his night-time voice and the one that I had trouble saying no to. I wrenched the door open and he smirked at me as he walked past me into my room. "Well, what the hell do you want?" I asked, going to my closet and pulling out my favourite t-shirt of Liam's that I'd found in the wash. I pulled it on, being careful to keep the towel wrapped tightly around me too.

"Hey, I was wondering where that shirt went," he said, nodding

29

at my t-shirt.

I gasped immediately thinking he was going to ask for it back. This was my favourite t-shirt. I put it on whenever I felt like being a slob and lounging around the house. "You're not getting it back, I love this shirt," I stated, waving my hand in a dismissive gesture.

"Fair enough. It looks better on you than it does me anyway," he replied, with a grin, looking at my legs.

I sighed in exasperation. Why does he have to be such a flirt? "Seriously, what do you want?" I repeated, walking over to the door and putting my hand on the handle, ready to kick his butt out if he makes anymore of his flirty comments.

"I just wanted to drop off my stuff. A change of clothes and things for tomorrow seeing as I'll be here tonight." He shrugged, dropping his bag onto my bed.

"And you couldn't just pass it to me, instead of coming in here?" I asked angrily. Why did he have to make everything so freaking difficult?

"I could have done, but then I would have missed the pleasure of seeing your hot ass in my t-shirt. I think it's very sexy when a girl wears her man's clothes," he purred, raking his eyes over me again, making me squirm.

I wrenched the door open and glared at him. "You're not my man, so get the hell out!" I shouted.

"Whatever you say, Angel." He chuckled and left, but not before shooting me his flirty wink.

I dried my hair off, straightening it and applied my make-up. Again, I hardly ever wear any make up, even to parties, so I just added a little silver eye shadow and some mascara, switching my clear lip gloss, for pink. I pulled on my midnight blue lacy bra and thong and looked through my closet. Parties at our house were always incredibly hot. Jake and Liam practically invited the whole school and everyone crammed in, making everyone sweaty and hot so I didn't want to go for too many layers. I pulled out a pair of black fairly short shorts and a tank top, then slipped on my silver long necklaces and my silver strappy sandals with a little heel. I looked myself over in the mirror. I had a nice figure, toned, not too skinny and curvy in all the right places. I took after my mom and had long legs and curvy hips, a small waist and slightly bigger than average breasts. I wasn't the most attractive girl around, but I was happy with myself and that was all that mattered to me.

Jake wouldn't like this outfit though. It probably showed way too much skin for his liking, even though I was completely covered -

and compared to the skanks he and Liam were used to hanging around with, I looked like a nun. I briefly considered changing before deciding against it, no it was hot and I wasn't going to get all sweaty and wear jeans just because he doesn't like guys to look his little sister.

I waited until the party was in full swing, that way Jake wouldn't tell me to go change like some little kid, in front of everyone. After about forty minutes, I made my way down the hall. There were people everywhere, some people were staggering around already. They must have only been drinking for an hour - it was pathetic. Jake spotted me and gave me the death glare that ran in the family, and pointed for me to go back to my room, mouthing the word *'change'* to me. I shook my head and smiled sweetly, mingling in with the party people, quickly heading to the other end of the lounge so he wouldn't know where I was.

"Hey, Sean," I chirped, as I spotted one of my best friends.

"Hey, girl. Wow, you are looking hot tonight," he said looking me over, but not in the usual perverted way guys had. Sean and I had been friends for a long time; he had been dating the same girl for the last two years and was completely besotted with her, which was really sweet.

"Thanks. You look good too," I replied, smiling and looking round for my other friends. "Where's Kate and Sarah?" I asked with a frown. They never missed these parties, for them it was just an excuse to drool over all the hot guys at school, mostly Jake and Liam.

"They're trying for your brother," he stated, pointing to the kitchen, and laughing.

I looked where he was pointing, to see Kate and Sarah both giggling uncontrollably at something that Jake had said. Kate had her hand on his arm, and Sarah was pressed against his side. Jake looked completely uninterested but he was enjoying the attention, the same as always. He was used to the two of them hanging on his every word, whenever they came to my house they would flirt with him shamelessly, and he would walk around topless, chuckling at their lustful expressions.

I rolled my eyes and turned my attention back to Sean. "No Terri tonight?" I asked, scanning the room for her.

Just then someone grabbed me from behind. I let out a little squeal before they spoke and I realised it was Liam. "You look incredible, but I definitely preferred the towel," he whispered seductively in my ear. His hot breath tickled down my neck, making

31

me shiver. I could smell the beer on his breath but he never got drunk, Jake did, but Liam always seemed to remain the one in control in case things got out of hand.

"Get bent," I growled, turning to walk away to the kitchen. I still hadn't even had a drink.

"Hey, Angel, wait for me!" he called, grabbing my hand as I continued to weave through the crowd of people making out and grinding against each other.

When I got to the kitchen I was greeted by the sight of a girl laying across my kitchen counter, and two boys doing shots off of her body. I recognised the girl easily by her red hair and lack of clothing. Jessica.

She let out an excited screech as we walked in. "Liam! Come on, baby, do a body shot," she purred seductively.

Liam gripped my hand tighter and gave me his puppy dog face, asking for help. I just laughed and pushed him towards her. "Go on, Liam, give the girl what she wants, you know you want to do a body shot," I teased, laughing hysterically at his horrified expression, which quickly turned to a smirk.

He gripped my hips and lifted me onto the counter, stepping between my legs so that our faces were inches apart. "Actually, I do. Lay down for me then, Angel." He gave me a wicked grin but I knew he was only messing around.

"Liam James, get your filthy man-whore hands off of me, now!" I whisper yelled at him, which made him chuckle again. He just shook his head, looking amused, and stepped back; pulling me easily from the counter and setting me back down onto my feet.

I grabbed a cup and poured myself three quarters of a cup of Vodka and added a splash of orange juice, downing a shot of vodka whist I was still pouring.

"Angel, take it easy there, alright?" He frowned at my drink shaking his head worriedly.

"No way. I'm getting wasted tonight, and there is no way I'm tidying up tomorrow." I patted his chest as I walked back to my friends.

After a couple of hours I was pretty drunk. I didn't really feel very steady on my feet, but I carried on dancing with my friends anyway. Liam was chatting to some of his team mates not too far away, and kept glancing at me.

"Seriously, Liam is checking you out!" Kate squealed in my ear for the fifth time.

"He is not! Don't be so stupid, Kate, he's probably just making sure I don't throw up, he's tidying up tomorrow." I finished my drink and dropped my cup on the carpet. Ha, let them clean that in the morning because I'm not! I started laughing hysterically, which made Kate giggle too. "I'm going to get another drink," I shouted over the music.

The song changed to 'She's like a star', by 'Taio Cruz' which is Liam's favourite song. I felt someone grab my hand and looked back to see Liam giving me a smile, one of the real ones, and I couldn't help but smile back. "Dance with me, Angel," he said, wrapping his arms around my waist.

I was so drunk at this point that I didn't even care that I was dancing with Liam; I wrapped my arms around him and tucked my face into his neck. He smelled amazing and I wondered what he would taste like if I licked him. Wait, did I just think about licking Liam like he was a Popsicle or something? I burst out laughing at my own idiocy. Liam pulled back slightly and gave me a *what the heck'* face, which just made it funnier. He rolled his eyes and shook his head, looking amused, as he pressed his body back to mine. The song wasn't really a slow song so we were swaying quite fast and half grinding against each other. I loved dancing, and he was really good at it, our bodies seemed to fit together perfectly.

I could feel him getting aroused but this didn't bother me. Liam has been pressing his erections on me since I was twelve and he was fourteen. He wakes up with one every day, and most of the time falls asleep with one too. I just ignore it. It was weird the first time it happened and really freaked me out. He had gone home that morning, so embarrassed that he'd almost cried, he'd spoken to his dad about it and then came back the next night and explained that it was normal for boys to have it happen because he was growing and it was all to do with hormones. I didn't know whether it was true or not, but I didn't have any reason to doubt him. It was embarrassing for us both for a month or so, then it was a joke for a while, now we just ignore it completely. He pulled back to look at me and gave me one of his nice smiles and my mouth pulled up into a smile in return. He actually looked really cute when he smiled like that, funny how I'd only just noticed and I'd known him forever.

Jake came out of nowhere. "Dude, what the fuck? That's my little sister!" he shouted at Liam, grabbing his shoulder and jerking him away from me.

"Jake man, seriously I was just dancing with her, that's her song!" Liam cried, looking really annoyed.

33

"Liam, you need to stay away from my sister, she's sixteen for fuck sake. You know what she's been through. She doesn't need guys like you chasing her around!" Jake shouted back, stepping forwards and getting in Liam's face. I could tell he was drunk by the slight touch of red to his ears, they were always the giveaway.

"I would never hurt her!" Liam growled, their chests almost touching.

"I don't give a shit! I said stay away!" Jake shouted.

I just shrugged and left them to it, I don't need to witness their fight, they'll be making up in a couple of minutes anyway, they always do. As I rounded the corner to the kitchen, I walked smack into a guy I didn't know. He was maybe a little older than me, probably Jake's age, he was really cute. He had black hair that was quite shaggy; it flicked across his forehead, and almost covered one of his brown eyes. He smiled and grabbed my waist steadying me as I swayed. I immediately flinched because he was touching me, but not too bad because the drink had numbed some of my brain.

"Well hello," he purred with his sexy voice.

"Hi." I smiled; he hadn't taken his hands from my waist so I took a step back to get some personal space.

"I'm Trent." He grinned; I noticed that when he smiled he had really cute little dimples.

"Amber," I replied, not looking away from his face, he really was handsome. I didn't recognise him from school. "You go to Penn State?" I asked, curious as to why I didn't know him if he was at the party.

He shook his head and smiled. "No. I'm actually just here to pick up my little sister, but I can't find her."

"Oh yeah? Who's your sister?" I asked frowning; someone has got one hot ass brother I can tell you!

"Jessica Sanders," he stated. I couldn't help my body's natural reaction; I turned my nose up a little, which made him laugh. "Not a big fan, huh?" he asked, still chuckling.

"Oh…. er…. sorry," I mumbled, looking at him apologetically and blushing like crazy. I can't believe I just made that face at his sister! What an idiot!

"Don't worry about it; I know she can be a pain in the ass."

"So, do you want me to help you find her?" I offered, looking round the kitchen for her. Nope, not in here. I giggled as I remembered that he'd just walked out of that room, so of course she wasn't there!

"Nah, she'll turn up. How about we get a drink instead?" he

34

suggested, nodding towards the drinks counter.

"Yeah OK, sure." I smiled as he grabbed two cups and a bottle of Jack Daniels.

We did a couple of shots of it and I was really trashed now. I leant against him heavily as we chatted and laughed about random stuff that didn't even really seem to make sense to me. Suddenly, he pushed me against the kitchen counter and pressed his body against mine. The familiar panic was starting to rise as my heart increased, he was inching his head forward towards mine. I felt my mouth go dry. Holy crap, he was going to kiss me! Did I want that? What if he puts his hands on me or something? My mind was spinning through the thoughts so fast that I couldn't even keep up with them all.

I gasped and pulled my head back, banging it on the cupboard behind me, hard enough to make my eyes water. He shook his head, looking at me a little bewildered and then crashed his lips to mine. I whimpered and pushed on his chest, trying to get him off, his hands went to the back of my neck holding me still and I felt him lick along my bottom lip. I clamped my mouth shut and pushed him as hard as I could, but he didn't budge. I started to freak out; I could literally feel the panic attack taking over as my heartbeat crashed in my ears.

The next thing I know, he was gone. I looked up, puzzled, to see Liam pinning him against the wall, his arm across the guys throat. He looked so angry that I actually started to feel sorry for the guy, who was now starting to turn a little red from not being able to breathe.

"You don't fucking touch her! What, you think you can just waltz in here and kiss her even though she plainly didn't want it?" Liam growled angrily.

I started to feel sick, literally, stared to feel sick. I jumped off the counter and staggered for my en-suite, where I threw up what felt like several liters of vodka. I groaned and flushed and moved back to sit down when I leant against someone's legs. I didn't freak out though, I could smell his aftershave, I knew it was Liam.

"You alright?" he asked, his voice sympathetic. But I couldn't answer; I just leant over the toilet and threw up another bottle of vodka. Wow, that's a waste of money! Liam, bless him, was rubbing my back in small circles and holding my hair up for me. After a few minutes I felt a lot better. "You want to go to bed?" he asked, looking at me concerned.

I nodded. "Yeah, I just want to brush my teeth." I struggled to get up off of the bathroom floor, but I was so uncoordinated that it didn't work out too well. Liam smiled and bent down, slipping his arms under me and picking me up easily as if I weighed nothing at all. He sat me on the unit next to the sink, grabbed my toothbrush and put on the toothpaste for me. I smiled weakly and brushed my teeth, making sure all of the alcohol taste was gone.

"Bed?" he asked, when I was done. I nodded and he picked me up bridal style and carried me back to my bedroom. He had pulled back the covers and was just about to put me in when I remembered I was still in my party clothes.

"Wait! I don't want to go to bed like this," I mumbled, looking down at my shorts and tank top, I still had my jewellery and shoes on too.

He nodded and set me down on my feet, but I could barely stand and I felt myself sway as my legs threatened to give out on me. Liam wrapped one arm around my waist, holding me up, and pulled my necklaces off. I got hold of the bottom of my top and pulled it over my head, getting tangled in the process and starting to laugh. I heard him sigh as he pushed me to make me sit on the bed and pulled my top off for me. When I looked up at him I saw he had an amused expression on his face. I laid back on the bed and unbuttoned my shorts, raising my hips as I pulled them down over my ass; he grabbed them and pulled them down slowly so I was laying there in my bra and thong. He held my legs up in the air as he took my sandals off one at a time.

"Nice," he purred, looking me over with his trademark smirk, but I didn't care, I just laid there, giggling, until my stomach lurched again.

"Oh no!" I gasped, trying to sit up, clamping a hand over my mouth. Quick as lightening, he picked me up again and carried me back to the bathroom, holding my hair again and rubbing my back while I emptied my stomach.

After I had brushed my teeth again, he slipped off his t-shirt and pulled it over my head. "There's another one to add to your t-shirt collection," he said with an easy smile, as he picked me up and carried me into my bed. He walked off towards the door. I thought he was going to leave and go back to the party, but he didn't, he just locked the door and slipped off his jeans, climbing into the bed next to me. I could still hear the party going on outside. Liam wrapped his arms around me and pulled me into his chest. I couldn't stop thinking about the guy kissing me in the kitchen. Before I knew what had happened, I'd started to cry.

"What's wrong, Angel?" he asked, looking at me concerned.

"That asshole stole my first kiss!" I wailed. Liam burst out

36

laughing and I felt even worse because of it. I can't believe he's laughing at me! "It's not funny, Liam! A girl's first kiss is important to her. Just because you're some kind of super slut who doesn't care, and probably doesn't remember his first kiss, doesn't mean that the little things aren't important!" I said angrily, slapping on his chest.

"Angel, calm down. He didn't steal your first kiss," he said sternly, looking right into my eyes making me feel weightless with his stupid bottomless, blue, man-whore eyes.

"What are you talking about? He did! He just kissed me and stole it," I croaked, a tear falling from my eye. He wiped it away with his thumb and shook his head.

"Yeah, he did just kiss you, but that wasn't your first kiss. I had that a long time ago," he explained, with a half-smile that made his face look beautiful. What the hell was he talking about? I'd never kissed him. I frowned, thinking back, trying to remember. "Remember when I hurt myself when I fell out of that tree in my front garden? I was thirteen and my freaking leg hurt so badly, and you asked what you could do to make the pain go away." He closed his eyes and shook his head at the memory, with a small smile playing at the corners of his lips.

I gasped. Oh my gosh, that's right! He'd asked me to kiss him and I did, well, twice actually. He said that it was still hurting and asked me to kiss him again. Right after that, Jake came out of the house and caught us; he punched Liam in the face for it. Oh crap, Liam had my first kiss! I wasn't sure how to feel about that, it was actually nice at the time. He was being really sweet that day; he was climbing the tree to get my ball that got stuck up there. I guess, that was a good thing, at least if Liam had my first kiss then it wasn't stolen by some asshole when I was drunk at a party.

I smiled at him and he smiled back. "That was my first kiss too, and I do remember it," he said softly, winking at me teasingly.

"Well you've had plenty more since then, and then some," I stated, meaning all of the girls that he had slept with.

"Yeah, but that was still the first and the best," he whispered, kissing the top of my head and pulling his arms tighter around me, tucking my head in the crook of his neck. We just laid there in silence; I didn't know what to say, so I just kept quiet.

After a little while I was still awake because of the noise coming from the party, it was only one o'clock so it would probably go on for at least another hour. I rolled over to see Liam watching me. "You can't sleep though that either, huh?" he asked, smiling.

I shook my head. "Why don't you go back out and make the

most of it. There's no point in us both laying here awake." I pulled away from him so he could get out of the bed.

He shook his head and pulled me back to his chest. "I'm fine where I am."

After about half an hour, I raised my head and looked at him, he was asleep and looked really peaceful and sweet, and not to mention hot. I'd never really looked at him that way. I knew he was gorgeous and had an awesome body, but it just never occurred to me to look at him in *that* way. My eyes moved to his chest. He really was incredible and had a perfect six pack. I reached out one finger and traced the lines of his muscles on his stomach, just wondering what they would feel like.

He shivered. "I'm feeling a little violated," he stated, making me jump and pull my hand away quickly.

I giggled because I'd gotten caught. "Welcome to my world, you make me feel like that all the time." I shrugged.

"I suppose I do, sorry," he said casually. Immediately I wondered why he wasn't like this all the time, if he was then I would probably be in love with him like every other girl was. "Hey, seeing as we can't get to sleep…. how about we play a game?" he suggested, sounding excited about it - which was probably a bad sign.

I rolled my eyes, trying not to imagine the stupid games that he would come up with. "I'm not playing a game with you, it'll be something like a strip game, or something else crude that's going to involve you seeing me naked," I said, frowning and pouting.

He laughed and gripped hold of my pouty bottom lip between his thumb and forefinger. "Don't pout, Angel. If the wind changes you'll get stuck like that," he joked, running his thumb along my lip. The movement made my mouth water for some reason. I stuck out my tongue and licked his thumb jokingly, expecting him to pull away and say it was disgusting. He didn't. Instead, he made a little moan in the back of his throat. The sound made something deep inside me tingle and throb.

He moved his head closer to mine and then stopped, his lips were a few millimeters away from mine. I couldn't breathe, my heart was racing, but it wasn't the usual fear I had, it was because I *wanted* him to kiss me. He seemed to be waiting for me to give him a sign to say it was OK. I gulped and closed the distance, pressing my lips to his lightly. It felt like he gave me a shock, my body started to tingle and throb with the need for him to touch me. A thousand butterflies seemed to take flight in my stomach, but I knew it wasn't because of the alcohol.

He responded immediately, pulling me closer to him and running his hands down my back. I raised my arms and put them around his neck, tangling my fingers into his silky brown hair. His lips were soft and fit perfectly with mine. He sucked lightly on my bottom lip and I opened my mouth, not really knowing what to expect from my first proper kiss. He slipped his tongue in my mouth and massaged mine slowly, tenderly. The taste of him was amazing as he explored my entire mouth; my whole body was burning, wanting more.

Suddenly, he pulled away making me whimper and wonder what I'd done wrong. He snapped his head up to my door, clamping his hand over my mouth to keep me quiet. "Shout that you're fine," he whispered. I looked at him confused.

"Amber! Open the door!" Jake shouted, banging loudly, making the door rattle slightly.

Liam nodded at me and took his hand off of my mouth. I cleared my throat quickly. "Jake, I'm fine. I'm tired so go away!" I shouted, trying to make my voice sound angry.

"Ambs, have you seen Liam?" Jake asked through the door. I looked at Liam, horrified. What on earth was I supposed to say to that? *Yeah, actually he's in the bed with me, half naked, and I've just had my tongue down his throat. Now can you go away, you're interrupting?* Yeah, I don't think that will go down too well with my brother!

"I went home," Liam whispered, nodding encouragingly.

"He said he was going home, Jake. Now go away," I shouted, biting my lip and hoping he'd buy it. Liam bent his head back down and touched his soft lips back to mine again, pulling away with a sigh when Jake shouted again.

"Amber, are you OK? You sound a little strange."

I giggled. "Yeah. I got sick so I came to bed, but I'm fine now. I'll see you in the morning. Oh and by the way, I'm not cleaning up, so you need to do it all," I teased, smiling at the thought of him cleaning the house on his own.

"Whatever, Ambs, we both know you'll help me anyway," Jake replied, laughing.

I looked back to Liam who smiled his beautiful smile at me and pressed his lips back to mine again, making the tingle come back instantly. His hand slid down my side slowly as he slipped his tongue back into my mouth, his taste exploding onto my taste buds. He reached the bottom of his t-shirt that I was wearing and slipped his hand underneath, running his hand up my thigh and touching my hip.

39

His fingers traced along the material of my thong, so that his hand was on my ass. My skin seemed to be burning wherever he touched me.

It was at that point that I snapped back into myself. This is way too fast. I pulled my head back and put my hand on top of his to stop him from moving it any further up my top.

"Oh sorry. Too fast, right?" he asked, looking a little guilty. I nodded, trying to get my breath back and calm my body down slightly. "That's OK, Angel. Let's just get some sleep then," he suggested, with a huge smile. He moved away from me slightly and laid on his back, pulling me tightly to his side.

I put my head on his chest and slung my leg over his and my arm across his waist; he reached down and took hold of my hand, intertwining out fingers. His lips grazed the top of my head and I closed my eyes, feeling happier than I had done for a long time. Just before I fell asleep I had a horrible feeling that this was a mistake that I would end up paying for tomorrow. I mean, I'd just made out with my brother's best friend, who is a total man-whore, and who only cares about himself.

Chapter 5

I woke in the morning with a pounding headache. My cellphone was ringing somewhere nearby. I stretched out my hand to get it, but I couldn't reach. I stretched a little further and managed to knock it onto the bed so I could answer it.

"Hello?" I yawned.

"Amber! Where the hell are you? We're supposed to be practicing," an angry male voice shouted. I winced away from the sound and tried to get up, but Liam was near enough laying on top of me. He was pinning me on my stomach, his arm and leg thrown over me, and he was using my back as a pillow. It was actually surprisingly comfortable.

"Justin?" I croaked, looking at my alarm clock, but the numbers were all blurry, I couldn't make it out. I squeezed my eyes shut then opened them to see that the time was now 8:42 a.m.

Shit!

"Yeah. Who the hell else do you think it's going be? You were supposed to be here at eight thirty, Amber. Are you coming or what?" he asked, clearly annoyed.

"Um, yeah, I'm on my way."

Liam groaned. "Tell him it's Saturday and I'm tired, Angel," he moaned into my back, making me giggle.

"Listen, Amber, kick that hot piece off ass out of your bed and get over here! We have a new routine, and you need to learn it," Justin said, sounding amused now, he'd obviously heard Liam. Justin was the only person that knew that Liam stayed with me, he didn't know the whole story as to why, but he knew that he did.

Liam drove me to my dance practice every Saturday, hungover or not. His two stipulations were that I buy lunch, and not tell my brother. Both of which were fine with me. Jake knew I danced but he

41

had never actually seen me do it, I had a feeling he wouldn't like it too much if he did. Liam and Justin got on really well, which actually really surprised me at first, because I wouldn't have thought that a macho ice hockey player could be friends with an openly gay guy who likes to wear something pink every day. Shows how much I know.

"I'll be there in a bit and I'll bring doughnuts to apologise, OK?" I offered sweetly. I didn't want him annoyed with me all morning; he would work me twice as hard.

He sighed. "Fine, just hurry up."

I wriggled a little and pushed my cellphone back onto the side. "Liam, Justin said I need to kick your hot ass out of my bed and get there, *fast.*" I chuckled.

He groaned and buried his face into my back. "Damn Saturdays are a pain in my ass," he muttered, rolling off of me onto his back. I turned my head to look at him; he was giving me his trademark smirk. "Your t-shirt's ridden up a bit there. Want me to get that for you?" he asked, looking down at my backside. I quickly shot my hands down to feel that his t-shirt that I was wearing, was now up bunched up around my waist, which meant he had a clear view of my ass in my thong. I didn't quite know where we stood after last night, but I think I had the right to tease him a little. It's not like he'd never seen me in my underwear before, he saw enough of me last night while I was being sick in just my underwear!

"No thanks. I got it." I climbed out of the bed and stripped off his t-shirt, throwing it in his face so I was just standing there in my bra and panties. "Thanks for the loan," I said with a smirk, walking seductively over to my closet, trying to find some sweatpants or something I could wear to dance in. I heard him gasp then moan quietly and I bit my lip to stop the giggle escaping. The bedsprings creaked; suddenly his hot breath was blowing down my neck, making my whole body break out in goosebumps.

"So, am I allowed to touch you today?" he asked quietly.

Jeez, is he really asking for my permission? I turned to face him; he was standing directly behind me in just his boxers, looking like a Greek God.

"Um…. I don't know…. do you want to?" I asked, a little unsure of myself. He'd been with so many girls before, all of them probably prettier than me, and that was my first real kiss last night for goodness sake, I bet I sucked royally at it! He nodded his head eagerly; his eyes were locked on mine. He wasn't even looking at my body even though I was almost naked, which made my stomach do a flip for some reason.

I stiffened as he lifted his hands, slowly, giving me the chance to stop him, he put them on my hips. His touch sent a hot flush to my skin and butterflies to my stomach. He pulled me forwards into his chest, and trailed his fingers slowly around to my back, one hand going up to grip the back of my neck lightly and the other hand tickling its way downwards. He brushed his hand over my ass gently, just once, before bringing it back up and putting it on the small of my back. His eyes didn't leave mine the whole time. Nervous excitement was racing through my body and I just stood there, frozen, not really knowing what I should do. This was all so totally new to me and I was almost scared to death, but in a good way somehow. He bent his head slowly and I felt my eyes widen, waiting for his soft lips to make contact with mine.

Just as they were about to connect, my cellphone rang again, making us both jump. We both looked at the phone, my heart was slowly returning to normal rate as I started to come back to reality. Liam was glaring at it, and I had the impression he was trying to shoot lasers out of his eyes to make it stop ringing. I giggled at his exasperated expression and pulled away from him to answer it. The caller ID said Justin, again.

I sighed and flipped it open. "I said I'm on my way!" I rolled my eyes even though I knew he couldn't see me.

"Just making sure you and your hot ass friend didn't go back to sleep," he said with a chuckle as he hung up. I snapped the phone shut and looked back at Liam; he was still watching me but was getting dressed at the same time. I smiled at him and he smiled back, it was nice. Usually, he changed into *asshole daytime Liam* in the morning, teasing me almost as soon as I wake up, but today he seems different. I couldn't help but wonder how long it would last. I went to my closet and grabbed a pair of black leggings and a tight white top that just covered my ass; I grabbed fresh underwear and went to the bathroom to change.

As I walked past him, he grabbed my hand, making me stop. "You know you have the sexiest ass in the world, right?" he whispered, just before he pressed his lips to mine lightly, sending what felt like lightning bolts around my body.

When he let go, I just looked at him a little shocked. "Yeah, I bet you say that to all the girls," I mumbled, shaking my head and walking into the bathroom closing the door and taking a deep breath.

What's wrong with me? Why was he making me feel like this? That's Liam for goodness sake! He's going to crush you and you're

43

going to end up like that damn slut Jessica, begging for his attention once he's finished and got what he wanted.

But he wouldn't do that to me. He'd spent every night with me for the last eight years. I needed him to be able to sleep, he kept my nightmares away. He wouldn't hurt me, would he? I trusted him to keep me safe, but could I trust him with my heart? I knew the answer to that was no, I couldn't, but for some reason I wanted to.

When I came out of the bathroom he was gone, but this wasn't surprising. I walked over to my window to lock it as usual and I saw a small white daisy on my window sill. I looked out of the window and smiled, these flowers grew just outside my window, he must have picked one for me when he climbed out, and left it there knowing I would see it when I locked the window. My heart skipped a beat and I smiled, a little confused. That was so unlike Liam to do something like that.

I sighed as I tucked the little flower into my pony tail and then headed to the kitchen, grabbing two juice boxes. I scribbled a note for Jake telling him that I had gone dancing, and that I would help him clear up later if he would let Kate and Sarah come over to watch a movie tonight. I knew he would go for it, this was my usual bribe for helping him clear up after his parties; they would come over to ours in the evening and he would pay for pizza and a movie. All he had to do was put up with two flirty girls hitting on him and Liam all night, as usually he came over too, if he didn't have a date.

I skipped out of the front door into his car that was already running outside my house. "Hey, got you this," I chirped, handing him the drink.

"Thanks. Got you this." He smiled, handing me a slice of toast.

I laughed. "That's a pretty good exchange," I said, smiling at him and eating it. "Oh, I need to go to Benny's and get doughnuts, if that's alright." I looked at him hopefully while we were driving down the high street. He nodded and was still beaming. "Why so happy today?" I asked, curious as to why he was smiling so much. He couldn't have had much sleep and I knew he was still tired, I could tell by his eyes.

"I had a good night last night that's all. I finally scored with some really hot chick that I've been after for a while." He winked at me, his genuine smile turning into his stupid smirk.

My insides felt like someone had shoved a chainsaw into my stomach. He had hooked up with someone, and then came on to me in the bed? That stupid jerk! I'd kissed him, a proper kiss too, and he had used some girl for sex before that! Ugh, the stupid man-whore, I *knew* I shouldn't have expected any different. I turned away so he couldn't see how hurt I was, and glared out of my window, refusing to cry. Crying is for the weak. I hardly ever let anyone see me cry, but some people we already behind the defences I had built so I couldn't help it. He pulled up outside Benny's and I jumped out, wanting to be away from him. I ordered twenty assorted doughnuts, heavy on the chocolate variety because they were my favourites.

When I got back in the car, Liam smiled. "Got enough there?" he joked, looking at the two huge boxes I had in my arms.

I just nodded and turned up the radio. "I like this song," I lied; I had no idea what it was but I just didn't want to talk to him.

He shot me a weird glance. "You hate rave music," he said, frowning and turning it down. Actually, he was right, I did hate that stuff, but I would rather that than talk to him, the lying slut.

We pulled up outside the studio where my crew rehearsed every Saturday, we were a street dancing crew and we were pretty good too. We had entered a dance battle last week against ten other crews in the area and had come second, winning over $1,000 in prize money. Not that we ever saw any of the money, it went straight on studio time and uniforms, music, and fliers or posters. I loved to dance, street dance was my favourite and anything that went with a hip hop beat got my vote. It had always been my dream since I was a little girl to have my own dance studio, maybe one day I'd get there, but it seemed highly unlikely.

"Hey, I'm so sorry guys, I overslept," I said, looking at them all apologetically as I walked in.

Justin pulled me into a big hug and I tried not to flinch away from him; he was wearing his trademark piece of pink in the form of a cap today. "That's OK. I'd oversleep too if I had that fine ass in my bed," he teased with a grin as he nodded over my shoulder towards Liam. I rolled my eyes and put the doughnuts on the table, grabbing a chocolate one quickly before they all went. I headed over to say hi to the other guys. There were eight of us in our crew, four girls and four guys. I was happily chatting with the guys, when Justin called everyone to start. "Seeing as we are already forty-five minutes late because someone couldn't drag her ass out of bed on time, we'd better get started," he stated, throwing me a mock glare and making me laugh.

We set to work on a new routine; it was hard and complicated and even had some pretty scary lifts. The worst one was where I was on Ricky's shoulders and had to flip off, turn in the air so I was facing backwards, then he would catch me as I fell down his body. Almost

45

instantly, I had to wrap my legs around his waist before leaning all the way back putting my arms on the floor and roll my body into the floor. Luckily we had mats, because it took over an hour for me to even land it once, and let me tell you, even landing on your back or stomach on a padded mat, hurts, *especially* if the muscled guy who is supposed to catch you, lands on top of you.

After about the twentieth attempt, I pushed Ricky off of me, laughing. I couldn't even get up I was so tired, sweat was running down my back. "OK, I officially give up on this for the day. My head hurts, my back hurts, my butt hurts, even my arms and legs hurt from holding on," I whined, laying like a starfish on the mat.

"Fine, it's nearly one anyway so we'd better clear the studio," Justin said, holding out his hand to help me up.

I shook my head, laughing. "Can't. I honestly can't move," I muttered, closing my eyes, trying to catch my breath. The next thing I know Liam was there, he grabbed hold of me and picked me up, throwing me over his shoulder as if I weighed nothing at all, and headed towards the girls shower room, laughing. "What the hell are you doing?" I cried, still annoyed at him for what he did to me last night.

"Helping you," he stated. I could tell he was smirking by his stupid sexy voice.

"Put me down!" I ordered, trying to wriggle free, but he just gripped me tighter.

I heard the shower turn on.

No! He wouldn't!

He did.

He stepped into the shower, putting me down under the spray, both of us getting completely soaked. I stood there, shocked. I had a change of clothes with me so it didn't really matter, but I didn't think that he did. Ha, stupid idiot, now he has to sit in his car in wet clothes!

He was laughing at me so I cupped my hands together and collected some water, throwing it at him; he laughed harder and gripped my waist, pressing himself to me under the shower. Water was running down his head, plastering his hair to his face, he looked sexy as hell. His clothes were slick to his body; I wanted to run my hands down him to feel the lines of his muscles. He bent his head forward and kissed me, wrapping his arms tightly around me and pushing me against the wall. He sucked lightly on my bottom lip and I gladly opened my mouth, eager to taste him again. He tasted even better today, probably because I was still half drunk when we kissed

46

last night so I couldn't appreciate it as much. His kissing was beautiful and was sending ripples of desire racing through my body.

Finally, he pulled away and we were both breathless. I looked into his eyes and I could see that they were dancing with excitement; I could also see something else that scared the life out of me because I knew I wasn't ready for that. I saw lust, plain and simple. Liam wanted my body badly. I gasped and pushed him back, stepping out of the shower quickly.

"Sorry, I shouldn't have done that. Too soon, right?" he asked, coming out of the shower and taking hold of my hand.

I turned back to look at him. I couldn't give him what he wanted; he could get that somewhere else. I mean, he was Liam James for goodness sake, he could have any girl he wanted, and he does! He already admitted he hooked up with someone last night before he kissed me. He was a player plain and simple and if I let him have my heart, he would break it, no doubt about it.

"Liam, what do you want from me?" I asked quietly, looking at my soaked sneakers.

He put his finger under my chin and lifted my face so I had to look at him. "Everything," he said simply.

My heart stopped, and then took off in a sprint at how sweet that sounded. Wait, it's just a line to get into your pants, Amber, calm down! "I can't give you that, not even close. Go find the skank that you hooked up with last night, I'm sure she's more than willing to do *everything* with you," I growled nastily, doing air quotes around the word everything, before storming off to get changed. My bag was already in here, I assume one of the girls put it in after seeing Liam and I in the shower making out. Damn it, that's embarrassing!

He grabbed my wrist and made me stop and look at him. "What skank are you talking about, Angel?" he asked, looking at me confused.

"The skank you screwed before you kissed me in bed! Damn it, Liam, you weren't even drunk and you've forgotten already? Wow, this one must have really meant something to you," I spat acidly.

He looked even more confused. "I didn't screw anyone last night, what are you talking about?" he asked, trying to pull me to him, but I stood my ground and wrenched my wrist out of his grasp, he didn't resist he just let me go; he knew I didn't like being restrained.

I gave him my death glare and grabbed my towel out of my bag, toweling off my dripping hair. I pulled the little daisy out of my ponytail and threw it at his feet. "Liam, you already told me in the car earlier that you fucked some chick you wanted, that's why you were

47

so happy," I growled. Was he seriously going to lie to me about it now?

Understanding crossed his face, his body seeming to visibly relax. "Actually, I never said I fucked anyone. What I actually said was that I finally scored with a really hot chick that I'd been after for a while," he stated, shrugging and smiling, as if this cleared everything up.

I shook my head, still angry. The wording didn't matter to me, it was all the same and I still felt betrayed and used. "Whatever, fucked, scored, it's all the same thing. You're a stupid freaking player and I can't believe I let you kiss me. Twice!" I cried. I could feel the tears threatening to come out, so I turned my back on him.

"You're misunderstanding what I meant!" he said desperately.

I span around to face him again. "Oh, I'm sorry! Explain please," I said sarcastically, waving my hand in a go ahead gesture.

"I was talking about you," he said quietly. I frowned, me? "I've been crazy about you since the first time I saw you, Angel, but your brother wouldn't let me anywhere near you. All this time it's only ever been you." He looked at the floor like a little lost boy and I couldn't breathe.

Did he really just say that? He liked me but Jake wouldn't let him near me? How could that be true? Anyway, he's a player who has sex with three or four different girls a week. How could it *only ever be me*? He's never even had a girlfriend, he just has dates!

He looked at me pleadingly, he was hurting I could tell by his face, but I didn't know what to do. If I took a chance I knew I would fall in love with him and there was a good chance he would break my heart into a million pieces, but I don't think I could stand to lose him. He had been a constant in my life and I needed him, probably more than I needed Jake. He stepped forward and took my face in his hands and bent his face to mine and kissed me, tenderly. I knew the decision had been made; this really wasn't something I could think through and reason out the pros and cons. When Liam kissed me, everything seemed right and whole, just like it should be. I kissed him back, wrapping my arms around him tightly, pressing into his chest.

He pulled away and grinned at me. "How about I buy lunch today, and we call it a date?" he suggested, looking at me shyly. I'd never seen Liam look shy or vulnerable in his life. The tender, pleading expression on his face was enough to set what felt like a hundred butterflies loose in my stomach.

I pretended to think about it for a few seconds and his face fell.

48

"OK," I finally agreed, smiling. He grinned happily before pulling me into another kiss that actually made me feel a little giddy.

He pulled out of the kiss just as I was getting slightly breathless. "I'd better go get some dry clothes from the car, give you a chance to get changed," he said looking me over with a satisfied smile on his face. "Not that you don't look sexy as hell in what you're wearing."

I looked down at myself, to see that my white t-shirt was now stuck to me and completely see through. I laughed uncomfortably and wrapped my arms around myself, blushing like crazy. He laughed too and bent to pick up the flower that I had thrown at his feet. He held it back out to me, smiling his beautiful smile.

"Thanks," I whispered, biting my lip as my face burned with embarrassment.

"Anytime," he said as he walked out of the door.

Chapter 6

I got changed quickly and walked out to the car. Liam was already there, leaning casually against the car, chatting happily with Justin and Spencer, another guy from my crew.

"Hey," I chirped as I walked up to them.

Liam smiled a beautiful smile at me. "That's my cue boys, gotta take the lady on our first real date. See you next week," he said, waving them away with a flick of his hand.

Justin's mouth fell open and he looked from Liam to me several times. "Date? But.... I mean.... what? I thought he was your brother's best friend! You don't even like him; you always say he's a man-whore asshole. Whenever I've said to you about how hot he was, you just said that you wouldn't touch his STD ass with a bargepole!" Justin said, frowning, and looking at me confused.

I groaned and closed my eyes. I was literally so embarrassed that I wished the ground would open up and swallow me. How could he just say that right in front of Liam? Not that I haven't told him that to his face on more than one occasion, but I still felt awful. I heard Liam start to laugh so I risked a glance at him, he didn't look angry or anything.

"Thanks, Jus," I muttered, giving him a look that should be able to kill him on the spot.

Liam reached out and grabbed my hand, pulling me to his side, still laughing. "It's a lady's prerogative to change her mind," he said to Justin with a wink, opening my car door for me.

"I'll see you next week, guys, and I promise I won't be late," I vowed, kissing their cheeks before getting in the car. Liam gave them both the typical man hug handshake thing, and ran round to the driver's side. When he started the car he looked over at me with a smile. "Sorry," I muttered, blushing again.

50

"Don't worry about it. It's nothing I haven't heard before out of your beautiful mouth," he replied with a grin.

I couldn't help but smile, he was full of the compliments today, but some part of me was worrying if he had said that to all the other girls. Was he expecting me to have sex with him after a couple of dates? Because if he was, then he was going to be very disappointed. I decided that we needed to talk about it. I mean, what was the point in even trying, if he was just using me for sex, and I wasn't planning on giving it up anytime soon?

"So, where shall we go for lunch?" he asked, snapping me out of my little internal discussion.

"Um…. I don't mind, what do you fancy?" I asked. He shot me a flirty look and a wicked smile. I rolled my eyes at him; he really is a sex crazed player! "To *eat,* Liam," I added, crossing my arms over my chest, trying to look stern.

He just laughed and started driving. "How about Chinese? You like that, right?" he asked, glancing at me from the corner of his eye.

"Yeah, I love Chinese food!" I chirped happily, grinning like I'd won the lottery. Jake hated Chinese food so we hardly ever had it; Liam smiled and drove us to the restaurant on the high-street.

We were now sitting, eating our food. We had been chatting happily for nearly an hour and I was again surprised by how easy it was to talk to him. I'd known him for twelve years and I'd never really just spoken to him properly about stuff. His leg brushed mine under the table and made me jump, not because of my fear, but because it sent a little jolt through my system, making the hairs on the back of my neck prick up and my pulse quicken.

I decided now was the time to sort it out, there was only one other couple in the restaurant so we could talk freely, but I just didn't know how to begin. "Liam, I think we need to talk about something," I said quietly.

He cocked his head to the side slightly and looked at me curiously. "OK. What's up?"

I took a deep breath, I just needed to get it out and see what he thought about it. "I really don't know what you want from me; I mean, you can have any girl that you want. I'm an emotional wreck for goodness sake… I mean…. I flinch every time anyone touches me. I…. I can't give you what you want," I rambled, frowning. Wow, that came out a little different than I thought, but at least it got the point across.

"You're worried about sex," he stated, looking at me knowingly,

51

not seeming to be bothered by this conversation at all.

I gulped and nodded. "I just…. I'm not ready for anything like that, so if that's what you want then there really is no point in starting anything," I said quietly, looking down at my plate and wishing the ground would swallow me again.

He put his hand under my chin and lifted my face up to look at his; he was smiling his beautiful smile. "I can wait as long as you want. I really am crazy about you, it's not about sex," he said tenderly, making my heart start to race.

Is he serious or is this a trick so I'll give it up sooner? "What if I said I didn't believe in having sex before marriage?" I asked, testing him.

His eyes showed his amusement, but he just kept his face straight. "Then I'd say how about we get married as soon as you're old enough. Eighteen is the legal age, right?" he replied, winking at me.

I laughed but was still unsure what he meant, I wasn't eighteen for another two years, is he saying that he'll wait two years for me? No sex until after marriage wasn't something that I believed in; I'd just wanted to see his reaction. "I don't believe in that, but I don't know how long it'll be, Liam, honestly." I chewed on my lip nervously.

"Angel, I said I can wait as long as you need. I want to be with you." He looked me right in the eyes as he spoke. I didn't see one ounce of doubt or trickery there and I felt hope building up inside me. Was he really that into me that he would wait for me?

"What about in three months' time when you still haven't gotten any, and some random girl throws herself at you, could you wait then?" I asked sceptically.

He laughed. "You really do think I'm some sex crazed player, don't you?" he asked. I nodded in confirmation. I didn't *think* it, I *knew* it, he slept around a lot! "Do you know why I've been with all of those girls?" he asked, suddenly looking uncomfortable and embarrassed.

"They give good head?" I asked sarcastically. Is he really going to go into details about his sex life to a girl he's just told he's crazy about and who is scared of having sex? Does he actually not have a clue?

He choked on his laughter, and shook his head. "No, Angel. The reason I went with all those girls was to try and get over you. I wake up next to you every day. You send my mind and body into a frenzy. I can smell your hair when I close my eyes, or I can imagine how your hand feels when you lay it on my chest. It kills me every day to be so close to you, but be so far away," he said, shaking his head and taking a deep breath, looking at me hopefully. "I thought maybe if I met someone else that I'd be able to stop thinking about you, but it didn't work. Nothing works. When I'm with them, I wish it was you. When they laugh or talk, I can't help but compare it to your voice or your laugh. It's always been you; it'll always be you, Angel."

I couldn't speak. What on earth do I say to that? I mean, I know he's a player, but I was killing him? That speech was so freaking adorable! "Oh," I choked out.

He burst out laughing. "Oh? That's all you can say?"

I nodded and laughed too. I still had no words to answer that little confession he'd just made. My head was still spinning and I knew if I said something now I would just make myself sound like an idiot. I leant across the table and took his hand, he smiled happily at me and that seemed to be all that was necessary.

My head was spinning with thoughts; I really didn't know what to believe. He just made that huge confession about how he feels, but does that mean he's not going to cheat on me? Well actually, we weren't even officially a couple. Liam only ever did dates; he's never had a girlfriend, so technically I have no claim on him anyway. I needed to be really careful, the more time I spent with this nice Liam, the more I liked him. I was in real danger of having my heart crushed.

My cellphone rang, saving us from the slightly weird silence. It wasn't an awkward silence though, just strange, like he seemed perfectly content just to hold my hand and look at me. The caller ID said it was Kate. "Hey, Kate, what's up?" I said cheerfully.

"Hey, Amber, want me to bring a movie for tonight?"

"Yeah sure. Nothing scary though." I smiled and slapped Liam's hand lightly as he tried to steal one of my spring rolls from my plate. 'What?' he mouthed to me innocently. I rolled my eyes at him and passed him my plate.

"I was thinking, Dawn of the Dead," Kate replied.

I gasped; is she kidding me? "No way! I'm not watching that, it'll scare the crap out of me!" I cried, horrified at the thought of watching a zombie movie. They made me so scared that I couldn't be alone for days afterwards; I had to pee with the bathroom door open for goodness sake!

I could hear her chuckling. "Please, Amby? I really want to see it," she begged, I could imagine the puppy dog look on her face right now.

Liam was giving me a quizzical expression so I put my hand

53

over the mouthpiece and whispered, "Dawn of the Dead."

He widened his eyes slightly before giving me his smirk. "Don't worry, Angel, I'll protect you," he whispered confidently, making me smile.

"Amby, please?" Kate begged again.

"Oh jeez alright fine, bring that damn movie," I muttered, defeated.

At least Liam would be there, he always kept my nightmares away. It would only be bad when I was on my own, like in the shower or something. I guess I could always make him stand outside the door and read to me or something while I was in there, it's not like he hasn't done that for me before. I looked at him a little shocked, actually the more I thought about it, the more this sweet, funny Liam, popped into my mind. He quite often did little things for me that I never took any notice of before. Had he always been sweet to me, but I was just too prejudice to see it?

"So, what do you think, is that OK?" Kate asked.

I snapped back to reality. Crap, I hadn't been listening to her at all! "Sorry, Kate, what? I didn't hear you, sorry. I was panicking about that stupid movie." I winced just at the thought of it.

She sighed. "I said that my mom and dad are going away for the weekend so do you think it would be alright if I just slept at yours tonight and tomorrow night? I don't really want to stay on my own," she said in a small voice. I looked at Liam and winced. If Kate stayed over that meant that he couldn't, because she slept in the camp bed on my floor.

"Um sure, Kate, you can stay over for the weekend. Jake won't mind," I agreed reluctantly.

Liam shot his eyes up to mine, and he shook his head. *'NO!'* he mouthed to me pleadingly. I just gave him an apologetic look and shrugged, I couldn't say no to her, she was my best friend.

"Great. Well I'll come over at about seven then, OK?" she chirped, sounding excited.

"Yeah, OK. See you." I snapped my cellphone shut and looked back at Liam.

"The whole weekend? I don't get to sleep for the whole weekend?" he whined, as soon as I had shut my phone.

"Sorry, but I couldn't say no. Her parents are going away for the weekend and she doesn't want to stay on her own." I looked at him apologetically.

He sighed looking defeated. "OK sure. But you do know you've just agreed to watch a scary ass zombie flick and I'm not going to be there for the next two nights," he stated with a cocky grin.

I gasped. I hadn't thought about that! I didn't sleep very well without Liam there, I had nightmares, bad ones, about my father, and now on top of that I would have zombie dreams too? Since I was eight years old I had only ever spent a few weeks away from Liam, like if one of us went on vacation, or one time he had chicken pox and I had to stay away from him for four days. Every time I was on my own, my dreams would be so bad that I would wake up screaming. I'd asked Jake to sleep in with me a few times when I was younger, but he didn't stop the dreams so I just stopped asking him.

I knew that Liam didn't sleep at all when he wasn't with me. He literally laid there awake, not being able to get comfortable. He always said that his bed felt strange because he hadn't slept in it since he was ten years old. He hated it when my friends came to stay and bitched about it the whole of the next day, dropping not so subtle hints that he wasn't impressed at having to sleep in his own bed.

"Well, I don't know why you're looking so cocky about it; you're not going to sleep too brilliantly either." I grinned, sticking my tongue out at him.

"Hmm, is that an invitation?" he asked, raising an eyebrow. I instantly realised what he was talking about, he was asking if I wanted to kiss him again because I showed him my tongue. I sure as heck did.

"Sure," I purred, looking at him seductively, knowing that he couldn't reach me over the table so he would have to wait until after we left the restaurant.

He immediately jumped out of his chair and bent down next to me, taking my face in his hands and kissing me, not seeming to care where we were or if people were watching. I took the initiative this time and traced my tongue along his bottom lip, he opened quickly and I slipped my tongue in. He moaned into my mouth, pulling me closer to him. The kiss was so good that it was making me slightly dizzy. He didn't once try to touch me other than holding my face, which I was surprised about. Maybe he wasn't just using me for sex after all. I smiled against his lips and he pulled away, smiling at me too.

"Thanks," he whispered, kissing me again quickly and then sitting back down opposite me as if nothing happened. OK, I am *so* not used to this whole dating and making out thing! "We'd better get going; I need to speak to your brother." He frowned, looking sad and a bit scared.

"You're not going to tell him, are you?" I asked, horrified at the thought of Jake knowing and going crazy.

He nodded. "Yeah, Angel. He's known that I've liked you all this time, but he didn't think that you liked me, so I need to talk to him about us actually dating." He winced as he spoke; I would imagine that he was thinking about the ass kicking Jake would give him when he told him.

"Liam, why don't we just leave that for a while, and then maybe in a couple of weeks, if everything is going well, then we can talk to him together. I mean, we don't even know if it's going to work out, do we?" I asked with a shrug. I didn't really see the point in talking to Jake and upsetting everything if this wasn't going to work out. In reality, how long would it last once he realised that I really wasn't planning on sleeping with him anytime soon? When he got bored or desperate, he would run away from me to the nearest easy lay, screaming as he went.

He looked a little scared. "You don't think it'll work out?" he asked, his voice sounded hurt.

"Honestly? I just don't think that you can wait, Liam. How long is it going to be before you decide that you've had enough and sleep with some bimbo?" I replied, hating the hurt expression that crossed his face.

"I promise I will never cheat on you, *ever*. I've waited too long for this chance; I'm not going to screw it up." He took my hand and I could see the honesty in his eyes, he truly believed that he wouldn't cheat, but he was a boy after all and his body would say something else eventually.

"Let's just wait a while, OK?" I suggested, pulling my hand away and waving for the waiter. He came over immediately. "Hi, can we get the check please?" I asked with a smile, he nodded and walked off.

"I'm just going to go to the bathroom. If he comes back before I'm back, then use this, OK?" Liam instructed, handing me his wallet and walking quickly to the bathroom.

I winced; I think I really hurt his feelings saying that. Damn it, I could be so stupid sometimes! I watched him as he walked away, my eyes unconsciously focused on his ass. Wow, he really does have a nice ass! Someone cleared their throat next to me making me blush because I had just got caught staring. I looked up and the waiter was standing there with the check.

"Oh, sorry! I didn't realise you were there," I muttered,

embarrassed.

"Don't worry about it." He handed me the receipt and bent down next to me so we were at the same level. He put one hand on the back of my chair and one on the table so I was trapped. My heart started to race. He was too close. "So, I've not seen you around here before. I definitely would have remembered a face as beautiful as yours," he said, his eyes were boring holes into me, as he looked like he was imagining me naked.

I squirmed in my seat. "Er no, I've not been in here before," I muttered uncomfortably, looking at the amount that was due and grabbing Liam's wallet from my lap.

"I'm Simon." He held out his hand for me to shake. I looked at it and gulped; I really didn't want to touch him so I just fiddled with Liam's wallet and pretended to be looking at something. I felt him playing with my pony tail and I felt sick. "So, what's your name?" he asked, with a flirty smile.

"Her name's touch her again and I'll break your face," Liam growled possessively from behind me. I physically relaxed.

The guy stood up immediately. "Sorry, I was just talking to your girlfriend that's all. No harm done," he said innocently.

"Right," Liam replied, sounding really annoyed. He reached out and took the receipt and his wallet out of my hands, looked at it and then handed the guy the money still glaring at him. My breathing still hadn't returned to normal, my heart was still racing. Liam held out his hand to me. "You ready, Angel?" he asked, not taking his eyes off the waiter. I took his hand and stood up, following him as he led us out of the restaurant. Once he closed the door he turned to me. "You alright? You look a bit pale." He stepped closer to me and put his lips on my neck. I wrapped my arms around his waist and pressed myself against him, letting his smell fill my lungs, his breath blew down my back and shoulders, making everything in my body relax.

I pulled away after a couple of minutes. "I'm fine now." I smiled at him reassuringly and he stroked the side of my face lightly. "Come on let's get back. I need to help Jake clear up so he'll buy pizza tonight," I teased.

He smiled and as we walked to his car, he slipped his hand in mine. I couldn't help but smile. It felt right for some reason; his hand just seemed to fit mine perfectly. It was so natural that it was almost too easy.

Chapter 7

It took a long time to clear the house. Someone had been sick in the back yard so I sent Jake out to clear that, while I worked on the kitchen, collecting all of the empty cups and bottles. It seemed like the party had gotten a bit out of hand when Liam and I had gone to bed, and my drunk ass of a brother hadn't bothered to stop it.

"This is the reason why I stay sober," Liam stated, scrunching his face up in disgust at the vase full of urine on the windowsill in the lounge.

"You stay sober to stop people from peeing in my mom's ornaments?" I asked, laughing hysterically.

He nodded. "Surprising, but true. There's always one who can't be bothered to walk to the bathroom," he joked, making me laugh harder.

He smiled at me, making my heart melt, and Jake walked in. "Wow, did I actually hear you two laughing at something together in here? That's a first," he said, looking at what Liam was holding and flinching.

"I'd better go sort this out," Liam muttered, walking off quickly. I could tell he was a bit uncomfortable lying to Jake, but I was really sure that a couple of weeks would be best, just to make sure this was what we both wanted.

"Jake, can Kate stay this weekend? Her parents are out of town and she doesn't want to stay in the house on her own," I asked, giving him my puppy dog face.

He grimaced. "Ugh! That girl does nothing but flirt with me, I wouldn't mind so much if she was older, but I mean jeez, she's my little sister's age! Ew!" he said with a fake shudder.

"So, you don't think a sixteen year old should go out with an eighteen year old?" I asked, trying to be casual.

He didn't buy it, he looked at me sceptically. "You're not interested in any eighteen year olds, are you?" he asked, narrowing his eyes at me. I saw Liam coming back down the hall way from the corner of my eye.

"No, I was talking about Kate," I lied.

He nodded, seeming satisfied. "No, I don't think they should. I mean, what sort of an eighteen year old would even look at a sixteen year old that way?" he asked, glancing at Liam as he walked past looking a little sheepish.

"It's only two years, Jake, no big deal. You're only freaked out because that's the same age as me. Just because you wouldn't date someone who's my age doesn't mean other guys feel the same way, right, Liam?" I countered, still trying for casual even though my voice cracked a little when I said Liam's name.

"Right. I know a lot of hot ass sixteen year olds," Liam replied, winking at me behind my brothers back.

"Yeah, but you can't date any of them!" Jake growled, turning to look at him and slapping him on the back of the head as he walked past. I met Liam's gaze and was a little shocked. Wow, Jake really *did* know he liked me, and by the look of it, he was very opposed to the idea of us being together. This could be even more complicated than I first thought.

Kate let herself in about an hour later. "Hey, Jake. Hey, Liam," she purred as she walked in, giving them both a flirty smile. I saw Liam chuckle under his breath as he smiled back.

"Hi, Kate." Jake smirked, giving her a flirty wink. He really didn't help himself, if he wanted her to leave him alone, then why did he encourage her?

"Come on, let's leave the man-whores alone," I joked as I grabbed her hand and dragged her to my bedroom. I saw Liam smirk at me from the corner of my eye and I stifled a laugh.

"I can't believe I get to spend the whole weekend here with you and your brother. Do you think Liam will stay here too?" she asked, her eyes sparkling.

"I don't know, maybe you should ask him." I smiled a little uncomfortably. I could just imagine her flirting with Liam right in front of me; I wasn't sure how I was going to feel about it.

She dumped her stuff on my floor and threw herself down on my bed. Suddenly she rolled over and grabbed my pillow off of my bed frowning at it, looking confused. "Amber, why does your pillow smell like cologne?"

I could feel my nerves bubbling up. "Er.... well I.... er.... Oh!

59

Liam borrowed it when he stayed here, so it must smell like him," I lied, stumbling over my words.

She buried her head in the pillow. "Mmm, I'm sleeping with this one tonight," she stated, holding the pillow tight.

I choked on my laughter. "Whatever, Kate. Let's go eat I'm starved." I pushed myself up off of the bed and walked towards the door so we could get the food ordered.

"I got this!" she chirped, waving a DVD in front of my face. Even the cover scared the heck out of me. I rolled my eyes and stalked out of the room plopping down onto the sofa next to Liam. He put his hand down onto the sofa next to mine and discreetly rubbed his little finger across mine when no one was looking.

"Have you ordered the food, Jake?" I asked, shifting sideways on the seat so that my knee touched Liam's thigh. I saw a smile play at the corner of his mouth.

"Yep, done. It'll be here in ten," Jake said, shifting up the other sofa a few inches because Kate had practically sat herself on his lap.

"So, Liam, will your fine ass be staying here tonight too? I'm more than happy to share my bed if you want. I may be scared from the movie, maybe I'll need someone to make me feel better in the night," Kate purred seductively.

I felt him shift his weight closer to me so my leg was on top of his more. "Nope, I can't. I'm busy tonight. You'll just have to manage without me." He shrugged and looked away to the TV.

"Oh well. It'll have to just be you then Jake, if you're interested," she purred.

I didn't hear his reply; my ears had started to ring. I actually started to feel jealous. It was the first time I had ever felt anything like that before, I wanted to stand up and shout at my best friend to leave Liam alone. I burst out laughing and then bit my lip to stop.

Everyone looked at me like I was crazy. "What?" Jake asked confused.

I shook my head, smiling. "Nothing, I just thought of a funny joke that's all," I lied getting up. "Anyone want a drink?" I offered, needing to change the subject. They all said yes so I made my way to the fridge grabbing four cans of Pepsi. As I shut the fridge door, Liam grabbed me from behind and made me turn around to look at him. He was standing so close I could feel his breath blow across my face.

"I'm missing you already," he whispered, kissing me lightly. I threw my arms around his neck and pulled him to me, deepening the kiss, tangling my hands in his hair. He stepped forwards making me move back, so my back was against the fridge as he pressed his body against mine. "I think we should just talk to your brother now," he murmured as he pulled away a couple of minutes later.

I shook my head, looking at him pleadingly. "No, just a couple of weeks that's all I ask."

He smiled a small smile. "OK, whatever you want. But can you stop your friend flirting with me? Tell her I'm taken."

My breath caught in my throat at his words. "Are you taken?" I whispered shyly.

He kissed me again, making my body tingle and yearn for more. "I'm definitely taken, if you'll have me," he replied, looking me straight in the eye. My insides were jumping for joy, my heart beating so fast that I could almost hear it in my ears, but my head was still telling me to be careful.

"I'll have you, if you'll have me," I bargained.

He gave me a wicked grin. "Absolutely. Whenever you're ready, I'll have you all the time," he said suggestively, waggling his eyebrows at me. I gasped and slapped his shoulder, making him chuckle. "Oh come on, I'm allowed to make slutty comments to you now, surely? I mean, you're my girlfriend so I have to use all my best moves on you," he said, faking hurt.

Did he just call me his girlfriend? My heart melted at the sound of that word coming out of his mouth. "Say that again," I whispered, pulling him closer to me.

"I'm allowed to make slutty comments to you?" he asked, looking a little confused.

I shook my head. "No, not that. The next bit," I murmured, putting my mouth inches from his.

"You're my girlfriend?" he asked. I nodded, my breath coming in small gasps, the sound of it made me feel like I was flying, I honestly can't remember the last time I was this happy. He smiled. "You're my girlfriend, Angel," he purred seductively, kissing my lips lightly. "My girl." He kissed me again. "The only one I want." He kissed me again, this time I didn't let him pull back, I held his head to mine and kissed him passionately, making him moan slightly and grip me tighter to him. Suddenly, he jumped away from me and moved to the side. I looked at him confused, had I done something wrong?

Just then Jake came round the corner, giving me a stern expression. "You need to have a word with your friend, seriously, she just grabbed my dick!" he whisper yelled at me. Liam and I burst out laughing at the same time. The doorbell rang and I ran to get it,

61

needing to be out of the room, I didn't really like being around the two of them together, it was kind of awkward.

After the food, Kate put on the stupid scary movie. I sat next to Liam. Which meant that Jake had to sit next to Kate on the other sofa - much to his obvious annoyance. The movie was awful; Liam slung his arm casually over the back of the sofa and was playing with my hair discreetly which made it slightly more bearable. About half way through I was honestly so scared that I scooted right up next to Liam and buried my face in his chest. I could feel Jake shooting daggers over at us but I couldn't help it.

By the time it got to the end, I was almost on his lap, much to his enjoyment. I could see the bulge forming in his jeans even though he put his arm over it to cover it quickly. I blushed slightly, knowing that I had caused that, because he was attracted to me and I was jumping all over him. My mind flashed to all the times that he'd been aroused near me before, in bed or dancing, and I wondered how many of them were caused by attraction as well. I bit my lip; maybe I'd ask him another time.

Finally, the stupid ass zombie movie was over and I breathed a sigh of relief.

"That was awesome," Kate chirped, grinning.

"Yep, best movie I've seen in ages," Liam agreed with a smirk, I knew he meant because I was sitting on him.

"I hated it! How can you say that was good? I mean, jeez, they're dead people who eat live people and turn them into flesh eating zombies too. And now I have to pee, and I'm scared to go on my own!" I whined, standing up and pouting. Why did I watch that stupid thing anyway? I knew it would scare me!

All three of them laughed at me, but Liam stood up. "I'll come with you and check the bathroom for scary un-dead before you go in, how's that?" he offered, nodding his head towards the bathroom in the hall, smiling.

"Will you check my bedroom too? And my en-suite?" I asked hopefully. He laughed; he obviously thought I was joking. "I'm not joking, Liam."

"Whatever you want, Angel," he agreed, smiling and following me up the hall. I stopped outside the bathroom door and waited for him to go in first. He came out a minute later, chuckling to himself. "It's a zombie free zone," he said shaking his head, grinning at me.

"Thanks," I mumbled, blushing and feeling like a little kid. I headed into the bathroom, leaving the door unlocked in case I needed to get out of there quickly. I knew I was being stupid but I just couldn't help myself. I washed my hands and stepped out, to see him leaning against the wall waiting for me, which made me smile.

"I thought I'd better wait for you. You never know what could be lurking in a dark hallway," he said, looking around slowly with wide eyes. My heart jumped into my throat as I threw myself at him, wrapping my arms around his waist tightly, burying my face into the side of his neck. He laughed. "Yep, best movie ever!" he stated, putting his arms around me and walking down the hall to the lounge. Before we turned the corner he pulled away and kissed me lightly on the lips.

Jake laughed as we walked into the lounge. "Seriously? You made him wait for you outside the door? That's low, Ambs. I hope you at least shut the door this time," he teased as I sat back down.

I nodded. "Yep I shut the door, didn't think he'd want to hear that," I confirmed, grinning. "How about we play on the Wii?" I suggested, trying to change the subject from my zombie phobia. Everyone nodded so Jake set it up. They decided on sports so Liam and Jake played boxing first. Kate moved over to sit next to me; the two boys were standing and playing in front of us.

"Hmm, I just can't decide which one has the cutest butt. Who do you think?" Kate said quietly but loud enough for the guys to hear.

"Ew! Seriously, what's wrong with you? That's my brother!" I cried, shuddering.

"Only one of them is your brother, Amber, the other is seriously freaking hot. And I think he has a soft spot for you," she whispered too loud again, making me cringe. I saw Jake shoot a death glare at Liam who looked like he was pretending he couldn't hear her.

"Right, yeah OK," I replied sarcastically, rolling my eyes. "Come on hurry up I want a turn," I whined, trying to change the subject. Kate really had no idea how close she was.

"Here, Angel, you can take my turn. I'd better get going anyway, it's almost midnight, my parents will be wondering where I am," Liam said holding the controller out to me. Kate jumped up and grabbed it, smirking and nodding towards my brother, signalling she wanted to play with him.

"Liam, would you check my bedroom before you go?" I asked, feeling pathetic and like a scared little kid.

He smiled but didn't laugh at me, which I found surprising. "Oh all right!" He forced a sigh, his eyes amused. By the look of him he actually quite liked the fact that I was asking him to do this, maybe he liked being all protective or something, maybe it was making him

63

feel needed. He stalked off towards my room and I got up and followed him after a couple of seconds. I closed my door silently, and leant against it. I watched him as he actually walked around my room, looking under the bed, and in the closet, before heading into my en-suite. As he walked back into the room, his eyes landed on me, he honestly didn't know I was there I could tell by his surprised face. Bless him; my boyfriend had actually checked my whole bedroom for zombies. My heart skipped a beat at the thought of him being my boyfriend.

"Hi," I purred seductively as I walked over to my bed and sat down.

"Hi," he replied with a small smile. He made no moves to come towards me; I think he was trying not to rush me. I patted the bed beside me and he eagerly trotted over and sat down.

"Thanks for checking my room," I whispered, playing with the neck of his t-shirt, tracing my finger along the skin there.

"Anytime. I'm just sorry I won't be here for you tonight. Try not to have too many nightmares, OK?" He looked at me with sad eyes; we both knew that I would have nightmares without him here.

I got onto my knees and moved to him, throwing my leg over his so I was sitting on his lap, straddling him. I wrapped my arms around his neck and looked into his beautiful blue eyes. He looked a little taken aback but his eyes danced with excitement.

"I'm sorry that Kate's staying over. I'm actually really going to miss you half crushing me to death in the night," I teased. I said it as a joke but to be honest I really was going to miss him tonight.

"Well, I'm really going to miss half crushing you to death," he joked, rubbing his hands on my back.

"Try and get some sleep tonight though, OK?" I pleaded. I really hated it when he went without sleep, it made me feel guilty because he only started sleeping here in the first place to comfort me and now he was stuck with it.

"I'll try."

I suddenly had the urge to kiss him and maybe tease him a little, but I was scared to do it. OK, just do it, Amber, what's the worst that could happen? It's Liam; he'll stop if you ask him to.

"Maybe I could give you a little something to dream about. Would that help do you think?" I asked, biting my lip and raising my eyebrows. He looked at me, his expression a little unsure; he obviously wasn't expecting this much physical contact so soon. I could tell by the bulge in his jeans pressing between my legs that he wanted physical contact, but I could also tell that he was letting me make the first moves.

"It might help," he said huskily, making my body tingle and my skin to heat up.

I leant forward and kissed him passionately, he made a small moaning sound as he slipped his tongue into my mouth. I ran my hands through his hair, loving the soft feel of it on my fingers. He didn't make any other moves, he just kissed me, but I wanted a little more so I pushed on his shoulders, making him lay down so that I was on top of him. I ran my hands down his chest and slipped my hand under his t-shirt, tracing it over his sculpted abs, making him shiver slightly.

He rolled me so I was under him, he broke out of the kiss and looked at me, our eyes locked together trying to slow our breathing. I gripped his t-shirt and pulled it up over his head, making him seem to stop breathing altogether. I looked down at his chest. He really was beautiful; I ran my fingers down it marveling that this boy wanted to be with me. He still hadn't moved, he just hovered above me, looking unsure what to do, so I put my hands back around his neck and pulled him back down to kiss me. He kissed me back eagerly. The kiss was getting hot; he broke it only to kiss across my cheek and down my neck. His hand moved slowly to my stomach and he slipped it under my top, tracing his fingers across the skin there. He continued to kiss downwards over my top until he got to my stomach then he hitched up my top and started kissing my skin. I felt his tongue trail across just under my belly button making me moan. I was getting a feeling down in my core it was like a burning ache but I tried not to think about it, the feeling scared the life out of me.

He pushed my top slightly higher and I felt him kissing the material at the bottom of my bra. I was still OK with this; I was enjoying it a lot more than I thought I would. I thought that this would just give him something to dream about, but I had a feeling I would be revisiting this tonight too. My top rose a little higher and I heard him make a soft moaning noise as it completely exposed my bra. His hand snaked up my stomach and he gently brushed his hand over one of my breasts, just once, before moving it away as if he was waiting for me to stop him. When I didn't say anything, he put his hand back there again and cupped my breast. I moaned again. It felt so nice to have him touch me; he brought his mouth back to mine and kissed me tenderly, still massaging my breasts gently.

I could feel his erection pressing into my thigh and I started to get a little panicky because this was getting too hot, too fast. Oh God I need to stop! I broke the kiss. "Liam," I said breathlessly. His eyes snapped to mine quickly and he took his hands off me, pushing himself up so that he was hovering above me, not touching me apart from our legs which were intertwined.

"Stop?" he asked, his voice sounding husky and full of lust. I gulped and nodded. He immediately pushed himself off of me completely and sat back on the edge of the bed, pulling on his t-shirt.

I sat up, blushing, feeling stupid and like a little kid. Jeez, I didn't even let him get my top off! "Sorry," I mumbled, not looking at him.

"Angel, you don't need to be sorry. We didn't have to do that. I told you, whatever you want. I'm not going to say that I didn't enjoy that though, because that would be a lie. That was the hottest damn thing that has ever happened to me," he said, shrugging.

I giggled at that statement. "The hottest thing that's ever happened to you? Yeah right, you've probably slept with over a hundred different girls and done goodness knows what *with* them and *to* them, and you didn't even get my top off before I freaked out," I said sarcastically, feeling like an idiot. He didn't need to lie to make me feel better.

"Angel, trust me that *was* the hottest thing that has ever happened to me. It's just you, you make me feel different. Even kissing you is different, it's a thousand times better than anything I've ever felt before. You make my body burn everywhere you touch me. I can't explain it." He frowned and shook his head as if he was annoyed at himself for not having the right words.

"I know what you mean." I smiled, kissing him lightly on the lips.

He grinned at me. "Now's where you're supposed to tell me that that was the hottest for you too," he joked, knowing that I hadn't kissed anyone but him and that jerk that kissed me at the party.

I pretended to think about it for a few seconds. "I've had better."

He laughed. "Yeah, I bet you have," he replied, shaking his head in amusement. I grinned at him and he sighed. "I guess I'd better go. Thanks for today; I had a really good time with you. Sleep tight, OK. Oh and by the way, that thing we just did that was supposed to help me sleep, well, I don't think that's going to have the desired effect. I think it's actually going to keep me awake all night thinking about it," he said, tracing his finger across my cheekbone.

I giggled. "Me too," I admitted, making him laugh too.

He stood up and held his hand out for me, I took it and he helped me up, we walked down the hallway hand in hand. He stopped at the corner and kissed my forehead before he sighed and let go of my hand. "Right, guys, I'm off. I'll see you tomorrow," Liam called as he walked towards the front door.

"Yeah, see ya," they both answered, still engrossed in their game of tennis on the TV. Liam smiled at me from the door but it was forced, I could tell it was almost hurting him to go, I smiled back and he shut the door. The moment the door closed my heart sank. The thought of having to spend two nights in my bed without him made me feel a little sick; it would have been horrendous even if we hadn't just got together, but now it actually felt like torture. I sighed and went back to the couch to watch Jake whip Kate's butt on the Wii.

That night was awful. I went to bed terrified of zombies, and even when I did go to sleep, I started to dream about my father. I hadn't dreamt of him for over five months. The last dreams I had were when Kate and Sarah stayed over for Sarah's birthday. Because the girls were here, Liam had to stay away, and I'd woken the whole house up with my screaming.

My dream tonight was bad. Jake was eleven and I was nine. We were playing in the yard to get out of the house because my father wanted to watch some football match on the TV. He'd been drinking all afternoon which made him even more temperamental. Jake and I were playing with his new soccer ball that he had got for his birthday a couple of weeks before. We weren't supposed to play with it in the yard, only in the park, but Jake wanted to show me this new trick he'd learnt.

He was kneeing the ball to keep it up in the air; I was laughing and counting how many times he could do it, being all proud of my big brother. He lost control of it, and instead of letting it drop to the floor, he tried to save it by kicking it back up with his foot. The ball flew through the air and hit the window. Luckily, it didn't smash, but it did make a loud bang. We both turned and looked at the door, waiting.

About ten seconds later, the back door opened and my father beckoned for us to come in. "Bring the ball," he hissed. His face was murderously angry, making me go cold. Jake grabbed my hand and forced me behind him as we walked in, picking up the ball in his other hand.

My father slammed the door, making me jump and whimper. Jake gripped my hand tighter. "Who kicked the ball?" my father asked nastily.

"I did. I'm sorry, Dad. It was an accident," Jake whispered, looking at him apologetically.

My father took the ball from his hands and put it on the counter, and then punched Jake so hard in the stomach that he actually lifted off the floor slightly. I put my hands over my mouth to stifle the scream that was threatening to come out of me. He raised his fist to hit him again, so I grabbed his hand to stop him. He turned to me and slapped me, hard, sending me flying into the wall, hitting my head. I could feel something trickling down the side of my face; my vision was a little blurry.

He turned back to Jake, hitting him again. He didn't just do it once, he punched him over and over, in the stomach and thighs until Jake was on the floor crying. I was begging for him to stop. He grabbed my arm and pulled me back up, grabbing a knife off of the counter. I couldn't breathe. Jake screamed at him to leave me alone and got up off the floor, pain stretched across his face from the beating he'd just sustained.

My father punched him in the jaw, sending him to the floor again. "It's OK. Cut me, do it. Just please don't hit Jake anymore, please!" I begged, crying and looking at my father pleadingly.

Surprisingly, he put the knife in my hand. I had the urge to stab him with it, but he had hold of my wrist so I couldn't. He grabbed Jake's ball from the counter and held it still. "Burst it," he ordered. I shook my head quickly. Jake loved this ball, it was his birthday present from me, I had saved my allowance for two months to buy it for him. "Burst it," he repeated in his cold voice. I could smell the alcohol on his breath as it blew across my face; the smell of it turned my stomach.

He gripped my wrist and made me shove the knife deep into the leather ball. I sobbed. He let go of my hand, taking the knife and throwing it roughly into the sink before walking off into the living room to watch the rest of his game as if nothing had happened. I looked over at Jake; he was sitting on the floor barely able to breathe. He looked awful.

I ran to him and he sat up, grabbing a kitchen towel and pressing it to my head where I had banged it, biting his lip to stop his crying. "Ambs, I'm so sorry. Are you OK?" he croaked, his voice barely above a whisper. The stupid boy was struggling to draw breath and he was asking me if I was alright? Jeez, I really did have the best brother in the world!

I jerked awake. I was crying, crying so hard that I could barely breathe. I wiped my face with shaky hands as I looked at the clock; it was almost four thirty in the morning. I reached over to hug Liam, but he wasn't there, he was at his own house. Oh God, I needed him! I grabbed my cellphone and snuck out of the room to the lounge.

'R U Awake?' I text him. Hopefully if he was asleep he wouldn't hear it, I didn't want to wake him up if he had actually managed to sleep tonight.

Almost immediately, my phone rang. "Angel, are you OK?" he asked as soon as I answered. I was still crying, I couldn't slow my breathing, my hands were shaking violently.

"No," I croaked.

"I'm coming over. Can I come in the front?" I could hear him sliding his window open and the wind blowing down the phone.

"Yes," I sobbed. I went to the front door and opened it, standing there waiting for him. I was only there for a few seconds before he ran round the corner and grabbed me into a hug, lifting me off my feet as he stepped into the house. I wrapped my legs around his waist and gripped tight around his neck. He immediately pressed his lips to my neck, breathing down my back and shoulders until my body relaxed. He moved to the lounge and sat on the edge of the sofa, still holding me tight with his mouth on my neck. When I was calm I pulled back to look at his worried face.

"Zombies?" he asked, looking a little hopeful. I shook my head and his face fell, he looked so sad but that quickly changed to anger, he was so angry it looked like a vein in his temple would burst. I just hugged him again without speaking; he knew I'd dreamt of my father, he didn't need to ask. "You want to talk about it?" he asked a couple of minutes later, stroking my back, soothingly.

"No." My voice was husky from crying so much. He nodded and continued to rub my back. "Did I wake you up, Liam?" I asked, suddenly feeling guilty for making him come all the way over here at half past four in the morning.

"No, Angel. I couldn't sleep," he said quietly.

I giggled. "The kiss didn't help then?" I joked, feeling better now that he was here.

"No, I knew that would have the opposite effect," he replied, grinning.

I smiled sadly at him. "Want to stay with me for a little while? I could set my alarm on my phone. We could sleep on the couch," I suggested. He grinned and laid us down side by side; I grabbed my cellphone and went through the menu screen until I came to the alarm function. "What time shall I set it for?" I asked, biting my lip, wondering what time Jake would get up, probably not before ten on a

Sunday.

"How about seven thirty?" he suggested, pulling me towards him. I set the alarm and put the phone on the floor where I could reach it easily. He draped his leg over mine and wrapped his arms tightly around me, our noses were almost touching.

I smiled and kissed him lightly. "Goodnight, Liam." I closed my eyes and sighed contentedly, feeling safe and secure in his arms.

"Goodnight, my beautiful girlfriend," he whispered, kissing my nose. I smiled at how sweet that was, and fell into a dreamless sleep within minutes.

Chapter 8

I woke to the sound of my phone alarm. I looked around wondering why I was in the lounge, then I remembered the dream. Liam was still asleep; as usual, his arms and legs were all over me, pinning me down with his weight. I smiled and looked at him for a few minutes before I decided to wake him up nicely for a change. Usually, I just elbowed him or pushed him off of me, I thought today I would be a little more creative, he'd like that.

I moved forward, pushing on his shoulder. He rolled onto his back, not taking his arms off of me, so he dragged me to his side. I raised myself up onto my hands and knees and moved so that I was straddling him, before putting my weight back down on him. I stroked his handsome face a couple of times before I pressed my lips to his lightly. He sighed a little in his sleep so I kissed him again, a little harder and longer this time. He started to get aroused and I stifled a giggle. OK, I know I'm new to all this, but this boy seems to lust after me a lot! It was a little embarrassing, but also at the same time it made me feel wanted, needed, and attractive. I kissed him again and ran my hand up his chest. He started to stir, his arms tightening around me, clamping me to his chest even though he wasn't even awake yet. I kissed him again and trailed my tongue along his lip. *That* caught his attention; he opened his eyes and looked at me, clearly shocked, but with a smile playing on the edge of his lips.

"I hope you're going to wake me up like this from now on," he said in his husky, sleep filled voice.

"Maybe, if you're lucky," I teased. He put one hand behind my head and pulled me back down to kiss him again. He nibbled on my bottom lip asking for entrance, but I pulled away instead, making him groan. "You need to go, Liam." I pulled out of his grasp and sat up, still straddling him. I could feel his erection pressing against my core, making me yearn for him in ways I hadn't even thought about until now.

He smiled and put his hands on my knees and just looked at me sitting on top of him. His eyes were so lustful that I was surprised he didn't beg me for sex there and then. He didn't even move; just laid there with a big contented grin on his face. This wasn't really a good position to be sitting in; the feel of him under me was turning me on so badly it was actually maddening. I wondered what it would feel like to have him touch me, to run his hands down my body; I bit my lip as a wave of desire washed over me. The feelings were so confusing, so foreign to me. I'd never wanted to even kiss anyone before, let alone the thoughts that were starting to form in my head right now.

"What are you doing to me?" I whispered, confused that I could feel this way, to actually want someone when usually I shy away from all physical contact because of what my father used to make me do.

"What do you mean?" he asked, looking a little confused. I shook my head; I couldn't explain it, especially not to him. I needed him to be able to wait for me, if I told him I was feeling like this, he would probably go full steam ahead and ruin everything. "Tell me what you mean, Angel. Please?" he begged; using his puppy dog face on me. Damn it! That has always worked and he knows it!

"I don't want to, Liam." I moved off of him and laid back down by his side.

"Please?" he whispered, looking at me with his begging eyes.

I sighed. "I don't know what's happening to me, one day I can't even stand to have anyone touch me and the next day I...." I trailed off, unsure how to finish that sentence without giving him the wrong impression.

"The next day, what?" he prompted, leaning up on his elbow so he could look into my eyes.

"The next day you're turning me on so badly that I can't even help myself," I admitted, blushing like crazy.

He laughed quietly, giving me his cocky grin. "You turn me on too."

"Yeah, that's half the problem," I stated, glancing down to see the tent he was sporting in his pyjama shorts, blushing again that I had just looked and he would have seen me looking. Oh crap, that is so embarrassing!

"I'm sorry if me being turned on turns you on." He smirked at me and I blushed harder, squirming at how uncomfortable this

72

conversation was. I slapped his chest and giggled out of embarrassment; he caught my hand and held it tight just looking at me.

"It scares me," I admitted, feeling stupid and childlike.

"I know it does, but I would never hurt you. If you ever felt like things are going too fast, you would only ever have to say, I promise." I couldn't doubt his sincerity; the truth of his words were clear across his face.

I leant forward and kissed him gently, before pulling away. "You really need to go. It's almost eight now."

He sighed and played with my fingers. "I really dislike your friend, it's her fault I have to leave," he mumbled, pretending to be annoyed. I laughed and got up off of the couch, pulling him up to his feet.

"You might want to calm down a little before you leave. What would the neighbours think if they saw you leaving my house like that?" I joked, nodding down towards his crotch, then blushing because I had just looked again.

He laughed. "They would think that I have an incredibly beautiful girlfriend, who has just kicked me out of her bed," he stated, shrugging casually. I grinned as he rearranged himself in his shorts so it was less noticeable, before kissing me again and going out of the front door.

I snuck back to my room. Kate was still asleep so I crawled in my bed, but I didn't go back to sleep, instead, I text Liam:

'Glad you got at least 3 hours sleep last night' I turned my phone onto silent so his reply didn't wake Kate.

'Me too. That couch is surprisingly comfy, better than my bed but that's prob because U were there' he replied, making me smile.

'U could always stay over tonight. Maybe I could sneak out to the lounge after Kate's asleep' I text him back.

'I like that idea! What R U doing today? Wanna do something?' he asked.

'Not sure, think I need to spend the day with Kate though seeing as she's staying here' I replied.

'That girl is ruining everything, first I can't stay over, now I can't spend the day with you! Strong dislike coming from over here' he text back, making me giggle.

We text each other back and forth for about an hour and I was glad that I decided to upgrade my phone package so that I got unlimited texts, otherwise this would be costing me a fortune.

I got up a couple of hours later, getting dressed and heading out to the kitchen. Liam was already over. I shouldn't have been surprised really; he was hardly ever at his house. He spent most of the day here when he wasn't at school, leaving around nine o'clock only to sneak back in through my window around ten thirty anyway. I smiled at him but quickly looked away because he was sitting next to Jake.

"Morning, Ambs. Where's Kate? Did you talk to her about not touching me?" Jake asked, making me laugh at his serious expression.

"She's in the shower. Anyway, you should be flattered that she likes you, though maybe she'll move onto Liam today," I teased, winking at him.

Liam groaned. "No way! I'm seeing someone," he stated confidently. I blushed slightly and shifted uncomfortably on my feet because he'd just said that to Jake.

Jake's face snapped in his direction. "You're seeing someone? As in, like, seriously? You don't do relationships," he said, frowning and looking at him disbelievingly.

"I crazy about her," Liam replied, shrugging. I made my way over to the fridge to get some milk for my cereal, trying to pretend I wasn't there. My heart was crashing in my chest. Oh God he was going to do it! He was going to tell Jake!

"Crazy about her? As in, you're not going to mess her around? She must be a really great screw," Jake said, smirking and slapping him on the back proudly. I choked on my orange juice.

"I've not slept with her. She believes in no sex before marriage." Liam smirked.

Jake looked like he nearly passed out, he was looking at Liam like he had grown another head. "You…. she…. what?" he stuttered, shaking his head violently.

Liam just laughed. "As of now, I'm officially off the market. So, Angel, tell your friend that I'm taken," he instructed, turning to me and giving me a wink.

"I will. Wow, so a reformed man-whore, maybe there is hope for you after all, Jake." I laughed, throwing a coco pop at him.

"No way, I give it a week and Liam will be back to his old self, sleeping with anything that moves," Jake stated confidently.

"I don't know Jake; he looks pretty serious to me," I said as I finished my breakfast. Liam smiled at me, he obviously liked what I said, showing my trust.

"Finally, you've learned to use the head that's attached to your neck," Jake joked, making me flinch at his words.

"I think it's sweet, Liam. She's a lucky girl; hopefully you won't break her heart," I muttered, looking down at my empty bowl, just hoping that he wouldn't hurt me.

"I won't," Liam stated confidently. I smiled as I walked back to my room to see Kate. I could hear Jake quizzing Liam in the kitchen and I didn't want to be there for it.

"So, what shall we do today?" I asked Kate as she was applying her usual ton of make-up.

"Hmm, I know, how about we go bowling? I could call Sarah and Sean. We could ask your brother and Liam to come," she chirped excitedly. I didn't really like bowling much, but my other friends loved it. We probably ended up going about one a month.

"Sure, I'll call them." I grabbed my cellphone and dialled Sarah's number.

"I'll go ask sex god one and two." Kate smiled, skipping out of my bedroom.

I followed behind her as Sarah answered. "Hey, Sar, want to come bowling?" I asked cheerfully, as Kate plopped herself down next to Jake on the couch, practically sitting on his lap.

"Yeah sure. What time?" she replied, sounding excited.

"We'll meet you there in, say, an hour?" I suggested, looking at my watch, it was only just after ten now so that should be fine.

"OK. I'll call Sean, I can pick him up on the way," she chirped.

I grinned because Kate was now flirting with Jake shamelessly. "OK great. See you there." I disconnected the call and leant against the wall, watching my best friend plead with my brother.

"Please come with us? Then you can see how skilled I am with balls," Kate purred, fluttering her eyelashes. Liam choked on his laughter, quickly turning it into a cough as Kate turned to face him. "Come on, Liam, I'll make it worth your while. I know you're a good player, how about you teach me a few tricks?" she said seductively, moving closer to him. He looked uncomfortable with her advances. I was actually enjoying him squirm. Usually, he would flirt back with her, but today he looked like he wanted to run away.

I decided to help him out. "Kate, will you leave them alone? I don't want my slut of a brother, and his reformed slut of a best friend, coming, if I have to watch you throw yourself at them all day," I scoffed, pretending to gag. I was actually getting quite annoyed that she was still looking at Liam like she wanted to eat him there and then. Liam looked at me gratefully, which made my heart seem to stutter slightly in my chest.

Kate grinned at me. "Hmm, well where's the fun in that?" she asked, winking at me and making me chuckle.

"We're going bowling in an hour anyway; if you want to come it's up to you. Sarah and Sean are coming, and maybe Terri too." I shrugged, plopping on the floor by Liam's feet, leaning against his legs. I could see Kate staring at me with shocked, wide eyes, so I quickly moved away from him, blushing like crazy.

"I don't mind bowling. What do you think, Jake, want to whip the girl's asses?" Liam asked, grinning.

Kate nodded quickly. "I'm definitely up for some whipping," she said enthusiastically. The boys both ignored her.

"Yeah OK. I like bowling I guess. Hey, Liam, why don't you ask your girlfriend to come along too? Or are you afraid that she'll take one look at me and think she's made a mistake and dump your ass for an upgrade?" Jake joked.

"My girlfriend wouldn't even look at you, Jake, so I don't have anything to worry about," Liam answered confidently; I could hear the amusement in his voice. I just blushed harder, trying to melt into the sofa and disappear.

"You have a girlfriend, Liam?" Kate asked, frowning. She looked like she was trying to solve a complicated math problem, her face all scrunched up in concentration.

"Yep he does. Some mystery girl who he's crazy about, apparently," Jake scoffed, rolling his eyes.

Kate's eyes shot to me for some reason. She looked like she was trying to bore a hole in my face. I gulped and looked away, not really wanting to lie to my best friend. She gasped and looked at me with wide eyes, then looked at Liam, then back to me, silently asking if it was me. Holy crap, what is she a mind reader or something? I nodded slowly, trying not to be obvious, making her gasp again and giggle excitedly.

"Let's go finish getting ready in your room, Amber!" she cried, jumping up. She was so excited that she actually clapped her hands like a child. I groaned internally, oh great, here it comes, the million questions.

"I'm already ready." I shook my head at her warningly.

"I *need* your help in the bedroom with something!" she hissed, looking like she would murder me if I didn't get up right now. I pushed myself up and I heard Liam chuckle from the couch. I rolled my eyes at him; he really had a big mouth at times! But it is a sweet mouth.

I followed Kate into my bedroom; she shut the door and grabbed me. "I knew it! That boy has been eyeing you for years!" she

76

cried, jumping up and down. I laughed at her excitement; she seemed almost as pleased about it as if it was her going out with him.

"He has not!" I smiled.

She dragged me over to the bed. "Oh be quiet! He is *always* looking at you. He finds any excuse to touch you. He flirts with you shamelessly, and is always telling you how hot you are." She sighed dreamily. "So, young lady, when were you planning on telling me, your best friend?" she scolded, playfully.

"Er well, we were going to keep it secret for a couple of weeks. Jake's really not going to like it." I cringed slightly at the thought of the warning look I'd seen him giving Liam earlier when we were cleaning after the party; he was really opposed to the idea of me dating him.

"Wow, yeah, I didn't think about that. Jake's going to be crazy mad!" she said with wide eyes. I nodded, playing with my hands in my lap. "So, when did all this happen? You were together at the party, right? He was staring at you the whole night, and he beat the crap out of Jessica's brother for kissing you."

I gasped, a little shocked. "He beat up Jessica's brother?" I asked. I remembered him pinning him against the wall, but then I ran off to be sick.

"Yeah. He was shouting at him to keep his filthy hands off you, and that you didn't want him to kiss you. He'd seen you trying to push him away, apparently. Liam hit him a couple of times before the team broke it up. Then he just disappeared after that, Jake said he went home." She eyed me curiously. I knew my face was red, I was a terrible liar. "He didn't go home, did he?" She smirked at me knowingly.

I took a deep breath and shook my head. She screamed, literally screamed, and about two seconds later Jake and Liam came bursting into my room.

"WHAT? WHAT IS IT?" Jake shouted, looking around like there was a fire or something.

"Er.... Er, it was a.... er," I stuttered, grasping wildly for something to say.

"Spider," Kate interjected quickly, pointing in the direction of my bathroom.

Jake sighed and walked in there, shaking his head disapprovingly. "Seriously, all that over a spider? I thought you were being murdered in here!" he scolded.

Kate smirked at me and Liam. He actually looked like he was

having fun watching me squirm. He winked at me, which made Kate laugh. I stuck my tongue out at him and he waggled his eyebrows at me, she just laughed louder at the two of us.

Jake walked back out, frowning and shaking his head. "I couldn't find anything in there."

"Oh, maybe it wasn't a spider; it might have just been a bit of fluff or something," Kate suggested, waving her hand for them to leave.

Jake rolled his eyes. "Jeez, Kate, you really are weird," he said, walking out and shutting the door behind him.

She turned back to me, looking excited. "I can't believe you lost your virginity to Liam James! Was it good? I bet he was good, right? He is so freaking hot! I'm so jealous!" she cooed, going off into a world of her own.

"I didn't have sex with him," I said quickly.

She snapped her eyes to mine. "You didn't? Well why the heck not? If that was me I would have jumped his fine ass there and then."

I giggled and shrugged. "Yeah I know you would, but that's just not me."

"OK, I know." She sighed, looking a little defeated. Suddenly her face brightened again. "So, what did you do then?"

"We just made out, Kate, that's all," I said honestly. We really hadn't gone much further than that, so it wasn't really a lie.

"You're so lucky. You have the hottest guy in school as your boyfriend and the second hottest is your brother. I mean, that's just greedy!" she scolded, waggling her finger at me in a mock annoyed gesture. "So, he called you his girlfriend! Has he asked you out? Like officially, you're a couple? Exclusively?" she asked, looking at me in awe.

I nodded, but grimaced at the same time. "Yeah he has, and yeah we are. But to be honest, I don't know how it's going to work out. I mean, he's such a player I'm honestly a little scared to let myself fall for him in case he cheats on me or dumps me or something," I admitted in a small voice, staring at the floor as all of my worries flashed through my mind.

She grabbed me into a hug, which immediately made me start to feel sick. My heart was pounding in my chest at her casual touch. I knew she was only trying to comfort me, but I couldn't help my body's reaction to touch. "I don't think he will. I mean, he's never had a girlfriend before, he's *never* been exclusive, so you have nothing to base your theory on. Technically, he's never cheated on anyone before." She gave me a half smile. I couldn't help but laugh at her attempt to make me feel better. I guess that's true, the fact that he's willing to be exclusive is a sign that he's into it.

"We'd better go anyway; Sarah and Sean will be waiting there for us. Oh and Kate, don't say anything to anyone, OK? Not even Sarah. I just want to see how it goes for a couple of weeks before Jake finds out," I explained.

"I won't, I promise," she vowed, crossing her heart. "So, is he a good kisser?" she whispered, as we walked down the hallway.

"Unbelievable," I replied, as we walked to the lounge.

"Damn it! Lucky cow!" she muttered quietly, making me chuckle.

Chapter 9

"So, are you guys coming or not?" I asked, because they were still sitting on the couch.

"Yeah, OK." Jake sighed. He obviously didn't want to come, maybe Liam was making him. He grabbed his keys and headed for the door. "I'll go get the car out of the garage. Meet you out there."

"Oh crap, I forgot my purse," Kate said, skipping off back to my room.

Liam immediately grabbed me and kissed me, pushing me against the wall gently. I wrapped my arms around his neck, gripping my fingers in his hair. "Mmm, I've missed you," he murmured against my lips.

"You did? I had no idea. Could you make it a little more obvious?" I joked, making him chuckle.

He kissed me again, sucking on my bottom lip lightly, asking for entrance. I eagerly opened my mouth for him; he slipped his tongue in, exploring every part of my mouth, making my stomach get butterflies. Someone cleared their throat and we jumped apart, thinking it was Jake. Thankfully it wasn't though, it was Kate.

She had the biggest grin on her face that I had ever seen. "You two look hot together," she stated, smirking at me.

Liam laughed and threw his arm around my shoulder. "Angel looks hot whoever she's with." He grinned and kissed my cheek, softly.

"Aww, that's so sweet!" Kate cooed, putting her hand over her heart, looking at him adoringly.

I rolled my eyes. "Oh, come on! We'll be late if we don't go now." I grabbed her hand and pulled her out of the door. I turned back and threw my keys to Liam, who locked the front door behind him. As he handed me back my keys, his finger brushed mine on

80

purpose, making me moan a little in the back of my throat.

"Hey, Liam, you don't mind riding in the back with Amber, do you? I really want to sit up front," Kate called from the car, giving me a wink.

I saw Jake shaking his head at Liam, obviously asking for help. Liam smirked in his direction. "No. That's fine if you want to ride up front." He glanced at me from the corner of his eye. I smiled at Kate subtly. I loved my best friend; bless her, she was giving me time with him.

I climbed in the back and Liam slid in next to me, pressing his knee against mine. I put my hands in my lap and smiled. He reached out and took my hand, holding it tightly, putting it on the seat in the middle of us and moved his leg so it was shielded from view in case Jake turned around. There wasn't really much chance of that though, considering he was driving, but I guess it's better to be safe than sorry. Liam's casual touch was sending sparks of electricity shooting up my arm. I bit my lip and looked out of the window, fighting the desire to grab him and kiss him until I couldn't breathe. After the longest, most excruciating car journey ever, we arrived at the bowling alley. OK, that a slight exaggeration, it only took ten minutes, but the whole time I was fighting with myself to just jump on him and hold him tightly.

There were eight of us bowling; Me, Liam, Jake, Kate, Sarah, Sean, his girlfriend Terri, and she had brought her brother, Mark, who was down from college. Liam seemed to have taken an instant disliking to Mark for some reason. He was being polite enough, but his smile didn't quite reach his eyes. I was actually having fun even though I was totally losing. I was terrible at bowling and only really came to be with my friends. The highlight of the whole experience was watching Liam bowl. When he bent to throw his ball, I got a perfect view of his perfect behind, and I could barely contain my enjoyment.

"Not too good at the whole bowling thing, huh?" Mark asked, sitting down next to me, smiling.

I laughed. "Nope, I never did get the hang of it," I stated, shaking my head in mock horror.

"I could teach you if you want. It's all about the positioning," he purred, suggestively.

I gulped nervously, but tried not to let it show. "Positioning, really? That's why I've been getting it wrong all these years?" I smiled, a little uncomfortable, but to be honest I liked flirting, as long as they didn't get the wrong idea and start trying to touch me.

"I'm somewhat an expert with positions. I would be more than happy to give you some lessons," he purred, leaning in closer to me, making me lean back to keep some personal space.

"Well, it's my turn right now, so what would you suggest?" I asked, standing up and choosing my ball.

He stood up and walked close behind me. "I would definitely suggest moving your hips with the ball. Maybe you should spread your legs further apart, give you more balance," he said, waggling his eyebrows.

I laughed at his suggestion; jeez, this guy is so obvious! "Well thanks for the tips; I'll see how it goes." I laughed and walked up to take my turn. My ball went straight down the edge and only hit one pin. My second ball went straight down the gutter. "Hmm, Mark, I think you may need to work on your tips. You kind of built my hopes up there, I feel kind of let down," I joked, pouting.

He laughed. "Wow, I've never let a girl down before," he said, smiling proudly.

"Cocky much?" I asked, laughing.

"Want to find out?" he teased.

"Hmm, let me think." I narrowed my eyes and dragged them down his body, slowly, from head to toe and back up again, making sure to bite my lip in a flirty manner. He was grinning wildly. "Could you turn around?" I asked, trying to hide my laughter.

"You want me to turn around?" he asked, smirking.

I nodded. "I'll need to view the back, I'm not sure if I want to accept your offer," I said dismissively. He winked at me and turned around, obviously thinking he was in luck. I bit my lip to stop myself from laughing and mouthed *'What an idiot!'* to Kate and Sarah who were giggling like mad girls on crack. "OK, you can turn back now," I said after a few seconds.

He turned back to face me. "Well, like what you see?" he asked, smirking at me confidently.

I leaned in close to him. "No, I don't, actually. You just don't do it for me, but thanks for the offer," I stated, smirking and winking at him as I walked back to the seats. I could hear my friends burst into loud laughter; Sarah slapped Kate a high five. Mark was just staring after me with his mouth open, obviously not used to rejection. I glanced at Liam, he looked hurt and angry.

Oh crap! What did I do? I was just flirting, I wouldn't have done anything! I tried to catch his eye but he just looked away at the score board, ignoring me. My heart sank.

Jake went to get some drinks in-between games so I took my

opportunity to speak to Liam; he hadn't even looked in my direction since the whole Mark incident. "Hey," I said, moving to sit next to him.

"Hey," he muttered, watching the people next to us bowl.

"Not talking to me?" I asked, scared he would say no.

He sighed. "Why did you do that?" he asked sadly, shaking his head, still not looking at me.

I grabbed his hand and dragged him off to the bathrooms. When we got into the ladies room, I shut the door behind us and locked it. "I'm sorry. I didn't realise that would upset you. I didn't mean anything by it. He was flirting with me, I was just joking around, that's all," I explained, trying to get him to look at me, but he just closed his eyes for a second before looking back at me again.

"Angel, that was hard to watch." He pulled me to his chest, looking into my eyes; I could see that I had hurt him badly.

"I'm sorry, Liam. Honestly, I didn't mean anything by it, I was just having fun. People don't know we're together I could hardly say, *'Mark, stop flirting with me, my boyfriend's sitting right there'* could I?" I asked, putting my arms around his neck.

He sighed. "I guess not." He still looked upset and I felt awful that I'd hurt him.

"You need to trust me though; I would never do anything to hurt you on purpose. I'm sorry." I pulled his face to mine and kissed him tenderly.

He responded immediately, kissing me back and pulling me closer to him. He slid one hand down and gripped it on my ass, it didn't even affect me at all, well, it did but not in any of the bad ways, I liked it, I wanted more. I grabbed his other hand and pulled it up my body, making it cup my breast. He pulled back, looking at me a little shocked; I smiled at him and pulled him back to me. He kissed me hungrily, massaging my breasts. His mouth travelled down my neck, making me shiver with desire. I slipped my hand under his t-shirt, tracing the muscles on his chest, making him moan. He slowly moved his hand down to the bottom of my top and slipped his hand under, trailing his fingers along my skin, moving it up slowly until he got to my breasts where he massaged them through my bra making me moan breathily.

After a few minutes, he pulled away, smiling at me, his eyes dancing with excitement. He put his forehead to mine, we were both breathing heavy. "I'm sorry. I didn't mean to be all possessive," he said, kissing the tip of my nose.

"You don't have anything to apologise for, silly. We've both

83

never done this before, so we need to find a way that works for both of us." I kissed him tenderly again, savouring the feel of his soft lips against mine.

He sighed. "I think we need to go back out now before people realise we're missing."

"Another minute won't hurt," I whispered, smiling flirtily. He chuckled and bent down to kiss me again.

That night we were all cramped into my lounge. Sean had brought Avitar round and none of us had seen it before so all seven of us were now sitting around, eating McDonalds. We were going to put the movie on after. I was leant against Liam's legs; Jake didn't seem to bat an eyelid, which we both took as a good sign.

Mark moved off of the couch. "Here, Sarah, you sit here, I'll sit on the floor," he suggested, as he plopped down next to me with a flirty smile. I shifted uncomfortably to get a little more space from him. I felt Liam stiffen, so I put my hand on his foot, rubbing my thumb across the top of it soothingly. "So, Amber, what do you like to do in your free time?" he asked.

"Lots of stuff. I like to dance and go to movies. You know normal *high school* stuff," I replied, adding definition to the words high school.

He laughed. "Wow, you really are a feisty one aren't you?" he said, shaking his head.

"You have no idea," I muttered, turning away, pretending to watch the TV.

"You don't want to talk to me?" he asked, faking hurt.

I let out an exaggerated sigh. "I'm just trying to watch this."

He looked at the TV, and laughed. "This advert for new sofas?"

I looked at the TV that I was pretending to watch, it was indeed an advert. Damn it! "Yep, I'm a sofa girl, you can never have enough sofas," I joked.

"You're funny." He laughed, scooting closer to me.

"Thanks, and you're too old for me," I stated, smiling sweetly.

"I'm only nineteen." He looked at me challengingly.

I nodded. "Yeah, but eighteen is my limit, so you're shit outta luck, bud," I said. I heard Liam laugh behind me.

"I could make you change your mind," Mark stated confidently.

I laughed humourlessly. "You know what, I'd bet you twenty bucks that you got nothing of interest for me," I replied just as confidently.

He chuckled darkly. "I'll take that bet, but you need to wait until your brother's not watching." He glanced at Jake a little nervously.

I sighed. "What is it exactly that you think I'm going to be interested in? You have a kitten in your pocket? Or maybe some candy? Or the answers to the test I have tomorrow in calculus?" I joked, making him laugh again.

"No. I'm going to kiss you, and you're going to love it." He shrugged, smirking at me again.

Liam's legs jerked behind me as he made a move to get up. I pushed back on his legs and started rubbing his foot again. "Really? If you kiss me I'm going to knee you in the balls." I smiled at Mark, innocently.

"You think that's going to scare me away from a hottie like you?" he asked, looking me over slowly, making my skin crawl a little.

"It's just a friendly warning." I shrugged, turning back to the TV which, thankfully, was now the movie and not a sofa advert.

"I'm pretty sure my money is safe. I've never had any complaints before," he whispered in my ear, making me go cold because of how close he was to me.

"Hmm, well there's a first time for everything," I said through my teeth, still rubbing Liam's foot.

When the movie finished, Liam went home to tell his parents he was going to stay over at ours and to grab a change of clothes. He actually had spare clothes in my room, but we couldn't exactly tell anyone that. Jake and Kate were making more popcorn. We were now going to watch Terminator Salvation, because most people hadn't seen it. I went to the bathroom. When I stepped out, someone grabbed me and pushed me against the wall. At first I thought it was Liam, but then I realised this guy wasn't tall enough. My heart started to race, the fear building up in my stomach. Mark laughed and crashed his lips to mine, roughly, gripping the sides of my face so I couldn't move away. I tried to push him away but he wouldn't budge. He nibbled my lip, asking for entrance, so I clamped my mouth shut and brought my knee up as hard as I could into his groin. He let go of me instantly, bending over, groaning.

"Told ya. That's twenty bucks you owe me," I said sweetly, as I stepped past him and made my way back to the lounge with a triumphant smile plastered on my face.

Liam was sitting back down on the couch so I quickly took the seat next to him before anyone else did. "You OK?" he asked, looking at me, smiling.

"Yep," I replied, popping the p.

He smiled. "What's so funny?"

I giggled. "Mark," I answered, grinning. Just then, Mark walked in to the lounge, limping slightly, his hand over his groin, looking like he was in a bit of pain. He threw a twenty dollar bill into my lap and sat down over the other side of the room.

Liam burst out laughing. "That's my girl," he whispered, making me smile.

After everyone had left, it was almost midnight. Kate and I went to bed, leaving Liam and Jake in the lounge. I winked at Liam as I went to bed and decided to put on my smallest pyjamas tonight so I could feel his skin on mine. I pulled on my pink short shorts that had purple lace along the trim. I paired it with a skin tight matching pink tank top with a bit of purple lace across the breasts. I looked in my mirror and suddenly got nervous. Maybe I should change, was this giving him the wrong impression? I bit my lip. No, it's fine, he'd seen me in this before so I'd wear it.

I went back into my bedroom, Kate whistled at me. "Wow, Amber, you should take a little trip to the kitchen and get a glass of water or something. Let Liam have something to dream about," she suggested, looking me up and down.

Actually, that wasn't a bad idea; otherwise he wouldn't get to see until the morning. "You think?" I asked nervously. She nodded eagerly, so I decided to do it before I wimped out. "OK," I agreed, laughing as I opened my door.

"Go on! Give him a thrill." She waved her enthusiastically when I hesitated at the door.

I took a deep breath and walked confidently down the hallway. The way our house is set out, you have to walk through the lounge to get to the kitchen. I strutted into the lounge in my tiny pyjamas. "Anyone want a drink?" I asked innocently, walking past Jake and Liam who were sat watching the sports channel.

"No thanks," Jake answered, not even looking at me.

Liam's eyes snapped to me, his gaze literally followed my every move, his mouth slightly open and his eyes wide. I bit my lip to stop from laughing. Oh yeah, totally worth it!

I grabbed two glasses of water and walked back out through the lounge, with Liam taking off what little clothes I had on, off of me with his eyes. Jake spotted him looking and slapped him around the back of the head. "Dude, stop perving on my little sister! Anyway, you have a girlfriend," he grumbled, clearly annoyed.

Liam rubbed the back of his head. "Right yeah, girlfriend," he mumbled, smiling.

I went back to my room, laughing my head off. "That was so funny," I told Kate, who was sitting up in bed waiting for me.

She started laughing too. "Did he like?" she asked, waggling her eyebrows.

"Yep," I confirmed, popping the p. I climbed in to bed with a smile on my face.

A little while later, I heard Jake go to bed so I knew Liam was on his own. "Kate, I'm going to go and see Liam for a little while," I said, once I knew that Jake would be asleep.

"Oh really? Give him another view of that sexy ass sleepwear?" she teased, smiling.

I giggled. "Something like that. Don't wait up, I might be a while." I winked at her as I climbed out of the bed, grabbing my cellphone so I could use the alarm function.

"Have fun, and don't do anything that I wouldn't do," she joked. There actually wasn't much that Kate wouldn't do, she'd had a few boyfriends and she definitely wasn't a virgin. I giggled and left the room, snaking down the hallway to the living room, where Liam was already laying on the couch under the spare duvet. I set the alarm for six; the usual *'get Liam out of my window'* time, and put it on the floor.

"Hey, Angel," he whispered, smiling at me and pulling the duvet out of the way so I could lay down next to him. I eagerly climbed in and melted my body against his. He sighed contentedly and wrapped his arms around me tightly. "That was not fair earlier, by the way," he scolded, as he kissed my forehead.

I smiled teasingly. "Really, you didn't like my pyjamas?" I asked, innocently.

"I *loved* the pyjamas, but not how you paraded your sexy ass right in front of me with your brother sitting there," he groaned.

"You think I have a sexy ass?" I teased.

"Hmm, I can't remember, let me have another look," he said huskily. I giggled and rolled over onto my stomach, putting my hands under my head.

He groaned again and slowly ran his hand down my back, across my ass and down one of my thighs before going back up the other one. His hand came to a stop on my ass, tracing the line of the lace, making me shiver. Jeez, what's happening to me? I actually want him to touch me. If he made a move to touch me, I wasn't going to stop him this time. He bent his head and kissed my shoulder, before moving down lower and trailing kisses across my back and

87

hips. He kissed to the bottom of the shorts and trailed his tongue across the very bottom of my ass cheek, just where it meets the leg. I gasped and stiffened.

He pulled away quickly. "Sorry, sorry. I got carried away," he said apologetically.

I blushed like crazy. "I liked it, Liam," I said huskily, my voice shaking slightly from the desire that was racing through my bloodstream.

"You did?" he asked, sounding surprised about it.

"Oh heck yeah," I admitted breathily, making me blush again. Wow, did I just say that? That's so embarrassing!

He moaned slightly and bent his head, tracing his tongue along the edge of the lace again. This time I couldn't help the little moan that escaped my lips. The sound seemed to encourage him, as he did it again, and slipped his hand up my thigh, massaging my ass and back. He kissed up my back, lifting the material of my top so he could kiss my skin. I rolled over so we were face to face and kissed him, pulling him down to me so his whole body was pressed onto mine. I could feel his skin against mine as I was glad I decided to go for the skimpy sleepwear. He was getting excited downstairs again, I could feel him pressed against my thigh, but I wasn't scared this time, I was encouraged. He brought his hands up and cupped my breasts; I let out a sigh when I felt his hot hand just through the material of my top because I wasn't wearing a bra. He moaned as he rubbed his thumb over my nipples making them hard. He was only wearing shorts so I rubbed my hands down his chest and stomach, just marveling at how toned and perfect he was.

He kissed down my neck and across my breasts through my top. My hands tangled into his silky brown hair as he kissed his way down my stomach, getting hold of my top with his teeth and pulling it up, slowly, exposing my stomach. I moaned and he brought his mouth down on my bare skin, licking it lightly and blowing on it, making my body almost vibrate with excitement. He slipped his hand under my top and slowly trailed it up towards my breasts, trailing his fingertips over them while he continued to kiss my stomach, but he was kissing higher now and my breathing was starting to speed in anticipation of him kissing my breasts.

Oh God, yep this is way too fast! "Sorry…. Liam…. stop," I mumbled.

He pulled his head back immediately, and smiled his beautiful smile. "You don't need to apologise, Angel." He bent his head and kissed me again gently. I smiled at him gratefully as he rolled off of me, pulling me close to his chest, running his fingers through my hair, looking at me lovingly. "You are so beautiful," he murmured, kissing my nose gently as he pulled my top back down for me. I giggled and shook my head. He really was full of these corny lines! Maybe that works for him to get the girls to sleep with him. He smiled, looking a little hurt. "You don't believe me," he stated.

"How many girls have you said that to, Liam?" I whispered, not really sure my voice would sound right if I spoke normally.

He sighed and looked a little defeated. "I can't change my past, Angel; trust me I wish I could. I've never felt anything for anyone else, I swear. I've never told anyone they were beautiful before, only ever you. Nothing else compares to you," he said, looking at me intently, willing me to understand. My breath caught in my throat at his sweet words. I squeezed myself closer to him and buried my face in his chest, breathing him in. He sighed happily and wrapped his arms tightly around me, kissing my forehead. "Goodnight, Angel," he whispered.

"Night, Liam," I murmured against his skin.

I had a feeling that the being careful not to give him my heart plan, had gone completely out the window. All I could do now, was pray that he wouldn't break it. I snuggled closer to him, laying my head on his chest and falling asleep within minutes. Just as I started to go under I thought I heard him whisper something that sounded like 'I love you', but Liam wouldn't say that, so it must have been something else.

Chapter 10

"WHAT THE FUCK IS THIS?" I heard Jake roar from nearby. I opened my eyes and looked at him. His face was bright red and he looked murderously angry.

"Jake, not so loud you're going to make my ears bleed! What's wrong?" I asked, sitting up. But as soon as I moved, I realised what was wrong. I was still on the couch with Liam. Oh no! I jumped up quickly and looked at Liam who had his mouth hanging open, looking completely shocked. OK, I need to salvage the situation quickly. "Damn it, Liam! Yuck! Did you have your hands on me?" I cried, pretending to shudder in horror. Jake looked at me, his face still angry, but he looked slightly confused now.

"I.... er.... don't.... what?" Liam stammered.

"What the hell were you doing with him, Amber?" Jake growled angrily, pointing at Liam who just looked confused at this point.

"I must have fallen asleep, I guess." I frowned, shaking my head as if I was confused too.

"Fallen asleep? Well, what were you doing with him in the first place?" he asked, shooting Liam another dirty look before turning back to me. OK, come on, think! Oh I got it; he'll have to accept this one!

"I had a bad dream, Jake," I mumbled, looking at the floor, and pretending to be upset.

He gasped and wrapped his arms around me, instantly, putting his chin on the top of my head. "Oh shit, Amber. It's OK," he cooed, rocking me slightly.

"I was upset and I thought you were out here, but you weren't. Liam comforted me, that's all. We must have fallen asleep," I whispered, feeling guilty that I was lying. I really wasn't ready for him to know yet, especially after the way he was just looking at Liam.

90

"I'm sorry, I just thought…. well, never mind," Jake muttered, pulling back to look at me. "You alright now?" I nodded, biting my lip to try and ease some of the guilt I felt. He looked over at Liam. "Sorry, man, I jumped to conclusions and er…. thanks for taking care of my sister."

Liam looked really uncomfortable and glanced at me; I gave him a pleading expression, begging him with my eyes not to say anything. "Yeah, no probs." He shrugged, rubbing a hand through his messy bed hair.

I quickly pulled out of Jake's grasp. "I'm going to go and get changed for school. What time is it anyway?" I asked, looking around for my cellphone. Why hadn't the freaking alarm gone off?

"It's not even six yet, Amber. I woke up early." Jake shrugged.

"Right, well then I'm going to go have some breakfast before I go in the shower. Er…. thanks, Liam, for last night," I said, blushing and giving him a small smile.

"It was definitely my pleasure, Angel." He winked at me, smiling happily.

Jake slapped him across the back of his head, making him wince. "Little sister!" he stated, rolling his eyes and stomping off towards the kitchen, leaving me and Liam in the lounge.

Once Jake had gone, Liam looked at me. "I don't like having to lie to your brother, Angel," he whispered, frowning.

"I know, but just a couple of weeks, please?" I begged, kissing him quickly on his lips and turning to run off in the direction of the kitchen. He grabbed my hand and pulled me back to him, kissing me again, before he gave me one of his beautiful smiles. I almost skipped to the kitchen because I was so happy. Jake was having toast, so I made two bowls of my favourite cereal, one for me, one for Liam. I carried them into the lounge and handed him one, before plopping down on the floor by the couch.

"Er…. thanks for this, Angel, but I don't like coco pops," he said, turning his nose up at the bowl.

I frowned at him, confused. He was always eating my cereal. Every day he had a bowl of coco pops. "Sure you do, you eat it every day." I looked at him like he'd lost his mind; did he think I was stupid or something?

He laughed and shook his head. "No I don't. I make a bowl of it every day and pretend to eat it, before you come in and snatch it off me," he said with a sexy smile and amused eyes.

"Why the heck would you make a bowl and pretend to eat it? Do you like to piss me off?" I asked, annoyed.

"No, Angel. I like to make you breakfast," he said simply.

I gasped at the revelation. He made them for me? "You make them for me? Every day?" I asked, my mouth hanging open, shocked that he would be so sweet and I had never even noticed. Every day I would come in and make some nasty comment to him about eating at home and leaving my cereal alone, and all this time he makes it for me? Jeez, that is so freaking sweet! He just shrugged as if it was nothing. All this time I thought he was just a jerk, when really he was being nice to me! Jake walked in then, so I couldn't say anything. I scoffed my breakfast and practically ran to my bedroom, grabbing my cellphone and texting him because as I couldn't speak to him:

'Thank you, that is really sweet! I never realised that you did that. I'll thank you properly later! X' I sent. I smiled to myself and went to take a shower.

As we stepped out of Liam's car at school, we were swamped by the usual hoard of girls wanting to paw Jake and Liam. I rolled my eyes as Jessica pushed her way to the front and wrapped her dirty little arms round my boyfriend's waist, looking at him with her come to bed eyes.

"Jessica, seriously you need to get off," Liam said sternly, unwrapping her from him and stepping backwards.

"Liam, baby, how about we skip first period and we go have some fun," she purred suggestively, rubbing her hand up his chest.

Oh my God, I was so jealous that I actually felt sick!

I turned and walked off as fast as I could, just wanting to be away from it all. After a minute I could hear Kate running to catch up with me, she grabbed my hand pulling me to a stop. "Seriously, I'm not in the mood," I almost shouted, turning to her, but it wasn't her, it was Liam.

"Hey, I just wanted to walk you to class." He frowned, looking at me sadly.

"Oh right…. er…. sorry. I thought you were with Jessica, having some *fun*," I said sarcastically, embarrassed that I had shouted at him.

He shook his head and stepped closer to me. "No, I'm not with her, I'm *with* you," he said sweetly, smiling at me and making my heart beat faster.

"Right, yeah sorry, I just…. I don't know…." I trailed off, blushing like crazy.

"You were jealous," he stated, seeming pleased about it. I nodded reluctantly not really wanting to admit it. "Good, I've been waiting for you to get jealous for the last twelve years," he said,

92

grinning like a crazy person.

I laughed. "You have? Well there you go then, it finally happened." I kicked my shoes in the stones; trying to distract myself from the jealous feeling I still had coursing through my veins. I guess I was going to have to get used to girls being all over him. He was Liam James for goodness sake; girls have always followed him around, begging for his attention.

"Remember the talk we had yesterday, the one about trust? Well, that works both ways you know. I will never hurt you, but you need to believe that too." He put his finger under my chin and tilted my head up, making me look at him.

I sighed; yeah OK I did say that I guess. "I do trust you, it was just hard to watch," I replied, smirking, mimicking his words from yesterday.

He laughed. "Yeah well, the word's out now that I have a girlfriend so that should put an end to the whole flirting thing," he said with confidence, brushing my hair from my face.

"You told everyone that you have a girlfriend?" I asked, shocked. OK wow, maybe he is more serious than I thought about making this work.

"Yeah, of course. I *do* have a girlfriend. I have the sexiest, most beautiful girlfriend in the world, who is yet to give me the thank you that she promised me by text this morning." He smiled his flirty smile at me and it felt like a thousand butterflies took off in my stomach.

I giggled and leant forwards until my mouth was almost touching his. "All good things come to those who wait," I teased, winking at him and walking off.

He groaned and caught me up quickly. "You don't think twelve years is long enough to wait?" he asked, faking shock, making me giggle.

"Hmm, not really. I think I'll make you wait a little longer." I blew him a kiss as I stepped through the doors to my history class. I heard him groan, but when I looked back he was smiling, watching me walk away. I purposefully swayed my ass, trying to look sexy; it must have worked because three boys from my history class whistled at me and made a comment about my sexy booty. I rolled my eyes. Boys!

I couldn't speak to Liam much at lunch, we were sat at the same table but everyone wanted to talk to him. "So, you really have a secret girlfriend?" Tim, one of his friends, asked, looking at him like he didn't believe him at all.

"Yep," Liam confirmed, looking extremely proud about it. Every

93

time he looked at me, I blushed like crazy, and was sure someone was going to notice.

"She must be one hot woman to have tamed the beast into settling down," Rick smirked.

Liam laughed, his eyes shot to me for a split second. "She is the sexiest thing alive, man," he said confidently.

"Really? She a good fuck?" Rick asked, picking at his sandwich.

"Dude, seriously, I'm not going to answer that about my girl," Liam stated with a smirk.

"I bet I could blow her out of the water," Rochelle flirted, running her hand down his arm.

He laughed. "You know what, you wouldn't stand a chance. My girl is incredibly beautiful, both inside and out." Liam shrugged, pulling his arm away, grinning. All the girls at the table aww'd and ahh'd. I smiled and tried to eat my lunch. I could feel Kate's eyes on me so I looked at her, she was grinning at me from ear to ear. I rolled my eyes at her, chuckling.

"He hasn't slept with her, she believes in no sex before marriage," Jake interjected, smirking. I swallowed a laugh. Had Jake really believed him when he told him that this morning? Everyone gasped and looked at Liam, who was grinning like crazy.

"No shit! You haven't slept with her?" Rick asked sceptically.

"No I haven't, but that's not really any of your business, guys." Liam shook his head, grinning. "I've got to go. I need to speak to coach about practice." He shrugged, getting up. Half of the boys got up too, following him out.

As soon as he was gone, all the girls started planning and scheming. They wanted to know who the secret girl was, and would stop at nothing to find out, then they each took out twenty dollars and put it into the middle of the table. I looked at them, confused.

"So, the next girl to nail him, wins the pot," Jessica said, with a smirk.

I gasped. "Seriously? He's just said he has a girlfriend and isn't interested, and you're betting on who's going to sleep with him next? What if his girlfriend sleeps with him next?" I asked, shocked. I can't believe these girls are betting on having sex with someone! It's a damn competition!

"Well, if she puts in her money then she can win, but she's obviously not giving him what he needs. He'll stray eventually. The next one to nail him wins, but I guarantee it won't be his girlfriend. He can't wait. No sex before marriage, yeah right! This is Liam James

94

we're talking about." She rolled her eyes, grinning. She was obviously very confident that she'd win.

Then I had an idea, I pulled out a twenty and dropped it into their pile. "The next one to nail him, right?" I asked, barely able to contain my grin.

"Yeah right! Like you stand a chance, Emo!" Jessica spat at me nastily.

"So, how much does the winner get?" I asked excitedly, ignoring her sneer.

She counted the money that was in the pile. "Well, there's two hundred and forty here at the moment, but once people hear of it.... well, I don't know.... the last time we did this, it was for Chris. It got up to six hundred and twenty, but Liam is way hotter, and by the looks of him untouchable, well, for the moment anyway." Jessica laughed, folding the money and putting it in her pocket, writing the entrants names onto a piece of paper. I laughed; wow, this is going to be easy money. Kate was laughing her head off.

"You going to put in as well?" Jessica asked Kate and Sarah politely.

"Nope, not me. I don't stand a chance." Kate shrugged, still laughing.

Sarah passed Jessica her money. "I'm in. Who could say no at the chance of all that money and they get to sleep with Liam James," Sarah said dreamily. I grabbed my two friend's arms and dragged them out of the lunch room to our next class.

I had to hang around after school, waiting for Jake and Liam to finish their hockey practice. I snuck into the rink and hid at the back so I wouldn't be seen. We weren't allowed in here during practice because their coach said that girls distracted the players. I loved to watch their hockey games; there was just something about the way they glided over the ice so fast and gracefully. They were doing sprints at the moment, skating from one line to the other as fast as they could, then they had to dribble a puck around a load of cones, and finally they were all taking turns shooting at the goal, with my brother doing his best to keep the pucks out. He was a really great goalkeeper, but he only played for fun. Liam on the other hand, had been offered a full athletic scholarship to one of the best collages in the country. He was hoping to turn pro - which apparently, he had every chance of doing because he had scouts falling all over him.

I found myself watching Liam skating. I'd watched him do this hundreds, if not thousands of times, but there was just something so beautiful about it. He took my breath away. I was watching the way his feet moved, the way his messy brown hair blew as he skated, the way the ice sprayed up as he stopped. And, of course, I noticed how unbelievably hot he looked in his uniform.

I snuck back out as practice finished and waited by Liam's car for them to shower. Sarah came up as I was standing there. "Hey, girl," she chirped, bouncing up and down a little in excitement.

"Hey, Sar. What's up with you? You haven't been sniffing those herbs again have you?" I teased. This was a running joke, Sarah had bought some 'herbs' from a friend of hers and lit them in her room to cleanse her aura or something. It had ended up being weed and she got high, running down her street half naked whist calling everyone on her cell to come and see the parade. She never lived it down.

"Ha ha! No, I've just spoke to Ashley who said that the pot for Liam's ass is now up to $1860! Can you believe that? So, I'm going to give it a shot when he comes out of practice," she said, bouncing on the spot and looking around for them.

I almost choked. $1860. Was that a joke? Holy crap! That means over ninety girls are going to be begging *my* boyfriend for sex, offering it to him on a plate and I'm scared to let him touch me. Maybe this isn't going to be as fun as I first thought.

About five minutes later, the boys came out. "Hi, Liam. Wow, you smell good," Sarah purred seductively as she leant in close to him.

He looked at her, a horrified expression on his face. I bit my lip, hard, so I didn't laugh. "Hi, Sarah. Listen, you might not have heard but I have a girlfriend, so…." he trailed off, shrugging.

"That's OK, I don't mind sharing," Sarah purred, putting her hand on his chest to make him stop in front of her.

He looked a little annoyed. "Sarah, seriously I'm not interested, OK." He moved her hand and got into the car, frowning.

I smiled apologetically at Sarah because she looked a little defeated. "There's twenty bucks I'll never see again," she pouted.

I laughed. "Hey, when I win I'll give you your twenty back." I winked at her teasingly, making her laugh as I climbed into the car.

Today was one of the days that Jake worked, so Liam always dropped him at the gym where he worked Monday to Wednesday evenings. Then Liam usually drove me home. "Shit, man, I think I've been hit on more times today than I ever have been. What the hell is that about? I tell people I've got a girlfriend, and all afternoon people have been begging me to fu-" He abruptly stopped talking, looking at me in the mirror as if he'd said too much. I laughed, bless him, he had no idea nearly a hundred horny girls were trying to sleep with him for a bet! "What's so funny, Angel?" he asked, raising his eyebrows at me in the mirror.

"You want to know why you've had all that extra attention today?" I asked, smirking.

"Yeah," he answered, looking a bit apprehensive.

Jake turned to look at me from the front. I smiled. "Well, there's a bet going around amongst the girls as to who can sleep with you first. The first girl to get you, wins the pot. It's pretty good money," I stated, still smirking. Jake burst out laughing, and Liam almost swerved the car into the other lane because he was so shocked.

"They're doing what? Don't they know I have a girlfriend?" he shouted, obviously really pissed off. His outrage seemed to make Jake laugh harder.

I nodded. "Yep, that's why they're doing it. They don't like the idea of you being attached, seeing as you're such a player, so they want to be the next one to sleep with you." I shrugged dismissively, pretending it was no big deal when I was actually worried sick about it. How long would he be able to resist all of this attention for?

"How much is the pot?" Jake asked, amusement still clear on his face.

"Over eighteen hundred dollars." I laughed. Liam nearly swerved us off the road again and Jake's mouth dropped open. He looked at Liam with a look of pure pride in his eyes. "Yep, twenty bucks each. So that makes about ninety girls wanting to be the next one you screw, Liam." I smiled at him in the mirror. He looked horrified, and honestly, a little scared.

"Holy shit, man! You know, you should just choose someone and screw them and split the money!" Jake said excitedly. Liam gave him the filthiest look in the world, like he'd just suggested skinning a puppy or something. Jake held up his hands apologetically. "Kidding. Jeez, I'm kidding!" he said quickly, but I could tell by his face that he was actually serious.

"So, that's why Sarah just hit on me outside the car! Who the hell else is in on this, Angel?" Liam asked, sounding really annoyed about it.

"Well, Jessica's arranging it. All of the cheer squad, most of the seniors, me, Ashley, Nadine," I replied, listing off the people that I knew, but Liam cut me off.

"You?" he asked, with wide eyes.

I nodded, laughing. "Well yeah, eighteen hundred bucks is a lot of money. Mind you, it was only at two forty when I put in, but still, I like to gamble," I joked, giving him a sexy smile in the mirror.

Jake looked like he was going to explode. "You? No freaking way! What the heck are you thinking?" he shouted at me, making me flinch. I hated to see Jake angry.

"Jake, it's a lot of money I just thought, you know, it'd be a laugh. You never know, I may get to lose my virginity to the famous Liam James," I teased, waggling my eyebrows at him.

Jake started to laugh, looking relieved; he obviously thought I was joking. I smiled and looked out of the window; I wasn't good at lying, if he asks me if I was joking then I would have to tell him the truth. "Jeez, Ambs, you scared me then! I thought you were serious." Jake laughed, slapping Liam on the shoulder proudly. "Eighteen hundred bucks that's awesome, Liam. I wonder how many girls you could bang in one night, if they all thought they were the one to win the bet."

I gasped. Oh crap! Great Jake, put that in his head, I'm sure that's all he needs to hear since his girlfriend's not willing to give it up! "Damn it, Jake, I have a girlfriend!" Liam cried, sounding a little exasperated.

"Yeah I know, but come on, girls are going to be pretty desperate to win, I bet you could get them to do anything," Jake smirked, waggling his eyebrows.

"Jake, just stop. I don't want anyone else; I'm crazy about my girl. I'm not going to screw it up with her," Liam stated proudly. He smiled at me in the mirror and my breathing started to slow down as my panic started to recede. Trust. I needed to trust him and stop assuming the worst all of the time.

We dropped Jake off at the gym and Liam drove us home. "You put in twenty bucks betting you would be the next one to sleep with me?" he asked, smiling at me cockily.

"Actually no, the bet is to be the next one to *nail* you." I shrugged, giggling.

He laughed and gripped my hand as we drove. "I can't believe that this is happening. I thought that once people knew I wasn't interested, that they would all leave me alone, not have more girls after me! I'm really sorry." He frowned and kissed the back of my hand softly.

"Don't worry about it; it's not your fault. I guess that whole trust thing is going to be needed a lot from now on, huh?" I joked, smiling a half smile, pretending I wasn't worried about all of the girls that would be throwing themselves at him for the foreseeable future.

We reached my house and he parked in his drive. "Hey, want

to come in? We can tell my parents we're together. I told them I have a girlfriend and my mom almost died, I swear," he said, chuckling and nodding towards his house with a hopeful expression.

"Wow, the whole meet the parents thing already?" I joked, pretending to be scared. "I mean, what if they don't like me?" I asked, wrapping my arms around his waist and putting my face in his chest, faking horror. He laughed and so did I. The idea of Liam's parents not liking me was seriously funny. They already thought of me as a daughter. Liam was an only child because his mom had some problems when she gave birth to him, which left her unable to have more kids, so she loved me and always said that Jake and I were part of the family. I loved them too; they were great people, kind, funny and thoughtful. Actually, just like Liam, though it just took me a long time to see past all of his bravado.

Chapter 11

He pulled me into his house, holding my hand, smiling excitedly. "Mom? Dad? You home?" Liam shouted, looking into the empty lounge.

I could hear voices in the kitchen. "Yeah, honey. We're in here," Pat called.

Liam smiled happily and dragged me to the kitchen. Pat was baking cookies and Rick was busy trying to eat the cookie mix straight from the bowl, making her laugh and hit his hand with the wooden spoon. I chuckled at the scene. They were always like this, she was the perfect housewife and mother, and he adored her and Liam, which was really sweet.

"Hey, Amber. Long time no see," Rick said, grabbing me into a hug, which made my heart race.

"Hey, Rick. Hi, Pat. How are you?" I asked cheerfully.

"We're great! Amber, I would hug you but I'm covered in cookies, honey." Pat frowned, holding up her hands in evidence.

"Yeah, I can see that! They smell so good," I said, eyeing the already baked ones on the plate on the counter. She passed the plate to me and I happily took one, smiling. "Thanks."

"Hey! You said I couldn't have one because they were cooling," Rick whined, pouting, making me laugh; she picked up a cookie and tossed it at him with a wink.

"Um guys, I was wondering if you wanted to meet my girlfriend. Maybe she could have dinner with us tonight?" Liam suggested, putting his hand on the small of my back.

A grin spread across Pat's face. She looked so happy that I actually thought she was actually holding back tears. "Oh, Liam! I'd love to meet her! I still can't believe you have a girlfriend. You spent all this time saying that there was only one girl for you and now

100

you're finally able to move on and actually date someone!" she cooed, practically bursting with excitement and pride.

"Yeah OK, Mom, tone it down a bit, huh?" Liam mumbled, rolling his eyes.

"So, what time is she coming? Have you met her, Amber? Is she nice?" Pat asked, beaming at me. I looked at Liam, unsure what to say. This whole situation was laughable. And did she say that Liam had always said there was only one girl for him?

"Actually, Mom, she's here right now," Liam said proudly, rubbing my back gently and smiling at me. His eyes bore into mine, making my whole body feel a little hotter. Pat jumped and wiped her hands on a cloth, quickly fixing her hair frantically, before she practically ran to the hallway. OK, weird! "Mom, what are you doing?" Liam asked, laughing; I noticed that Rick was staring at Liam's hand on my back, a wide grin on his face.

"Well, is she parking the car or something?" Pat asked, looking back at Liam before glancing at the front door again. He laughed harder and Rick and I chuckled too.

"Mom, this is my girlfriend. Her name is Amber Walker." Liam beamed proudly at me as I pressed myself closer to him.

Pat's face snapped to look at me, shocked. Slowly, her face turned to happiness, then complete bliss, as she laughed and ran to me, grabbing both me and Liam into a big hug. "Oh my gosh! Finally, you two got together? Finally!" she almost screamed, jumping up and down on the spot.

Liam wrapped his arm round my waist and pulled me impossibly closer to him. "Yeah, finally," he confirmed, rolling his eyes, but looking amused at the same time. Rick put his hand out to Liam. They shook hands in a very grown up gesture, before he pulled him into a bear hug.

After all of the excitement had died down, we had dinner. It was really nice to be sat with Liam's parents like this, they honestly didn't stop smiling. Every time Liam and I touched each other, Pat would sigh happily, beaming at us.

"Right, you boys can clear the table!" Pat ordered, grabbing my arm and pulling me to the lounge. "I am so happy for you two. Liam's told you he's been in love with you for years, right?" she beamed. My breath caught in my throat at her choice of words. She thought that Liam was in love with me? He wasn't in love with me, was he? Did he really whisper that he loved me last night before I fell asleep?

"Er, he told me he's liked me for a long time, yeah," I mumbled, a little uncomfortably.

She rolled her eyes. *"Liked*, jeez that boy has been smitten with you from the get go. I mean, he still calls you Angel for goodness sake!" she laughed.

I looked at her, confused. "What does that have to do with anything?" I asked, frowning. I really loved Pat, but sometimes she can be a little crazy.

"He's never told you why he calls you that?" she asked, smirking at me. I shook my head, and she chuckled darkly. "The first time we met you was at Liam's sixth birthday party. You'd not long moved in and we thought it would be nice, you know, to invite the neighbours to the party," she started, nodding enthusiastically.

"Yeah, I remember. You had balloons everywhere, and a clown that did magic tricks." I smiled; the James' always did throw the best parties, even kids parties.

"That's right. So anyway, you and your brother came to the party and as soon as you walked through the door, Liam just stared at you. He literally couldn't take his eyes off of you. You smiled and said happy birthday to him, but he couldn't even speak to you, so you walked off to go dance. He turned to me, and do you know what he said to me?" she asked, her eyes tearing up. I shook my head. What the heck is she going to say? This is freaking me out a little! "He said in a deadly serious tone, *'Momma, am I dead?'* And I said *'no honey, you're not dead'*, and he shook his head, looking all confused about something. Then he pointed to you dancing and *said, 'if I'm not dead, then why is there an Angel in our house?'"* she stated, clasping her hands together and beaming.

I gasped. Holy crap! That's why he calls me Angel? My heart was racing and my palms were sweaty. I think Liam really is in love with me, but am I in love with him? I don't think so, at least, not yet. But I could easily see myself falling in love with him.

"That's why he calls me that? Are you serious?" I asked, unsure if she was joking or not.

"Totally. Ask him if you don't believe me, but from the moment he saw you he was in love with you, it's plain on the look on his face. I'm surprised you never noticed." She shook her head, chuckling.

"I never noticed because he was always so mean to me. He was always pushing me over, or pulling my hair, calling me names." I frowned. Why did he do all of that if he was in love with me?

"Your brother made him stay away. He beat Liam up after his birthday party that same year and told him to stay away from you," she said, laughing and shaking her head. "That brother of yours sure is protective, bless him," she said, smiling fondly.

"Yeah, I know. Liam and I talked about it and we decided to keep it from Jake for a couple of weeks, just until things settle down. I'd really appreciate it if you'd not say anything to him if you see him." I winced at the thought of Liam and Jake fighting. I definitely wanted to put that off as long as possible.

"I won't say anything, but I don't think you should leave it too long, otherwise it'll only get harder."

I smiled gratefully. "Yeah, just a couple of weeks."

Suddenly, Liam jumped over the back of the couch and landed next to me, wrapping his arm around my shoulder and pulling me to him. When I turned to smile at him, he kissed me, nibbling my lip, asking for entrance. Jeez, did he forget his mom was sitting there watching us?

I pulled away quickly, making him groan. "Angel, I haven't seen you all day," he whined, pouting like a little kid. I laughed at the word Angel; did he really call me that because he thought I was an Angel when he was six years old? "What are you laughing at, beautiful?" he asked, stroking the side of my face with the back of one finger.

I bit my lip to make me stop and shook my head. "Nothing," I lied, smiling at him. He bent his head forward and kissed me again, asking for entrance and I pulled away again. "Liam, seriously, your mom is watching us," I whispered to his puppy dog face. We both looked over at Pat who was staring with a huge grin on her face, like she was watching the cutest thing in the world.

Liam stood up and held out his hand to me. "Let's go listen to some music in my room." He frowned a little at his mom who was still watching us like some kind of crazy happy woman.

I grabbed his hand and let him pull me up and into his room. I hadn't been in his bedroom for years. I think the last time I was in here was probably about two years ago when I came in to change my clothes after we had a huge water fight and Jake and I had gotten locked out. His room was much the same as it was then, but it now had more stuff on the walls. Like his signed hockey shirt that he had gotten for his birthday from his parents this year, and his trophies that were all lined up on some shelves.

He put on some music quietly and I walked over to the bookcase to see two framed photos. One was of Jake, Liam and I at the park where we had gone for a picnic when we were kids, I was probably eleven or twelve. The other photo was of me and my dance crew, taken at one of the competitions that we had entered. I picked it up and looked at it curiously.

"I love that photo," Liam said, smiling at it as he stood next to me.

I held it out to him. "When did you take this?"

"About two months ago at the club on Richmond. You won first prize and you were jumping all over the place, excited." He smiled and rubbed his thumb over the picture, before putting it back down.

I walked over to his bed and sat down. "Wow, your bed *is* uncomfortable! No wonder you like sleeping at mine," I joked, running my hand over his duvet. He laughed and came and sat next to me. I couldn't help but notice that he looked so handsome when he laughs. I pushed him down on the bed and moved so I was straddling him, I put my forearms near his head and bent down so that our faces were almost touching. "So, Liam, I want you to tell me something," I breathed, running my hands through his hair.

"Can I kiss you first? Then I'll answer anything you want." His gaze flicked down to my lips for a split second, before returning to my eyes.

I crashed my lips to his. His arms immediately went around my waist, pulling me closer to him, one of his hands tangling in my hair. He traced his tongue along my bottom lip slowly and I didn't refuse him this time, I opened my mouth, eagerly. His taste exploded into my mouth as he slipped his tongue in, massaging mine passionately, making me moan. Kissing Liam seemed to get better and better each time. I was burning with the need for him to touch me, but I was also conscious that his parents were just down the hall and knew that we were in here together. I pulled back after a few minutes, we were both breathing hard. He was running his hands slowly down my body from the top of my head down to my waist and back up again, looking at me lovingly.

I was a little startled by the look on his face. What his mom said was true. He really was in love with me; I could see it in his eyes.

"So, what is it you want to know, Angel?" he asked, gripping both of his hands on my ass and squeezing gently. I was almost distracted by his hands; I mean, if he just moved them a bit further down and towards the centre more, they would be exactly where my body was screaming for him to be. I shook my head to clear away the lustful thoughts, and smiled at his handsome face.

"I want to know why you call me Angel."

He gasped and blushed slightly. I smiled reassuringly at him. He groaned and shook his head quickly. "No way. I'm not answering that," he whined, giving me the puppy dog face that I couldn't resist.

"Come on, you said you'd answer anything I wanted," I

encouraged. He frowned and shook his head. OK, I'll try another tactic. "Please?" I begged, pecking his lips. "Please?" I whispered, kissing him again. "Please?"

He moaned and took a deep breath as I kissed down his neck. "I call you Angel because, I honestly believe that God put an Angel on this earth just for me," he admitted, cupping my face in his hands making me look at him. I took in a shaky breath. So it was true what Pat said. My heart was racing in my chest as he continued to speak. "The first time I saw you I thought you were an Angel straight from heaven. You were so beautiful that you took my breath away. You still do, every day."

"That has to be the sweetest thing I have ever heard, Liam," I murmured, kissing him tenderly. He kissed me back and rolled so I was underneath him. "I could kiss you all day," I whispered, as he kissed down my neck, nibbling gently on the skin and making me moan breathlessly.

"Mmm, that sounds like a good plan," he mumbled against my skin. I wrapped my legs around his waist and pulled him closer to me, kissing him with everything I had. He pinned my arms above my head and kissed me again before trailing kisses across my cheek to my ear. "I love you, Angel," he whispered.

My heart stopped and my body began to tingle but I didn't know what to say. "I…. I…. Liam…. I…."

He kissed me again, stopping me from speaking. I felt his grip loosen on my wrists, so I wrapped my arms around his neck, pulling him closer to me. "You don't have to say anything. I've felt like this about you for years, but you've only just stopped looking at me like your brothers asshole best friend. I just wanted to say the words to you, that's all. I've been waiting to say them for a long time," he said, smoothing my hair away from my face. I wrapped my arms around his neck tightly and kissed all over his face, before finally kissing him long and hard on his perfect mouth.

Chapter 12

We must have fallen asleep because I woke up with Liam wrapped all over me. I looked at his clock. Holy crap, it was past nine! Jake would be home already. I nudged him awake. "Hey, I gotta go, it's after nine," I stated, urgently trying to unwrap him from me.

He groaned. "Ten more minutes, Angel," he muttered sleepily.

I laughed; he looked so cute when he was sleepy. I giggled as I tickled him. "Liam, it's not morning, it's still night-time, but I've got to go. Jake will be wondering where I am!" I explained, finally prying him off me and jumping up. He groaned and pulled me back down to him, holding me tight against his body, smiling sleepily. I giggled. "Will you stop! I need to go," I said, laughing as he nibbled my earlobe.

He shook his head. "No, I don't want you to go," he muttered, as he kissed my neck. I pushed him up and he groaned. "But I'm going to miss you," he whined, making me laugh even harder.

"I'll see you in an hour. Anyway, I have homework to do," I said, with a shrug.

He sighed in defeat. "Yeah, me too," he admitted, pouting slightly. I climbed out of his bed and went to the door. "Hey wait. I'll walk you out." He grabbed my hand as we walked down the hallway.

I stuck my head into the living room. "Bye, Pat. Bye, Rick," I called.

"Goodbye, honey," Rick replied, not taking his eyes off the TV.

Pat smirked at me. "Bye, Amber. Did you guys have fun?" she asked, giving me a wink. I blushed like crazy and nodded not sure that my voice would come out if I tried to speak. Liam rolled his eyes and pulled me to the front door, where he pushed me against it lightly and kissed me until I was dizzy.

"I'll see you at half past ten, OK?" he whispered, caressing my cheek.

I walked quickly to my house, turning back to smile at Liam as I walked in the front door. Bless him, he was standing on his porch checking to make sure I got home safe and I live like thirty feet from him.

Jake was sitting on the sofa, waiting for me. As I walked in the door he looked at me, his eyes tight with anger. "Where have you been? I've been worried! You could have left a note or something," he said, shaking his head disapprovingly.

"Sorry, I was over at Liam's. Pat asked me to stay for dinner, and I thought, seeing as you weren't here, that I'd go so I wouldn't be here on my own," I said with a shrug.

"I love Pat's dinners!" he moaned, his angry expression leaving his face, to be replaced by a jealous one.

"Well you missed a good one too, she made a homemade pie and everything," I teased, smiling wickedly as he groaned.

"Well, I enjoyed my grilled cheese," he joked, making me laugh.

"I'm going to go do my homework." I turned and started towards the hallway so I could go to my room.

"Ambs, wait a minute. I need to talk to you about something," he said, patting the couch next to him, looking sad.

I plopped down next to him. "What's up, Jake?" I asked, concerned, he looked really upset about something.

He took a deep breath. "I spoke to Mom tonight."

I smiled. "Yeah? Is she OK? Is she coming home?" I asked, getting excited, thinking about seeing my mom sooner than a couple of weeks. I'd missed her like crazy and the time that she was here always seemed to go too fast.

He shook his head. "She told me something, but I don't want you to freak out about it. There's nothing to worry about, I promise." He took my hand and looked at me, smiling sadly.

Oh crap, this is going to be bad! "What is it?" I asked, already imagining the worst. We were going to have to move to china. She'd lost her job. She was getting remarried - but I suppose that wasn't necessarily a bad thing, unless he was a jerk. Hundreds of things were running through my mind, but the last thing I expected was what Jake said.

"Our father has been in contact with her. He wants to see us, apparently, make amends for what he did," he spat through his teeth, his sadness turning to blind rage.

I couldn't breathe. My lungs just refused to work. My heart was beating way too fast as my body started to shake. He was coming back. He wanted to see us. The last time I saw that man, he had ripped my school shirt off me and had pinned me to the floor while he undone his pants. He was about to rape me when Jake and Liam came in and beat the crap out of him. Oh God, he was coming back. I replayed all of the beatings he handed out to me and Jake, all the touching that happened when I was alone with him, the whispered words and secret smiles. My vision started to get black spots as I hyperventilated. I was going to die I could feel it; my body was shutting down, unable to deal with the memories and the pain.

I was vaguely aware of shouting. "Just let go. I can help her!" a voice I recognised, shouted.

"Call 911 for fuck sake. She can't breathe!" Jake shouted.

"Jake, let go of her! I got this, I promise," the voice said urgently again.

I was jostled slightly and then I felt two strong arms go around me, pulling me into a hard chest; there was a beautiful smell that I recognised as Liam.

Oh thank you God, Liam's here! My heart rate started to slow as I felt him press his lips to my neck and breathe slowly and calmly down my back. I tried to match my breathing to his. I concentrated on the feel of his steady heartbeat against my chest and the black spots slowly started to fade. After a few minutes I regained control of my arms and I wrapped them tightly around his waist, clinging to him as if he was the only thing keeping me from falling off the edge of the world. My father was coming back, but I was with Liam, he wouldn't let anything hurt me, I knew that. So I started to feel safe in his arms. After what seemed like forever, I was able to pull back to look at him.

"You alright now?" he asked, putting his hands on either side of my face and pressing his forehead to mine.

I nodded and licked my lips, they tasted salty for some reason, and then I realised I was crying. I wiped my face and sniffed. I slowly became aware of my surroundings; I was still in the lounge. I looked over to see Jake sitting there, shocked, staring at me and Liam. His mouth was hanging open, his eyes wide. I thought about stepping back, but I couldn't. I couldn't move away from Liam, he was my safety; he was the one I needed, the one that would keep me sane through all of this.

Jake walked over and pulled me from Liam's arms, making me whimper. He wrapped me in a tight hug. "Damn it, Amber. Don't ever do that to me again! I thought you were going to die! Shit, you scared me," Jake ranted, as he rocked me back and forth gently.

"I'm OK," I said weakly. I looked back to Liam for reassurance and saw that he wasn't there, the panic started to rise in my chest as my breathing started to get shallow. "Where's Liam?" I choked out, tears flowing down my face again. Oh God, he left me!

Jake hugged me tightly. "Shh, it's OK. Just breathe, Shh," he murmured, but I couldn't, my lungs were too tight. "Shit!" Jake gasped looking at me. "Liam, get in here quick!" he almost screamed.

Liam ran back into the room, holding a glass of water which he put down on the table roughly, spilling half of it, before wrapping his arms around me. "It's OK, Angel," he whispered, putting his lips to my neck again.

After a couple of minutes, when I could pull back, I smiled at Liam gratefully.

Jake looked murderously angry. "What the fuck? You two are together, aren't you?" he roared.

Liam just held up a hand to stop his rant. "Look, Jake, you and I will talk about this, but now's not the right time after what just happened. I need to make sure she's OK," he said sternly, ending the conversation.

Jake looked at me apologetically and nodded. "I'm sorry, Amber, but I had to tell you, to make sure you knew, but I promise I'll never let him hurt you. You don't need to worry about anything. I'll kill him before he touches you," Jake said, taking my hand.

I smiled but I had a feeling it would look more like a grimace. "I know that, Jake. I'm sorry I freaked out and scared you." I raised a shaky hand and swiped at my tears again.

"That's OK. Just don't do it again," he said, smiling at me. I laughed weakly and nodded.

Liam handed me the glass of water and I drank it gratefully. I noticed that Jake was watching Liam's every move, glaring angrily. "Stop looking at him like that, Jake, he's done nothing wrong," I said, frowning.

He shook his head and clenched his jaw, taking a deep breath, obviously trying to calm himself before speaking. "You two are together," he said simply, looking between the two of us for confirmation. I shifted uncomfortably in my seat. OK, so much for a couple of weeks.

"Yes," Liam answered, nodding. His arm wrapped tightly around me. I cringed into him, wanting this to be a dream. Not only is my abusive father coming back, but my brother was now going to beat the crap out of my boyfriend.

"How long?" Jake asked. His jaw was still tight but he seemed to be doing well with his control.

"Since Friday," Liam replied quietly. He looked really guilty, and I knew it was my fault because I asked him to lie about it.

"He wanted to tell you straight away, Jake, but I wanted to wait. I don't want you two fighting. Please?" I begged, looking at my brother, giving him my puppy dog face.

"You like him, Amber?" Jake asked, closing his eyes, looking sad and disappointed.

"Yes," I admitted, still begging him with my eyes to accept it and not go off on one or blame Liam for it. I would hate it if they fell out over me.

He nodded but didn't open his eyes. "What was that what you did, Liam? How did you do that? Calm her down like that?" he asked, opening his eyes and looking at him gratefully.

"I don't know. It's just something that calms her down that's all. I've always done it," Liam said with a shrug.

"Always done it? You've done that before?" Jake asked, looking confused.

"Yeah, I've had to calm her down a few times," Liam replied sadly. I thought about what he meant, all the times that he had seen me cry, probably every single night up until the age of fourteen.

"What? When? I've never seen you do that," Jake protested, shaking his head, looking confused. I drew in a shaky breath. Now he's going to find out that Liam sleeps in my room. I crossed my fingers and prayed that this went well, that Jake was OK and not too angry with his best friend. Liam looked at me for permission to tell him, I nodded and chewed on my lip knowing this needed to be brought out into the open sooner or later.

"Jake, please don't freak out," I begged, moving my body so it was in front of Liam's slightly, in case Jake lunged for him or something. My small move might just deter him from beating the crap out of my boyfriend.

"Jake, man, nothing ever happened, I swear," Liam promised. Jake looked at him, his expression even more confused. "When I was ten, I saw her crying on her bed through my window. So I snuck over to make sure she was OK, and I ended up falling asleep in the bed with her." Jake glared at him like he wanted to murder him there and then. "It happened again the next night, and the next. She would be crying, so I would sneak through her window. After a while it was just a habit," Liam said, frowning slightly.

Jake jumped up with his fists clenched. His eyes tight, and

glaring at Liam. As quick as lightning, Liam grabbed my arm and pulled me behind him protectively. Jake's eyes flashed before his face calmed. "Why did you just do that?" Jake asked, sighing and looking at Liam intently.

"Do what?" Liam asked confused, still holding me behind him.

"Move my sister behind you like that," Jake said, his face completely calm now.

Liam shook his head as if he didn't understand the question. "I didn't want her to get hurt, that's all."

Jake sat back down and dragged his hand through his blond hair. "You really like my sister?" he asked, looking at the floor.

"Jake, I'm in love with your sister, you know that." Liam sat back down on the sofa and pulled me to sit down next to him.

Jake nodded. "And you've slept in her bed before, when we were kids," Jake stated, as if trying to make sure he had the facts straight.

"Not just when we were kids, that's what I was trying to say. She used to cry, and so I would sneak over to comfort her every night. It just became a habit, and now neither of us can actually sleep properly without the other there," Liam admitted, frowning.

Jakes face shot up. "You still sleep in her room? Every night since you were ten? Damn it, Liam. Shit! Motherfucking, stupid asshole!" Jake ranted, not really able to get the words out, taking a step forwards his fists clenched again. I winced. Oh God, here it comes!

I held up my hands, trying to stop him. "Jake, remember when I used to wake up screaming all the time?" I asked desperately. I needed to make him see reason fast before they ended up fighting.

He nodded and winced. "Yeah, that stopped though when you were like eight or something."

I nodded. "Yeah, I was eight. That was when Liam started sleeping in with me. I don't have nightmares anymore, because of Liam," I said, smiling and squeezing Liam's hand.

"You do! I've had to sleep in with you a few times since then," Jake protested.

"Yeah you did, but I still had the nightmares even though you were there," I countered. Jake flinched and nodded, probably at the memory of me screaming the house down in his bed. "I've only had a few nightmares since then, the only times I ever have them is when Liam's not there. Like if he's on vacation or something," I explained, looking at Jake, watching as understanding shot across his face. We were all silent for a while. Liam was stroking the back of my hand;

Jake was just staring at the floor.

After what seemed like forever, Jake looked at Liam. "Liam, if you hurt my sister, best friend or not, I will kill you," Jake warned. I could see that he meant it.

"I won't, I promise," Liam vowed, smiling reassuringly.

"Right, well, I'm going to bed. I guess I'll see you in the morning, make sure you lock the door before you two go to bed," Jake instructed, getting up and leaving us sitting there on the sofa, shocked.

I looked at Liam; he just looked stunned as I felt. "Wow, that was easier than I thought," he mused, smiling at me and putting his hands either side of my face.

I smiled, just pleased that it was finally out in the open. "Want to go to bed, Liam? I'm not in the mood for homework; I just want to go to sleep." I just needed to lie in the bed and have him hold me for a little while.

He nodded and kissed my nose. "Yeah, I just need to go back home first. Jake called and said you were freaking out, so I just ran out of the house without even telling my parents where I was going." He stroked my face with his thumbs softly, just looking at me with a sad smile.

"OK. I guess I'll just go to bed and see you when you're ready," I said, getting up and pulling him towards the front door.

"Hey, can I use the door now that Jake knows?" He grinned.

I laughed at his excitement, but shook my head. "No, your parents might see.... unless you tell them you're staying here," I suggested.

He smiled happily. "I would love to walk through your front door and get in your bed; I've never done that before."

I took out my keys and gave them to him. "Make sure you lock it after, OK?" I kissed his cheek and made my way to my bedroom.

It was nearly ten o'clock but my body felt so exhausted from all the emotional drama that it felt like I hadn't slept in days. I pulled off my clothes and slipped on my favourite t-shirt that used to be Liam's. I fell asleep instantly. A couple of minutes later I felt two arms wrap around me and a heavy leg slung over mine. I smiled and pressed back into him. My boyfriend. The one I needed when things went wrong.

It's weird, but when Jake pulled me away from Liam tonight, I felt strange, like I'd left my heart behind. I didn't realise up until then, how strongly I was connected to him. He literally was everything to me. When I felt his arms wrap around me earlier, I felt like I was home, all my panic started to recede. I felt like, as long as he was with me, I'd be alright.

I snuggled into him and heard him whisper, "I love you," right before I fell back into a deep dreamless sleep; I didn't doubt his words this time.

Chapter 13

I woke at six with my alarm going off. I groaned because I'd forgotten to cancel it. I guess I don't need to kick him out of my bed early anymore. I rolled over and hugged Liam. He always slept through the alarm; I swear he would sleep through an earthquake. I nudged him gently, deciding to play a joke on him.

"Six o'clock," I said, nudging him again.

He groaned and slowly got up out of the bed, still half asleep. "OK, Angel. I love you; I'll see you later." He kissed my forehead and got out of the bed, his eyes only half open. I couldn't help myself, I burst out laughing. He looked at me, confused. "Shh! What are you laughing at?" he asked, frowning, pulling on his jeans.

"You," I teased, smiling happily.

"What about me? What have I done?" he whispered, climbing back onto the bed and crawling on top of me. He pressed every inch of his body to mine but still keeping all of his weight off of me somehow. He looked into my eyes, smiling happily for a little while, and then understanding crossed his face. "Shit! Your brother knows! Then why the hell did you wake me up, Angel? I don't need to leave," he whined.

I wrapped my arms around his neck and pulled him in for a long kiss. "I was just kidding around. I forgot to cancel the alarm so I thought I'd use the extra time and we could make out."

He grinned. "You wanna make out?" he teased, kissing down my neck. I gasped as he reached the sensitive spot near my collarbone.

"Mmm," I breathed, running my hands down his back, scratching slightly with my nails, making him moan. He climbed back under the covers, and kissed me tenderly and softly, holding me close. He made no moves to take things any further than that, which

I loved. He really was adorable.

We walked out of my bedroom a little after seven thirty. Liam pushed me onto one of the kitchen stools, grinning to himself like the cat that got the cream. "Hey, I get to make you breakfast without getting shouted at today," he chirped.

I laughed and watched as he made me a bowl of cereal; he smiled and put it in front of me, before making some toast for himself. "You don't eat cereal?" I asked, watching him scoff four slices of toast.

He shook his head, turning his nose up. "I don't like cereal; it's gross and all soggy." He faked a shudder, pretending to gag.

I laughed again. "You really are weird, Liam," I teased, smiling at him.

He grinned. "You know, it's kind of weird, you being all nice to me over breakfast."

"I could be mean to you if you want," I offered, shrugging.

He laughed and shook his head. "No. I'll get used to it eventually." He walked over to my side. I turned to look at him and he brushed my hair behind my ear, his fingers lingering on my cheek, making me blush. "You really are the most beautiful thing in the world," he murmured. My heart skipped a beat at the honesty in his voice, his blue eyes were burning into mine, making me feel like the only girl in the world.

"Cut that crap out! I might have given my blessing but I don't need it shoved in my face over breakfast," Jake growled as he walked into the kitchen to make some cereal. He slapped Liam on the back of the head on the way past as usual.

We all laughed and Liam stepped behind me, wrapping his arms around my waist, leaning his head on my shoulder. "Thanks, Jake. I know you said stay away but..." Liam trailed off, looking at my brother gratefully.

"Whatever, Liam. We're fine. Just don't make us have a problem, OK," Jake replied, smiling a friendly smile.

Liam's arms tightened around me. "I won't." He kissed my shoulder lightly and Jake fake gagged, making me laugh.

"Well, come on then, lovebirds, I suppose you need to get to school a little earlier so that you can announce you're together," Jake stated, rolling his eyes.

Liam grinned and nodded. I gasped and shook my head fiercely. "No way! We can't do that," I said, looking at Liam. He looked really hurt for some reason.

"Why not?" he asked, taking my hand, and looking a little confused.

I glanced at Jake; he really wasn't going to like this. "Er, well, I sort of have a bet going on. The next one to sleep with you will win the pot. I could really use that money." I looked at Liam uncomfortably, but he just started to laugh hysterically.

Jake almost choked on his drink. "No way! You can't do that!" he cried, shaking his head violently. "I don't want to know that you two are having sex. I don't!"

I laughed at his annoyed and disgusted face. "Jake, we're not having sex." I shrugged, making his face relax a little. "But when we do, I definitely want to win the pot. I won't if people know I'm his girlfriend already." I looked at Liam, unsure if he would go along with this or not.

"Angel, I don't want you to want to be with me for some bet." He frowned, looking a little hurt.

I smiled seductively at him. "You think that's the reason I'm going to want to have sex with you? Trust me, lover boy; it won't be to do with the money, that'll just a perk."

He leant in and put his mouth to my ear. "So what will be the reason?" he breathed, sending a shiver down my spine.

I bit my lip. "Hmm, I'm not sure but it'll have something to do with you begging me on your knees," I teased, smirking at him.

He laughed and kissed me, pulling me close to his body, sending ripples of desire racing through my bloodstream. He pulled away to look at me, lust written clear across his face. "I'd happily beg you right now you know."

I patted his chest and stepped away before I dragged him back to my bedroom and ripped his sexy ass jeans and black button down shirt off his flawless body. "Oh I know, lover boy." I laughed, trying to catch my breath.

I glanced at Jake who was staring at us eyes wide, his mouth hanging open in shock. "Guys, I seriously can't take these PDA's," he said, grimacing and shaking his head.

"It's OK, the PDA's done. I just think we should keep this quiet for a little while. Why not make a little money for doing something that would happen eventually anyway? That's how I look at it," I said, shrugging.

Liam and Jake looked at each other. "I guess. But will you be able to win? I mean, was the bet to make me break up with my girlfriend or something?" Liam asked, frowning.

I giggled and shook my head. "Nope, I made sure of that. It's definitely just the next one to *nail* you, as they so eloquently put it."

Liam shook his head, looking a little disgusted. "I can't believe girls do that sort of thing."

Jake laughed. "You know what? I think I might announce that I've got a girlfriend next. Then I can just pick someone and we can split the money," he said brightly, as if he was serious.

Liam grabbed my hand and pulled me towards the door. "Come on, let's get to school before you brother has any other bright ideas." He laughed, shaking his head at Jake.

Liam winked at me in the mirror as we pulled into the parking lot. There were more girls than usual waiting for them. They all made a beeline for Liam as soon as his door opened. Jessica, as usual, was at the front.

I laughed. "Good luck, boyfriend," I teased, winking at him as I walked off, swaying my ass on purpose. I knew he was watching me. When I got to the door I glanced back over my shoulder to see him pulling a girl's arms off of him, a distasteful expression on his face. He must have had about twenty-five girls round him, he looked extremely pissed off. I laughed and went to find my friends; as usual, they were hanging out by our lockers.

"Hey, guys," I chirped, as I got up to them.

"Wow, someone's in a good mood today! Any particular reason?" Sean asked, looking confused at my happy face.

"Nope, no reason in particular. I just watched Liam getting hounded by like twenty-five girls. He looks really annoyed about it, that was pretty funny," I explained, grinning wildly. Just then he walked past me with Jake. He had a girl flirting with him on either side, and about another ten walking behind him. I burst out laughing and he shot me a dark look, making me laugh harder.

"I'm not surprised he has all those girls after him. Do you know how much the pot is now?" Kate asked, smirking at me.

I nodded. "Yeah I know, Sarah told me it's like eighteen hundred dollars or something. I can't believe it." I shook my head disapprovingly, and tried not to imagine what it would feel like to win that much money.

Kate, Sarah and Sean exchanged a look, before bursting into laughter. "No, that was yesterday's total. Today it's up to four thousand two hundred," Kate said. I felt the colour drain from my face as my heart sank. Holy crap! That's like, oh God I can't even work it out! Like two hundred girls, all wanting to sleep with *my* boyfriend!

"Oh my God! Really?" I asked as I swallowed the lump that

117

was rapidly forming in my throat. The thought of all those girls throwing themselves at my boy, literally made me feel a little ill. Kate nodded and looked a little sympathetic; as if she knew what I was thinking. Sarah and Sean just looked excited because they obviously had no idea I was with Liam. Luckily, the bell rang, so we all made our way to class.

At lunchtime I decided I would start making my play for Liam. People needed to at least see that I was trying. I couldn't just announce that I had slept with him, so I needed people to see me putting in the effort. I hadn't talked it through with Liam, but a little harmless flirting over lunch shouldn't be too hard. As I carried my tray of food across the lunchroom to our usual table, I turned to my friends.

"Guys, I'm going to go make my play for Liam for the bet. Let's go sit with my brother today, OK?"

Kate gave me a knowing look and winked at me and we all walked over to the jock table. The jock table was almost full of girls, all of them flirting shamelessly with Liam. I smiled at his expression; he looked even more pissed off now than earlier. I looked at the girl sitting next to Liam; she'd finished her lunch and was staring at him intently, a flirty expression on her face.

"Hey, Sally. I just heard that someone hit your car in the parking lot, was there much damage?" I asked innocently.

She gasped and jumped up. "Shit! That's my mom's car!" she cried, as she turned and ran off. I heard my friends burst into laughter behind me as they took seats further down the table.

"Hi, Liam." I smiled at him as I plopped down in the chair next to his.

"Hey, Angel," he replied, grinning at me. I looked around to see I was getting the death glares from all the girls nearby, obviously because I had earned a smile already. "Someone hit Sally's car?" he asked, eating his tuna sandwich.

I shrugged and shook my head. "Nah. I just said that because I wanted to sit here."

He burst into laughter. "I knew you wanted me," he teased, winking at me.

"Well, who doesn't," I answered, smirking and looking around the table at the girls who were all trying to kill me with their eyes. I grabbed my bottle of water and pretended to try to open it. "Liam, can you open this for me?" I asked, pouting slightly.

"Angel, if you keep pouting, the wind will change and you'll get stuck like that," he joked, grinning and taking my bottle from me. He opened it easily and passed it back.

"Thanks." I smiled, ignoring his remark. "Wow, I never realised how strong you are. You must work out a lot, huh?" I purred, trailing my finger down his bicep, biting on my lip seductively. He looked at me lustfully, his eyes fixed on my mouth. Just from the pained expression on his face, I could tell he wanted to kiss me. He didn't answer. "So? Do you work out a lot? Because you must do, I mean, your body it's, mmm...." I trailed off, looking him over slowly.

He gulped. "Er, I guess, yeah a bit," he muttered, still looking at me a little shocked and bewildered.

I didn't want this to go too far, I was only setting the scene for my victory at the moment. I broke eye contact and started to eat my food, slowly, letting the fork linger in my mouth longer than necessary. "Oh God," I moaned, closing my eyes chewing slowly. "This is so good," I breathed. I heard him moan slightly next to me and I knew my sex noises were getting to him. I looked over at him. "Liam, you should try this," I purred seductively. He had a pained look across his face as he stared at me with his mouth slightly open. He shook his head slightly, as if trying to push a thought away and I swallowed my giggle. Oh crap, he is so going to make me pay for this later.

"Er, OK yeah," he said. I smiled and grabbed a forkful of my pasta and guided it to his mouth to feed him.

A bit of the pasta fell off the fork onto his jeans. "Oops, I'm so sorry!" I winced, looking at him apologetically.

"Don't worry about it, Angel." He smiled and brushed it off with his hand.

OK, I could make this work to my advantage! I grabbed a napkin and wiped his jeans with it. It was on his mid-thigh so I made sure to wipe just a little higher, as I looked up at him through my eyelashes. I heard him gulp noisily as a slight bulge started to appear in his jeans which he quickly covered with his arm.

"There. All done," I flirted.

"Er.... thanks," he muttered, closing his eyes and sighing.

I grinned triumphantly. Hah! Take that, girls! I looked around the table to see they were all staring at me. Either a shocked or angry expression was plastered on every female face. I giggled, and winked at Jessica who had turned red with annoyance.

"I'd better go. I've got to speak to Mrs Francis about my science project," I said, getting up and smiling broadly.

Liam grabbed my hand and pulled me back to the seat. "What was that about?" he asked, looking slightly confused.

119

I shrugged and grinned at him. "Am I not allowed to be friendly to you, Liam? I mean, you *are* my brother's best friend after all. You're always hanging out at my house so I just thought I'd be civil."

"Civil, right," he replied, smirking at me.

I shot him a wink and got up to go to my friends. As I walked past Jessica and the cheerleaders I bent down to whisper in her ear. "Beat that," I teased, laughing my ass off.

I grabbed Kate's hand, making her walk a little in front of Sarah and Sean who were chatting about some art gallery that Sarah wanted to go to at the weekend. Sarah was a bit of an art freak. "Kate, I think I need to go on the pill. Do they still do the drop in family planning clinic on Rose Street after school?" I asked. She nodded in confirmation. I knew she would know, she had a little accident about a month back with a broken condom and went there for the morning after pill.

"Yeah, from four until eight," she replied, glancing over her shoulder to make sure no one could hear us. "So, you're going to take the plunge, huh? I think it's great. You should definitely go on the pill. You want me to come with you?" she asked casually. I knew she meant it; she was the best friend a girl could ask for.

"I'm not ready yet, but I don't want to get caught short or anything, I mean, it must take a while to get in your system or something. You don't mind coming with me though? I'd really appreciate it," I admitted, looking at her gratefully. I was a little nervous about going on my own, and I didn't feel right asking Liam to come. It wasn't exactly a guy thing to do.

"Of course not! You've been there with me loads of times." She linked her arm through mine. "I have my car today too, so we don't even need to walk."

I grinned. "Thanks, Kate." I sighed happily and we made our way to our lockers. I grabbed all the books that we needed for the afternoon, shoving them into my bag. "I just need to tell Jake that I'll meet him at home. I'll see you in class," I explained, turning in the direction of Jake's locker. I spotted Jake and Liam chatting to some of their other friends from the team. "Hey, guys," I chirped as I got up to them. They all looked at me, I knew that some of the guys on the team liked me; it was obvious in the way that they stared at me. No one ever made a move though - that was probably Jake's doing.

"Hi, Amber. How are you?" Casey asked, looking me over slowly.

"Good thanks, you?" I asked politely.

"All the better for seeing you," he replied, smirking at me.

Jake punched him in the arm, making me laugh. "Dude, little sister!" he cried angrily.

"Jake, I just wanted to tell you that I won't be coming home with you tonight. Kate needs me to go do something with her after school. I'll just see you at home later," I said, smiling. I could see Liam frowning looking slightly disappointed.

"Well, I'm working tonight, so it would have been Liam taking you home anyway," Jake replied, shrugging casually.

I glanced at Liam and smiled. "Right, yeah, I forgot. Well I'm sorry I'll miss that." He smiled back and my heart almost stopped because he was so handsome. I turned to walk off before stopping again, an idea forming in my head. I turned back to him and looked at him, teasingly. "Oh, and by the way, Liam, the pot stands at over four thousand bucks now. That's over two hundred girls."

His eyes went wide. "No shit?" he asked, looking shocked, and quite frankly, a little scared. Jake was laughing his ass off, and the other boys were looking around like us three had gone crazy.

"No shit," I confirmed, winking at Liam and walking away, giggling at his disgusted face.

After school, Kate drove us to the family planning clinic. I took a number and because I hadn't been there before, I had to fill out a ton of forms about my personal details, current sex life and my medical history. After about an hour of waiting, I was called through to a white sterile room where a lady was waiting there for me.

"Hi, Amber. Come on in," she said, smiled and pointed to a chair.

"Hi," I croaked nervously, sitting down opposite her.

"You don't have to be nervous. I'm not going to bite!" she chuckled. I smiled nervously. "So, what can I do for you today?" she asked, flipping through the forms that I'd filled in.

"Well, my boyfriend and I are getting pretty serious and are talking about having sex, so I wanted to go on the pill. Is that something I can do here, or do I need to go to my own doctor?" I asked, playing with my hands, blushing.

She smiled kindly. "You can certainly do that here. It says here that you're a virgin," she said, flipping through my forms again.

"Er, yeah I am." I blushed harder, wishing the ground would open up and swallow me.

"You don't need to be embarrassed, Amber. I think it's great that you're here. I see so many young girls who don't think about going on the pill until it's too late. It's refreshing to have a young girl being so responsible," she stated, patting my hand. I breathed a sigh of relief and smiled. I thought I was going to get a lecture as to why I shouldn't be having sex at my age and how I should be waiting. "OK, I just need to get some information, like blood pressure and weight and such. Then we can talk about which one will suit you best, alright?"

After I had done my blood pressure and weight and worked out my BMI we were both sat back down near her desk. "Right, well I recommend that you go for the combination pill. You take it every day, at the same time each day for three weeks, then you don't take it for a week which will be when you have your period. It's very effective and it's what most young girls go for," she explained, smiling.

I nodded and smiled because everything seemed to be falling into place. "That sounds good."

She grabbed her pad and scribbled a prescription. "You can get this filled right next door. I've given you a three month supply so I can check how you get on. Next time, if all's OK, then we'll go for six months," she explained.

"Yeah, thank you." I smiled gratefully because she had made this so much easier on me than I thought it would be.

"So, I'll give you a leaflet to read, but the important things to note are: you have to take it at the same time every day, and you have to take it every day apart from your week off." She smiled and handed me the prescription. "Make sure you read the leaflet about what you do if you miss one, or if you vomit after you take it, because that can stop it working. I'll give you some of these to keep you safe until you are into the swing of your pill, OK." She grabbed a handful of condoms and put them in a brown bag for me.

"Oh thanks," I mumbled, taking them gratefully.

"Well, thanks for coming in, Amber. I'll see you in three months." She stood up and held out her hand to me, signalling the end of the appointment.

I shook it, smiling. "Thank you." I walked out of the door, grinning from ear to ear. Wow, that was easier than I thought!

"Hey, how'd it go?" Kate asked, getting up from her seat.

"Yeah great. I need to go fill my prescription, and then I'm all set." I linked my arm through hers, pulling her towards the door.

"Wow, I can't believe you're going to have sex with Liam James!" she squealed, excitedly.

"Not yet I'm not. I need to know he can wait for me. I'm not ready for that yet," I said honestly.

"He'll wait for you. He looks like he's crazy about you." Kate smiled happily and I sighed. I really hoped that was true. I filled my prescription and Kate dropped me home. Jake was still at work so I made myself sandwich and sat at the table to do my homework. Once I had finished, I glanced at the clock. It was only eight o'clock; I had another hour until Jake came home.

I grinned and grabbed my phone, dialling Liam, barely able to contain my excitement. "Hey, Angel," he answered, sounding ridiculously happy.

"Hi. Want to come over?" I asked, chewing on my lip in excitement.

"Hell yeah. I'll be right there," he answered and hung up. I ran to my room to quickly check my hair. I laughed to myself when I realised that I had turned into one of those girls that thought they had to look perfect for him. I walked back to the lounge, just as he walked in the front door.

"Hi." I grinned.

He swept me up into his arms and kissed me passionately, making my heart race and my stomach flutter. After a while he pulled back. "Hi," he breathed, making me shiver with happiness. "So, where were you? I missed you," he murmured, putting his face in my hair and breathing deeply.

I giggled and pulled away. "Wow, what are you some kind of creepy hair smelling guy?" I joked, grabbing his hand and pulling him to the couch and pushing him down.

He laughed and gripped my waist, and pulled me onto his lap so I was straddling him. "I missed you so much today. I hated seeing you and not being able to touch you. Also, what the hell was that at lunchtime? Do you enjoy teasing the crap out of me?" he asked, frowning.

I ran my hands through his silky brown hair and giggled guiltily. "I have to set the scene for my victory. I can't just rock up to Jessica and be all like *'yeah, I won the bet'*, can I?" I asked innocently.

He shook his head, still frowning. "But that was over the top. I mean, do you know how hard that was for me not to jump you?" he joked.

I nodded and bit my lip so I didn't laugh. "Oh yeah, I could tell that was *hard* for you," I teased, raising my eyebrows knowingly, making him chuckle.

"Mmm, whatever. Where did you go anyway? I was hoping to spend some time with you tonight." He pulled me closer to him and kissed down my neck, making me bite into my lip as my skin broke out in goosebumps.

I pulled away and stood up, walking over to my school bag to get the brown bag from the clinic. I sat back on his lap and held the bag out for him to take. He looked at me, confused, and then looked in the bag. His face turned from confusion, to understanding, to happiness, to being annoyed. Wait, annoyed? Why on earth would he be annoyed with me?

"You went to do this on your own?" he asked, frowning at me angrily.

I shook my head, a little confused by his reaction. "I didn't go on my own, Kate came with me," I amended, wrapping my arms around his neck again.

"Why didn't you tell me? I would've come with you," he said, pulling me closer to him, the annoyed expression still on his face.

"Liam, I just thought that, you know..... it's not really a place where you take your boyfriend. I wanted to go on the pill; Kate offered to come with me." I shrugged; I didn't really see why he was so angry about it.

"Angel, I love you, I would've come with you. I wish you would've told me," he said, looking at me sadly.

"What difference does it make? I didn't think you'd want to go," I muttered, confused. Why the heck is he being all hurt and annoyed? I just went on the pill so I could have sex with him! Shouldn't he be happy about that fact?

"You didn't think that I'd want to go? Angel, this is about me too, I want us to do things together. We're a couple, a team. I feel a little hurt that you'd think I wouldn't want to go," he explained, kissing my forehead.

"Liam, I'm sorry, honestly. I didn't really think about it like that. I just thought that most guys wouldn't be interested. I thought you'd be pleased that I took some initiative," I said, looking at him apologetically, begging him with my eyes to understand that I didn't mean to hurt him.

"I am pleased that you took the initiative, but I'm not most guys. I love you. Most guys aren't in love with their girlfriends like I am. This was a big thing for you to do, and I should have been there for you," he explained, kissing me tenderly.

I took in a deep breath feeling guilt settle in the pit of my stomach. I didn't think about it like that. "I'm sorry I didn't tell you or ask you to come with me. I have to go back in three months for a check-up, want to come with me then?" I asked, smiling and putting my forehead to his.

He laughed. "Nah, it's not really my thing," he teased, turning his nose up and shrugging.

I laughed and slapped him playfully on the shoulder. "Asshole," I muttered jokingly, making him laugh harder. I pushed him down onto the sofa and laid on top of him, kissing him. By the time I pulled away, we were both breathing heavy. He was staring at me lustfully and I could feel he was aroused already. "Liam, just because I'm going on the pill, doesn't mean that I'm ready for anything more. You know that, right?" I asked, grimacing, hoping I hadn't got his hopes up and now he was going to be expecting sex.

He smiled and tucked my hair behind my ear. "Angel, I know that. It's fine. We'll go as slow as you want. As long as I still get to do this." He pulled my face back down to his again. I smiled against his lips and felt happier than I had been in years, he was just too sweet. I just prayed I would be ready soon, before he got bored or desperate and went chasing after that skank Jessica.

After making out and cuddling for about an hour we heard a car pull up. "Damn it, that must be Jake's ride," I whispered, trying to push myself away from Liam. I sat up, smoothing down my hair, hoping that it didn't look like we'd been fooling around for the last hour.

Liam laughed and pulled me back down on the couch with him. "Jake can handle this. Come on, he has to get used to it eventually. He's going to see us kiss from time to time," he said, chuckling against my neck. I smiled as I weaved my fingers into his hair, I heard the front door open and Liam snapped his head up to look, a small smile playing on the edge of his lips. I actually think he was enjoying teasing Jake.

"Oh come on, guys! Seriously, what did I say this morning about PDA's?" Jake whined, slinging his keys on the table.

Liam groaned and rolled his eyes as he sat up, pulling me up to sit next to him. "Better?" he asked, grinning wickedly.

Jake sighed and rolled his eyes too. "I'll get used to it, I guess," he grumbled. Liam grinned at me and I couldn't help but smile back. He threw his arm over my shoulder and held my hand with his other arm, playing with my fingers.

Jake came in and plopped down on the sofa opposite, looking at us grumpily. I laughed at his disgruntled expression and stood up. "I'm going to go do my homework. You boys can entertain yourselves for a while, right?" I smirked at them both in turn. I had a feeling that they needed a little 'boy bonding time' after the revelations last night. Jake and Liam were best friends after all.

"Yeah. Want to play Halo, Jake?" Liam asked excitedly. Jake jumped up to set it up and I smiled to myself happily. Yep, they were back to normal. I grabbed the brown bag and made my way to my bedroom, giggling as Liam slapped my ass and whistled at me. I'd already done my homework, so I decided that a nice long soak in the bath would be good. I ran a bath and added a lot of bubbles, before grabbing a book and settling into the tub. I lost myself in the story.

I was so engrossed in the story that I didn't hear the door open. "Now *that's* sexy," Liam purred from right next to me.

I screamed and almost dropped my book in the water. "Shit! You scared the crap out of me, Liam!" I cried, trying to slow my heart that was trying to break my ribs. I brought my knees up to my chest and tried to cover myself up so he couldn't see anything inappropriate. Lucky for me, there were still quite a few bubbles which helped.

He laughed. "Sorry. Hey, can I get in?" he teased as he knelt down next to me and put his fingers in the bath. He pulled them out quickly and shook his head. "Never mind. That's freaking freezing!" He frowned and dried his hand on the towel.

"Liam, will you get out of here? This isn't funny!" I cried, blushing.

He grinned his cocky little smile and bent over to kiss my lips just for a split second before he turned and walked back for the door. "I was kidding. I didn't actually realise you were in here. You should get out though, that water is really cold. Have you been in there all this time?" he asked, shaking his head.

"It is a bit cold," I admitted. Now that I was out of the story I didn't even realise that the bath was stone cold and I had goosebumps all over me. Liam smiled and turned to go back to my bedroom, closing the door to give me some privacy. I pulled the plug out and threw my book onto the side as I stood up. Grabbing the towel off of the side and wrapped it around myself tightly. I realised as I climbed out of the tub that I didn't bring any clothes in here to change into. I was actually really cold now and my teeth were chattering. I couldn't stay in here all night, I'd just have to go and get some pyjamas. It was no big deal; Liam had seen me in a towel before.

As I walked into my bedroom I noticed that he was lounging on my bed. "Hey," I muttered, feeling a little uncomfortable as I pulled on a pair of shorts under the towel.

"Jeez, Angel, you could have got hypothermia or something," he scolded, looking at me worriedly. He grabbed my hand and pulled me to the bed, sitting me on the edge as he went into the bathroom, coming back with another towel. He rubbed my arms and shoulders, drying me quickly.

I was glad I decided not to wash my hair, instead, putting it in a messy bun, otherwise that would have made me even colder. He wrapped his arm around me, putting each of my prune like finger tips into his mouth, warming them one at a time. Oh my God, that's sexy! I bent my head and kissed him, seeming to catch him by surprise. After a second or two he responded, kissing me back. I sucked on his lip softly and he opened his mouth, allowing me to slip my tongue in. He moaned in the back of his throat and I wrapped my arms around his neck, gripping his hair roughly, tugging slightly. He pulled me closer to him, deepening the kiss. After what seemed like forever, but still wasn't long enough, he pulled away breathing heavy. His lips didn't leave my skin though, instead, he kissed down my neck, sucking on the skin near my collarbone, making me gasp and squirm.

I was still freezing cold and my teeth started to chatter again, ruining the moment. He pulled back, laughing. "Let's get you under the covers and you can get warm." He pulled off his t-shirt in one easy movement and I couldn't help but stare at his sculpted chest. I felt movement and my vision went black for a few seconds, interrupting my ogling. I smiled as I realised he'd pulled his t-shirt over my head.

"Liam, if you wanted to make me hot, all you need to do is take your clothes off," I purred, biting my lip and looking over his chest and abs, wanting to run my tongue over them.

He laughed and wrapped his arms around me. "Angel, you couldn't possibly be any hotter, trust me. That would be illegal," he replied, kissing me again. I pulled the damp towel off and threw it on the floor as he picked me up. I wrapped my legs around his waist as he carried me up to the pillow end and pulled the covers back, climbing into the bed with me still attached to his front like a baby monkey. He pulled the covers completely up over our heads and pulled back to talk to me in the semi darkness. "I missed you tonight. Why didn't you stay and play with us?" he asked sulkily.

"I thought you and Jake needed a little time together. You haven't really spoken to him on your own since he found out about us. He's still your best friend, so you're just going to have to find a balance. You can't spend all of your time trying to get in my pants, you know," I joked.

"But I love trying to get in your pants," he whined playfully, giving me the puppy dog face, making me giggle. I was warming up now. His body heat pulsing into me and our hot breaths tangling under the duvet, made it seem almost steamy under there. Then again, that might have just been the passion I felt burning inside me. "I guess you're right. Jake was fine tonight, he actually said it was nice to see you happy, which I took all the credit for of course," he said cockily.

"All the credit? Wow, that's an inflated ego you have right there," I teased, smiling at the double meaning, about the bulge in his jeans that was pressing onto me. He laughed and stroked the side of my face with the back of his fingers.

"You'd better not be naked with my little sister, James!" Jake growled warningly from near the door.

Liam pushed the cover back off of our heads, grinning guiltily. "Jake, dude, a little more warning would be nice."

"Oh, Jake, get a grip! What do you want? And have you ever heard of knocking?" I asked, pushing the covers back further so he could see I had a t-shirt on.

"I knocked. You just didn't hear through all the flirting," he replied, smirking. We all laughed and Jake shook his head. "Anyway, I just wanted to tell you, Ambs, that Mom's coming home on Sunday."

I grinned; I hadn't seen my mom in three weeks. "Yeah? Awesome!" I cried happily.

Jake nodded, his smile matching mine. "Yeah. OK well, I'm going to bed. Keep the noise down in here; I don't want to hear anything."

I laughed and couldn't resist teasing him some more. "Jake, you might want to borrow my iPod, we're warming up for the bet," I joked, winking at him.

Liam burst out laughing and Jake just glared at me, shaking his head disapprovingly, closing the door behind him. "Angel, you are just too funny," Liam said, kissing down my neck.

"Shut up, JAMES," I replied, mimicking Jakes tone jokingly.

Chapter 14

I woke in the morning with a huge smile on my face. The sun was shining, the birds were singing, and I had woken up next to the world's most sexy boy, who just so happened to be in love with me. I smiled against his arm that I was laying on and pressed back into him, feeling his hard chest press into my back where he was spooning me.

"Liam?" I whispered, turning my head in his direction.

His arms tightened around me as he slowly opened his eyes. "Hey," he mumbled, lifting his head so he could kiss me. "Wow, I love waking up knowing that you're finally mine." He laid his head back down and sighed contentedly. "So, can we tell people we're dating today?" he asked happily, grinning from ear to ear.

"Um…. no. Not today. I still need to do a bit more prep work on that," I replied, running my hand down his chest, tracing the bumps of his muscles.

He groaned. "By, 'prep work', you don't mean you're going to flirt and make me horny as hell again like yesterday, do you?" he asked, looking at me pleadingly.

"You'll have to wait and see, won't you? Oh, and I give you my permission to touch me a little today if you want," I offered casually. I turned to face him, propping my head up on my elbow so I could see him better.

"Mmm….. touch you, like this?" he purred. His fingers trailed across my body slowly, from my face, down my neck, across my breasts and stomach, finally settling just on the inside of my thigh. His hand was so close to my core that I couldn't stop the little moan that escaped my lips.

He traced his fingertips across my leg, making me whimper. Damn, I wanted him so badly but I just couldn't, not yet. "Don't,

Liam," I begged. I said the words but I moved my hips unconsciously, trying to get closer to his hand.

He laughed, putting his lips so they are almost touching mine. "Promise you won't tease me too hard today at school," he murmured against my lips as he moved his hand away to the outside of my thigh.

"I won't tease you too much. I can't promise you won't get hard," I teased, twisting his words.

He crashed his lips to mine and I could feel he was smiling. "You're such a damn tease! I don't even think you realise what you're doing to me," he growled, kissing my neck gently. Jeez, I knew exactly what I was doing to him, I could feel it!

I kissed him back passionately and he pulled away after a couple of minutes, just as I was getting really into it. "I better go." He kissed me again as he climbed out of the bed.

"OK. I'll see you in a bit," I replied, watching as he pulled on his clothes. He winked at me as he climbed out of my window, heading back to his house. Even though Jake knew, Liam still needed to keep up the pretense for his parents. He couldn't exactly been seen leaving through the front door when he was supposed to be in his bed.

I climbed out of bed and skipped to the bathroom for a shower. When I was dry, I stood there looking through my closet for a long time. I needed something different to wear today. I wanted Liam to look like her really wanted me in front of everyone because I didn't want to keep lying about our relationship. I pulled out a denim mini skirt and a plain black V-neck short sleeve top. I smiled as I looked at the outfit. This would definitely work. I got dressed and looked myself over in the mirror, the skirt was short but not too short that I looked like one of the skanks, and the top was fitted but not too much, just enough to hint at what was underneath. I grinned and pulled on a pair of ballet flats, completing the outfit.

I grabbed the little bag that I got from the family planning clinic and pulled out my box of pills. Scanning the packet, I found the first one and swallowed it quickly, smiling to myself. I skipped to the kitchen. Liam was chatting to Jake with his back to me; there was already a bowl of cereal on the counter waiting for me. I felt my heart melt a little at his thoughtfulness.

"Good morning," I chirped. Liam was just drinking a glass of water and as he turned around, he almost choked. Jake slapped him on the back roughly and I just laughed. Yep, that was the effect that I wanted! His eyes were wide and hungry as they looked me over slowly; making me blush as I imagined the thoughts he was having about my body. He still hadn't spoken. "Liam, you want to take a picture? It'll last longer," I joked, eating my cereal.

That seemed to snap him out of the private fantasy he was having. "You're not wearing that today are you?" he asked, frowning slightly.

I looked down at myself wondering what he meant by that. I didn't look that slutty. "Yeah, why?" I asked, confused. I thought he liked the outfit; he certainly looked like he did!

He walked up and wrapped his arms around me from behind. "Angel, how the hell am I supposed to concentrate all day, knowing that my beautiful girlfriend looks like a freaking sex goddess? Are you torturing me on purpose?" he whined, kissing the side of my neck and running his hands up my exposed thighs.

I giggled and elbowed him in the stomach. "Well then you'll just have to exercise some control won't you," I teased, pulling away after grinding on his erection discreetly.

He groaned and moved so that he was behind the counter, probably so Jake couldn't see he was so excited. "You are so not playing fair," he whined.

I just laughed and grabbed my bag. "Ready to go, Jake?" I asked, smiling at my brother who looked like he was trying to ignore our little exchange but was failing miserably.

"Yeah. I think Liam needs another minute to calm down though," he stated, laughing, making Liam roll his eyes. I giggled at his warning expression. Jake grabbed my shoulders and pushed me out of the door. I was still laughing at Liam.

The morning flew by and finally lunchtime was here. I was so excited to see Liam that I couldn't stop smiling. "What the hell's wrong with you?" Sean asked, looking at me like I'd lost my mind.

"Nothing, just having a good day. Plus, I'm hungry and we're now going to eat," I lied smoothly.

"You gonna make another move on Liam?" Kate asked, smirking at me knowingly.

I laughed. "Oh heck yeah. Just watch Jessica's face. I'm going to make him want me today." I grinned happily. This was going to be great and Jessica was going to hate every second of it.

"No doubt about it," Kate agreed, laughing.

"Oh! So that's what the skirt's for!" Sean stated. A look of understanding crossed his face.

I laughed and nodded. "Think it'll work?" I asked him, actually wanting his opinion.

He nodded. "Oh yeah it'll work. All the guys in school have been talking about your killer legs today. I must say that even I, who am totally in love with my girlfriend, have checked you out," he admitted, shrugging.

I slapped him on the shoulder playfully. "Ew! That's gross, Sean. You're one of my best friends! Best friends don't perv on each other!" I stated, faking a shudder.

"Actually, I've been checking you out too," Kate joked.

"Me too," Sarah added, making us all laugh harder.

As we walked into the canteen, laughing, I could actually feel some of the guys looking at me. Now that Sean had said about it, I realised I did have a lot more male attention than normal.

We bought our food. "I'll be right back, guys," I said, grinning as I made my way over to the table where the jocks sat. My friends all went to sit at our usual table, watching me with curious eyes. I watched Liam as I approached. As usual there were about ten girls hanging around him, flirting shamelessly. He looked like he was really pissed off.

"Seriously, Rebecca, if you touch me one more time I'm going to go speak to someone about it. This is bordering on sexual harassment," Liam growled, glaring at her and knocking her hand off of his thigh. She looked extremely put out as she stood up and stormed off. The rest of the girls were smirking at her back. You could practically read their thoughts on their faces: *One less girl for competition.* I stifled a giggle and sat down at the table. Jake wasn't there, so I decided to make the most of it and really push it today.

"Hi, Liam," I purred, smiling at him seductively.

His face lit up as he saw me. "Hi. You had a good morning?" he asked happily. I pouted and shook my head. His face dropped and he put his arm around my shoulder, looking at me concerned. "What's wrong, Angel?"

I stood up and sat on the table in front of him, propping one foot on the bench in-between his legs so my foot was almost touching his crotch. He didn't seem to notice though; he was still watching my face, worriedly. "I hurt my leg in gym class. It's really sore. Do I have a bruise?" I asked, opening my legs slightly and pointing to my inner thigh. His eyes instantly dropped down to my legs. I'm betting he had a clear view of my panties because a pained, and hungry expression crossed his face. I felt a little like a slut for doing this but at least no one else could see what he was seeing otherwise I wouldn't have done it.

He put his hand on my calf muscle and slid it slowly all the way up my leg to my inner thigh, moaning quietly as he did it. "Nope, no bruise," he stated in his sexy voice, making me burn in need as he massaged my thigh.

"Hmm, really? It's so sore," I lied, smiling at him. He was smirking at me; his expression told me that he knew he was driving me crazy. "How about you kiss it better for me?" I suggested, raising my eyebrows, trying to look sexy. I heard some of the guys groan as they were obviously watching the exchange. Lust crossed Liam's face as he nodded with a little sexy smile and bent his head towards my leg. Just before his lips touched my skin, I moved my leg away. "Actually, you'd better not. I thought you had a girlfriend," I teased.

He laughed and shook his head at me, narrowing his eyes, obviously disappointed he didn't get to kiss my leg in front of the whole school. "I do have a girlfriend. I love her more than anything," he said, his voice full of honesty.

I smiled as my heart melted. "Well, you shouldn't be doing this then, huh?" I teased, smirking at him and climbing down from the table. I grabbed my lunch tray. "It seems fine now anyway. Maybe if it starts hurting again later, I'll give you a call," I flirted.

He groaned as I winked at him and walked off to my table of friends. I could hear the boys all making slutty comments behind me about how hot that was, and how they would definitely 'tap that', and the girls all saying what a whore I was. I giggled and plopped down at our table. Kate grinned at me knowingly, and Sarah and Sean were watching me with their mouths wide open.

"You were *so* in there! I really think you might win the bet!" Sarah said, looking at me in awe.

I couldn't help but laugh at her; she was looking at me like I was some kind of goddess or something. "I could use four thousand bucks," I admitted, laughing. I just hoped Jessica actually paid up once she realised I was his girlfriend all along.

When we finished eating, I was walking along with my group of friends, when someone grabbed my hand and jerked me to a stop. I squeaked, a little shocked, and turned to see Liam grinning at me as he dragged me to the nearest empty classroom. I giggled as I watched my friends walk off without me, not even noticing I wasn't behind them anymore. He closed the door and looked at me, trying to pretend he was annoyed with me but there was no way I was falling for that, he enjoyed himself I could tell.

"Angel, that was way too much," he stated as he stepped

closer to me.

I stepped back and bumped into the wall. "Too much? I thought it was pretty perfect," I replied playfully.

He laughed and pressed his body to mine. "You're pretty perfect." He brushed my hair away from my face gently, looking at me tenderly. I put my arms around him and pulled him closer, then moved my hands down to grip his ass. He smiled that sexy little smile at me and pressed his lips to mine gently; I whimpered slightly and pulled him closer, wanting more.

He pulled away to kiss down my neck, his hands roaming down my body, across my legs. One of his hands slid under my skirt, tickling his fingers on my ass teasingly. I felt him sucking gently on my neck. "Liam, are you giving me a hicky?" I asked, giggling.

He stopped sucking for a second and pulled his mouth away from my skin. "Mmm hmm, I'm branding you," he murmured, before sucking on the same spot again. After a few more seconds he pulled away to look at it, inspecting his handiwork. He looked extremely proud of himself and was grinning from ear to ear.

"Right, and do I get to brand you?" I teased.

"Sure, if you want to," he agreed, shrugging but actually looking a little hopeful. Did he actually want me to brand him? He pressed his lips to mine again, seeming to set my body on fire. Jeez, how on earth did he do this to me? He was the only guy I had kissed for goodness sake. Yet here I am, letting him put his hand on my ass! I grinned as he tipped his head to the side, giving me access to his neck. Just as my lips touched his skin the bell rang.

He groaned and pulled away, looking at me with the cute puppy dog face again. "Skip with me," he pleaded, pouting slightly.

Skip with him? Oh crap I hated skipping school, that just wasn't me at all! "Um, Liam, I can't." I was torn, I really wanted to spend time with him, but I just couldn't bear the thought of my teachers knowing I missed class unnecessarily.

"Please?" he begged, bending his knees so we were at the same height.

His blue eyes were killing me. I couldn't say no to him. I sighed heavily. "If I get caught, then you're in deep trouble," I warned. If I got detention, I would make sure he got one too.

He laughed; a beautiful smile stretched across his face as he pulled out his cellphone and called Jake to tell him I wasn't feeling well and that he was taking me home. "Yeah, she's fine. No she said she feels a little dizzy, that's all. No, no, I got it. OK great. See ya," he said into the phone, grinning and shooting me a wink. He slid his phone back in his pocket and grabbed my hand, pulling me from the classroom out to his car. "Jake's going to get a lift to work. So, as long as I get you home by nine, he won't even know we skipped," he said happily.

I rolled my eyes at him. "Like Jake really believed that I was sick! He knows we're skipping." I shook my head, laughing. Jake wasn't stupid, he just didn't want to say anything.

"Well then, Angel, what shall we do?" Liam asked, pulling out of the parking lot quickly before anyone noticed us leaving.

I shrugged easily. "I don't mind. Whatever you want." As long as it involved spending more time with him, I would do anything.

He grinned. "Want me to take you skating again?" he offered.

"Sure, why not. I need to change first though; I'll get frost bite on my butt otherwise." I laughed as his eyes immediately shot down to my legs again. I text Kate to tell her I was skipping and asked her to collect any work that I missed.

When we pulled outside my house, Liam went to his house to get something he said he needed, and I ran in and slipped on some jeans. I ran a brush through my hair and added a quick sweep of mascara. As I left my room, I grabbed a sweater so I didn't get cold.

I ran back to the car, excited for some alone time with him. He smiled as I climbed in. "Hey, brought you this," he said, handing me one of his hoodies.

I frowned at it, knowing I had one of my own. Why would he bring me this? "Er.... thanks?"

"It's for your peachy little ass. I told you I'd bring one so you didn't get wet and cold like last time. Although, I have every confidence that you'll be skating on your own by the end of the lesson," he boasted, grinning.

"Well, I'm not sure I want to skate if you're not touching me," I purred suggestively.

He smiled. "Hmm, I never thought of that. Hopefully you won't catch on too quickly then." He waggled his eyebrows at me, making me laugh.

Skating was fun. He was right, I was a lot better this time. It was probably due to the fact that he was such a good teacher, and because we spent almost all day here last time. He was so much fun to be around. He skated backwards just like he did before, holding both my hands, making jokes, and chatting. I only fell a few times and each time he would break my fall or catch me and pull me up. I looked at him as we skated, he was smiling broadly and my heart skipped a beat. He was so handsome, kind and patient. I could feel myself falling for him. I knew it wouldn't be long before I was head over heels for him.

"Hey, how about you show off a little? I love to watch you skate," I suggested, gripping onto the side for dear life so he could let go of me.

He kissed me before skating off backwards, he turned sharply and skated forwards so fast that it actually scared me. My heart was hammering in my chest at the sight of it. If he fell while skating like that, he would be seriously hurt. The thought of him being hurt terrified me. He did a few laps, showing me his skills like jumping and skating on one foot. I'd always loved to watch him skate. It looked so beautiful and graceful, but I never really lusted after him for it, until now. He looked so sexy when he was skating, so powerful and masterful.

Liam wanted to play hockey professionally, he had already been scouted for a really good team but needed to be in college before they could sign him. He'd been offered a full athletic scholarship to a really great school in Boston, which would mean that he would have to move away when school finished in a few months. The time apart was going to kill me. I was going to have nightmares every night when he wasn't there, not to mention the heartache I'd feel watching him leave. I hated the fact that he'd be so far away and that girls would be falling all over him. I sighed, refusing to think about it. I needed to trust him. And I did, I trusted him completely, I believed that he loved me and that he didn't want to hurt me.

When he came back to me, he skidded to a stop, sending an ice spray off over the side. "Is that showing off enough for you?" he asked, wrapping his arms around my waist and kissing me tenderly.

"Oh yeah. My man can skate alright," I confirmed, grinning at him.

"Mmm, say that again. I like that," he growled, in a husky sexy voice that made my insides tremble.

I wrapped my arms tightly around his neck and pulled him in close. "My man can skate," I purred seductively, looking into his eyes. I could feel the burning passion sizzling between us. He bent his knees so we were on the same level, held me tight and then stood back up, lifting me off my feet. He started to skate gently around the rink. I wrapped my legs around his waist while he skated around, occasionally doing small spins and changing to skate backwards. His eyes never left mine. It was the most erotic and sexy thing that had ever happened to me, and my whole body was yearning for him.

"I love you so much, Angel," he whispered.

I smiled. My insides were bubbling with happiness and passion. He was driving me crazy; I wanted him and needed him. As I looked into his beautiful blue eyes, I could see all of his love for me shining through and it made my heart beat way too fast. Suddenly, it hit me like a truck, I loved him too. Maybe I'd always loved him, I wasn't sure. He had kind of crept behind my defences and wormed his way into my heart, but I had always refused to look at him that way. He made me feel safe, wanted, needed and special; I didn't ever want to let him go. I loved him like crazy, more than anything, he was the one thing I needed out of life.

I opened my mouth to tell him I loved him too, but he spoke first cutting me off. "Let's go for dinner," he suggested, skating off the ice rink and sitting me down on the bench. He got down on his knees and took my skates off for me. I just watched him as he did it, unable to keep the smile off of my face. Was this boy really mine? How did I get so lucky?

After we got our shoes back on, we drove to a little Italian restaurant that he said made the second best lasagne in the world. "Second best?" I asked, laughing.

"Yeah. Your lasagne kicks ass," he stated, holding my hand tightly as we followed the waiter to the table.

"You do know that you've got me now, you can stop with the compliments," I teased, laughing. He grinned and shook his head, rolling his eyes like I was being stupid.

The food was good and the restaurant was really cute, it had candles on each table and was really quite romantic, he was so much fun to be around there wasn't one awkward silence. I couldn't help but wonder how I didn't know anything about him before we got together. I guess it was because the only personality he ever showed me was the asshole side, which actually, didn't seem to be a part of his character at all.

"Liam, can I ask you something?" I asked, too curious not to ask.

"Sure. Whatever you want." He shrugged, taking a mouthful of his drink, watching me curiously.

"Why were you always such a jerk to me? If you've liked me all this time, why were you always pushing me over when we were kids and being such an ass to me? You do know that I used to hate you, right?" I asked, raising my eyebrows, looking at him apologetically.

He laughed. "You know, there's a thin line between love and hate. Maybe you loved me and didn't realise," he suggested, grinning. I smiled because that was exactly what I was thinking earlier.

"No, Liam. You were a complete ass to me. But most of it was an act, right? So why did you do it?" I asked, needing the answer, it was killing me because I just didn't understand.

"Jake." He shrugged.

"Jake? I don't get it." I gave him my best 'what the hell' face.

He smiled sadly. "Jake really didn't want me near you. He beat the crap out of me a couple of times when we were kids for it. He's really protective of you. It was just easier to keep myself away from you if you didn't actually want to be with me. I thought that if I made you want to stay away from me, then I wouldn't have to try as hard," he said, frowning.

Wait, he pretended to be an asshole so I wouldn't want to be with him because of Jake? Damn that boy!

"All those years, Liam, it just seems like a waste." I sighed and shook my head; if he'd have told me then maybe we could have been together for longer. "You know, I always thought you had a split personality," I told him, laughing.

He laughed too. "You did? Why?"

"Well, I always thought of you as daytime Liam, who was an asshole, jerk and a man-whore, flirt. Then there was night-time Liam, who was adorable and sweet and caring. I've always liked night-time Liam," I said honestly.

He smiled happily. "Well, the night was when I would stop trying to push you away. I decided that since Jake didn't know about it, that I could be myself and enjoy my time with you. Just so you know though, both of my personalities have loved you forever," he said, shrugging and grinning at me.

Aww, he's so freaking sweet! I reached out and held his hand tightly. "I wish you'd told me sooner, I really did hate you at times," I admitted sheepishly, making him laugh.

"Yeah? Like the time I cut your stuffed bear's head off and threw him in the trash?" he asked, laughing. I gasped at the memory of it, I'd forgotten about that! Jake had got my bear out of the trash and put him back on my bed for me and fixed his head.

"Yeah, you jerk!" I scolded, fighting a smile.

"You know I never really did that, right? I pretended to cut his head off and I hid it up my sweater and put him back on your bed a couple of hours later," he said, still chuckling.

138

"No way! Jake told me he got him back for me!" I laughed.

He shook his head. "No. That was one of the times he kicked my ass. He caught me sneaking into your room that day. I'd told him I was going to the bathroom," he said, laughing and shaking his head.

"I can't believe my brother kicked your ass. That's just too funny."

"I'm just glad he didn't kill me for dating you. I can hold my own in a fight, but Jake's a damn psycho when it comes to you." Liam frowned, shaking his head slightly, a smile pulling at the corners of his mouth.

"Yeah, well, you better make sure you don't hurt me then, huh?" I teased.

He nodded. "I would never hurt you, ever." He squeezed my hand gently, looking right into my eyes, his whole demeanor showing me the truth of his words.

I believed him, I didn't think he would ever hurt me on purpose, but I knew he would break my heart sooner or later. When he went to college and we were apart, even if he didn't cheat, that was going to hurt badly. Even if we weren't dating it would be awful being without him, but now it would be like torture. I pushed the thoughts out of my mind. I couldn't think about it, not until it happened and even then we could get through it. I loved him enough to wait for him. I just hoped that he would feel the same in four months' time when all the college skanks were throwing themselves at him and I was a three hour drive away.

"Right then, you ready to go?" Liam asked after I had eaten a massive piece of chocolate cake all to myself. I nodded and he threw some money on the table, holding out a hand to help me up.

I grinned. "You know you're shaping up to be the best boyfriend in the world," I said happily.

"I love it when you call me that." He grinned and wrapped his sweater around my shoulders as we walked out into the cold.

I gripped hold of his hand, not wanting to let go. As we got to the car he even opened my door for me. "Such a gentleman, Liam," I teased.

I watched him walk round to the driver's side. He was just so handsome, and he was mine, I couldn't help but smile at that knowledge. I'd never dreamed I would ever have anything like this with a guy. When I used to think about dating it would scare the life out of me because I couldn't let people touch me, and all the time I had the perfect guy who was in love with me, who held me and kept

139

me safe every night, and I didn't even know. How could I have been so stupid?

When we got back to my place, it was only eight o'clock. Jake wouldn't be home for another hour so we had the house to ourselves. "Come here, I want to talk to you," I said, pulling him towards the sofa. He looked a little worried and nervous. I pulled him down next to me, sitting close to him. I could feel the passion building and I knew it wouldn't be long before I would be ready to take things further with him. I'd never felt like this before and although we had only been together for five days, I'd known him forever. I trusted him like no one else and I knew he wouldn't hurt me. I wasn't worried about him not being able to wait for me, I could see in his eyes he would wait as long as I wanted, and that knowledge was pushing me forwards. If I doubted he would wait for me, then there would be no way that I would feel like this. I gripped his hand tightly as I just looked at him, trying to find the right words to express my feelings for him.

"What's wrong, Angel?" he asked quietly, frowning rubbing circles in the back of my hand.

Oh crap, could I say it? I was so embarrassed; I'd never said anything like this to anyone before.

I took a deep breath and willed my voice not to show the nerves I felt inside. "I love you, Liam," I said honestly. He looked at me, shock clear across his face. His mouth was hanging open, his eyes wide as he took in what I said. I couldn't help but laugh. "OK, that's not how I imagined your reaction." I winced, waiting for him to say something.

He pushed me down onto my back, rolling on top of me. "You love me? Seriously?" he asked, the shock leaving his face to be replaced by excitement.

I nodded, feeling my cheeks heat up slightly. "Yes, I love you."

He laughed and kissed me passionately. When he pulled away his eyes were sparkling with happiness. "Thank God! I thought you were going to dump me or something. You looked so serious that I thought you didn't want to be with me," he said, shaking his head, grinning.

I laughed. "You did? That's why you were looking nervous?" I asked, giggling.

"Say it again," he whispered.

I wrapped my arms around his neck and pulled him closer to me, his mouth about an inch away from mine. "I love you, Liam James," I whispered.

"I love you too, Amber Walker." He kissed me, hard, and I couldn't help but kiss him back with the same intensity. I ran my hands down his back and gripped the bottom of his t-shirt, pulling it up over his head, trailing my fingers down his chest, just marveling at how flawless he was. His hands were roaming all over my body hungrily; he gripped the bottom of my top and started pulling it up slowly, as if he was waiting for some sort of reaction. I felt my love for him bump up another gear because of how thoughtful and patient he was with me. I smiled against his lips and he pulled away, looking at me curiously.

"OK?" he asked, concern colouring his voice.

I nodded and pushed him off of me so I could sit up. I gripped my top and yanked it off over my head, throwing it to the floor. He was just watching me in shock. I pulled him back to me, kissing him deeply. His hands were everywhere while we made out but he didn't do anything I didn't want him to. It was perfect and sweet. An incredible end to an incredible date. After a while he pulled away and laid next to me, we talked happily for awhile.

At nine, he sighed. "Jake's going to be home soon, maybe we should get dressed," he suggested, looking a little reluctant as his fingers trailed over my bra and stomach.

I nodded. "Yeah. I don't think he'd be best pleased if he came home and found out that you'd seen me with no top on, James," I said with mock horror. He laughed and sat up, grabbing my shirt from the floor and passing it to me, kissing me again tenderly.

When we were both fully dressed again, we sat watching TV until Jake came home. I couldn't keep the smile off of my face, Liam loved me and I loved him and everything was perfect. Jake came home and they played on the Wii while I did my homework, trying unsuccessfully, not to watch Liam's ass as he stood in front of me. At ten he went home to change his clothes and see his parents for half an hour before he would sneak through my window tonight. I could barely contain my excitement at being with him again.

"So, how are you two getting on?" Jake asked curiously, when we were on our own.

I grinned happily. "Really good actually. Thanks for not freaking out and hurting him or anything," I said, grimacing at the thought.

He smiled sadly. "That's OK. Just be careful, he's a player, I don't want you to get hurt." He looked at me worriedly. He always was overprotective, but I guess growing up the way we did he always felt he needed to protect me from our father. I guess that urge never left, even after my father did.

I smiled and shook my head. "He won't hurt me," I stated confidently.

He laughed. "Such confidence in a guy who's never managed to hold down a girlfriend before," he mused, shaking his head.

"Jake, Liam's a great guy, he won't hurt me. He loves me."

He sighed and nodded. "I know he does." He frowned disapprovingly as he said it. I don't think that Jake would ever approve of anyone I brought home; he was just so damn overprotective. He'd always been the best brother a girl could ask for. "So, do you need to talk to me about Dad or anything?" he asked, wincing as he said the word dad.

I closed my eyes; I had been putting off even thinking about that man coming back. "I don't want to see him," I said quietly.

He pulled me into a hug. "OK, then we won't see him." He rubbed my back soothingly, looking at me worriedly, as if he thought I was going to have another panic attack like the last time we spoke about him.

"You can see him if you want to," I said, feeling a little guilty. I didn't want to stop Jake from seeing him if he wanted to.

He laughed humourlessly. "Actually, I *need* to see him." He shrugged, and my heart sank, I didn't want Jake anywhere near that asshole.

"OK, well if that's what you want...." I trailed off, trying not to cry.

Jake pulled out of the hug and looked at me sadly. "I don't want to see him, Amber, I want to kill him," he stated, shrugging casually, making me laugh. I slapped his shoulder making him laugh too. "I promise I won't let him hurt you, never again." He kissed the side of my head gently, his whole body tense. I knew Jake always felt guilty that he didn't do something sooner. I don't think he'd ever forgive himself for it, but it was an irrational belief, none of it was his fault, yet he took all the blame for it not ending before it did. I think he forgets that he went through it too; he only ever worries about me. He never really talks about the fact that he probably got hurt twice as much as I did because he was always protecting me. He always seems to forget that he was a child at the time too, that he couldn't have done anything about it anyway because he wasn't strong enough.

"You know you're the best brother in the world, right?" I told him, smiling happily.

He nodded, smirking at me. "Yeah, I know," he replied cockily, making us both laugh again.

I sighed, feeling exhaustion creep in. "I'm going to bed. Night, Jake." I kissed the top of his head as I went to my room, locking the door behind me out of habit.

I put on my pyjamas and just as I was about to fall asleep, I heard my window open. I smiled happily as Liam climbed in the bed behind me, wrapping his arms around me. "Hey, you," I mumbled sleepily.

He kissed the back of my head gently. "Hey, yourself," he replied, as I snuggled back against him.

"I love you, Liam." I grinned as I said the words; it just got easier and easier to say each time.

"I love you more, Angel." I sighed and closed my eyes, drifting off to sleep, safe and warm, wrapped in his embrace.

Chapter 15

~ Liam ~

I had been with Amber for a week now, and it'd honestly been the best week of my life - of anyone's life, probably. She was just so perfect. I'd wanted her for so long that I was a little worried that if I ever did get her, that she would never be able to live up to what I had imagined. I'd put her on such a high pedestal that I was surprised she actually had enough oxygen to breathe. But being with her was better than anything I could have ever imagined.

I couldn't wait for tonight. As usual, there was a party at Jake's - the after game celebrations. I was definitely planning on dancing with my girl tonight. I pulled on a pair of ripped jeans and a white button down shirt and headed over to their house. I was so excited to see her that I could burst into song any moment. I still couldn't believe that someone like me would be lucky enough to have someone like her fall in love with them. She could have any guy she wanted; she was beautiful, smart, funny, and kind. Practically every guy in school lusted after her, not that I could blame them; her body was just out of this world, all that dancing…..

I struggled to watch her at her dance practice every Saturday, it was such a freaking turn on seeing her jumping around, shaking her ass. She honestly made my mouth water I wanted her so badly. It would be even worse tomorrow because I'd actually had my hands on that pert little ass that would be shaking around.

I went straight to their kitchen, helping Jake sort out drinks and snacks as usual. Amber was probably in her room making herself look unbelievable, just to tease the life out of me again. She'd insisted on flirting her pretty butt off with me every day at school for the stupid bet. Every day it got worse and worse as she bumped it up

144

another gear. She was getting more confident now; she knew exactly how much she affected me, and definitely used it to her advantage. Not that I minded, she was having a good time doing it and seeing her enjoying herself made me happy.

Amber had been getting more and more into our relationship since she told me she loved me, taking things further and further. I was a little worried at first. I didn't want her to think all I wanted her for was sex, I'd told her I would wait and I would wait as long as she needed. I truly loved her more than anything in the world. If I thought she would say yes, I would ask her to marry me right now, but I just didn't want to rush her or pressure her into anything, we had all the time in the world.

Jake had been great so far too. He seemed to like the fact that Amber was happy so he didn't give me too much flack about dating her. We did have a few words the day after he found out about us, but I'd never tell Amber about that. It was basically just threats of decapitation and castration - which I knew he meant. Not that it mattered, I wouldn't be the one to hurt her or end this relationship, that was definitely up to her. All I wanted was to take care of her and make her happy.

An hour later, people started arriving for the party. I watched the hallway, waiting for her. Usually, she didn't come out of her room until the party was in full swing, so I knew I had a little while. I spotted Jessica walk in and I groaned as I grabbed Casey, pulling him in front of me so she wouldn't see me. She had been pissing me off so badly all week with all the flirting, well, they all had. I couldn't believe that girls do that sort of thing, and jeez what they were offering, it was literally anywhere, anytime, and anything I wanted. I didn't even want to think about what Jessica had offered me, the dirty little tramp. My subconscious mind wandered to the couple of times we'd been out and had sex, I shuddered a little at the thought.

Casey was laughing his ass off. "Seriously, Liam, just man up and fuck someone get it over with," he said, laughing.

I rolled my eyes at his stupid comment. "Whatever, the only one I'll be with is my girlfriend. I'm not interested in any of these skanks." I waved my hand dismissively as a couple of girls eyed me from across the room. Someone grabbed my arm, squeezing gently to get my attention. Oh for goodness sake why can't they leave the hell alone? "Look, I'm not interested! I've got a girlfriend!" I growled angrily as I turned around.

My breath caught in my throat, Amber was standing there in a little black dress that clung to her shapely body and came to her mid-thigh. Her hair was half up and curled, and her eyes were sparkling with amusement. I couldn't breathe. She was so beautiful that it was unreal. All I could do was stare at her like an idiot. Oh crap, I'm staring! OK come on, Liam, say something.

Say anything.

Liam, freaking say SOMETHING!

"Um…. Hi, Angel," I mumbled, my voice sounding tight. Wow, that was real smooth, Liam! God, I'm such a dick! I was so turned on it must have been obvious to everyone.

She grinned, her smile lighting up her whole face. "Hi, Liam," she purred in her sexy voice. I mentally groaned. OK here it comes; she's finally going to kill me. I really didn't think I could take her flirting with me while she looks like that.

"You look beautiful," I said honestly, looking her over again.

She grinned and did a little twirl, making the dress rise up a little. My heart started to beat faster. "You like?" she asked biting her lip. Did I like it? Was she kidding me?

I nodded and stepped closer. I could smell her perfume making my head slightly fuzzy. "I love," I confirmed.

She giggled and closed the distance, pressing her chest to mine. I couldn't help but put my hands on her hips, feeling the silky material under my fingers. "You know what? I think you'll like what's underneath even more," she whispered in my ear.

I tightened my grip on her as she tried to step back, holding her to me tightly, not wanting to let her move away from me. "Don't tease me tonight, Angel. Seriously, you look too hot, I can't take it," I pleaded.

She laughed and gripped the front of my shirt, pulling me impossibly closer to her. I looked into her eyes, feeling myself being drawn in. "I'm not teasing, Liam. By the way, your clothes look so damn hot on you, but I've got a feeling they'll look even better on my bedroom floor later," she said quietly, making me groan. I closed my eyes. Seriously, she was killing me. She kissed my cheek and pulled away quickly, heading off into the crowd of people, leaving me standing in the middle of the kitchen with a freaking boner as usual.

I turned back to Casey who was looking after Amber too. "Damn, she looks hot tonight. I think I might go see if I can tap that fine ass," he said, waggling his eyebrows as he went to go after her.

I grabbed his arm and shook my head, looking at him warningly. "No way, Casey. Just stay away from her, she's taken."

He looked at me curiously, then his eyes went wide. "She's not your…." he trailed off, looking at me shocked.

Oh crap. Oops, well now he knows! I nodded slowly. "Yeah," I confirmed. I couldn't help the proud grin that stretched across my face that someone finally knew about us.

He burst out laughing, shaking his head. "Jake is gonna have your balls when he finds out. Seriously, he's going to tear you a new asshole."

I grinned and slapped his shoulder. "He already knows." I shrugged easily, smiling as his face turned to shock.

"No way! Did he beat the crap out of you?" he asked curiously.

I laughed and gestured down at myself. "Does it look like he beat the crap out of me?" I asked, chuckling.

He suddenly looked pissed off. "All that freaking time I never asked her out because I thought Jake would cut my balls off, and he didn't do anything? Damn it, I knew I should have asked her out!" he grumbled, looking annoyed.

"Too late now," I teased, slapping his shoulder again as I went to get a drink.

I grabbed two shots of vodka and went to go and find her and tell her that Casey knew. I didn't bother telling him not to say anything; I wanted this out in the open. I couldn't care less about the money. In a couple of years, when I was playing hockey professionally, that would seem like peanuts and I could give her anything she wanted.

I spotted her dancing with Kate and Sean off to one side. I grinned as I wrapped my arm around her waist, making her jump. "Hey, girlfriend," I whispered in her ear. She smiled at me over her shoulder as she ground her ass across my crotch, making me yearn for her again. I pulled her tighter against me and danced behind her, I handed her one of the shots.

"Thanks." She smiled gratefully as she downed it, wincing.

"So, I've got something to tell you," I admitted sheepishly.

She turned to face me. "What's that then?" she asked, grinning. Her excited expression told me that she obviously thought it was something good.

"Casey knows you're my girl," I said quietly, bending close to her so no one could hear.

She gasped. "He does? How?" she asked, clearly shocked, as she looked around suspiciously.

"I told him by accident. He was going to come and make a move on you, I told him to stay away," I admitted, smiling apologetically, hoping she wouldn't chew me out for ruining her plan with Jessica and the bet.

She rolled her eyes and stepped closer to me. "Big mouth," she scolded jokingly, as she wrapped her arms around my neck, dancing with me again. I pulled her closer to me wrapping her in my arms tightly, loving the feel of her body against mine. She smiled happily. "Well then, Liam, if people are going to find out, we might as well give them a show," she flirted, raising one eyebrow playfully.

What the hell does that mean? She giggled and pulled my face down to hers, kissing me, hard. I heard people gasp and start talking hurriedly around us, but I didn't care. I was kissing the girl of my dreams and she loved me. I pulled her closer, tracing my tongue on her lip, wanting more. After a minute or so I pulled out of the kiss and started kissing down her neck, making her moan quietly. I smiled against her neck because I knew that people were watching. Finally, no more pretending, no more listening to the guys talk about her and wanting to beat the crap out of them. I pulled back to look at her, she was grinning at me, looking so freaking hot it was unbelievable.

"I love you, Liam," she said, her eyes locked on mine. I heard some other people gasp again.

"I love you too, Angel," I replied, immediately.

I knew people were talking about us, and literally the whole room was staring, but I just didn't care. All I could focus on were her beautiful eyes and how they were looking deeply into mine, driving me crazy. I pulled my arms tighter around her, not wanting the moment to end. I loved the way her incredible body was swaying against mine, turning me on so badly that it was almost unbearable. We danced for about an hour. Now that people knew about us, I didn't leave her side, wanting more time with her. I never got to spend time with her at parties; usually, I was either too busy making sure nothing happened to their house because Jake was always off of his face, or hooking up with a girl out the back.

Tonight was the best party ever, just because I got to hold her hand and kiss her. Even the girls didn't hit on me, which made a nice change. I hung out with her and her friends. Kate was actually really funny, I'd not really spoken to her properly before. Usually, the only time she spoke to me was to flirt with me, so it was weird to have a normal conversation with her.

Just after midnight, Amber pressed herself to me tightly. "I'm tired, Liam. Want to take me to bed?" she asked, raising her eyebrows teasingly. Oh crap, I thought all the flirting and teasing would stop now that people knew!

I laughed and rolled my eyes. "Sure, Angel." I would love to wrap my arms around her sexy body right now. She grinned and turned to walk off; I put my hands on her hips following her through the throng of people, to her bedroom. As soon as we were through the door she turned to me with her face playful and I knew that the teasing wasn't over with yet. I groaned quietly. Jeez, I loved this girl more than anything, but she was driving me crazy!

She locked the door and stepped up close to me, pressing her toned body to mine. Her hands ran down my chest, slowly, making me so freaking hard it was embarrassing. Surely I should be immune to her charm by now? I mean, I'd been in love with this girl for twelve years, how the hell could she still turn me on like this? No one ever compared to my Angel, she literally was the world's most perfect girl.

I bent my head down to kiss her, tracing my tongue along her soft full lip, wanting to deepen the kiss. She tangled her hands in my hair and I couldn't help but pin her against the wall, pressing every inch of my body against hers. She moaned in the back of her throat and I felt happiness bubble up inside that she loved kissing me as much as I loved kissing her.

I bent my knees and wrapped her tighter in my arms as I stood up, lifting her off of her feet. She wrapped her long legs around me as she unbuttoned my shirt slowly; her fingers lingering over my skin, making me get goose bumps. Every single touch from Amber was like nothing I'd ever felt before. All those girls I had slept with just to try and forget her, were nothing compared to her. I wished with all my heart that I had waited and that she would be my first, but everything felt like a first time with her anyway. Every touch was ten times better than anything I'd ever felt before, it was like every place her skin touched mine, felt like she burnt me slightly, but in a nice way. She made me so nervous too. I didn't want to do anything she didn't want, but I was also so scared that I wouldn't be able to please her and I didn't want to ruin anything.

I pulled out of the kiss, peppering little kisses down her neck, sucking on the hickey I'd given her a few days ago to make it darker. I loved that mark on her. Knowing that she was mine made me crazy. I walked over to the bed, laying her down and climbing on top of her as I ran my hands down her body. When I got to the bottom of her dress, I slipped my hand under, tracing it back up her toned thigh, making my way higher so I could grip her ass. I couldn't help but moan at the feel of it. Knowing that I was the only one that she would let near her like this, made me feel like the luckiest guy in the world.

She pushed my shirt off of my shoulders and ran her hands back down my chest. When she got to my jeans she immediately started unbuttoning them too. I stiffened slightly. What the hell is she doing? She rolled me onto my back and sat up, straddling me, looking so sexy it was unreal. She chewed on her lip, looking a little nervous about something.

"You OK?" I asked curiously, rubbing my hands on her thighs reassuringly. What on earth is she nervous about? She nodded and took hold of the bottom of her dress, pulling it up over her head, shaking her hair after, making it fall loosely around her beautiful face. I looked at her in her strapless black lacy bra and matching thong, and a thousand lustful thoughts were bombarding my brain at once. I wanted her so much it was unreal. This was the furthest we'd gone, I'd seen her with no top on but not almost naked like this. She was incredible. She bent down and kissed me passionately, pulling back to look at me, still looking a little nervous but excited at the same time.

"Do you want me, Liam?" she asked.

Crap, is that some sort of joke or something? "Angel, I've wanted you forever."

She smiled making my heart beat faster. "Make love to me," she whispered, kissing me softly.

My heart stopped. Did she just ask me to.... no, no way, she said something else and then you're going to look like a dick when it turns out you heard her wrong!

"What?" I asked weakly, pushing her hair behind her ear.

"I'm ready now; I want you to make love to me." She blushed slightly, looking even more adorable because of how sweet and innocent she was.

I rolled her onto her back. Does she think she has to give it up to me? Jeez, does she not believe me when I say I'll wait for her? "Angel, I'll wait as long as you want. I promise I can wait," I vowed, willing her to believe me. I would never ever touch another woman again, they just didn't interest me, they never did.

She laughed. "Well I'm sorry, Liam, but I just can't wait for you any longer. I need you to be ready now," she teased, gripping her hand on my ass.

I laughed; she was so damn funny. "Oh you can't wait for me, huh? Well that's not very fair; you're kind of putting undue pressure on me to perform," I joked. My heart was returning to normal rate now that I realised she was only joking. She smiled and ran her hands down my chest again, when she got to my jeans she slipped her hand inside, rubbing me through my boxers. What the hell? Oh crap, is she not joking? "Angel, what are you doing?" I asked breathlessly. Shit, that feels good!

"Liam, stop talking," she whispered, pulling me closer as she pushed my jeans down.

OK, I'll just go with it until she tells me to stop; I knew she felt comfortable enough to ask me to stop, which I loved. I loved that she had faith in me not to rush her or pressure her. I kissed her hungrily, brushing my hands over her bra, loving the feel of the lacy material. I unclasped it, pulling it off, slowly, waiting for her to stop me. I was so nervous that my hands were shaking slightly. Her breasts were perfect. I bent my head kissing all over them, making her arch her back and moan breathlessly. OK, so this is a first, not been this far with her before! I kicked my jeans off that were now almost to my knees and ran my hands down her body, stopping as I got to her panties, my hand brushing over them gently, which made her raise her hips trying to get more. I smiled slightly as I rubbed her through her panties, making her moan and grip her free hand on my shoulder tightly.

Her eyes were locked on mine. "Make love to me, Liam," she whispered.

Shit, she *was* serious! I stopped and pulled back, not taking my eyes from hers. There was no sign of indecision; she had made up her mind. All I saw on her face was love, happiness and need, and I would bet anything that my face looked exactly the same.

"Angel, I can wait," I promised again.

"I know you can, but I'm ready now." She nodded, looking at me softly.

"Shouldn't your first time be special? In a nice hotel or something, with rose petals and candles all scattered around?" I asked, frowning. I could book one for tomorrow night if she was really ready.

She shook her head. "It will be special, Liam. It'll be our first time. That's special enough for me. Please?" she begged, running her hand down my back.

My whole body was rejoicing at the thought of being with her, but my head knew I had to be sure she wasn't doing this for the wrong reasons; I'd never forgive myself if she regretted this in the morning. "This isn't about the bet is it?" I asked curiously.

She laughed and shook her head. "I couldn't care less about the bet. I trust you, I love you, I want you to make love to me."

I felt my heart skip a beat as I got so freaking excited and nervous at the same time that I swear it would kill me. "I love you too, Angel, more than anything." I bent down to kiss her again softly, knowing I needed to take it slow and gentle, I just prayed to God that it didn't hurt her too much.

I ran my hands down her body, loving the feel of her soft skin under my hands as I kissed her passionately, showing her how much I loved her and wanted her. I hooked my thumbs in her panties, pulling them down slowly, teasing her, getting my own back. She was digging her fingers into my back, her breathing speeding up with excitement, making me even hotter for her. I kissed down her body, running my tongue across her breasts and down over her stomach, pausing to bite just below her belly button, making her gasp and raise her hips. I sat up and pulled her panties the rest of the way off and just looked at her. She was sheer and utter perfection, laying there naked and vulnerable. I knew I would never be able to look at another girl again without comparing her to the sight of my Angel, as she just lay there, blushing. She was obviously embarrassed that I was seeing her naked for the first time.

"You are so beautiful, Angel," I whispered. She smiled and gripped her hand around the back of my head, guiding my mouth back to hers. I felt my heart swell as I kissed her passionately, showing her just how much I loved and cherished her before I prepared myself to make love to her for the first time.

I smoothed her hair away from her sweaty forehead. She was grinning at me and looked so happy it made my heart skip a beat. "I love you, Angel." We laid there trying to slow our heart beats. I pressed my face into the crook of her neck kissing her, feeling her rapid pulse under my lips. I felt happier than I had ever felt in my life. After a minute or so, I pulled out of her and rolled to my side. I tightened my arms on her, pulling her close to me, trailing my fingers over her naked, sweaty body, lingering on her breasts. "I'm sorry I hurt you," I said quietly. I felt awful that I was the one to have to cause her pain, but I guess every girl had to go through that the first time.

She laughed. "Liam, that was so totally worth it," she teased, pressing her body closer to mine, snuggling into my arms.

I laughed. "Well I'm glad you enjoyed it," I stated, smirking at her. I'd never had any complaints before, but I'd never actually cared if the girl enjoyed herself before. Usually, I just did what I wanted; I'd never actually taken the time to think about it - funny how that was so different with my Angel. All I cared about was her; my feelings were secondary to hers.

"I definitely enjoyed it. Did you though? I mean, I didn't know what to do or anything, should I have done something different?" she asked, chewing on her lip, looking at me worriedly.

I laughed and kissed her forehead. "Angel, that was the best thing that ever happened to me. It was perfect, you're perfect, and I love you so much," I promised.

She snuggled closer to me, taking my hand and interlacing our fingers; she sighed contentedly and closed her eyes. "I love you too, Liam," she whispered, kissing my chest gently. I couldn't help my body's reaction; I started to get turned on again. She was so close and now that I'd had her once I couldn't get enough. I moved my hips back so she didn't feel me getting excited again. That was her first time; she was bound to be sore so she didn't need to know about my body's slutty reaction to hers.

But I'd moved too late, she must have noticed. She raised her head and looked down. She looked back to me a little shocked. I smiled apologetically and she giggled. "Seriously? Already?" she teased, as her fingertips trailed down my chest, making me shiver.

"I'm sorry; it'll go in a minute. You're just too damn sexy. You should rest, you'll be sore," I said a little sheepishly. She raised her eyebrows, a slow smile spread across her face as she rolled me onto my back, straddling me, looking like a freaking sex goddess sitting on top of me.

"I'm OK. This time I want to have a try, tell me if I do something wrong," she said, kissing me passionately.

Holy crap, this girl is freaking awesome!

I woke early the next morning. Amber had to be at dance practice at eight thirty, it was now only just past seven. I couldn't keep the smile off of my face. Last night was incredible, the best night ever. Hearing her moan my name was the best sound in the world. She enjoyed herself too which made it even more special for me. It hadn't hurt her too much, well, she said it didn't anyway. It couldn't have been that painful because she had me make love to her again after. I wrapped my arms tighter around her, loving the feel of her naked skin against mine. I just laid there and watched her sleep until her alarm went off. She was so damn beautiful; she honestly was just like I would imagine an angel to look.

She snuggled closer to me as she opened her eyes, a slow smile spreading over her face as she looked at me. "Hi, boyfriend."

I couldn't help but smile back. "Hi, girlfriend." She wrapped her arms around me tightly as she sighed contentedly. "How are you feeling today?" I asked, running my fingers through her messed up sex hair.

She smiled. "I'm good, a little sore, but extremely happy," she stated, giggling.

I rolled on top of her, pressing my body to hers. "A little sore, huh? I could kiss that better for you," I flirted.

She bit her lip, looking at me excitedly. "Oh you can, huh?"

I nodded, grinning wickedly. "Oh yeah." I smirked at her before kissing my way down her body, barely able to contain my excitement.

Chapter 16

~ Amber ~

After finally prying myself off of Liam on Saturday morning, I literally couldn't keep the smile off my face. He was so incredible last night and it was better than I ever thought it could be. He was so sweet and patient and tender with me, taking everything slow and easy. I couldn't have asked for a more loving boyfriend.

"Come on then, lover boy, let's go," I ordered, pulling on some sweats and a tank top ready for dance practice.

He grabbed my waist and kissed the back of my neck. "OK. But please try not to shake that fine ass in my face too much, or I might have to rip those sexy sweats off of you and take you right in front of your crew," he growled, biting my neck gently.

I couldn't help but laugh at that comment. He'd never said anything like that to me before and I blushed like crazy as I slapped his shoulder. "Get out of my room, man-whore," I joked, pushing him away, laughing. He gripped my hand, tugging me along behind him, grinning happily. I couldn't help but stare at his ass as he walked in front of me up the hallway. Wow, he'd made me into a pervert too!

Dance practice was great. I seemed to finally be picking up the lift that I was having trouble with last week, so at least I didn't fall on my ass too much. By the time we finished I was tired and sweating. Liam sat there patiently watching as usual, joking around with Justin. He seemed to be smiling more than normal. I guess it was hard for him, waiting a whole week for sex, I bet he'd never done that in his life. He was probably just pleased to have finally gotten some last night after all the teasing I'd done recently.

Wait, had we only been dating a week? I laughed to myself - wow, I was a slut. I slept with a boy I'd been dating for a week; I never thought I would say that! It seemed like we'd been together forever because everything was just so easy and I'd known him for so long.

When we were finished practicing, we went to a little café and bought sandwiches, taking them over to the park to eat them. Liam sat under the shade of a tree, opening his legs for me to sit between them. Just as I was about to sit down, he stopped me. "Wait, Angel." He shrugged off his hoodie and laid it on the floor for me to sit on.

"Thanks." I smiled gratefully, sitting down and leaning back into his chest, eating my food. As usual, Liam inhaled his food and wrapped his arms around me, rocking me gently while I finished eating. I never thought I would ever have anything like this with a guy. Whenever I'd thought about dating, it had scared the hell out of me because I didn't ever want a man to touch me like that. After what my father did with all the touching, I guess I was a little scarred. All the time I'd thought I didn't ever want a boyfriend, I never realised I already had the perfect boy who was sweet and kind and kept me safe every night.

"I could stay here forever," I mumbled, closing my eyes, sighing in contentment.

He kissed the side of my head. "Not regretting sleeping with me then?" he asked.

I turned to face him, pretending to think about it. "That depends. Are you going to leave me now I've given it up?" I joked.

He smiled at me wickedly. "Hmm, I just might," he answered, kissing me gently.

I smiled against his lips. "Well maybe I should get in there first and dump your hot ass. Save myself the embarrassment," I suggested, raising my eyebrows, smirking at him.

He laughed and laid down on his back, pulling me on top of him, holding me close. "If you dump my ass I'm going to be begging you until the day I die for you to take me back," he stated, running his hand down my back.

"Begging on your knees?" I asked, laughing.

He nodded, looking at me gravely. "Yep, whatever it takes. Everywhere you go, I'll be following behind you, begging for another shot. I'll be just like an obsessive stalker," he joked, rolling so I was under him.

"Sounds like that would be a pain in my butt. Maybe I just should keep you then." I smiled, shrugging.

He nodded. "Good plan," he agreed, kissing me passionately, ending the conversation.

After an hour in the park we went home to tidy the house. As usual the place was a mess. Jake had already started. We had to do a really good job this time because my mom was due back tomorrow. She had no idea there was a raging party in her house every week. I even roped in Kate to help with the cleanup, but to be honest as soon as she showed up neither of us got much done. She followed me around wanting to know every single detail of last night - how was he, what was it like, and every other detail you could think of. I refused to answer the more personal questions, like how long he lasted, and how big he was.

Finally, we were cleaned up and settled back with pizza and a DVD. "So now that these two are paired up, Jake, that just leaves you and me," Kate said to my brother, smiling flirtily.

He smirked at her. "You're too much of a good girl for me, Kate," he told her, grinning wickedly.

She laughed. "And who told you I was a good girl? Anyway, even if I was, maybe you could corrupt me." She raised her eyebrows, looking him over slowly.

I cleared my throat theatrically, gaining their attention. "Stop. The movie's on. No flirting through horror movies, that's the rule, you both know that," I scolded, trying to sound stern. Jake shot me a thank you smile. I rolled my eyes. He really didn't help himself; he'd walked straight into that one. If he didn't want her to hit on him then why set himself up for it?

I snuggled closer against Liam, watching the rest of the movie. When it was finally done, Liam went home as usual to keep up the pretense for his parents. With my mom due home tomorrow, we needed to make it look like he stayed at his house. I don't think my mom would like to hear that the boy from next door sleeps with her daughter every night. I kissed him hungrily at the door, before skipping to my room, deciding on a nice long soak in the bath. I was a little sore from having sex, and on top of that dancing for hours this morning made my muscles a little tight. I slipped in the bath, closing my eyes, blissfully happy.

"Hey, you," Liam said from the door way a little while later.

"Hey," I greeted, not opening my eyes.

"Another cold bath?" he asked, laughing. I shook my head and glanced over at him. He was leaning against the doorframe, one leg slung casually over the other, his arms folded across his chest, a smirk on his face. He looked sexy as hell.

"Actually, it's warm this time. Want to get in?" I offered.

He looked a little shocked. "Seriously?" he asked, standing up straighter, looking ridiculously eager.

I laughed and nodded in confirmation. "Seriously."

Quicker than I thought possible, he was naked and in the bath behind me, wrapping his arms around me.

Sunday flew by incredibly fast. I was really excited to see my mom; I hadn't seen her for just over two weeks. She wasn't actually due back until next weekend but she wanted to come back this week instead. It was now just after six o'clock, and she was due home any minute. I was sat on Liam's lap in the lounge, practically vibrating with excitement. When I heard her car pull up outside, I ran towards the door, squealing happily.

Jake jumped up at the same time as me and grabbed me round the waist, laughing as he threw me on the sofa. "Me first, shrimp," he stated, running for the door ahead of me, making me laugh.

I followed him out of the door and attacked my mom into a hug. "Hey, Jake. Hey, Amber!" she chirped, hugging us tightly. Liam went straight to the trunk and pulled out her luggage. When she pulled out of the hug she was smiling with tears in her eyes. "I missed you guys," she said, kissing us both happily, "Hey, Liam. Got a hug for me?" she asked, grinning.

He laughed and nodded. "Always, Margaret," he said, hugging her tightly.

"You got more handsome," she stated, patting his cheek affectionately.

He laughed. "I don't know about that," he answered, shaking his head, grinning. I bit my lip; he'd definitely got more handsome in my opinion. My mom loved Liam, she always had done. He spent a lot of time over at our place, and since my father left she became really close with Pat and Rick once she was 'allowed' to socialise.

"So, what have I missed?" she asked, looping her arm through mine, walking off towards the door, leaving the boys to carry her bags.

I grinned knowing that she was going to freak out when I told her about Liam. "Um, not much. I fell in love," I said happily.

She gasped and pulled me to a stop, looking at me so shocked that I couldn't help but laugh. "You…You what?" she stuttered, looking at me with a bewildered expression.

I smiled and made her walk into the house, pulling her into the kitchen. "I got a boyfriend," I confirmed, grinning like a mad person.

"Oh, Amber, I never thought you would be able to! I'm so proud of you, honey. I know how hard it is for you to let people near you," she cooed, hugging me tightly, tears glistening in her eyes again. Liam and Jake walked in; both of them leaning against the kitchen counter. Liam shot me a little wink and I smiled in response. "Well, what's his name? Do I get to meet him while I'm here? Oh wait, does Jake know?" she asked, whispering the last part, probably thinking she was dropping me in something with my overprotective big brother.

I laughed and looked at Jake who was in the process of glaring at Liam again. "Yeah, Mom, Jake knows," I confirmed, chuckling.

"Well? Who is it? What's he like?" she asked, beaming at me excitedly.

"Well, mostly he's a pain in the ass. He's cocky and way too confident. But on the plus side, he's extremely hot," I stated, watching Liam's face as he tried not to laugh.

"Looks don't last long, Amber! You shouldn't base a relationship on how someone looks!" she scolded, her eyebrows knitting together in disapproval.

I couldn't help but laugh. "Don't worry, Mom, I'll kick him to the curb when his looks go," I joked.

"You'd better not!" Liam warned, moving to my side, wrapping his arm around my waist.

My mom looked between the two of us a few times, a shocked expression on her face. Her eyes flicked to Jake, her expression bewildered and confused. Jake nodded somewhat reluctantly. All of a sudden, she started laughing and shook her head. "I should have known! All that teasing and stuff, I didn't realise it was sexual tension," she said, laughing harder as Jake snorted angrily.

"I don't want to know!" Jake growled, covering his ears quickly, shaking his head as we all just laughed.

My mom pulled me into another hug. "I'm so pleased for you, Amber. He's such a good boy," she whispered.

"I know he is," I agreed as she let me go. I took hold of Liam's hand, pressing my side against his. I couldn't help but wish I could take him in my room and have him rub his hands all over my body again, I hadn't been with him since this morning and it felt like forever.

"Congratulations, guys," she chirped, smiling. Liam squeezed my hand, grinning happily at me, making my heart melt. My mom smiled a little sadly, looking at Jake first, then me. "Guys, I need to talk to you about something. There's a reason I came back a week early," she admitted, her voice hard and serious.

Jake stiffened, and his face hardened. "We don't want to see him if that's what you're going to say," he said sternly, moving to stand next to me protectively.

My mom shook her head. "It's not that simple. I don't want to have to say this, he's put me in such an awkward position and I'm sorry," she said quietly. Liam and Jake both moved closer to me unconsciously, so I was completely wedged between the two of them. Jeez, what the hell are they getting so worried about? He's not here now!

"Mom, what are you talking about? I won't let that asshole anywhere near Amber," Jake growled angrily.

She started to cry so I pushed away from the boys and wrapped my arms around her. Crap, this was bad. Whatever it was, she was really upset about it. "What's wrong?" I whispered, willing myself not to cry too. I hated seeing my mom upset, she was always the strong one.

"I need to sit down," she said quietly, swiping at her face roughly, wiping the tears away as she took a deep breath. I followed her into the lounge, sitting on the sofa, barely able to breathe. Thoughts of the two of them getting back together, him wanting to move back in, him demanding to see us, even him wanting custody of us, all these thoughts were whizzing through my brain so fast that it made me feel sick. Liam sat next to me, wrapping his arm around me tightly. I pressed into him for support, waiting for her to say it.

"Your fathers moved to this town," she said quietly.

Jake jumped out of the seat. "Motherfucker! I told him to stay away!" he shouted angrily, looking like he wanted to smash something.

My mom nodded. "Jake, he wants to get to know you two again. He says he's sorry and that he's changed. He wants you to give him another chance."

"You mean he wants another chance to try and rape Amber?" Jake shouted. I flinched as the memories rushed back. Liam's arm tightened around me, his hands clenching into fists.

My mom shook her head, looking at him pleadingly. "Jake, I don't like this any more than you do, so please stop shouting at me! I hate that I'm the one to have to tell you this, but it's not my fault," she said, crying again now.

Jake sighed and shook his head, kneeling down in front of her pulling her into a hug. "I'm sorry. I shouldn't be taking this out on you," he said, still sounding angry. I pressed my face into Liam's

160

shoulder, breathing him in. I felt him put his lips on my neck and I concentrated on the feel of his breath blowing reassuringly down my back, trying desperately not to freak out. After a minute of silence, Jake spoke. "Why has he come back? Why didn't you just tell him we didn't want to see him?" he asked.

She closed her eyes and smiled sadly. "He remarried. He has a son who's one, he's your half-brother. Apparently, the woman that he married has a son already. He's seventeen. Your father wants you to get to know his new family," she said, sneering slightly at the 'new family' bit at the end.

Holy shit, I had a little brother, and a step-brother?

Jake jumped up. "That fucker should have been castrated! He shouldn't be allowed to have more kids!" he cried, gripping his hands in his hair tightly.

"I needed to come back today and speak to you because the elder boy, Johnny his name is; he's going to be starting your school tomorrow. He knows about you two," she said, looking at me apologetically.

Jake kicked the coffee table, hard, sending it flying over. Liam jumped up and stood in front of me protectively as Jake shouted profanities and kicked the table over and over again, probably hurting his foot. I stood up and pushed past Liam, batting off his hands as he tried to stop me going near my brother. I grabbed Jake's arm, making him stop and look at me. His face was pure rage and I think if my father was here tight now, he'd be dead. That man really needed to stay the hell away from Jake. I wrapped my arms around him tightly, knowing I needed to calm him down before he hurt himself. The only way to calm Jake down when he went crazy like this was to make him think I was upset, that usually snapped him out of his rage pretty quickly.

"Jake, stop. You're scaring me. Please?" I whispered, clinging to him for dear life.

He was shaking with anger as he wrapped his arms around me. "It's OK. Shh, everything's OK. I'm sorry," he murmured, rubbing my back, his overprotective nature kicking in.

"I'm sorry," my mom muttered, sobbing behind us.

I pulled out of Jake's arms and went to sit next to her. "It's OK, Mom. None of this is your fault. We'll figure it out. Neither Jake or I want to see him, so we just won't see him," I stated, pretending it would be that easy.

"What about this boy, Johnny, your stepbrother? He's going to be at your school tomorrow. He knows who you are but he doesn't know about what happened back then. Your father told me that his new family thinks that you don't want to see him because of the breakup of our marriage, nothing else," she said shaking her head.

Jake laughed humourlessly. "Yeah, why would the spineless bastard tell his new wife that he beat the crap out of his old family for years before finally trying to rape his own daughter? Not something you can bring up in normal conversation is it?" he spat nastily. I flinched again. I hated the word rape, it was awful.

"Jake! Will you stop fucking saying that?" Liam cried, glaring at him angrily as he sat down in front of me, taking my hand.

"Sorry, Ambs, I didn't think," Jake mumbled apologetically.

I shook my head and faked a smile. "It's fine, Jake, don't worry." I waved my hand dismissively, pretending that I was unaffected by this whole situation. "What's the baby's name?" I asked my mom, wanting to know about the little brother I now had.

She smiled sadly. "Matt."

I smiled. Matt. It was cute, I liked it. I could feel the hysterics building inside me though and I knew I needed to be on my own. "Well, there's not much we can do about it now, I guess. We'll just have to see what this Johnny guy is like tomorrow. But I don't want anything to do with that man ever again," I stated matter-of-factly as I stood up. "I'm going to lay down. I have a headache," I said as I started to walk off. I needed to get out of here before I had a meltdown in front of Jake - that would just make him crazy again.

Liam grabbed my hand. "Want some company?" he asked quietly, looking at me with the puppy dog face. The damn boy knew I couldn't say no to that face.

"Yeah, OK." I nodded slightly and started walking off towards my bedroom.

"I'll just be a minute. I'm just going to help Jake clear up the table," Liam said, nodding towards the broken wooden mess that used to be our coffee table.

I nodded and walked off quickly. I could hear them whispering behind me, I knew they were talking about me, but I just couldn't bring myself to care. I curled into a ball on my bed and sobbed as I thought about it. My father was in this town and wanted to get to know us again. He had a new family. I couldn't help but wonder if he treated them nicely and loved them, and if he did treat them nicely and love them, why the hell couldn't he have done that to us? Why didn't he love us?

A few minutes later Liam walked in, wrapping his body around mine, letting me sob on his chest until I fell asleep. The last thing that went through my brain was that I knew everything in my life was just too perfect. I knew I shouldn't have got my hopes up for a happy ending. I'd never have a happy ending.

~ Liam ~

"What's the baby's name?" Amber asked her mom curiously. She was being so calm about it. I knew this was probably killing her inside but she was putting on an act - probably for Jake's benefit. Her eyes were tight; her hand was holding mine a little too hard for her to be alright.

"Matt," Margaret replied, looking sad.

Amber smiled. "Well there's not much we can do about it now, I guess. We'll just have to see what this Johnny guy is like tomorrow. But I don't want anything to do with that man ever again," she stated, as if it just didn't matter that the man who beat her, sexually abused her for years, and finally tried to rape her, was coming back and wanted to see her again. She stood up and let go of my hand. I instinctively jumped up too. Jake was still really angry, I knew he wouldn't ever hurt Amber on purpose but if he went off on one she could get hurt by accident, so I needed to be there just in case. "I'm going to lay down. I have a headache," Amber mumbled, walking off without so much as a tear. This was bad; she seriously was going to freak out any minute I could tell by how her shoulders were hunched slightly.

I grabbed her hand. "Want some company?" I asked, praying that she wasn't going to shut me out.

"Yeah, OK." She nodded slightly and walked off without waiting for me.

I needed to speak to Jake first, make sure he wasn't going to go around there without me or anything. "I'll just be a minute. I'm just going to help Jake clear up the table," I lied, nodding at the splinters of wood scattered across the floor. She nodded and walked off quickly. I watched her walk up the hallway before turning to Jake. "Don't you dare go there on your own. I'm serious, Jake. If you want to go, then I'll come with you," I whispered to him warningly.

He frowned but nodded reluctantly. "I'm not going to go unless I need to. If he doesn't come near us then I don't want anything to do with him. If comes anywhere near her though, I'll kill him," he growled.

I nodded, I knew he would, I could tell by his face. Stephen Walker was in some deep shit, because if Jake didn't kill him, then I would if he came anywhere near my Angel. "Listen, I need to go in there and make sure she's alright. I'll speak to you about this later. Don't do anything rash, Jake," I said sternly. He nodded and I practically ran down the hallway to her. I let myself in her room; she was curled into a ball on her bed, sobbing her heart out. I hated seeing her like this; it brought back memories when I used to see her like this every night since she was eight. The sight of it now was breaking my heart.

I laid down in front of her and wrapped my arms around her tightly, throwing my leg over hers, pulling her closer to me as I rested my chin on the top of her head. If he ever touched her again I was going to kill him. I won't let her live her life afraid of a man. I didn't care if I ended up doing time for it - so long as she was safe, that was all I needed.

After about half an hour of her sobbing hysterically, her breathing became deeper. I pulled back slowly and looked down at her. She was sound asleep. Her face was red and puffy, it was stained with tears, but she still managed to look like the most beautiful girl in the world. I kissed her forehead gently and wiped her tears away, untangling myself from her as gently as I could.

I snuck out of her bedroom and found Jake sitting on the sofa; his mom was in the kitchen making dinner. I sat down next to Jake letting my eyes wander over his face. He looked so stressed; I hadn't seen him like this for a couple of years. The last time I saw him like this was when his dad got in touch about two years ago, when we were sixteen. That was about a year after we had beaten the crap out of him and kicked him out. Apparently, Stephen had wanted to see them again to make amends, or so he said anyway. Jake had freaked out, just like earlier, and in no uncertain terms told his dad that if he ever came near Amber again, that he would rip him to pieces. It was just lucky that that conversation happened over the phone; otherwise that asshole would be rotting in some unmarked grave right now.

"Alright, Jake?" I asked, gripping his shoulder, squeezing affectionately.

He sighed and nodded. "Is she OK?" he asked quietly.

I shook my head. "No," I admitted sadly. I winced as his face turned harder; I hated to see Jake so angry. "She's asleep now though."

"You need to help me, Liam," he mumbled, closing his eyes.

"Of course," I agreed, nodding quickly. I'd do anything it took to keep my Angel safe, anything in the world.

"I don't want her on her own. One of us needs to be with her at all times. Can you stay with her while I go to work during the week?" he asked, looking at me hopefully.

I smiled a little guiltily. "I always do, Jake. Don't worry. Everything will be fine. She'll be fine." I smiled reassuringly. I would never let anything hurt her again. I'd let it go on when they were kids and I never forgave myself for that. I mean, if I'd just said something to my mom or dad, maybe it would have stopped before it got too far.

He nodded. "Yeah, I know. Listen, about tomorrow, I don't know how she's going to react to this Johnny kid. I know he doesn't know anything, but what if he starts asking her why we don't see him? He could upset her at school. She'd hate that. She'll have years of this now," he said sadly.

"Jake, we'll just have to see how it plays." I took a deep breath and decided to tell him what I had been thinking about since his mom first said that asshole was back in town. I wasn't sure how Jake would react to my suggestion though; hopefully he'd see that I was thinking about her. "You know I'm off to college in a couple of months. Well, I was going to turn down my scholarship to Boston and go to college closer to here so I could still stay with her, but if the worst comes to the worst, I'll take her with me to Boston. She can transfer schools," I suggested, shrugging, waiting for his reaction.

I'd been thinking about this a lot over the last few months, since I received my offer letter. That college was an awesome opportunity for my career, but I didn't want to go. I didn't want to leave Amber even before we got together, but I don't even think I'd survive it now that I finally had her. I was thinking about either going to a local college, or asking her to come with me to Boston. The trouble was that Amber was only sixteen, so I was sure I was going to take the first option and stay here with her. Now that this situation had come about though, I was back to the asking her to come with me plan. I could take her away from it all; we could have a fresh start where she wouldn't be reminded about him every day, where she wouldn't have to worry about bumping into him every time she stepped out of the house.

I expected Jake to go crazy at me for even suggesting that I take her away from him; it surprised me when he didn't. He just nodded. "Thanks, man," he said sadly.

"I'm going to go and ask your mom if I can stay the night," I said, standing up and heading to the kitchen. Margaret was still upset; her eyes were red from crying.

She smiled sadly when she saw me. "Is she OK, Liam?" she asked, looking towards the hallway as if expecting her to come out.

I nodded. "She's upset, but she's sleeping now. Margaret, do you think I could stay with Angel tonight? We won't do anything, I swear. I just want to be there for her when she wakes up," I pleaded. I would be staying in her room regardless; I just thought it would make things easier if everyone knew I was in there.

She came over and hugged me tightly. "You're a good boy, Liam, you always have been," she said with a tear in her eye.

"Is that a, *'yes, you can share a bed with my daughter, Liam'*?" I joked, trying to lighten the mood. It worked, she laughed.

"Yeah, OK." She nodded, rolling her eyes and sniffing loudly.

I kissed her on the cheek. "Everything's going to be fine. Jake and I will watch out for you both," I promised as I hugged her tightly.

She nodded. "I know you will. Just watch out for Jake for me too. I have a feeling he's going to do something rash and get himself in trouble," she said, frowning.

"I'll watch him. Don't worry about anything." I smiled and rubbed her back gently. "I'm going to go grab some clothes and stuff from mine. I won't be long." I turned and practically ran to my house, trying to be as quick as I could.

My mom was ironing in the lounge. "Hey, Mom. I'm staying with Angel tonight," I informed her as I breezed past without waiting for an answer. I shoved fresh clothes and my school books into a bag, before heading back out to see my mom. I hadn't seen her since Friday morning when I came out of my room, pretending I'd stayed the night here as usual.

"How are you and Amber getting on?" she asked, grinning happily.

I smiled, thinking about just how great we were getting on before all of this happened an hour ago. "Awesome. Really awesome," I admitted.

She beamed at me happily. "You two are being careful, right?" she asked, looking at me warningly.

I smiled and nodded. "Yeah, Mom, Angel's on the pill," I stated, rolling my eyes. She had never asked me about my sex life before and now all of a sudden she was interested? "Listen, I've got to go. Margaret's back so she's making dinner. I just came back to grab my clothes." I shifted the bag on my shoulder, looking at the door longingly; I just wanted to get back over there as quickly as I could in case she woke up.

My mom looked at me curiously. "Margaret's home and she's letting you stay with Amber?" she asked, looking a little shocked. I smiled, knowing that under normal circumstances Margaret would have kicked my ass just for asking to stay, but what with everything going on she didn't seem to mind.

"Yeah, she said it was fine." I kissed her on the cheek. "I'll see you tomorrow night about nine when Jake gets home from work, OK?" I called over my shoulder as I walked towards the door.

She sighed dramatically. "It was nice to see you, Liam," she called sarcastically.

I laughed. "Love you, Mom."

"Love you too," she called, just as I shut the door.

I ran back to Amber as quick as I could, she was still asleep in the same position. It was only seven thirty; maybe she'd sleep all night. I laid down next to her again, just looking her over. Instantly, she snuggled closer to me, the same as she did every night. I wrapped her tightly in my arms and closed my eyes, trying to think of anything other than the worst memory of my life. The image of walking in on her father trying to force himself on her while she laid there bruised and bleeding on their lounge carpet. After he left, she admitted that her father had been touching her since she was about five. After that confession, she never spoke of it again. I think she buried it so deep inside her that she kind of pretended like it didn't happen or something – like denial I guess. The only time that you ever saw effects from it, where when people touched her and she panicked.

A little while later, Jake brought in two plates of food. He looked at Amber with a pained expression on his face. "You think we should wake her and get her to eat something?" he whispered.

I shook my head. "No, let her sleep. If she wakes up hungry then I'll make her something," I said quietly, as I started scoffing my pasta, hungrily. He sat on the foot of her bed just watching her sleep for a little while. "She'll be alright, Jake," I promised.

He sighed and nodded. "Yeah I know. G'night, Liam." He smiled sadly as he took my empty plate and Amber's untouched one and slipped out of her room. I wrapped myself back around her and watched her sleep until I couldn't stay awake anymore.

Chapter 17

~ Amber ~

When I woke up in the morning my head was pounding. I groaned. I really didn't need a headache on top of everything else that was going to go wrong today. Liam was still asleep so I crept out of the bed, trying not to wake him. I headed to my bathroom for a shower. I stood under the spray, trying desperately not to cry as I thought about my father and his 'new family'. What on earth was I going to say to this Johnny guy? I sighed and got out of the shower, wrapping myself in a towel.

Silently, I tried to convince myself that this boy Johnny probably won't even want to talk to me today and that I was getting myself all worked up over nothing. It wasn't this boy's fault that my father married his mother and made him move here. Hell, he probably needed a friend right now because he would have just left everything and everyone he knows behind.

Walking over to the bed, I looked down at Liam. He looked so peaceful that I almost didn't want to wake him up. I sat on the edge of the bed and took his hand, knowing we needed to get ready for school. "Liam?" I whispered. He woke up almost straight away, which was unlike him, he usually took forever to wake up in the morning.

"Hey." He sat up and looked at me sadly.

I smiled reassuringly; he was worried about me I could tell. "Hi," I replied, moving onto the bed with him and pulling him back down with me. "I'm fine. Stop stressing," I promised, smoothing out the frown lines on his forehead.

He sighed and shook his head. "I'm here if you want to talk to me. You know that, right?" he asked, looking at me intently.

He really was just too adorable to me sometimes, I really didn't deserve it. "I know, Liam, but I'm fine. Let's just get this over with and see what this guy says today," I suggested, shrugging. He bent his head and kissed every inch of my face, making me giggle before he pulled away to go in the shower.

When we pulled into the school parking lot an hour later, Kate came bouncing up to the side of the car with a huge grin on her face. She wrenched open my door. "I'm officially in love!" she announced to me proudly.

I laughed. "Really? OK, well…. congratulations," I replied sarcastically, whilst rolling my eyes.

She laughed. "I'm serious. There's a new guy started today, and he is *hot*!" She fanned her face dramatically. I stopped dead in my tracks; I bet that was him, my new stepbrother. Well that's just perfect, now Kate's going to be falling all over him and I'll be forced to hang out with him. Great, just freaking great.

"New guy?" I asked quietly. Liam rubbed his hand down my back gently.

"Oh, heck yeah! You should see him, he's yummy. But you've got Liam so I've called dibs," she said, grinning and skipping along beside me. "I don't know his name yet, Hottie McTottie suits him though." She waggled her eyebrows at me and I couldn't help but laugh at her.

Jake threw his arm around her shoulder. "You know, I'm not used to you not wanting me, Kate. I'm not sure I like this new behaviour," he stated, giving her his flirty smile.

She sighed dreamily. "I'll always want you, Jake, there's just some fresh meat to drool over. I guess you'll have to work harder for my attention from now on," she teased, winking at him as she shrugged off his arm. He actually looked genuinely shocked and a little pissed off. "So, I need to find out everything about him, want to help me?" she asked, linking her arm through mine.

Hell no I didn't.

"His name's Johnny," I told her, shrugging and trying to go for the casual approach.

She laughed. "Psychic much? You've only just pulled up, how do you know his name's Johnny?" she asked, shaking her head, looking amused.

"He's my stepbrother."

She stopped walking and looked at me, shocked. "You're kidding me," she gasped, with wide eyes.

I shook my head. "Apparently, my father remarried, and his wife already had a son. If it is him that you saw, then he's seventeen and his name's Johnny," I said, shrugging as though it was no big deal.

She squealed and linked her arm through mine excitedly. "This is awesome! You can introduce me and I'll have the advantage over the skanks." She was grinning from ear to ear.

"I don't know him. I can't introduce you," I replied quietly. I really didn't want her falling all over him; I wanted to keep my distance from anything even remotely connected to my father.

"You are so damn greedy, Amber! Seriously, the hottest guy as your boyfriend, the second hottest as your brother and a very close third is your damn stepbrother?" she cried, looking at me with mock anger.

I was just about to answer when Jessica and three of her little clones came over, all of them looking at Liam hungrily. I couldn't help but smile as Liam's arm snaked around my waist. "Hey, Jessica. Have you got my money?" I asked, grinning.

She sneered at me. "Yeah right. As if, emo girl." She turned to Liam and smiled seductively, making his arm tighten on my waist. "You didn't sleep with her, did you, baby?" she purred confidently.

I heard Jake groan behind me. "I can't hear this! I'm going to my locker. Ambs, if you need me today then call me, I'll leave my cellphone turned on," he said, as he walked off quickly.

"Well, baby?" Jessica asked, putting her hand on Liam's arm.

He grinned and shrugged. "A gentleman never tells," he stated, kissing the side of my head.

I laughed. "Well that doesn't really help with the whole claiming the money thing, lover boy," I teased, rolling my eyes.

He sighed dramatically. "Fine. Jessica, you owe Angel four thousand dollars," he said, looking at me lovingly.

She stamped her foot on the ground and I couldn't help but laugh. "How the hell could you do this to me?" she almost screamed at Liam. "You were supposed to be with me! You can't sleep with some little whore!" People were stopping to watch now as her face got redder and redder. Maybe she'd forgotten to breathe.

"Jessica, we went out like twice," Liam countered, looking uncomfortable.

"I don't care how many times we went out! I'm head cheerleader! We're supposed to be together. You're not supposed to be with some brown haired, grey eyed, little freak," she screeched, waving her hand at me distastefully.

I couldn't help but laugh. *Brown haired, grey eyed, little freak? Where the heck did that come from?* "Wow, Jessica, be careful, we'll have a pack of dogs here if your voice gets any higher," I joked, laughing.

She turned her anger to me. "You! You stole my boyfriend! I was the secret girlfriend and you slept with my man," she shouted, pointing at me accusingly.

Kate burst out laughing next to me. Oh no, she did not just go there!

I stepped closer to Jessica, looking at her warningly. "Yeah I did, and wow he was good. I take cash, or a cheque with a bank guarantee card, whatever's easier for you. Oh, and Jessica, if you ever scream like that at me again I'm going to break your face. You understand?" I growled, angrily.

She flinched away from me slightly; I grabbed Liam's hand and dragged him away into the school, with Kate skipping along behind me, laughing her ass off. "You should have bitch slapped her. I would love to see that," Kate chirped happily.

Sarah and Sean came running up then. "You won the bet?" Sarah cried with wide eyes.

Wow, news travels fast in this school!

Liam laughed and kissed me, tangling his fingers into my hair. "I'd better go. It'll give you some time to gossip about me before class," he said, smirking at me cockily. "I love you, Angel." He kissed me again gently, before walking off quickly in the direction of his locker.

I stood around, filling in my friends about how we were secretly dating, and yes I had won the bet. I had my doubts as to whether I would get the money though. Kate opened her big mouth and told them that the 'hot new guy' was my stepbrother. I was secretly glad when the bell rang so I could escape to class. I didn't want to keep talking about Johnny. I hadn't even met the guy yet and he was already too big a part of my life.

I made my way to English and sat in my usual seat, next to Kate. A few minutes later he came in. I knew it was him without even looking, I could tell by the way Kate gripped my arm way too tight. I glanced up and looked. He was totally hot; I could see what she was talking about. He wasn't as tall as Liam or as well built. In fact, he was a little lanky, but he totally pulled it off. He had on ripped jeans and a black t-shirt with a black hoodie over the top. He had brown eyes, his brown hair was a lot longer than Liam's and was messy and a little shaggy. He looked a little shy, his shoulders hunched a slightly as if he was nervous. I could definitely see the appeal he held, and so could every girl in the class who was now staring at him lustfully. I laughed; the poor kid didn't know what he was in for. Once Jessica got her claws into him he'd be done for.

Kate nudged me with her elbow, making me look at her. She mouthed the word 'hot' and fanned her face, nodding excitedly, making me laugh harder. That boy really was in some big trouble.

"Class, this is my new student, Johnny Brice," Mrs Stewart said, smiling at him warmly. He turned to the class and smiled uncomfortably.

"Told you! Seriously hot," Kate whispered.

Sure he was hot, but he had nothing on my Liam. "He's cute," I confirmed, nodding in agreement.

"Johnny, tell us a little about yourself," Mrs Stewart suggested.

He shifted uncomfortably on his feet as he looked around the class nervously. "Er….. well, I've just moved to Timberfield with my mom and stepfather. I have a little brother who's one. And I like to skate?" he said, making it sound more like a question.

"OK, well I'm sure you'll be very happy here. How about I pair you with someone for my class then they can show you to your next class after?" Mrs Stewart offered. I groaned. There was no way she would pick me, that's the kind of thing that just happens in cheesy stories. I sank down in my seat, looking at my book, praying for a break. "Jessica, are you volunteering?" Mrs Stewart asked. My head snapped up and I breathed a sigh of relief. Kate cursed under her breath and put her hand back down, she was obviously volunteering too.

Johnny made his way across the class to sit next to Jessica, who was busy undoing another button on her already slutty shirt. He smiled at me as he walked past my desk. "Hi, Amber," he said quietly.

"Hi, Johnny," I replied, a little shocked. How the hell did he know my name? I watched him sit next to Jessica, she immediately starting flirting her ass off with him, while he just seemed to be nodding politely, looking uncomfortable.

Kate looked at me with wide eyes. "I thought you didn't know him," she whispered, frowning at me, looking a little confused.

I shook my head. "I don't. How the hell did he know who I was? I've never seen him before," I replied.

The teacher cleared her throat. "Right then, if we're all done talking, how about we start the lesson?" she asked sarcastically. I grabbed my book and sunk further into my seat, trying not to look in his direction.

As soon as the bell rang I jumped out of my seat and

practically ran from the room, not wanting to chance another meeting. I silently prayed over and over in my head that he wasn't in anymore of my classes. Thankfully, the rest of the morning went past with no more run-ins with my new stepbrother.

People were talking to me a lot today; everyone was asking if Liam and I were an item, they wanted to know how long we'd been together. Blah, blah, blah, it was the same thing over and over and I was already bored of it.

"Hey, Angel," Liam purred, grabbing me from behind as I stood in the lunch line with Kate and Sean.

"Hi." I smiled, feeling instantly happier now that he was near me.

"How's your day been?" he asked, kissing my neck, making me squirm.

I sighed. "Well, I've been answering the same questions over and over. It was so bad that I'm actually considering getting: '*Yes, I am dating Liam. Yes, I have won the bet. Yes, he is a good boyfriend. No, my brother didn't go crazy,*' tattooed across my forehead so I don't need to keep repeating myself," I joked, shrugging. He laughed and held me tighter. "Aside from the repeating myself, I had a class with my stepbrother. He knew who I was. And oh yeah, he's walking in right now with that skank Jessica, who by the way, looks like she wants to kill me. So my day's not going too good, boyfriend," I stated, discreetly nodding towards Johnny.

"He knew who you were?" Liam asked, turning me slightly so he was hiding me from Johnny's view.

"Yeah. He said hello to me as he walked past," I replied, frowning, still not understanding how he recognised me.

Liam laughed and looked at me as if I said something stupid. "He probably didn't know who you were, Angel, he probably thought you were hot. Can't blame him there," he purred, grinning at me as his hand moved down to cup my ass.

I rolled my eyes. "Liam, he walked past and said '*hi, Amber'* so I think he knew who I was," I stated sarcastically.

He frowned and looked over his shoulder before chuckling wickedly. "He doesn't look too comfortable with Jessica."

"Well who the hell would look comfortable near Jessica? Oh yeah, you didn't look too stressed when you were hanging all over her," I teased, smirking at him.

He turned his nose up, faking a shudder. "Don't remind me about my former life without you, Angel. I'll have nightmares," he said

173

with mock horror, making me laugh.

I grabbed a couple of sandwiches and drinks. Liam insisted on paying and carrying the tray as usual. I headed over to his table and sat down next to him. Jake was already there with some of his boys from the team, my friends all sat down too, taking the last seats. I ripped open my sandwich and was just about to take a bite when a shadow fell over me.

"Hi," Johnny said smiling, he was blushing slightly.

I gulped, feeling my stomach sink a little. "Er, hi."

"You mind if I sit with you?" he asked, looking at me hopefully.

I saw Jake tense from the corner of my eye. I looked around at the full table. "Um…." I trailed off, biting my lip.

"Never mind, don't worry. I just thought I should introduce myself." He shrugged, blushing harder, shifting on his feet uncomfortably.

Kate kicked me under the table. "Ouch! What the hell was that for?" I asked, rubbing my leg. She glared at me. I knew exactly what it was for, I had to ask him to sit with us for her sake or I wouldn't hear the end of it this afternoon. Oh God, kill me now! "It's fine, Johnny. Grab a chair, you can sit on the end here," I suggested, moving my tray over so he could put down his plate and drink.

He grinned and relaxed. "Thanks, Amber," he said, smiling gratefully as he walked off to get a chair from a couple of tables away.

I turned to Kate, frowning. "That freaking hurt, Kate! Seriously, he's not that hot!" I whisper yelled at her.

"Yeah he is." She nodded enthusiastically, laughing and I ended up laughing along with her. Damn slutty girl.

Johnny sat down on the end of the table. "So, this is weird, huh?" he stated, grinning sheepishly.

I laughed uncomfortably. "Wow, that's an understatement and a half. You think it's weird, try unnerving and awkward," I joked, making him laugh.

"I'm not that bad," he whined, faking hurt.

I decided to just get it out there and ask what had been bothering me all morning. "How do you know who I am?" I asked quietly.

He smiled. "Stephen showed me a photo of you. I haven't seen one of your brother though, so I have no idea who he is," he explained, shrugging.

My dad had a photo of me? I wasn't really sure how to feel about that. Why the hell would he have a photo of me, and not Jake?

I didn't even want to think about that question too much in case I came up with an answer I didn't like.

I pointed at Jake. "He's right there. Jake, Johnny. Johnny, Jake," I said, waving a hand between them in introduction.

"Hey, how's it going?" Jake growled, his face was hard and not at all friendly. Johnny squirmed in his seat a little - Jake could be quite intimidating if he wanted to be.

"Yeah, good thanks. It's good to meet you," he replied nervously.

Kate kicked me again under the table in the exact same spot as before, making me wince. I glared at her warningly; she obviously wanted an introduction too. "Johnny, these are my friends, Sean, Sarah and Kate. This is my boyfriend, Liam," I stated, introducing everyone that was at our end of the table.

Johnny smiled warmly. "Hey, sorry, I'm bad with names. I'll probably forget in like half an hour," he admitted, wincing.

Kate turned on her flirt mode, tossing her hair over her shoulder, smiling seductively. "I'm terrible with names too. We have something in common," she purred, looking him over slowly. He laughed, looking uncomfortable. It didn't look like he was used to female attention at all.

"So, what school did you go to before here?" I asked, trying to help him out slightly.

He smiled at me gratefully. "I actually went to an all-boys school in Mersey," he answered, shrugging. OK, that explains the blushing and being uncomfortable. I could almost see Kate's brain ticking over thinking about teaching him new tricks and breaking him in. I couldn't help but feel sorry for the poor boy.

"An all-boys school? Well that's no fun," Kate smiled, eating a potato chip, obviously trying to look sexy.

Liam burst out laughing next to me. "Kate, leave the poor guy alone, it's his first day," he teased.

Jake looked at Kate with a slightly annoyed expression on his face. It suddenly dawned on me what was happening. Jake was totally crushing on Kate! "I saw that, Jake," I stated, grinning at him knowingly. He flinched and tried to look innocent. Yep, totally jealous! "So, what classes do you have this afternoon?" I asked, turning back to Johnny, trying to keep the conversation going. I felt a little sorry for him; he was obviously like a fish out of water here. He pulled out his schedule and handed it to me. I glanced over it and almost choked on my sandwich - he had every single afternoon class with me. "I have the same ones," I said quietly, handing it back. Liam rubbed his hand on my leg gently and I leant against him for support. Johnny seemed like a nice guy but I didn't want him near me all the time. The occasional conversation I could probably deal with, but what if he went home and my father asked about me? He would know way too much stuff about me for my liking.

"Yeah? Awesome! You think you could show me the way and stuff?" he asked hopefully. I nodded slowly, I couldn't exactly say no.

Jessica came strutting over; she now had only two buttons done up on her shirt. "Hey, Johnny. Want to come and sit with me?" she asked, twirling her hair around her finger.

"Jessica, you missed a few buttons there, sweetie," I said innocently.

She glared at me. "It's supposed to look like this, Emo freak," she spat nastily.

"Actually, yeah I think you're right. I saw that shirt worn exactly like that on the hooker on the corner last night," I replied, smiling kindly.

"You hang out on street corners?" she asked, grinning, obviously thinking she had won.

"When I'm meeting with your mom I do." I shrugged.

Liam and Johnny burst out laughing. "Bitch," she mumbled as she stormed off. Kate and Sarah slapped a high five, giggling like mad girls on crack.

"You're funny," Johnny said, grinning at me.

"Yeah, I think maybe I just ruined your chances of nailing her today. She'll give you another chance tomorrow though so don't worry," I teased as I started eating again.

He turned his nose up. "She's been driving me crazy all morning; she's bitching about some girl who stole her boyfriend. What kind of guy would go out with someone like her anyway? He must be a right ass," he scoffed, shrugging.

The whole table, apart from Liam, burst out laughing. "Er, that ass would be me. But we weren't going out," Liam stated, shaking his head.

Johnny blushed like crazy. "Oh sorry," he mumbled, wincing.

I wrapped my arm around Liam. "Don't worry, lover boy, your taste has improved since then," I cooed, pulling him closer to me.

"Angel, my taste has always been the same. Forbidden fruit." He leant in quickly, biting my neck, making me giggle. Jake cleared his throat and Liam pulled away with a sigh and rolled his eyes. I let Kate talk to Johnny for the rest of lunch, adding in the occasional question or answer when I needed to. He was actually a nice guy. It

176

would have been easier if he was an jerk, then that way I would be able to brush him off and not feel like a piece of crap about it after. I showed him to his classes and he sat next to me when he could. When the bell rang for the end of the day I breathed a sigh of relief.

"So are you headed straight home?" Johnny asked, smiling, as we walked to my locker.

I shook my head. "No. I need to wait for Jake and Liam to be finished with their practice."

"Yeah, what does Jake play?" he asked curiously.

"Ice hockey."

"Cool. You know, I could give you a ride if you want," he offered. "My mom and Stephen bought me a wicked car for my birthday," he added, smiling broadly. I felt my heart sink at the sound of his name again, the way he used it in casual conversation scared the crap out of me.

"Um, thanks for the offer, but I'll wait for them. Liam usually comes over after because Jake goes to work," I said quickly.

"Where does Jake work?" he asked, leaning against the lockers.

"Benny's gym." I rammed my books into my bag with way too much force bending all the pages, because I was getting uncomfortable.

"Jake doesn't seem to like me much," Johnny muttered, looking a little sad.

I smiled reassuringly. "He doesn't know you. It's just weird for us that's all. We haven't seen our father in three years, then all of a sudden he turns up here and bang, we have another brother and a stepbrother. Jake doesn't like change," I explained, trying to skirt around the issue a little.

He nodded, looking thoughtful. "Yeah, I guess it's hard. So, do you think maybe I could wait with you until their practice ends and we could get to know each other a bit more? I mean, I don't want this to carry on being awkward for either of us, I'm here now so I think we need to make the best of it," he asked, looking at me hopefully.

Holy shit buckets! I didn't know what to say, so I said nothing, I nodded and shut my locker.

"You want to sit out front? I usually sit under the tree and wait," I said as we walked out of the building.

"Sounds good," he agreed, following me with a little smile. I walked to the big oak tree where I usually sit and do my homework and sat down leaning against it. He plopped down in front of me, picking a couple of blades of grass, playing with them nervously.

There was a little daisy next to my foot, so I picked it and tucked it into the back of my ponytail because it reminded me of the one that Liam picked for me before dance practice after that first night we kissed.

I was so uncomfortable that I squirmed on the spot, trying to think of something to say. "So, your little brother, Matt…. Well, I guess he's my brother now too, anyway what I was going to say is, what's he like?" I asked curiously.

He grinned. "He's cute. He's a pain in the butt, especially when he cries in the night, but he's cute. I have a picture if you want to see," he offered, pulling his wallet out and handing it to me. I smiled and eagerly flicked it open, wanting to see the little baby. My breath caught in my throat as I looked at the picture, it wasn't just the baby, it was a family picture. I looked at my father; he was smiling proudly with one arm around his new wife and the other around Johnny who was holding a little blond boy. My father looked older, his hair had changed and gone a little greyer, but his eyes were the thing that caught me. I remember his eyes being hard and cold and always angry, but he was different here, smiling and warm, he looked friendly and kind.

"Cute, huh?" Johnny said.

I tore my eyes away from my father and looked at the little baby; he was cute, chubby, blond hair, brown eyes and a big smile. I looked at the lady in the picture; she had brown hair and grey eyes just like my mom and me. She looked nice. "Is this your mom?" I asked, pointing at her.

He smiled and nodded. "Yeah. Her name's Ruby," he said, taking his wallet back when I was done.

I couldn't get the image out of my brain of my father smiling. Had he changed? I looked Johnny over, he looked happy, no bruises or cuts, no telltale limp or wincing or anything. "So, do you get on with him then?" I asked curiously, watching his face for his reaction.

"Matt? Yeah he's OK. It'll be better when he's older and he can do more stuff," he answered, shrugging.

I gulped. "No, I meant my father," I clarified, trying not to flinch at the thought of him. Johnny shrugged and nodded, but didn't say anything. "It must be hard having a guy come along though after years of it just being you and your mom," I stated, trying to push for an answer. Was my father hurting him too, or maybe the baby, or his mom? I was immediately thankful that he didn't have another girl living with him. The physical abuse was bad; Jake got the brunt of it, but the sexual abuse, that left mental scars that I knew I still wasn't over. Memories of those Sunday's flashed through my mind and I bit the inside of my cheek to stop from crying.

He nodded and looked at the floor. "It was a little hard, but they've been together for over two years now, so…" he trailed off, shrugging. I opened my mouth to push the issue further but he cut me off. "So how long have you and Liam been together?" he asked, pulling out some more grass and rolling it in his hand to make a ball.

I smiled at the thought of Liam. "A week and a half."

"He's your brother's friend, right?" he asked.

"Yeah. I've known him since I was four," I confirmed, loving talking about Liam. I was actually really missing him, I gotten used to seeing him all day over the weekend so it was hard going back to only seeing him at lunchtime. "So, tell me some more about you," I suggested, laying down on my belly and propping my head on my hands, watching him.

He laid down too and chatted about his life, his likes and dislikes. He was a keen skateboarder and entered competitions and stuff at the weekends and did stunts and tricks. He missed his friends. He'd never had a girlfriend. His favourite food was chicken curry. I'd just started to tell him mine when I spotted Liam jogging towards me across the parking lot, looking so handsome that he was almost painful to look at. I jumped up and grinned as he wrapped his arms around me, lifting me off of my feet and crashed his lips to mine. I kissed him back hungrily.

He pulled back after a few seconds. "I need to have some alone time with you," he whispered as he kissed me again, gentler this time.

I smiled. "What, right now? Can't you wait until we get home?" I joked.

He shook his head. "No, but I can wait until the parking lot at the back of the gym after we've dropped Jake off," he suggested, grinning wickedly.

"In your dreams, Liam," I said, laughing and rolling my eyes.

"Probably," he agreed as he put me down, holding me close to his side, laughing at my horrified expression. Johnny pushed himself up and was standing there awkwardly. "Thanks for looking after my girl for me," Liam said, smiling a friendly smile.

"Yeah, no problem," Johnny muttered nervously, kicking his shoes in the grass. Jake walked over, looking between me and Johnny with a confused expression. "Well I guess I'll see you guys tomorrow. Thanks for letting me hang with you, Amber," Johnny said, smiling.

"Yeah, it was fun. Hey, let's see this car of yours before you go," I suggested, nodding back towards the parking lot. He grinned proudly.

"What car have you got?" Jake asked curiously as we all started walking. I knew that would catch Jakes interest. I smiled and pulled Liam a little bit behind, letting Jake and Johnny go ahead, giving them a little time. Jake needed to see for himself that Johnny was OK before he would stop scowling at him. By the time we caught up with them, Jake was sitting behind the wheel of a midnight blue BMW Z4, rubbing his hands on the dashboard lovingly.

"Oh shit, this is a nice car," Liam purred, tracing his hand over the roof with wide eyes. He grabbed my hand and pulled me close to him. "When I'm a millionaire hockey player, I'll buy you one of these," he stated, tangling his hand in my hair, looking into my eyes making me feel slightly weightless.

I pressed myself to him and bit his chin gently. "I'd rather have a Ferrari," I joked.

He sighed dramatically. "Wow, OK, I hope I get signed to a good team if you're going to be this demanding," he replied, as he kissed me, making me yearn for him to run his hands down my body. After another ten minutes of drooling over Johnny's car we finally left and went to drop Jake at work. I jumped into the front seat and held Liam's hand all the way home, excited for some private time. Not that it would be easy with my mom home for the week, but I'm pretty sure we'd manage. Even just a cuddle on the sofa sounded like heaven right about now.

Chapter 18

The next morning, after Liam had snuck out of my window, I went to the kitchen to see Jake sitting there chatting to my mom. "Good morning," I chirped happily.

My mom looked at me a little shocked. "What are you so happy about this morning?" she asked, smiling.

I grinned and suppressed a giggle; I couldn't very well tell her that my hottie of a boyfriend had just given me a very good reason to be smiling before he climbed back out of my window. So instead, I just shrugged. "Why not?" I countered, looking anywhere but Jake. He probably knew the exact reason for my happy, satisfied face. "So, Jake, anything you want to tell me?" I teased, sitting down next to him.

He shook his head, looking confused. "No. Should there be?" he asked, raising an eyebrow suspiciously.

"You, crushing on my best friend perhaps?" I suggested, nudging him with my shoulder gently.

He gasped and spilt a spoonful of cereal onto the kitchen counter; he composed himself quickly and smirked at me. "I'm not crushing on your best friend. That's your job, remember?" he said sarcastically. I couldn't help but laugh, him being all defensive wasn't helping his case, if he felt nothing for her then he would have just gone along with it or made some slutty comment.

"Yeah OK. Whatever you say, Jake. I've got my eye on you. Just don't hurt her," I stated, grabbing a bowl and making some cereal.

Liam walked through the door, and I would imagine that if my face looked like his, then that's probably why my mom was asking what I was so happy about. He was grinning from ear to ear. "Morning," he greeted, giving Jake one of those cheesy fist punches on the way past.

"Good morning, Liam. Breakfast?" my mom offered, holding up some bread.

He nodded, smiling gratefully. "Sure, Margaret, that'd be great." He wrapped his arms around me from behind. "Hey, Angel. I missed you last night," he purred.

I heard my mom 'aww' quietly and I tried not to laugh. "Oh you did, huh?" I said, slapping his hand as he moved it down between my legs under the counter.

He laughed and moved to stand next to me. "Absolutely I did. I liked sleeping in with you the other night. Maybe your mom will let me sleep in with you from now on," he said, looking at my mom hopefully.

"Don't push it, Liam," she replied, rolling her eyes.

He laughed. "Hey, it was worth a shot!" he stated, brushing my hair behind my ears and looking at her a little sheepishly.

"You always were cheeky," my mom muttered, smiling as she put three slices of toast in front of him.

"I was just asking Jake about him crushing on Kate," I told Liam, wanting to change the subject from my sex life and him sleeping in my bed. I'd spoken to Liam about Jake and Kate last night. He said that he hadn't noticed anything, but he was going to watch him today for me.

"You're not crushing on a sixteen year old, are you Jake? What the hell kind of eighteen year old would even look at a sixteen year old that way?" Liam asked with fake shock, using Jakes words from a couple of weeks ago.

Jake glared at him warningly. "Ha ha. You two are hilarious," he grumbled, shaking his head as he walked off to get dressed.

When we pulled into the parking lot at school, there was a crowd of people hovering around Johnny's car. He was standing there awkwardly, looking really uncomfortable while the boys talked to him about his car and the girls flirted shamelessly, trying to get him into the back of it by the looks of it. Jessica, as usual, was at the front.

"Wow, we really have some sluts at this school!" I whispered to Liam.

He nodded, looking unimpressed. "Yep."

"Maybe you should go and help him. He looks really uncomfortable," I suggested, looking at Liam pleadingly.

He sighed and rolled his eyes at me. "Why must you be so damn nice all the time?" he asked, kissing me gently before walking off in the direction of Johnny's car. I watched him wave his hand in a buzz off gesture, making half of the boys walk off immediately. He threw his arm around Johnny's shoulder, grinning as he guided him away from the crowd towards the school, while Johnny looked at him gratefully. I smiled to myself; I really did have the most adorable boyfriend in the world.

Kate skipped over to me. "Where's your hot ass of a brother?" she asked. Jake cleared his throat behind her. She turned and grinned at him. "Sorry, I should have said, hot ass of a *stepbrother*," she corrected, winking at him.

His face dropped slightly but he quickly put on a smirk. "Finally realised I'm not interested but you're still trying to get in with the family, huh?" he teased.

She laughed. "Something like that. Maybe I've just gone off of blonds, or maybe you've lost your mojo," she countered, smirking back at him. I almost choked on my laughter. Jake loved the chase I could tell, he'd never wanted anyone he couldn't have before and I honestly think he wanted Kate now just because she wasn't interested. I dragged her in through the doors and spotted Liam and Johnny chatting against his locker.

"Hey," I greeted, smiling as I wrapped my arm around Liam's waist.

"Hey, Amber. How are you today?" Johnny asked politely.

"I'm excellent. You?" I asked trying not to laugh as Liam's hand slipped down the back of my jeans, rubbing his hand over my ass softly.

"I'm good." He nodded in agreement. Kate was smiling at him seductively next to me.

"I was just telling Johnny about Ice Hockey," Liam interjected, squeezing my ass gently. I smiled sweetly at him as I elbowed him in the ribs. Damn pervert boy! He pulled his hand out of my jeans chuckling to himself.

"Yeah, I'm going to come to the game on Friday. You think I could sit with you?" Johnny asked, looking at me hopefully.

"You can sit with me if you want to," Kate offered, licking her lips slowly as she looked him over.

He blushed and smiled at her timidly. "Thanks. I'd like that," he agreed quietly.

"Come on then, let's get to class," I suggested, rolling my eyes. Those two were *so* going to get it on, because by the look on Kate's face she wasn't stopping until he was hers, and he seemed to like her too. I turned to walk off but stopped as I spotted Jessica walking up to me with a hateful expression on her face. She practically threw a brown envelope into my hands as she glared at me.

"I still think you cheated, but people say that it's only fair that you get the money, so there it is, Emo bitch," she growled angrily.

Holy crap! Did she just give me over four thousand dollars? I actually won the money?

Kate stepped closer to me. "Jessica, you better back the hell off before I make you," she spat angrily.

I smiled happily. "It's OK, Kate, there's no problem. Thanks for this, Jessica," I said, waving the envelope proudly.

"Make sure you don't lose it," she stated with a smirk on her face.

I had no doubt in my mind that she had some sort of plan that probably involved me dropping this money down a drain or setting fire to it somehow. Suddenly, I had a great idea that would seriously piss her off. I grinned happily as I turned to Liam. I stepped up close to him as I shoved the money down the front of his jeans, pushing my whole hand down there too. Liam grunted and looked at me, shocked.

"Look after that for me, boyfriend. I'll get it out later," I purred suggestively, as I pulled him down to kiss me. I heard people cheer and clap, guys calling things like 'oh yeah' and 'nice'. I smiled against his lips and pulled back. I glanced over in time to see Jessica storm off in the opposite direction.

I burst out laughing; Liam grabbed me and kissed me again, lifting me off of my feet. The bell rang and people started heading off to their classes. I lingered behind with Liam, not wanting to break the kiss. I can't believe I won four thousand dollars! What the hell can I buy with that?

He put me back down on my feet gently a huge grin on his face. "That was so funny, her face was a picture," he said, laughing.

"Your face was a picture," I countered, flicking his nose gently.

"Yeah well, I wasn't expecting you to push money into my pants like some kind of stripper." He grinned and shook his head amused. "So, what are you going to spend your money on then, Angel?" he asked, as he pulled the envelope out of his jeans and handed it to me.

I shrugged, grinning. "I have no idea. What shall we buy? It's half yours."

"I don't need anything, I already have everything I could ever want right here," he said, gripping his hands on my ass.

"My ass, that's all you want?" I asked, laughing.

He grinned. "Technically, it's my ass now, right?" He smirked at me before kissing my neck.

"For now," I teased as I pulled away. I fanned myself with the envelope. "Now that I've got what I want, I'm just not sure there's anything in this relationship for me anymore."

He laughed and rolled his eyes at me as he wrapped his arm around my waist. "Come on, I'll walk you to class," he suggested, leading us down the corridor.

I held the envelope out to Liam. "Will you look after this for me? I don't really trust myself with it, I'll probably lose it." I winced at the thought of losing all that money.

He smiled and took it, folding it in half and slipping it into his inside jacket pocket. "And what if I lose it?" he asked.

I smiled as we reached my class; I pulled him in close, crushing my body against his. "Then you'll just have to pay me in kind," I breathed, pecking his lips and walking off into my class quickly.

Jessica glared at me as I walked in and sat down next to Kate and Johnny in the seat they had saved for me. Lucky for me, my teacher was late too otherwise my tardiness would have earned me a detention.

The next month passed really quickly. Liam was still the most adorable boyfriend in the world, taking me out on dates and buying me flowers and chocolates. Jake was still overprotective as usual, nothing would ever change there. My mom went back to work but was due home again in two weeks because she had to stay on for some launch of a new product or something. Kate was still flirting her butt off with Johnny - much to Jake's disgust. Liam told me that he'd spoken to Jake about her, apparently, he didn't want to be with Kate, he just didn't like the fact that she was falling all over someone else when she used to be into him. He felt a little left out apparently. So, to rectify the problem he slept with a few extra girls and made himself feel a lot better.

Our relationship with Johnny had changed a lot too. He was actually a really close friend of mine now; he was such a nice guy and seemed to be growing in confidence every day. I think maybe that had something to do with Kate's influence. They had been out together a couple of times, and Kate told me that he'd kissed her last night which she was positively glowing about. She actually really liked him, and I think he liked her too, which was sweet.

Johnny had been coming to watch the Friday hockey games

with us and for the last two weeks, he had even come to our 'after game party' for a couple of hours after too. We never spoke about my father, he never asked me anything about him and I didn't bring him up. Occasionally, he would mention him in passing, something to do with his life or home and every time it would make me feel sick and slightly panicky.

Today was Sunday and I was going with Johnny to watch him in a skateboarding competition. When he pulled up just after lunch time, I kissed Liam goodbye and giggled at his pouty face. "Stop pouting, Liam. I'll be back in a couple of hours," I said, laughing.

He sighed dramatically. "But why can't I come? Sundays are *my* days," he grumbled, frowning.

I smiled. "Liam, I told you, he could only get one guest pass. He asked me to go with him! Stop whining. I'll see you later," I instructed, kissing him again as I stood up. "Love you," I vowed as I grabbed my keys and cellphone.

"Love you more, Angel," he called as I opened the door and ran to the car.

"Hey," Johnny greeted, smiling, as I got into his shiny little sports car.

"Hey. You already psyched and ready for the competition?" I asked, grinning.

He nodded. "Yeah, I'm a bit nervous though. The new trick that I've been practicing keeps going wrong. I'm gonna look like such a dick if I fall on my face," he groaned, grimacing.

"You won't fall on your face, Johnny. Have some confidence," I replied sternly.

He smiled and rolled his eyes, driving us to the skate park where they had set up a huge half pipe ramp thing. Johnny had been trying to teach me a few things about skating but to be honest, like most things sporty; it just went in one ear and out of the other. If it wasn't dancing, then I just wasn't really that interested.

Usually I liked to watch Liam play, but that was only to perv on him in his uniform. The ramp they had set up was absolutely huge. I felt a little sick when I looked at it. It was so high, at least fifteen foot high on each side. "Um Johnny, are you sure about this?" I asked, as we walked up to the signing in booth. Johnny handed over our competitor passes and we were given yellow wrist bands and waved in.

"Amber, I'll be fine, don't worry." He laughed as he dragged me over to the skater area where people were hanging around waiting to go on and practice.

"Shit, Johnny, it's so high! What if you get hurt?" I asked, swallowing the lump in my throat.

"Hey, cut that out right now. You told me in the car to have some confidence, I expect you to do that same," he said grinning at me. Jeez, I had confidence, but that would hurt if he fell from there! We sat there watching the other skaters have their turns. The tricks that they were doing blew my mind, somersaults, handstands, everything that you could think of.

The whole time I just felt worse and worse. I wasn't even sure if I could watch him do it. After about an hour, Johnny was called up to go and get ready, and my heart started trying to break out of my chest.

"Oh God. Please be careful," I begged.

"I'll try. But if I die, you can have my car," he replied, winking at me.

"Only if I can re-spray it pink," I joked, trying not to show him I was terrified. He laughed and walked off quickly to the area to warm up for a few minutes.

When it was finally his turn, I couldn't breathe. I watched him climb the stairs to the top of the platform and position at the end with the board tipped up waiting to go. He smiled down at me and I tried to smile back - I'm pretty sure my expression looked more like a grimace though. The whistle blew, and he tipped off. I squeezed my eyes shut, listening to the people clap and cheer, but I didn't want to see. I knew that the minute I opened my eyes, he'd fall and break his neck.

After an hour, well, it felt like an hour anyway, it was probably only about a minute, people were clapping like crazy so I chanced opening my eyes. Johnny was walking down the stairs, no broken bones, no blood. I jumped up and clapped along with everyone else, deciding to pretend I'd watched. Next time I'd have to tell him I couldn't come. I just wasted his spare ticket by not even watching it.

He jogged over and hugged me tight. "That was awesome!" I chirped enthusiastically.

He laughed and shook his head. "Yeah? Did it look good through your eyelids?" he asked, laughing harder.

I looked at him apologetically. "I'm so sorry! I couldn't watch it, Johnny. I felt so sick. I was so scared, I just couldn't," I said apologetically.

He shook his head. "Don't apologise, it's fine. I landed it though," he boasted, grinning wildly.

I nodded. "I know, I heard people cheering," I said a little sheepishly. I felt incredibly guilty. He'd brought me here to watch and give him support and I couldn't even do that. I guess I was a useless stepsister.

We sat back down and he gave me a play by play of everything that I'd missed while we waited for the scores and stuff to be counted. Johnny was one of the last to go on, so we didn't have to wait too long before the results were announced. When the guy walked on the stage I gripped his hand nervously, praying he had been scored well.

"OK, so we had some excellent tricks today. The judges were very impressed, so congratulations," the guy stated on the little platform. "Right so, in reverse order. Coming in third place with a score of forty-four points out of fifty, is…. Johnny Brice," he called.

I squealed and jumped on him excitedly as he laughed. "Oh God, Johnny, that's awesome! I'm so proud of you," I enthused, almost crying.

He grinned. "Thanks, Amber. I'd better go get my trophy." He nodded at the stage. I stood there cheering and clapping like an idiot while he went up and got his little silver trophy. He ran back and hugged me spinning me in a circle.

"Johnny, that's so good. Let me see it." I practically snatched it out of his hands and looked at the little silver trophy with a little man on a skateboard.

"I'm really pleased with forty-four points. That's my best score." He grinned, proudly.

"Hey, shall we go get something to eat to celebrate? My treat," I suggested, happily.

"Sure. I just need to get changed first though; I can't really go out like this." He looked down at his ripped t-shirt, skater shorts and dirty sneakers, pulling a face.

Why the hell would he need to change? "Johnny, I don't care what you wear," I said honestly, as we started walking back to his car.

He laughed. "Amber, I look a mess. These are my competition clothes. I always wear the same thing; they're like my lucky clothes. They're all ripped and dirty. Besides, I'm all sweaty and stuff," he countered, shrugging. We climbed into his car. "I'll just nip home and change, and then we can go," he said as he pulled out of the parking lot.

Oh shit! He wants me to go to his house? I started to feel sick. I couldn't go, I didn't want to see my father, I couldn't. I closed my eyes, willing myself not to freak out. Liam wasn't here so I didn't want to have a full blown panic attack.

"I can't," I whispered.

He glanced at me, confused. "You can't go to dinner?" he asked, looking at me like I was crazy, probably because it was my idea in the first place.

I shook my head. "I can't go to your house, Johnny. Please, I can't see him," I begged as he continued to drive in the opposite direction to my house.

"Stephen?" he asked, frowning. I nodded, unable to speak through the lump in my throat. My hands were shaking. I closed my eyes and thought of Liam, trying to stay calm. I thought of the colour of his eyes, how his hair felt when I ran my hands through it, the sound of his voice.

"You OK?" Johnny asked, sounding concerned.

I nodded weakly. "I don't want to see him, Johnny," I whispered, turning in my seat to look at him.

He was trying to watch the road and look at me at the same time. "Why not?" he asked quietly. I shook my head. I couldn't talk about it, especially not to him, that was his stepfather for goodness sake, he lived with him.

"I just don't, please." I begged him with my eyes.

He sighed and shook his head. "He's not there anyway. He went away for the weekend with my mom and Matt. They're not due back until late tonight," he said.

He wasn't there?

"Are you sure?" I asked, my body was starting to relax.

He nodded and smiled reassuringly. "Positive. They went to Mersey for the weekend to see my grandparents. They're not getting back until like ten or something."

I looked at him to make sure he wasn't lying or trying to trick me or something. He looked like he was telling the truth. Johnny was a really nice guy, he wouldn't do something like that to me, he wouldn't lie. "OK," I agreed quietly.

He smiled and looked back at the road. "So, do I get to know why you and Jake hate Stephen so much?" he asked curiously. I closed my eyes; I really didn't want to have this conversation with him, with anyone. Even Kate didn't know any details about my father and my childhood.

"Johnny, I don't want to talk about it. It's in the past, I prefer it to stay there," I replied, praying that he would drop it.

He nodded, looking a little disappointed and sad. "OK. Well, if you ever need to talk to me about anything, you can. You know that, right?" he asked as he pulled onto a really nice looking street. I nodded looking out of the window; the houses were huge, with big expensive cars in the drives. He pulled in to a driveway and I glanced up at the huge pale blue house. It looked like my dad had certainly done well for himself.

"You sure he's not here?" I asked nervously, as I got out and walked to Johnny's side.

"I'm sure. The car's not even here," he confirmed, waving at the empty drive. I relaxed and followed behind Johnny closely, up to the house. I was barely able to breathe. As he opened the front door I gripped hold of the back of his t-shirt. He chuckled. "Amber, there's no one here," he assured me, shaking his head as he wrapped his arm around my shoulders, pulling me into the house. The house was gorgeous. "Want a drink?" he offered, leading me into the kitchen.

"Um, sure." I looked around at all of the expensive ornaments and furniture. "You could fit my whole house into your lounge and kitchen," I said, smiling.

He laughed. "This is house is nice, but it's too big for just us. I don't know why they had to buy such an expensive one."

"What does my father do now then?" I asked curiously, as he handed me a can of Pepsi.

"Stocks and shares. He's some big broker or something, I don't really understand it. He makes a lot of money though," he said casually.

He was still doing that then, that's what he did when we were kids. I didn't want to talk about him anymore; being in his house was freaking me out more than enough.

"So, you and Kate, huh?" I teased, trying to change the subject.

He blushed and nodded. "She's nice," he muttered nervously.

I grinned at his blush, he really was adorable. "She said you kissed her." I raised my eyebrows excitedly, waiting for details. I'd had her version of the 'perfect kiss' now I wanted his.

He grinned. "Yeah, did she say if she liked it?" he asked, blushing harder.

Oh hell yeah she did! "Yeah, she liked it a lot," I confirmed, waggling my eyebrows at him.

He laughed. "Well thank goodness for that." He sounded so relieved that I couldn't help but laugh too. "I was thinking about asking her out, properly, you know, being exclusive. Do you think she'd go for that?" he asked, looking at me hopefully.

I grinned at his worried face. "Hell yeah she'd go for that." Kate really liked him, she would definitely be exclusive.

He laughed and messed up the back of his hair. "Awesome! Thanks, Amber."

"Go get changed then and let's go eat. I'm starved," I instructed, nodding to the hallway.

"OK. I'll be five minutes."

I shrugged. "You can shower and stuff if you want, I don't mind waiting."

"Are you saying I smell?" he asked, laughing, as he made his way to the hall.

"Well, I was trying to be polite," I joked. He laughed and skipped off up the stairs.

I sat down at the kitchen counter, happily drinking my Pepsi, playing with his trophy, when I heard the front door open and a lady talking. "No, I just need to give him some medicine and put him to bed," she said.

I felt my breath catch in my throat.

"Well, he hasn't stopped fucking crying," my father snapped, sounding annoyed.

I jumped out of the chair so fast that I nearly fell over. I moved to the other side of the counter, needing to put something between us if he was coming in here. My heart was crashing in my chest. I couldn't breathe properly. There was a door behind me; I grabbed the handle, desperately wanting to get away before he came in. I couldn't see him; I couldn't let him see me. Rattling the handle I quickly realised that the door was locked. I could feel the tears starting to prickle in my eyes.

"I'm sorry, Stephen. I'll put him to bed in a minute, he'll sleep it off," the lady said quietly.

"He fucking better, he's giving me a headache," he growled angrily.

I rammed my hand into my pocket, grabbing my cellphone. Who I was planning on calling I don't know. Liam and Jake were too far away, and Johnny was probably in the shower. There was no one, no help; I was alone in my horror. I turned around facing the door, waiting for him to come in. I felt sick. Oh God, was I actually going to throw up?

The lady walked in, carrying a whining little blond boy in her arms, stroking his back soothingly. Her eyes snapped to me and she jumped a mile, obviously not knowing I was in here. "Hi, sorry, I didn't realise Johnny had friends over," she said, smiling at me warmly. She was very pretty, brown hair and grey eyes, just like my

191

mom's and mine. I nodded, unable to talk.

"Johnny's got friends over?" my father asked as he walked through the door.

I felt dizzy, my legs were weak, he looked almost exactly the same, just a little older, a little less hair and more greys. His eyes were hard and stern like they used to be, not like the photo that Johnny showed me. He hadn't changed at all.

He looked at me, his eyes raking over every part of my body while I just stood there, unable to move, unable to breathe. I felt like I was a kid again. I was terrified, and this time I had no Jake to protect me. The man that ruined my childhood, my brothers childhood, was standing less than fifteen feet from me.

"Amber," he said quietly. He smiled and I felt bile rise in my throat.

Chapter 19

"Amber?" the lady repeated, looking between him and me. "Your daughter, Amber?" she asked, a smile tugging at her lips. My father nodded, his eyes not leaving mine. I felt like a deer trapped in the headlights of an oncoming car, and all I could do was brace myself for the impact. "Well, it's great to meet you at last. I've heard so much about you from Stephen and Johnny that I feel like I already know you," the lady chirped, smiling warmly at me. I tried to smile back and pretend that everything was fine, that I wasn't about to pass out any second, that I wasn't about five seconds from screaming the house down.

"You too, Ruby," I replied quietly, dragging my eyes away from him.

"What are you doing here, Amber?" my father asked, raising his eyebrows and smiling a half smile. The sound of his voice sent chills down my spine as I tried desperately not to remember my childhood. I had nightmares about his voice, his eyes, the way he stood so straight, and how his fists were always clenched, just like they were now.

"I….. I came with Johnny. He's…. he's getting changed," I stuttered. Immediately I was mentally scolding myself because I was stuttering. His old rules were coming back, stand tall, speak clearly, no mumbling.

Ruby smiled. "Well, it's great that you're here. Would you like to stay for dinner? I think we're getting a takeout because there's not much food in. We weren't due back until later tonight, but Matt's been ill all weekend so we came back early," Ruby explained as she kissed the baby's head softly. She seemed really nice, too nice for this abusive asshole. I shook my head, I couldn't speak again. My hands were shaking so I clasped them together tightly, trying to

193

remain in control and not slump into a pile on the floor and sob. "You sure? It's no trouble. We'd love to have you stay for dinner, wouldn't we, Stephen?" she continued, smiling at him, completely oblivious that I was living my worst nightmare right now. He nodded, his gaze travelling the length of my body, making me go cold.

"I'm sure, thanks," I said quietly, my voice breaking at the end.

The little boy started crying again. Ruby's eyes went wide as she looked at Stephen. "I'll just give him some medicine and put him down for a sleep," she said, heading over to a cupboard pulling out a medicine bottle and spoon.

My father walked a couple of steps towards me and I shrank back against the door, my breathing coming out in shallow gasps. I thumbed my phone open and dialled Johnny - he was the closest person, if I could just call him and somehow tell him to get the hell downstairs, then we could leave.

"How have you been, Amber? I've been trying to see you for years but your brother wouldn't let me," he stated, sneering on the word brother.

He'd been trying to see me and Jake didn't tell me? Why the hell wouldn't he tell me something like that? Knowing Jake, he probably thought he was protecting me. I looked at Johnny's mother for help; she was putting the medicine bottle back now.

"I've been fine, thank you," I answered. I glanced down at my phone, it was still trying to connect, Johnny wasn't answering. Damn it!

"I'll just put Matt to bed, then I'll be back and make some coffee or something," Ruby suggested, smiling kindly at me.

"OK, love," my father replied, his eyes not leaving mine.

I gulped; I couldn't be here with him on my own! "Can I come with you?" I asked desperately. Ruby looked at me a little shocked. "I'd like to see Matt's room, if that's OK," I lied quickly. There was no way I was staying in here with him.

"I don't think that's a good idea, Amber. Matt's not well. You can see his room another time," my father interjected before Ruby could answer.

Ruby smiled. "I'll be right back." She headed out of the room with the little boy clinging around her neck.

I stepped to the side and almost ran out of the room after her. Just as I passed him, he grabbed my wrist, yanking me to a stop, almost making me fall. I felt the scream trying to rip itself out of my throat but I swallowed it back down, I couldn't show him how much power he had over me.

"You look beautiful, Amber. Just like your mother when she was your age. You always were a fucking peach," he purred, licking his lips as he trailed his hand across my cheek.

I brought my knee up and kneed him as hard as I could in the groin, yanking my arm from his hold and streaking for the hallway as fast as my legs could carry me. I had no idea where I should go though. I came here in Johnny's car so I didn't want to just run out of the house with nowhere to go. So instead, I ran up the stairs, streaking down the hallway until I spotted a door with a *'Enter at your own risk'* hazard sign hanging on it. That one *had* to be Johnny's. I didn't bother knocking as I burst through the door, slamming it behind me and bursting into hysterical sobs as I leant against it.

"Amber! What the hell?" Johnny gasped. I looked up he was standing there in just a towel, his body wet from getting out of the shower. I pushed myself away from the door and threw myself at him, hugging him tightly, ignoring the water dripping on me from his hair as I sobbed against his neck. "What's wrong? Amber, for goodness sake! What's happened?" he asked desperately as he rubbed his hands up my back trying to soothe me.

"I need to go home. I need to go, right now!" I cried. My legs were barely holding me up; he was supporting most of my weight. I was probably hurting him because of how tightly I was clutching at him, but he didn't complain.

"What's wrong?" he asked, pulling back to look at me.

"Johnny, please?" I choked out.

He nodded and pulled me over to the bed making me sit down. "I need to get dressed," he said, blushing. I nodded and closed my eyes, trying to picture Liam, I needed to calm down, I couldn't go into meltdown here. I could hear him moving around, getting dressed. Less than a minute later he took my hand. "I'm ready. Let's go," he stated, pulling me up gently. I clung to his hand tightly as he led me across the room to his door; he stopped with his hand on the handle. "You promise you'll tell me what this is about later?" he asked, looking at me pleadingly. I nodded. I'd agree to anything he asked for if he would just get me the hell out of here. He wrapped his arm around me, pulling me close to his side as he opened the door, leading us quickly down the stairs. I stiffened as his mother walked out of the lounge. "Shit! What are you doing home?" he asked, shocked.

She smiled a little sadly. "Matt's not well. He was sick last night and he's been grizzly all day, so we just came home early," she explained, holding her arms open for him. He stepped away from me

195

and I felt my breath catch in my throat at being on my own. He hugged her quickly. "Missed you," she cooed, patting his back.

He smiled and kissed her cheek. "You too. Look, Mom, I need to take Amber home, her brother needs her," he lied, moving back to me quickly.

She smiled sadly. "Are you sure you can't stay for dinner, Amber? Stephen would love to spend some time with you."

Spend some time with me? Is she freaking kidding me? I shook my head. "I can't," I whispered.

My father walked around the corner and I shrank into Johnny's side, pressing against him so hard that it actually hurt. His arm tightened around me even though he didn't know why I was acting like this. He really was a great stepbrother.

"Hi, Stephen," Johnny greeted, stiffly.

"Hi, Johnny. Getting cosy with my daughter?" Stephen asked, his voice hard making me flinch.

"I need to go," I whispered desperately, digging my fingers into his side.

"I'll see you guys later," Johnny said, turning and pushing me in front of him putting himself between me and my father as we walked to the door. I practically ran to his car, watching the front door the whole time in case he came after me. I knew he wouldn't though. He needed to keep up the act for his wife and Johnny, but that didn't stop the panic from rising in my chest.

Johnny was watching me worriedly as he sped down the streets. "Are you alright, Amber? You look really pale, you're shaking," he said, taking my hand.

I nodded. "I want to go home," I choked out.

"OK, shh I'll take you home." He rubbed his thumb over the back of my hand as he drove to my house. I squeezed my eyes shut. He really hadn't changed at all; the way he looked at me turned my stomach. Oh God, I needed Liam!

After about ten minutes of trying to think of anything other than my father, we pulled into my drive. I burst out of the car and ran for the house, praying that Liam was still over. I threw the door open and spotted him sitting on the sofa playing PlayStation with Jake.

They both glanced up as I came in. Liam grinned at me happily before his face fell. He jumped up from the sofa as I ran to him. "What the hell?" he shouted angrily, glaring at Johnny who came in behind me. I threw myself at him, sobbing. Jeez, I needed him; he was the only thing that kept me sane when my world started to fall apart. He wrapped me tightly in his arms, turning me away from

Johnny, his whole body tense and stressed.

"What the hell is going on?" Jake shouted, stepping towards Johnny, looking really angry.

"I don't know. I was getting changed then she just freaked out and started crying. Jake, I didn't do anything!" Johnny cried sounding a little scared.

Jake grabbed my arm, pulling me away from Liam. "Has he hurt you, Amber?" he asked fiercely, pointing at Johnny accusingly.

I shook my head, trying to speak. They thought Johnny had hurt me? "I went to his house. He wasn't supposed to be there," I sobbed, my legs gave out from under me. Liam grabbed my waist before I slumped to the floor and picked me up quickly, he sat down, pulling me onto his lap, rubbing my hair away from my face and kissing my cheek.

"Shh it's alright, Angel. Everything's OK," he cooed.

"Who wasn't supposed to be there? Someone needs to tell me what the hell happened, RIGHT NOW!" Jake shouted getting angrier and angrier.

"Dad," I croaked.

Jakes eyes went wide his hands clenched into fists, his jaw clamped tight. I felt Liam's arms get tighter around me. "You saw him?" Jake asked, his voice sounding truly menacing. I nodded and watched him glare at Johnny again as if this was somehow is fault. "You took her to your house and let that asshole near her?" Jake growled, making Johnny flinch.

"I didn't know he was there! He wasn't supposed to be there. They came home early while I was in the shower," he protested, holding his hands up innocently as Jake looked like he wanted to murder him there and then. If looks could kill Johnny would be dead right now.

"What did he do, Angel?" Liam whispered, pulling my face around to look at him. I shook my head. Could I tell them? If they found out I had no doubt that they would be going round there in the very, very near future, and then they'd get in trouble. "Tell me," Liam ordered.

I hugged him tightly, I couldn't lie to him. "He....he grabbed my arm. He said I... I looked beautiful, just like my mom at my age, and that I was a f...fucking p...peach," I whispered, barely able to get the words out, my voice hitching and catching through my sobs. Liam's arms tightened around me, so tight that it was actually starting to hurt my ribs. "Liam, you're hurting me," I whined, gripping my hands into his hair. His arms loosed instantly but his whole body was so tense

197

that he was probably giving himself an ulcer.

Jake grabbed his keys off of the side. "I'm going. You coming, Liam?" Jake asked, heading for the door. Oh hell no! I couldn't let them get in trouble!

Liam lifted me off of his lap and sat me on the sofa. "Watch her," he said to Johnny sternly, as he stood up to leave.

"No!" I screamed, grabbing Liam's hand. "Jake, no!" I begged.

"I won't let him hurt you again," Jake growled.

"He won't. He won't come near me. It was my fault; I shouldn't have gone to Johnny's. I shouldn't have taken the risk. Please, please don't. I can't see you get in trouble. I need you. I need both of you. Please don't leave me on my own," I begged. I squeezed Liam's hand for emphasis. "Please," I begged pulling him closer to me again.

He sighed and looked at Jake. "She's right, Jake. We can't go without him doing anything first. He'll just get away with everything, and we'll be the ones in trouble," Liam reasoned.

I relaxed. Liam was seeing sense; he always thought things through, not like Jake. "What do you mean by, *hurt her again*?" Johnny asked quietly.

All three of us looked at him. Jake spoke first. "Nothing. I think you should go, Johnny." He nodded at the door, signalling for him to leave.

Johnny shook his head. "No. Amber, you promised you'd tell me what this was about," he stated, looking at me pleadingly.

He's right, I did say that. Jake looked at me, letting me make the decision. "I did say that," I confirmed, nodding and closing my eyes, pressing myself to Liam again. Jeez, this was going to be so damn hard!

~ Liam ~

I pulled her back onto my lap, wanting her close to me. My heart still hadn't returned to normal from seeing her sobbing like that. I was so angry that my jaw was aching where I was clenching my teeth together so tightly, trying to stay in control. I wanted to go around there and beat him until there was nothing left of him, but she was right, we'd be the ones getting in trouble then and she didn't need any more stress right now.

Jake motioned for Johnny to sit on the couch opposite us, and he sat down next to him. Both of them looked stressed. Amber curled herself up into a ball on my lap, pulling her knees up and tucking her face into the side of my neck. I rocked her gently as I listened to Jake telling Johnny about the abuse when they were kids, how their father had tried to attack Amber, and how we'd kicked him out three years ago. He left out the sexual abuse that no one really knew very much about because she refused to talk about it. The whole time Johnny just sat there, playing with his hands. Why didn't he look shocked at all of this? If someone sat there and told me that their father had abused them for years, I think I'd at least be a little shocked, wouldn't I?

After about ten minutes I glanced down at Amber to see she was asleep in my arms. She looked so sad and vulnerable; her face was still red from crying. I'd never let anything hurt her again. I waved to Jake to get his attention. "I'm going to put her to bed," I whispered, standing up and trying to keep her still as I carried her to her room, laying her on her bed. She whimpered and snuggled closer to me, so I laid down with her for a couple of minutes until she was back in a deep sleep. I kissed her forehead and went back to the lounge

Johnny had his head in his hands. Jake looked really angry again. "What's wrong?" I asked, looking between the two of them. Jake looked at me, he looked really stressed and worried. I didn't see Jake like this very often, he was always so strong and it actually made me feel a little sick to see him like that now.

"He's doing it again. He's hit Johnny and his mom a few times," Jake growled, looking disgusted. Damn it! I told Jake we should have called the police instead of just kicking him out, but he insisted he didn't want Amber to go through that. And now he was doing it to someone else!

"My mom was talking about leaving him last year. Then we moved here instead. She said it was a fresh start and that we should all start over, but it hasn't helped," Johnny said sadly. I knelt down next to him and put my hand on his shoulder. I didn't really know him that well, he was more Angel's friend than mine, but I knew he was a good kid.

"Johnny, does your mom still want to leave him?" I asked, looking at Jake, who looked like he was ready to explode any minute. I'd have to keep a close eye on him. If the time came then I'd be there at his side, but we couldn't go rushing into anything, it would need to look like self-defence.

Johnny shrugged. "I haven't spoken to her about it since we

199

moved here, so I don't know. I know that she's scared for Matt. He hasn't hit him yet, but he's only a year old," he replied, his voice breaking.

I squeezed his shoulder supportively. That asshole was a real sick piece of work. Jake sat down next to him and patted his back awkwardly. As guys, we weren't really too good at support. Angel would be perfect for this; she was so damn loving and kind.

"Johnny, you need to tell your mom that he's done this before. It could be the push that she needs to leave him before he does anything to Matt," Jake said kindly.

Johnny nodded, standing up. "I'll go home and speak to her when I can."

"Johnny, if you ever need help you call me. Day or night, understand? And if you need a place to stay for a few days, your mom and brother too, then you can stay here," Jake said fiercely. He meant it, Jake was a great guy and he would never let anyone hurt his family or friends, I guess technically Johnny was his family too.

"Thanks. I'll wait until he's not there, and then I'll talk to her." Johnny nodded, looking really sad, and a little scared.

"Call me and let me know how it goes. And I'm serious about the place to stay, my mom won't mind, and she's not even due home for another two weeks," Jake stated, walking Johnny to the door. He put his arm around his shoulder. "Everything's going to be fine," Jake assured him. Johnny looked like a little lost boy, he didn't look ready for this at all, but I guess he'd need to man up quickly like Jake did when he was younger.

"I don't think you should tell Amber any of this stuff. She doesn't really need anything else to worry about, and I don't even know what my mom's going to say about it all," Johnny muttered, frowning.

I nodded. That was probably a good idea. If Angel knew any of this she would be getting herself all worked up, worrying about Johnny and Matt, and for all we knew his mom might not even want to leave him in the first place. We could tell her when the time comes. "Yeah, good idea," I agreed, nodding.

"OK thanks. See ya." He smiled sadly and headed out of the house.

Jake shut the door and pressed his forehead against it. "Liam, you need to give me one good reason why I shouldn't go round there and slit his throat," he growled, his whole body stiff.

"Because then you'd be in jail, and Angel wouldn't have her big brother here to protect her," I said quickly, knowing that Amber was the one thing that would keep him calm and restrained.

Jake turned to me and did something I'd never seen him do in his life; he slumped down against the door, pulled his knees up to his chest, and cried. I felt my insides squirm at the sight of it. I was so angry again that I needed to remind myself of the exact same reason I couldn't go around there and slit his throat. I sat down next to Jake and put my arm around his shoulder while he cried. I don't think he'd ever had a proper release before.

~ Amber ~

Things had been really strained for the last week between me and Johnny. I knew that he knew about what my father had done to us, well, some of it anyway. Jake assured me that he didn't tell him too much about me because he knew I wouldn't want people knowing about it. I'd told Johnny that I didn't want to talk about any of it, which he respected. He seemed to hang out with Jake and Liam more than he did me and Kate at the moment. They were always off talking in hushed whispers, and would stop whenever I went near them. I wondered if they were talking about me, but to be honest I really didn't want to know. I didn't want to talk about that man ever again, so if they were happy to talk about me and leave me out of it, then good.

When I woke up on Friday morning, Liam was already up and getting dressed quietly. "Hey, are you doing the walk of shame?" I teased, wondering why he was sneaking out of my room. He never woke up before me.

He laughed and pulled his t-shirt on before climbing back in the bed. I hooked my fingers in his belt loops, pulling him closer to me. "The only shame I have is that I have to get out of your bed. I would happily stay in bed with you forever, but I have something I need to do today so I've got to go." He kissed me softly, causing the usual little flutters in my stomach that his kissing evoked in me.

Something he's got to do? What's that about? "What have you got to do, lover boy?" I asked, pulling him closer to me, stopping him from getting up.

He smiled and rolled onto his back, pulling me on top of him. "Nothing interesting. I just need to sort something out for college that's all," he replied, looking uncomfortable. Was he lying to me? I looked at his face, his eyes were a little tight, he was definitely looking uncomfortable about something.

"Liam, is something wrong?" I asked worriedly. Oh crap, is he seeing someone else or something?

He smiled and tangled his fingers into my hair. "Nothing's wrong. Don't worry your pretty little head about anything. It's just a couple of scouts want to meet with me, and this is the only time they could come," he explained, still looking uncomfortable.

I nodded, he obviously had something he was trying to keep from me, he'd tell me eventually. I trusted him. I was sure that he wouldn't cheat on me - that had just been a stupid spur of the moment thought. I knew he loved me. I bent forward and kissed him, pulling away to bite his chin, he loved it when I did that. His hands tightened on my waist as his breathing started to speed; I smiled and bit his earlobe.

He groaned. "Angel, I need to go. Don't tease me," he whined.

I smiled against his neck and sat up, pouting, deciding to have some fun with him before he left. I sighed dramatically. "OK, well I guess I'll just have to shower alone then."

He groaned again. "Angel, don't do that to me, it's not fair you know," he grumbled, frowning.

I couldn't help but laugh at his lustful expression as I climbed off of him. "Well, have fun with your scouts. Go impress them with your awesome talents, lover boy," I instructed, kissing him again softly.

He brushed my hair behind my ear. "I love you. I'll see you after school."

I frowned. He wasn't coming to school? "You're not coming to school after?" I asked, disappointed that I wouldn't get to see him much today.

He sighed and shook his head. "No, I'll see you after though," he countered, kissing me again as he climbed out of the bed.

"Liam?" I called just as he was about to walk out of the door. He stopped and looked back at me, curiously. "I love you too, and good luck with the scouts. Just remember, they'll be lucky to have you, not the other way around," I said honestly. Scouts were falling all over themselves for Liam, he didn't need to work too hard to impress people, his skills spoke for themselves. He smiled and winked at me before heading out of the door.

I showered and went out to get some breakfast; Jake was sitting there in pyjamas even though it was almost time to leave. "Hey, you'd better hurry or we'll be late," I scolded, frowning at the thought of a detention.

He shook his head. "I'm not feeling well, so I'm not going. I've asked Casey to drive you because Liam's with the scouts," he said quietly.

Jake hardly ever got sick. I walked over to him a little worried, and put my hand on his forehead. He didn't feel hot or anything. "I don't think you have a temperature. What's wrong?" I asked, concerned.

"I feel sick that's all. I'm going back to bed. Casey will be here in fifteen minutes," he replied, standing up and heading towards the hallway.

"You want me to get you anything, Jake?" I asked.

He shook his head. "I'll be fine, Ambs. See you later." He waved over his shoulder and disappeared into his room.

Casey was funny on the drive to school, I always liked him and he didn't hit on me once, which was great. The guys all seemed to have stopped making their comments to me since I'd been with Liam. When we pulled up, I spotted Kate, Sarah and Sean so I skipped over to them

"Hey," I chirped, smiling.

"Hey, Amber. Where's Jake and Liam?" Sean asked, looking over my shoulder.

"Liam's meeting some college scouts," I said proudly. "And Jake's sick," I added, turning my nose up. I hope he doesn't throw up anywhere and leave it for me to clean up!

"Yeah? Johnny's sick too. He called me this morning," Kate said, pouting. He still hadn't asked her out like he said he was going to. I hadn't told her what he'd said about her, I thought it would be better coming from him.

"Johnny's sick too? I hope there's nothing going around." I winced at the thought of being sick, I hated throwing up.

"Me too. Come on, let's go to class," Kate suggested, linking her arm through mine and pulling me towards the building.

School passed unbelievably slowly because I didn't have seeing Liam at lunch time to look forward to. The morning and afternoon just blurred into one long Liam-less day, and on top of that I started to feel a little sick too. My stomach felt queasy and I couldn't even force anything down for lunch.

Great, now I'm getting sick!

I tried calling Jake to see how he was feeling, but there was no answer. He was probably asleep or something. Kate was dropping me home because the boys weren't here today. She dropped me at the front and I walked into the house, feeling exhausted, all I wanted to do was go to sleep.

As I walked in through the front door I saw suitcases and boxes and black trash bags full of stuff all piled up in the hall. What the hell is all of this? "Jake?" I called.

I could hear voices in the kitchen so I made my way in there, only to see Liam, Jake, Johnny, and Ruby who was holding a little kid in her arms which I assume was my little brother, Matt. I hadn't officially seen him apart from the back of his head last week. What the hell are they doing here? Wait, I thought Kate said Johnny was sick - he didn't look sick.

"Hey. What's all this? You guys having a conference?" I teased. Ruby smiled at me weakly, her eyes were slightly pink, like she'd been crying. I felt my back get stiff at the sight of her sad face.

Liam came over and wrapped his arm around my waist. "Angel, we've got something to tell you," he said softly. I gulped because of the tone of his voice; this was going to be bad whatever it was.

Jake stepped forward. "He's been doing it again, Ambs. They've left him. I said they could stay here for a while. Mom said it would be fine," he explained.

Ruby started to cry again softly. I looked up at Johnny. He'd been getting abused and he didn't tell me? I could feel myself getting angry with him. He knew what that man had done to us; he should have known he could talk to me! I opened my mouth, about to shout at him, but his expression stopped me. He looked so sad, guilty, and actually a little scared. I pulled out of Liam's arms and hugged Johnny tightly. God, he had been abused by the man of my nightmares too, I shouldn't be angry with him, he didn't need that on top of everything else.

Suddenly, everything made sense to me; he never liked to talk about him either. When I asked him if he got on well with him, he always looked really uncomfortable. He was so tense when I was at his house last week when he saw my father.

"You could have talked to me," I whispered, feeling the tears fall down my face slowly, grieving because I knew exactly what he had been through and how he was feeling right now. At least I had Jake and Liam to look after me then; but Johnny was the eldest, he probably felt like he was the one protecting his mom and brother.

Johnny hugged me back. "I didn't want to upset you; we've been planning all week. Jake and Liam helped us pack up our stuff today while he was at work. He's away for the weekend. He's not due back until Sunday morning."

I pulled back and kissed his cheek. "Everything's OK now. Don't worry, he can't hurt you anymore," I said sternly. I turned and hugged Ruby even though I didn't even know her; she just looked like she needed a hug right now. The baby in her arms was gorgeous; he looked just like her, but with blond hair.

"You alright, Ambs?" Jake asked, concern colouring his voice.

I gulped noisily. I was feeling sick actually. I guess I was a little overwhelmed by everything. I couldn't actually take everything in. "Actually, I feel a little strange," I admitted, rubbing a hand over my face.

"Angel, you look a little pale. Do you want a drink or something?" Liam asked, walking towards me.

Damn, I was so hot! My lips and fingers were tingling; I started to feel a little dizzy.

Chapter 20

I was vaguely aware of an annoying beeping noise; my head was pounding and throbbing on one side. I squeezed my eyes shut trying to make the pain go.

"Angel?" Liam said from near my head.

I groaned and turned my head towards his voice. I felt terrible, like I was in some kind of bubble. I finally opened my eyes to see him leaning over me, looking gorgeous as always, except right now he looked stressed. He was frowning, his was jaw tight.

"Hey," I croaked, trying to smile and ignore the pain in my head.

"Thank God. You scared me." He bent his head and kissed my forehead softly, seeming to breathe a sigh of relief.

"OK. If I could just get in and have a look," a female voice said sternly.

I glanced around and had no idea where I was. I was on a little bed, all strapped in. This was a little room of some sort with shelves and cupboards all along the walls - except we were moving; I could feel the vibrations from the road.

Liam moved to the side and a lady in a green jumpsuit leaned over me. "Hi, Amber. How are you feeling?" she asked, shining a little light in my eyes.

I pushed her hand off of me, looking for Liam again. "Where am I?" I asked, panicking slightly. How the hell did I get here? I was in the kitchen, then I felt a little sick....

"You're in an ambulance, sweetie. You passed out and hit your head pretty hard on the kitchen counter," she explained, taking my hands and putting them down on my chest. "I just need to check you over. You've been unconscious for about twenty minutes." She flicked the light into my eyes again, nodding, seeming satisfied.

"Does your head hurt?" she asked, touching behind my ear lightly. Pain shot through my head and I hissed through my teeth. "I think you'll need a couple of stitches here," she stated, nodding to the side of my head.

I reached out a hand to Liam. He immediately took it, and kissed my fingers, his eyes not leaving my face. He looked really stressed. After another couple of minutes we pulled into the hospital and they started to wheel me out on the little bed.

"I can walk," I protested, feeling stupid for being wheeled into the hospital on a bed.

"Sorry, sweetie, it's standard practice. You arrive with lights, you go in on a bed," she countered, winking at me. I smiled weakly and Liam laughed, but it wasn't his usual laugh, it was tight and humourless.

We were wheeled into a little cubical and left on our own. "What happened, Angel?" Liam asked, bending over me and brushing his hand over the side of my face softly.

I shrugged and then winced as the movement made my head hurt again. "I don't know. I just felt a little dizzy, then I woke up to you in the ambulance," I explained. That was all I could remember.

"You scared the shit out of me. Don't ever do that to me again. Promise me," he instructed, making me giggle at just how serious he was. He wanted me to promise him that I'd never pass out again?

"Liam, I can't promise something that I have no control over," I teased, still laughing. He sighed and bent forward, kissing me lightly, setting my body on fire. He pulled back when the curtain opened and a doctor walked in.

"Oops, sorry. Shall I come back later?" the doctor asked, grinning. I laughed, embarrassed to have been caught making out in a hospital.

"Yeah, could you give us five minutes?" Liam joked, making the guy laugh. He held my hand tightly as the Doctor looked in my eyes and checked my head, scribbling on his pad.

"So, you passed out, Amber, have you been feeling alright today? Have you taken anything that you shouldn't have?" he asked, watching me a little suspiciously.

"Like drugs or something?" I asked, shocked. Did I look like a damn drug addict? He nodded, looking at me expectantly. "No, I haven't taken anything. I've been feeling a little off today, a bit queasy," I admitted.

He scribbled again. "Have you eaten?"

I thought about it - had I eaten? I had some toast for breakfast, but I didn't eat lunch because I felt sick. "Um, not really. I felt sick at lunch."

"Hmm, that's probably your problem right there. Are you under any sort of stress or anything at the moment? Doing exams, that kind of thing?" he asked, scribbling again.

Stress. Wow, that's an understatement. My abusive father moved back to town, bringing with him a whole new family. A week ago I saw him again for the first time since he tried to force himself on me. I found out just now that he's been abusing his new family and they're now moving in with us for a while. Actually, how long were they staying with us? Did someone mention that? I'd have to get Johnny in with Jake, and Ruby and Matt can share my mom's room, then when my mom comes home I could....

"Amber?" the doctor said, snapping me out of my own little world.

"Oh right. Um, yeah, life's been kind of stressful lately," I stated, biting my lip at just how much of an understatement that really was.

"Well, stress can do funny things to you. You really need to eat properly. I'm going to run some bloods to make sure there's nothing else going on. I'll get someone to come in and stitch your head and I'll keep you in for a couple of hours just to check everything's alright after that bump," he stated, smiling kindly.

He went to the cupboard and pulled out a needle. I looked at Liam with wide eyes. I hated needles. When the doctor came over to me, Liam bent his head and kissed me.

I closed my eyes and melted my lips against his. Jeez, he tasted so damn good!

"OK, all done. I'll get these sent up they should be back in an hour or so," the doctor announced, throwing the needle in the trash and writing on a little vial. I glanced down at my arm to see a little piece of white tape holding a cotton wool ball to the inside of my elbow.

"Did you do it?" I asked, shocked. Wow, I didn't even feel it!

The doctor and Liam laughed. "Yep, all done. Ah, the power of distraction," the doctor mused, grinning. I smiled at Liam; I'd have to take him with me for every shot I ever get from now on.

"OK, so a nurse will be in to stitch your head in a few minutes. You'll probably be here for two or three hours," he said, heading over to the curtain.

I nodded. "Can my boyfriend stay with me?" I asked hopefully as I clung to Liam's hand. I didn't want to be in this sterile little place on my own.

"Sure, that's fine. Just one visitor though, so you might want to tell the crowd asking about you, to go home," he suggested, chuckling as he left and pulled the curtain back around.

Crowd, what's that about? I looked at Liam, he smiled. "They all came. I literally had to push Jake out of the ambulance when they said only one person could ride with you," he said, looking a little guilty about it.

I smiled and squeezed his hand. "Well I'm glad I woke up to you instead of Jake. So thanks."

He bent his head and kissed me lightly. "I'm glad too." He sighed. "I'd better go and tell them you're fine, and that they should go home," he said, standing up.

"Hurry up though, OK?" I asked, giving him my begging face.

He smiled. "I'll be as quick as I can," he promised, kissing my forehead and leaving quickly. I closed my eyes and listened to the noisy ward and waited for him to come back.

Liam was back within five minutes with a pre-packed sandwich and a drink. "Hey, I'm not sure if you're allowed these yet, so you'll have to wait until the nurse comes to stitch your head. I didn't miss that, did I?" he asked worriedly.

"No, you didn't miss it." I smiled at how thoughtful he was all the time.

He sat down on the little chair and held my hand. The nurse came in a few minutes later and stitched up my head, apparently, I needed six stitches. I made Liam distract me the whole time, he was actually the best painkiller known to man. Maybe I should try to bottle him somehow, and then sell it. I'd be rich!

Finally, after an hour and a half, the doctor came back. "Hey, so I've got your blood test results back and it appears it wasn't the lack of food that made you pass out," he said, looking at me seriously. Liam tensed next to me, squeezing my hand, leaning so far forward in his chair that it wouldn't surprise me if he fell off any second.

"OK, so what was it?" I asked curiously. It couldn't be anything bad. I was only sixteen for goodness sake, I didn't smoke, didn't drink very much, I wasn't overweight, I exercised regularly. I mean, I shouldn't be able to get ill, should I?

"You're pregnant," he stated.

I burst out laughing. Damn, that was funny, he almost had me there. I shook my head, still chuckling. "Seriously, what was it?"

He looked from me to Liam. "You're pregnant," he repeated.

I stopped laughing immediately. I couldn't be pregnant. No, this was a mistake. "I can't be, I'm on the pill. I've taken it every day; I've not missed a single one. I take them at exactly eight o'clock every morning," I protested, shaking my head, it had to be something else. I looked at Liam; he was looking at the doctor, his mouth hanging open.

"Well, when was your last period?" the doctor asked.

I looked at Liam again. "Two weeks ago. I'm on the pill where you stop taking it for a week, so it was definitely two weeks ago. I'm due to have my next one the week after next," I said positively.

"And your period, what was it like? As heavy as normal?" the doctor asked, scribbling on his pad again.

As heavy as normal? I thought about it. Actually, it was really light, but that was because I was on the pill, Kate said it made your periods lighter. "It was light but I definitely had one, two weeks ago. I can't be pregnant," I said sternly.

"Sometimes you can still have very light periods through pregnancy. It's called spotting. How long have you been on the pill?" he asked curiously.

"Six weeks," I replied, quietly.

This couldn't be right. Please tell me this is some kind of huge mistake, or even one of those hidden camera shows and people are going to jump out and shout 'Gotcha' any minute.

"And when you started taking it, did you take it on the first day of your period?" he asked.

I shook my head. "It was a couple of weeks after my period. What difference does that make?" I asked, starting to get nervous.

"Right, well, when you start taking the pill you need to start on the first day of your period and then it will be effective straight away. If you take it within five days, it will be effective after two weeks, but if you start on any other day then you need to start your second packet before it takes effect," he explained softly.

So that means it didn't even start to work until two weeks ago when I started my second pack and we had been having unprotected sex the whole time! Liam was still staring at him. He hadn't said anything at all, I wasn't even sure if he was breathing. He was sitting so still that it was like he was a statue.

"I'm going to get a portable ultrasound machine and we'll have a little look, OK?" the doctor suggested, smiling kindly as he disappeared out of the curtain.

"Liam?" I whispered. He was honestly scaring me a little, I'd never seen anyone be so still in my life, it wasn't natural. He didn't answer. The doctor came back and I watched as he squirted some gel on my stomach and pressed a little thing that looked like a small microphone to my stomach, rolling it around.

Oh crap, please let this be a mistake.

He stopped, holding it still and nodded. "Yep, definitely pregnant. I'd say from the sizes here, you're about four, maybe five weeks. You want to see?" he offered, holding the little handset out to me.

"No," I refused, pushing it away quickly.

I didn't want to see because then I wouldn't be able to do what needed to be done. I couldn't have a baby, we were too young, it would ruin everything. We'd only just got together; there was too much going on. Liam would be leaving me for college soon, we couldn't have a baby. I wouldn't ruin Liam's dreams, he'd always wanted to play hockey and I wouldn't take that away from him. I couldn't look at the little handset; I couldn't see the little baby in there because I needed to stay strong.

"You don't want to see?" the doctor asked, looking a little confused.

I shook my head. "No. I want an abortion," I said sternly.

Liam moved. Oh thank God, finally!

"An abortion? What? Why?" he cried, shocked.

I looked at him; he was looking at me, horrified, as if I'd just suggested clubbing a seal or something. "Because it needs to be done," I said, looking away from his intense stare. I turned to the doctor. "Can I get it done today? What do I need to do?" I asked, nervously.

"Well, there's two ways; a medical abortion, which is a pill today and tomorrow, which would basically bring on a period. Or there's a surgical one which would need to be done under general anaesthetic and we would basically remove everything," he explained in his business like tone.

I cringed. I hated the sound of both of those, but I needed to do this. I couldn't think of it as a baby, a tiny little Liam, because otherwise I wouldn't be able to get rid of it.

"Can you give us a minute?" Liam requested. The doctor nodded and walked out quickly. "Angel, what the hell are you doing?" Liam asked once we were alone. He took my hands, looking at me like I had lost my mind or something.

"Liam, we can't have a baby! I'm sixteen. You're going to college. We can't," I explained, shaking my head.

He shook his head. "Angel, think about this, please? I love you,

you love me. I want us to have kids one day. I mean, shit, this is A LOT sooner than I thought." He blew out a big breath, running a hand through his hair, nervously.

"Liam, we can't. You're going to college in Boston for goodness sake; I can't raise a baby on my own. Don't be ridiculous!" I cried, shaking my head. He wasn't thinking this though properly.

He climbed onto the bed, laying next to me. "Angel, just hear me out, OK?" he pleaded. I nodded and looked at him, unable to see what he could say to make this right. There was nothing he could suggest, there *was* no other way. "I love you more than anything in the world. Before this happened I was going to reject my scholarship and go to a college here instead," he started. I opened my mouth to tell him he was being stupid, but he covered my mouth, looking at me pleadingly. "I wanted to ask you to come with me to Boston. But I can't ask you to move away from your home and Jake and your friends, so I decided to stay here with you instead," he said, shrugging.

Jeez, he is so damn adorable and sweet and thoughtful. But how the hell does any of this relate to us having a baby, meaning that he probably wouldn't get to go to college anyway as he'd have to drop out and get a job? I'd have to drop out of school without even graduating.

He smiled as he continued to try and convince me. "We could make this work; I know my mom would help out. I'll go to college and get a job in the evenings and weekends to earn some money. You'd have to either finish school by correspondence, or we could get a childminder so you could go to school. Or maybe even my mom would do it," he suggested, looking at me hopefully. "That's our first baby in there, Angel. That's a baby that we made together. Can you just think about it, please? It'll be hard for a little while, but once I get signed by a team, I'll be able to give you anything you want. Both of you," he cooed, rubbing his hand over my stomach lightly.

"Liam, I don't want to ruin your future," I whispered.

He smiled and kissed me lightly. "Angel, *you're* my future," he countered, slipping his hand under my top, and placing his hand on my stomach.

I looked at his gorgeous face; his blue eyes were sparkling with love as he stroked his hand across my stomach. "I didn't do this to trap you," I said nervously.

He laughed and rolled his eyes. "You trapped me when you were four years old. You were wearing a dark blue dress with a bow on the back, and little white socks. The first time I saw you I was trapped. This," he drew a little pattern on my stomach with one finger, "this is a bonus. Sure, I wasn't expecting it for about five or six years, but still…. it's a bonus," he said, grinning.

Could we really do that? He would stay here with me? "Would you really stay with me here and give up your scholarship?" I asked a little shocked. He worked so damn hard for that scholarship, it was such an awesome opportunity, and he would give it up for me and a baby?

He smiled. "Angel, if you want to get rid of the baby because you don't want it, then I could understand, but don't do this for me. I *want* to stay here with you. If you weren't pregnant I'd still be turning down the offer," he vowed, scooting closer to me on the bed, wrapping his arms around me.

I buried my face into his chest and closed my eyes; I wanted to have kids with him one day too. I could see myself holding a little baby that had Liam's blue eyes and messy hair. Granted, when I pictured it I was a lot older than I am now, but I could still see it, and I liked it. Maybe we could make this work. The baby wouldn't be short on love, and once people got over the shock of it, they'd understand. I had no doubt in my mind that Liam's mom would help out too. And Jake, once he got over the initial anger of everything, he'd be a great Uncle.

Liam pulled away from me slightly. "I swear I'd be the best dad in the world," he promised.

I smiled; I didn't doubt that for a second. I kissed his lips, wrapping my arms around his neck, pulling him closer. I loved him so much, more than anything. I knew we could make it work, a little family. He pulled out of the kiss to look at me with a hopeful expression on his face.

"OK," I agreed.

He grinned and kissed me again, moving so he was half on top of me. I noticed he put none of his weight on my stomach, he was being super gentle. He kissed down my neck, getting lower and lower. He hitched my top and kissed all over my stomach before pulling up to smile at me.

"I love you," he whispered.

I pulled him closer to me. "I love you too, baby daddy," I teased, making him laugh.

He wrapped his arms around me, laying close to my side. I rested my head on his chest and I listened to his heart beat flying as I slipped one hand down my body, resting it on my tummy, rubbing my fingertips over it lightly.

I kissed Liam's chest. How the hell could such an adorable, gorgeous, sweet, kind, funny, talented and responsible boy, want me? How could he love me as much as I can see he does? I couldn't help but smile. Laying in Liam's arms, I actually felt like the luckiest girl in the world. I got to have a baby with the man I love.

After a couple of hours I was discharged. Apparently, Liam was to wake me up every hour to make sure I didn't have concussion or anything. We'd agreed not to tell anyone about the baby yet. It was so early and we were only just getting our heads around it - we didn't need any interference from anyone else.

"Shall we call a cab or something?" I asked as Liam walked me out of the hospital, holding me tightly to his side.

He grinned. He'd been doing that a lot for the last couple of hours; I actually think he was really excited about being a dad which I had never seen on an eighteen year old before.

"No. Jake left us his car. He went home with Johnny and gave me his keys," he explained, guiding me to the parking lot. He helped me into the car, even putting on my seatbelt for me. His hand lingered over my stomach as he pulled it away.

My head was pounding; the painkillers they gave me were starting to wear off. I rested my head back against the headrest and closed my eyes. It was going to be hard lying to Jake. I hated lying and was actually really terrible at it, but it needed to be done for a few weeks. We just needed to let the whole abusive father thing settle down first, that would give us a chance to sort out everything in our own heads. I still had the money from the bet, I hadn't spent any of it yet so that would help with all of the things we needed to buy for having a baby.

When we pulled up at my house, I didn't even get out of the car before Jake attacked me into a hug. "Shit, you scared the hell out of everyone, Amber!" he scolded.

I smiled and hugged him back. "Sorry, Jake. I didn't exactly plan to pass out in front of everyone and bang my head, did I?" I replied sarcastically as I rolled my eyes. Why the hell is he mad at me for getting sick?

He sighed and pulled back. "So, what did they say? Why did you pass out in the first place?" he asked, looking concerned.

Oh crap, what do I say?

"Stress apparently. That, and she hadn't eaten all day," Liam interjected, coming round to my side. I silently thanked God that Liam was better liar than I was.

Jake looked at me, clearly annoyed again. "Why the hell didn't you eat all day?" he asked accusingly.

I smiled and let Liam lead me in to the house. "Let's just get her in and let her sit down, Jake, then you can shout at her all you like," Liam suggested, shaking his head with a small smile.

Jake followed us in and sat next to me on the sofa, Johnny and Ruby came and sat down too. Everyone was looking at me worriedly. "Stop worrying, guys. It was lack of food, apparently. Sugar low or something. I'm fine now, honestly," I assured them, nodding, trying not to look too guilty. I just hoped that Jake didn't go too crazy when he found out, and that he didn't beat the crap out of Liam or something. Maybe I would tell him on my own, calm him down a little before he saw Liam.

"The bang to her head needed stitches. I need to wake her up every hour to make sure she's OK, so I'll be staying over tonight," Liam stated, more for Ruby's benefit than anyone else's, Jake already knew he'd be there anyway.

I yawned. It was almost nine now and I just wanted to go to bed, it had been a long stressful day. "I'm going to bed, guys. Oh, and Ruby, it really is nice to meet you again. I'm sorry I didn't get a chance to talk to you properly earlier," I said, smiling apologetically.

She chuckled slightly. "We'll talk tomorrow, honey, don't worry. If you need anything in the night then let me know. Jake said I could sleep in your mom's room, just so you know where I am, alright?" she asked kindly.

Wow, she really is nice!

"OK. G'night, guys. And you, lover boy, go get your stuff if you're staying here," I instructed, smiling at Liam.

He stood up quickly. "OK. I'll be back in a bit then." He kissed my forehead gently before heading for the front door to tell his parents he was 'officially' staying over.

I went to my bedroom and looked at myself in the mirror. My hair was a mess, I had a plaster thing stuck behind my ear over the stitches, I looked tired but I couldn't help but smile. I didn't bother with pyjamas as I slipped into the bed; I wanted to feel Liam's skin against mine. After about fifteen minutes he came in, looking so handsome that it made me want to cry. I rubbed my hand over my stomach lightly under the sheets. I hoped I had a little boy in there, and he would be just like his daddy.

Liam stripped down to his boxers and climbed in the bed with me. He gasped suddenly and pulled back to look at me. "Are you naked?" he asked, a little shocked.

I smiled. "Yep. I thought you should make the most of me before I get all fat and ugly," I teased.

He grinned and rolled on top of me, hovering above me, barely touching me. "Angel, you will never be ugly," he whispered, looking at me adoringly. "And the bigger you get, just means I have more of you to love," he added, slipping his hand down to my stomach. I smiled as I pulled his mouth down to mine.

Having Johnny, Matt and Ruby stay with us was actually awesome. Ruby made pancakes on Saturday morning, and I spent the day chatting to her and playing with my gorgeous little brother. She was planning on staying in town because Johnny didn't want to change schools again.

Kate came over in the afternoon, and Johnny *finally* asked her to be exclusive - which she obviously jumped at. They were so sweet, being all cuddly and flirty. Kate would say stuff that would make Johnny blush. He was just too innocent - but knowing Kate he wouldn't be that way for too long if she had her way. Liam kept shooting me little knowing smiles and would touch my belly at every single opportunity.

On Sunday, Ruby, Johnny, Kate and Matt went to the zoo for the day. They wanted to get out and do something to take Ruby's mind off of the fact that my father was due home from his business trip today. He would come home to find the note that she left him, and that all of their stuff was gone from his house. She had gotten rid of their phone numbers and bought new sim cards for their cellphones so he had no way of contacting them or knowing where they were. But sitting around worrying about it wasn't helping anyone, so they wanted to do something to keep them occupied.

I was sat on the sofa, reading, with my legs on Liam's lap while he played PlayStation with Jake, when the phone rang. I moved to get it but Jake got there first. As he answered it his whole body tensed up. "What the hell do you want?" he growled, jumping off of the sofa. I sat up so fast that it almost made my head spin. "Are you fucking drunk?" he almost screamed down the phone. I watched him, feeling sick, knowing that my father was on the phone. "Yeah, so what? What are you gonna do about it, old man?" Jake spat, going red with anger. "We don't want to see you, so fuck off. No. She doesn't want to see you. I swear, if you come near her again I'll kill you," he growled, turning his back to me. "Actually, you know what, screw it, come over, come over right now. We're home, come on over and let's talk about it," Jake suggested.

What the hell is he doing? "Jake?" I cried, scared.

"Sure. You remember where the house is, right? Absolutely. See you in a bit," Jake said, hanging up and throwing the phone across the room. Luckily it landed with a thump on the other sofa and didn't break. Did he just tell him to come over?

"Jake, he's not...." I trailed off, unable to finish the sentence.

Jake turned back to look at me, his face hard. "Yeah. Go next door," he instructed.

I looked at Liam for help. He was looking at Jake; he had the same hard expression on his face. "Liam, tell him this is stupid!" I whispered, with tears falling down my face. Liam didn't look at me; Jake and him were locked in some sort of silent exchange with their eyes. I jumped off of the sofa and grabbed the phone planning on calling him back to cancel it. I couldn't let him come here, not with those two looking like that.

Jake pulled the phone out of my hands. "He's not going to stop harassing you, Ambs. He wants to see you. He's also really angry that Ruby's left him. He knows that I helped them; a neighbour saw my car in the drive. He's seriously pissed at me, so I just need to tell him to back the fuck off," he said, pulling me into a hug.

I shook my head, that wasn't what he was planning at all, they weren't going to *tell* him anything, Jake and Liam were going to beat him senseless and *show* him to back the fuck off.

"Please don't, you'll get in trouble. Please?" I whispered. My insides were squirming with dread.

"Not if he starts something first," Jake replied, fighting a smile.

Chapter 21

~ Liam ~

Crap, this was bad. The first thing that shot through my brain was that I needed to keep Jake under control. Sure, I wanted to kill that asshole as much as he did, but we seriously needed to be careful. If we literally jumped him as soon as he walked in, we'd be liable, and I'd promised his mom I wouldn't let him do that. I wouldn't let Jake go to jail for that asshole, Angel needed her big brother, especially now with the baby coming. The second thing that sprung to mind was that I needed to get my girl and my baby the hell out of here, now.

"Angel, let's go, I'll take you to mine," I stated, grabbing her hand and pulling her away from Jake.

She wrenched her hand out of mine and glared at me. "I'm not going anywhere! I won't let you do this, either of you. You can't beat the crap out of him, you'll get in trouble. You're being freaking stupid!" she shouted. Tears rolled down her face as she spoke.

"Angel, you need to leave, *now*," I ordered. She wasn't staying here near that man, no way, because if he even looked at her the wrong way I wouldn't be able to restrain myself, let alone keeping Jake under control.

She shook her head fiercely. She always had been stubborn, usually I loved that about her - but not right now I didn't. Fine, if she wants it that way then screw it. I grabbed her, wrapping her in my arms, lifting her bridal style. "Liam, don't you dare!" she shouted, her face getting red with anger as she struggled to get down. I shook my head, I'd deal with her anger later, she wouldn't stay mad at me for long and a night of the silent treatment would be totally worth it, just so I knew she was completely safe. She started sobbing and wrapped her arms around my neck as I carried her out of the house.

Damn it, she was killing me! I hated to see her cry.

I kissed the side of her head. "Shh, everything's going to be fine, I promise. I just need to you safe so I can concentrate on keeping Jake calm, OK?" I said honestly.

We reached my house and I opened the door quickly, heading over to the sofa. I sat down and held her on my lap, rocking her gently. "Please don't get in trouble, Liam, please," she begged, hugging me tighter.

"I won't. I need to go next door now. You stay here; don't come over until I come to get you. You understand? Can you do that for me?" I asked desperately.

She sniffed and pulled away without looking at me. "Just go then," she snapped angrily, moving off of my lap to sit on the sofa. She really didn't like this at all.

I groaned, hating her angry expression.

"I love you, Angel. I just need you and our baby safe," I explained as I kissed her cheek, rubbing my hand over her flat stomach. I fought the urge to smile thinking of my baby growing inside her, that lucky little baby gets to be closer to her than anyone for the next eight months. She nodded and closed her eyes; silent tears were still falling down her face.

I stood up and turned to leave. "Liam?" she called just as I got to the door. I turned back, hoping for a smile. "I love you too. If you get sent to jail for murder then I'll wait for you," she stated with no emotion in her voice at all. It wasn't a joke; she really thought I was going to jail.

I didn't answer, I just left. There was no answer for that. She was seriously annoyed with me and I would have a lot to make up for after this. I'd never done anything that she didn't want before and I hated doing it now.

I ran back to Jake's. He was pacing in the lounge, looking murderously angry. "Jake, you need to listen to me," I said, grabbing his shoulder and making him face me.

"I know, I know. I can't do anything unless he starts anything. I just want to talk to him and tell him to get the fuck out of our lives, but if he comes near me, I swear...." He gritted his teeth. He didn't need to finish the sentence, I already knew what he would do and it wouldn't be painless either.

After about ten minutes a car pulled up outside. I grabbed Jake's arm as he jumped up from the sofa. "Calm the fuck down, Jake. Understand?" I ordered. He nodded and I headed to the door. I opened it and the asshole stood there looking at me angrily. My hands were itching to choke the life out of him. I hadn't seen him since we threw him out of the door followed by all of his stuff, three years ago, but he looked exactly the same as I remembered.

"Liam James, you've grown a bit, huh?" he stated, sneering as he looked me over.

"Stephen Walker, you stopped molesting young girls?" I countered, my hand squeezing the door handle so tightly that my fingers were hurting.

He glared at me and pushed past into the house. "Where the fuck are Jake and Amber?" he asked angrily.

"I'm here. And Amber's out," Jake said calmly. Maybe he was going to be calm after all.

"You little shit! You always were fucking trouble! Where the fuck is my wife and son? And I'm taking Amber with me too," Stephen shouted, heading towards the hallway at the back. I could feel my anger rising every time he said my Angel's name. I took a couple of deep breaths; I needed to be the strong one.

Jake started to laugh. "Yeah, OK," he said sarcastically. I think he was trying to goad his father into starting something. I think he was planning on letting him get a couple of hits in first so he could say it was self-defence.

"Where are they?" Stephen practically screamed. He always did have a bad temper.

"I'm telling you now, old man, that if you ever come near my sister again, I'll kill you," Jake growled. "Do you understand me? You need to leave town. Now. There's nothing left here for you now. Ruby doesn't want you either, no one wants you," he spat.

He smiled slightly as Stephen stepped closer to him with his fists clenched. "This is all your fucking fault! You and Amber had to open your filthy mouths and tell Johnny about what happened. You've ruined everything for me, everything, you worthless piece of shit. I should have fucking pushed your mother down the stairs or something when she told me she was pregnant with you," Stephen shouted angrily.

Damn it, he was an asshole!

Jake grabbed him and slammed him against the wall, knocking his breath out of him.

Crap! I grabbed Jake just as he was about to punch him and pulled him away. "Not like this! Jake, not like this," I shouted, trying to restrain him.

"Let me go! I'm gonna fucking kill him. Liam, let me go!" Jake screamed, trying to throw me off of him.

"Jake, calm down!" I heard Amber say.

My blood went cold at the sound of her voice. What the hell was she doing here? We all turned to see her standing in the doorway. I let go of Jake quickly and went to go to her, but that asshole was between me and her. He grabbed her wrist. She flinched and tried to pull her arm out of his hold.

"You! You fucking ruined everything!" he screamed at her.

"Let her go, now!" I growled through my gritted teeth, barely able to contain my anger. I could hear my heart beat drumming in my ears; I was so angry that my hands were shaking. I was going to kill him in three seconds if he didn't let her go.

He turned to look at me, hate clear across his face. "Fuck you! She's my daughter," he shouted, yanking her roughly closer to him. She turned and tried to push him away. His face turned hard. I lunged forward at the same time he slapped her hard across the face.

I grabbed his shirt and punched him full in the face, enjoying the satisfying crack his nose made as my fist connected with it. I pulled back my arm and punched him again and again, ignoring the pain each blow caused in my hand. After the fourth or fifth punch his body was going a little limp so I shoved him against the wall so I didn't have to hold him up, and punched him over and over. I put all of my hate into it, all the anger and hurt and helplessness that I'd ever felt when I would watch my girl cry herself to sleep. I would never let this man hurt her again. He slumped to the floor, wrapping his arms around his head, but I didn't stop, I couldn't stop. So I started kicking him instead.

Suddenly, Jake grabbed me from behind and slammed me face first into the wall. What the hell is he doing?

"No! I'm not done! Get the hell off me. Jake, get off!" I shouted, trying desperately to get him off of me so I could kill the man that made my Angel's life a misery. I shoved myself away from the wall trying to get free.

"Amber's hurt, Liam," Jake said, shoving me back against the wall again, his arm across the back of my neck.

"Just get off me. Let me finish it!" I cried, still struggling against his hold.

"LIAM, AMBER'S HURT!" Jake shouted.

Wait, what did he say? Amber? Oh my God.

"What? Where? Where is she?" I asked desperately. I didn't see her get hurt, he slapped her and she fell and all I could see was him. Shit! He let go of me and I turned to look for her, she was laying on her side, curled into a ball, her eyes squeezed shut, her jaw tight, her whole face was the picture of pain. I felt sick as I ran to her side, bending over her quickly. "Angel?" I whispered, bending over and stroking her red cheek where he had slapped her.

She whimpered and tried to move, making a strangled gasping noise. "It hurts, Liam. Please, it hurts so much," she cried, looking at me desperately. She looked terrified; she looked so scared that I felt like my heart would stop beating at the sight of it.

"What hurts, Angel?" I asked, trying to sooth her as I bent and kissed her sore cheek. I needed to get her some ice or something then it would be alright, she'd have a wicked bruise for a week or so but it'd be alright.

"My stomach," she croaked, sobbing, turning her face into the floor, crying hysterically.

Her stomach hurts? I looked down at her stomach, she was cradling it protectively. I could see blood seeping down the leg of her jeans. My heart stopped, I couldn't breathe. All I could see was the blood, all I could hear was her sobbing and whimpering.

~ Amber ~

I heard the car pull up so I jumped up and ran to the window. I flinched as I saw him get out of the car and stalk angrily towards the house. I felt sick. I couldn't let them do this; they were going to get in so much trouble. I couldn't bear to lose either of them. I didn't want Jake to get in trouble, but it seriously would kill me if Liam was in trouble for this.

I bit my lip, thinking. Maybe I could just go over and be another witness, then that way when he starts something first I could say it was self-defence too. Another witness would definitely help their case. Oh crap, Liam is going to kill me for this! I ran out of his house towards mine. I could hear shouting coming from inside and I stopped, I felt the familiar fear that I always felt when I was a child. I couldn't move from the spot, it was like I was frozen. I could hear his voice, shouting, and my blood ran cold - but that was Jake and Liam in there, they were always looking out for me, always. I could do this for them, all I had to do was witness him throwing the first punch.

I crept to the door; it wasn't shut, just pushed to. "This is all your fucking fault! You and Amber had to open your filthy mouths and tell Johnny about what happened. You've ruined everything for me, everything, you worthless piece of shit. I should have fucking pushed your mother down the stairs or something when she told me she was pregnant with you!" my father shouted angrily.

I whimpered because of the horrible words he'd just spoken to my brother. My father always was a nasty piece of work, but that was low even for him.

I heard a bang and a groan, so I pushed open the door, to see Liam holding Jake, trying desperately to keep Jake away from my father who was standing up against the wall looking at them angrily. "Not like this! Jake, not like this!" Liam shouted, at Jake as he thrashed in his arms.

Jake wasn't calming down. His face was red with anger, the only thing that could stop him when he was like that, was me. He hated to see me upset or anything, he was so overprotective.

"Jake, calm down!" I pleaded desperately.

He stopped moving, and Liam pushed him away, looking at me shocked and a little scared. He moved towards me and I saw my father move at the same time, he was so much closer to me than Liam, and he was blocking Liam's path. I didn't even have time to move away before he grabbed my wrist, squeezing hard, his face angry and red. I flinched as he squeezed harder making pain shoot up my arm. I tried to pull my arm away quickly, but he wouldn't let go.

"You! You fucking ruined everything!" he screamed at me, digging his fingernails into my skin. I couldn't breathe.

"Let her go, now," Liam ordered, looking so angry that it actually scared me.

My father turned to face him, still holding me tightly. "Fuck you! She's my daughter," he spat, pulling on my arm, making me lose my footing and stumble closer to him. I could smell the alcohol on his breath, making me feel sick. I twisted and pulled on my arm, trying to get free. He still didn't let go so I put my hand on his chest and shoved him as hard as I could. He didn't budge an inch. I saw his hand move and I closed my eyes knowing he was going to hit me.

His hand connected with my face, making me feel like my whole head had exploded. I fell back and crashed into the sideboard. Pain like I had never felt in my life shot up through my stomach and lower back. It was like someone had stabbed me. I clutched onto the sideboard, trying to stay on my feet as I hissed through my teeth. Jake ran over and grabbed me pulling me down onto the floor, sitting us down, leaning against the sideboard.

"Shit. Ambs, are you OK?" he asked desperately, cradling my head to his chest.

I wrapped my arms around my stomach, trying to breathe through the pain. "No," I croaked. Oh no, I was losing the baby! "Liam? Where's Liam?" I asked, opening my eyes and looking round for him, but I could barely see anything because my eyes were filled with tears. I could hear a grunting and groaning noise. Oh God, he's not...... Please tell me he not doing that! I blinked and looked over to see Liam punching my father over and over; his face was the picture of rage. He wasn't going to stop until he was no longer breathing. This was it. Liam was going to be taken away from me and I was losing his baby. I felt my heart breaking into a million pieces.

"Go stop him," I whispered, barely able to talk.

"No. Let him kill him," Jake growled angrily.

I shook my head. Oh God, please! "Jake, go stop him! For me, please? I need him. Tell him I'm hurt. I need him," I gasped as a wave of nausea washed over me, making me retch. "Liam?" I called desperately, but it was barely above a whisper.

Jake moved. "I'll get him," he said quickly as he jumped up. I rolled onto my side, pulling my knees up to my chest, holding my stomach. Oh please don't let me lose this baby! I squeezed my eyes shut against the pain; a couple of seconds later Liam stroked my cheek making it sting again.

"Angel?" he whispered, sounding so concerned it was breaking my heart all over again. How could I tell him I was losing the baby? He was so happy about it, how the hell could I say the words? I wanted to wrap my arms around him and have him hold me and make all this go away. Liam could make this OK, he could make everything OK.

I moved to get up but a fresh wave of pain hit me, making me gasp. "It hurts, Liam. Please, it hurts so much," I mumbled, looking up at this perfect face. He looked so worried about me. I was losing everything. He was going to be in jail and I would be on my own. How was I going to live without him?

"What hurts, Angel?" he asked, as he bent his head and kissed my cheek.

"My stomach." I couldn't look at his face when he realised I was losing the baby, I didn't want to see the hurt and devastation there. I turned my face into the carpet and sobbed. This was entirely my fault. I should have just stayed at his house like he told me to. If I was there now then baby would be safe, and Liam wouldn't be facing jail. He had only hit my father because I was there, he wouldn't have done that if I had just stayed. Why couldn't I have just stayed there like he told me?

"Jake! Call an ambulance!" Liam shouted desperately. He was stroking the back of my head gently. "Shh, everything's OK. It's OK, Angel," he cooed. I felt his arm wrap around me, so I turned my head back towards him. He was laying next to me. How the hell is he still comforting me? This is all my fault - why is he not shouting at me?

"I'm so sorry," I said honestly. This was going ruin everything; he wouldn't want me now that I'd killed our baby.

He bent his head and kissed my forehead. "Angel, you have nothing to be sorry for," he whispered, moving closer to me. His hand rubbed circles on my stomach, so softly that I could barely even feel it.

"This is my fault," I cried, sobbing again. He shook his head fiercely and pushed himself away from me. I felt my heart breaking. I knew it; he was going to leave me now. He got up and moved over to my father who was trying to get up off of the floor and started punching him again, shouting a string of expletives.

Jake tackled him to the floor. "Stop it! Go to Amber, now!" he ordered, looking at him angrily.

Liam nodded and ran back to me. "I'm gonna pick you up, OK?" he said softly.

I shook my head, I didn't want to move. "No, don't. Please don't," I whispered. The pain was so bad that I felt sick. He looked like he was in pain too as he fussed over me, brushing my hair away from my face, kissing me gently, murmuring soothing words.

"Where's the freaking ambulance?" he screamed at Jake.

"On its way. What's wrong with her?" Jake asked, kneeling at my side. I squeezed Liam's hand, not wanting to see them fighting about it if Jake freaked out about the baby.

"She's pregnant, Jake," Liam explained, kissing my cheek.

"P.... pregnant?" Jake stuttered. Liam nodded, looking at me worriedly.

"I'm gonna make you pay for this, you little shit!" my father shouted from the door. Jake and Liam both moved to get up but I grabbed Liam's hand, I didn't want to be on my own again.

"Get the fuck out before I kill you myself, and if she loses her baby I swear to God, you're dead," Jake growled venomously.

"Jake, please," I whispered, not wanting anymore trouble.

"Baby? She's pregnant? The little slut," my father growled.

Liam was so angry that his whole face was red as he moved to get up again. Just then I could hear sirens getting louder. Liam's face snapped to mine, he smiled weakly. "It's alright now, Angel, helps here. Everything's going to be fine," he said softly. I looked up to see that my father had gone; Jake was standing at the door waiting for the ambulance.

Liam was looking at me, his gorgeous blue eyes tight with worry. I loved him so much, how am I going to cope when he leaves me and go to college, and all I have left is what could have been?

The paramedic came over with Jake. "What's happened?" he asked Liam.

"She's pregnant. Angel, did you hit your stomach or something?" Liam asked, holding my hand tightly. I nodded, scared to move in case the pain got any worse, I couldn't cope with much more.

"How far along is the pregnancy?" the paramedic asked.

"Five weeks," Liam answered, looking at him pleadingly.

"OK. Well let's get you to the hospital; I'll check you over in the ambulance. Does it hurt anywhere else, Amber?" the paramedic asked.

"My back's hurting, and my hips." I winced as he guided me to move onto my back.

He nodded. "That can sometimes happen. It looks like you might be having a miscarriage," he said, apologetically. I nodded in agreement. I knew that already, there was no way I wasn't having a miscarriage, this was just too damn painful to be anything else. Liam held my hand the whole time on the way there, just watching me, not speaking. His face was the picture of grief. He was hurting badly; I could see the pain on his features as he looked at me. He wasn't going to forgive me.

When we got there I was wheeled into a little cubicle and a doctor came in almost immediately. "OK, Amber, I'm going to have to have a look and see if your cervix is open," he explained, pulling on some gloves.

I looked at Liam, horrified, gripping his hand tighter. "Shh, everything's OK. I'm here. Everything's fine," he soothed, rubbing his free hand over my face gently. I cried out as pain shot through me, making fresh tears fall as the doctor did his examination. Liam kissed them away softly, looking at me, heartbroken.

"I'm sorry, your cervix is open, you're miscarrying. We need to do a procedure to speed things along. You're only five weeks so this is that safest and easiest way," the doctor said, throwing his blood smeared gloves away.

"What procedure?" Liam asked.

"It's called an ERPC. It's a surgical procedure. It will need to be done under general anaesthetic and we'll remove all traces of the pregnancy," he explained, looking at me a little sadly.

Surgical procedure?

"That's safe?" Liam asked, gripping my hand tighter.

The doctor nodded. "It's the safest way. We could leave it to expel itself over the next week or so, but that would come with a higher risk of infection. It's best for Amber if we remove it all quickly."

I nodded. I wanted this over; I didn't want to be bleeding heavily for a week, especially if it was as painful as this the whole time. Liam looked at me, waiting for me to make the decision. "OK," I muttered, closing my eyes.

"Right, well, I'll go and make sure there's an operating room free. It's a very quick procedure. You'll come back down here after," the doctor stated, nodding at Liam as he left quickly.

I sniffed and turned to Liam. "I'm so sorry, Liam, this is all my fault."

He gasped, and shook his head fiercely. "Will you stop saying that! This isn't your fault, Angel. Stop blaming yourself. That asshole did this, not you." He bent over me and kissed my forehead softly.

"No. I shouldn't have left your house. You told me to stay there. I should have listened to you, and now I've killed our baby," I sobbed, feeling my heart break all over again.

He climbed onto the bed carefully and wrapped his arms around me, trying not to move me. "None of this is your fault; you didn't kill the baby, Angel. It's just one of those things. You know I'm a firm believer of everything happens for a reason; we weren't supposed to have this baby. You're not to blame. If anything, this is my fault, if I hadn't told him to get off of you he might not have hit you," he said quietly. I shook my head and buried my face in his chest, clinging to him tightly, this wasn't his fault, none of it was his fault. "I love you," he whispered over and over in my ear, until the doctor came back and took me off to the operating room.

Liam walked along the side of my bed until I got to the room and he wasn't allowed any further. He kissed me softly, his eyes bright with sadness and pain. "I'll be right here when you wake up. I love you more than anything," he promised.

I smiled at his words. He still loved me, he still wanted me. I just hoped that he wasn't just saying these things because I was upset and in pain. I prayed that he really did still want me after what I'd done.

~ Liam ~

As soon as she was through the doors and out of my sight, I slumped onto the floor and put my head in my hands. My whole body was hurting. She was in so much pain and there was nothing I could do. We'd lost the baby, and for some idiotic reason she was blaming herself for that asshole doing this. I squeezed my hands into fists, pressing them against my eyes, trying not to think about him. The more I thought about him, the more I wanted to get the hell out of here and rip his head off - but I couldn't do that. I needed to be here for my girl when she woke up. She didn't need anything else to worry about right now.

I believed what I had told her earlier. If we were meant to have this baby, then we would have. She wouldn't have lost it if it was meant to be. I'd always believed that everything happens for a reason - but that didn't stop it hurting like hell to lose this baby. A perfect little baby that I imagined would be just like its momma in every way. I closed my eyes and rested my head back against the wall, waiting for her to come out. I barely even noticed when Jake came and sat next to me, wrapping his arm around my shoulder.

"She lost it," I mumbled.

Jake's arm tightened around my shoulders. "Yeah. She'll be OK, Liam," he assured, squeezing my shoulder.

I was actually surprised that he wasn't kicking the crap out of me for getting his little sister pregnant, but to be honest, I just couldn't care less. He couldn't cause me any more pain than I already felt, the only one that could hurt me more than this was my Angel. She was the only one that had the power to kill me.

After about forty minutes they wheeled her out of surgery, she was still asleep from the anaesthetic. I jumped up quickly, looking her over. "Is she alright?" I asked desperately, skipping along beside the bed as they pushed her down the hallway.

"Everything went well. We removed everything. She'll be fine. She should start to come around from the anaesthetic within the hour. We'll keep her in overnight, and let her go tomorrow afternoon sometime. She'll have to take it easy for a day or so," the doctor confirmed. I nodded and followed her into her room, sitting beside her bed, holding her hand tightly. Jake and I sat silently next to her bed, there was nothing to say, nothing could make this any better.

After about half an hour, she moved her hand in mine. I jumped up quickly as her eyes fluttered. This was the second time in three days that she'd woken up to me like this and I just prayed to God that she never did it again, because I couldn't take any more of this.

"Hey, Angel," I murmured, stroking her face lightly, it was sore looking and was already starting to bruise where he'd slapped her.

She turned her head in my direction but didn't open her eyes. "You stayed," she breathed, a small smile playing on the corner of her mouth.

She honestly thought I would leave her?

"Of course I stayed." I kissed her gently. She whimpered and gripped the front of my shirt weakly as she kissed me back.

"I love you so much, Liam," she whispered.

"I know you do, but I still love you more," I countered. No one ever loved anyone as much as I loved her.

Jake cleared his throat so I pulled away, still holding her hand tightly. He leant over and hugged her. "I'm sorry you lost your baby, Ambs," he said, looking like he genuinely meant it.

She nodded and smiled sadly. "Yeah, me too," she replied, her voice breaking as she spoke.

"I'm gonna go and call Ruby and Johnny. I'll call your parents too, Liam," Jake said, kissing her cheek before disappearing out of the curtain, giving us some privacy.

"Will you lay with me?" she croaked.

I nodded and climbed carefully onto the bed with her. "Are you in pain or anything?" I asked as I wrapped my arm over her gently.

"Not really. It's sore, but nowhere near as bad as it was." She winced as she moved on the bed.

I closed my eyes and buried my face in the side of her neck. "You need to stop scaring the shit out of me. You're seriously going to give me a heart attack soon," I teased, trying to lighten the mood.

She laughed humourlessly. "I'm so tired, Liam." She turned her head, nuzzling against mine.

"Go to sleep then, Angel," I cooed, pulling the sheets up higher around her to keep her warm.

She drifted in and out of sleep for a few hours. They gave her some more pain meds, but she said she was OK. After a couple of hours they let her get out of the bed to go to the bathroom as long as she was accompanied by two nurses - which she didn't appreciate at all.

At nine o'clock the nurse came in, smiling sadly at me. "I'm sorry but visiting hours are over now. I'm going to have to ask you to leave," she said apologetically as she settled Amber back into her

229

bed.

"Seriously? Can't I stay? I won't be any trouble, please? I'll sleep in the chair, you won't even know I'm here," I begged, giving her the face that seemed to work so well on Amber.

She sighed and rolled her eyes. "Fine. But if anyone asks, you snuck in here. Understand?" she asked, smiling and shaking her head.

I grinned. "Thanks." Wow, that face worked on other people too.

Jake said his goodbyes, promising to be back first thing in the morning, and bring me and Amber a change of clothes. Once he was gone, she scooted over on the bed, wincing but trying not to show me it hurt.

"I'll sleep in the chair, Angel," I protested, grimacing at the thought of rolling on her or something.

"Please, Liam?" she begged.

Damn it, why can't I say no to this girl? I sighed and kicked off my sneakers, climbing onto the bed with her. She snuggled into my chest and cried herself to sleep.

I woke really early in the morning to someone shaking my arm. I looked up to see two men standing there, both of them were looking at me sternly. What the hell? Oh crap, I'm going to get in trouble for sleeping in here!

"Liam James?" one of them asked.

I nodded and sat up quietly. "Yeah," I whispered, trying not to wake Amber. Too late, she stirred and jumped as she saw the two guys standing there.

"Liam James, I'm arresting you on suspicion of Grievous Bodily Harm. You do not have to say anything, but anything you do say may be used against you in a court of law. You have the right to an attorney. If you cannot afford an attorney, one will be appointed to you," he stated, as he took hold of my arm.

GBH? That asshole is pressing charges?

Chapter 22

~ Amber ~

I sat up quickly. "What the hell?"

Liam put his hand on my shoulder. "Don't get up," he said sternly. Jeez, the damn silly boy was being arrested and he was still worried about me?

"This is stupid! You can't arrest him, it wasn't his fault!" I cried desperately, looking at the two men who were watching Liam put on his shoes. Why the hell is he being so calm about this? Did he expect something like this to happen?

"There's been a serious complaint, Ma'am. We need to investigate," the man stated, not even bothering to look at me.

"Angel, everything's fine. Don't worry," Liam assured me. Fine? How is this fine? He turned to look at the guy holding his arm. "Can I kiss my girlfriend goodbye? She's just had a miscarriage," he pleaded. The guy's face softened slightly and he let go of his arm. Liam bent over and kissed me softly on the lips. "I love you, Angel. Don't start to stress about me. You need to rest," he instructed, stroking my face gently.

As he went to pull back, I panicked. I couldn't let him go, I needed him. I threw my arms around his neck and refused to let go. "Please don't take him, please? This wasn't his fault, this was my fault, everything was my fault. I should have just stayed at his house. I shouldn't have gone home, please?" I begged, gripping my hands into Liam's hair, sobbing on his shoulder.

"Ma'am, you need to let go now," the same guy stated. I tightened my grip on Liam, probably hurting him but he didn't complain. "Ma'am!" the guy barked.

Liam rubbed his hands up my arms gently, unclasping my

hands from his hair. When he was free of my arms, he pulled back to look at me. He was stressed and worried, I could tell by his eyes. "I love you," he vowed, kissing me gently on the lips again.

"I love you too," I whispered, not trusting my voice to speak again.

Liam stood up and the guy immediately pulled his hands behind his back, putting on handcuffs. Liam's eyes didn't leave mine as I felt my heart breaking all over again. I thought after losing the baby that nothing could be more painful. I was wrong.

I watched as they led him out of the room leaving me on my own. I felt sick. I couldn't let them do this, this wasn't his fault. I could press charges as well, then they would see that my father hit me first, and then Liam would get let off because he was defending me. But they wouldn't let him off for that, would they? Defending me is one thing, but he went crazy, they'll never believe that what he did was self-defence.

I put my hands over my face, trying to think of something. Either way, Liam was getting in trouble for this because my father had pressed charges, even if I pressed charges against my father, Liam's charges would still stand. Self-defence or not, he was still going to be charged with GBH because he *did* do it even though he was provoked. I couldn't take the risk that he would be let off. What if he wasn't? What if he got sent to jail for this, and I lost him?

The only thing I could think of was getting my father to drop the charges. I grabbed my phone and called Jake. He answered on the second ring. "Jake, Liam's been arrested," I said simply.

"What the hell? No way!" he shouted, making me wince away from the phone slightly.

"Jake, look I'm due out of here this afternoon, so can you bring me some clothes ready for that?" I asked, trying to stay calm.

"Yeah, I'll be there in like twenty minutes," he agreed. I could hear him crashing around in the background, probably throwing all of my stuff in a bag or something.

"Thanks." I snapped my phone shut, pressing it against my forehead, thinking. Was there any other way? I just couldn't see another option.

My hands were shaking, I was scared as hell, but I dialled my father's house number. It rang for a long time. Just as I was about to give up, he answered. His voice was thick with sleep; it sent a shiver down my spine. I squeezed my eyes shut. "Hello?" He somehow managed to sound terrifying with one word.

"It's Amber," I said, swallowing the lump in my throat.

He laughed. "And what can I do for you, Amber?"

"I want you to drop the charges against Liam," I answered, trying to sound confident.

He laughed again. "I'm not dropping the charges, that fucker broke my nose! You should see what he did to my face," he shouted, making me flinch. How is it that he still scared the life out of me, and he was only on the phone?

"Please, please don't do this, please?" I begged, trying not to cry.

He sighed. "You want me to drop the charges?"

"Yes," I answered, wiping the tears off of my face.

"Come to my house and we'll talk about it," he stated, sounding amused.

Go to his house? Oh my God, is he kidding me?

"Please drop the charges. You know you hit me first, please?" I begged, feeling the bile rise in my throat, he liked holding this over my head I could tell.

"Come to my house and we'll talk about it," he repeated.

I looked up at the clock; Jake would be here in about ten minutes. "Can I bring Jake?" I asked, knowing that was the stupidest question I'd ever asked in my life. Why on earth would I be allowed to take Jake? If he was anywhere near him then we wouldn't need to worry about charges, because he would be buried by the side of some road somewhere.

"No. Leave that fucker out of it!" he growled.

Oh God, can I do this? Can I really go there and talk to him? Was I strong enough? I knew the answer to that question. I would do anything for Liam, even if I had to kill my father myself to stop him pressing charges. No victim, no crime.

I swallowed my fear. "OK, I'll be there within the hour," I said quietly as I snapped my phone shut, trying desperately not to have a panic attack. I needed to be strong now.

I laid back down in the bed and tried to calm myself. I couldn't be too freaked out when Jake came, otherwise he wouldn't want to leave me on my own. I laid there, counting the foam tiles on the ceiling, trying not to think about anything else. I got to 867 before Jake ran into the room. He looked really tired and stressed. I would bet my bottom dollar that he didn't sleep too well last night. He pulled me into a hug gently and I tried not to wince as it hurt my stomach and hips.

"Shit, Ambs, this is bad." He shook his head, looking both angry and worried at the same time.

233

I nodded; I needed to get him out of here quickly. "Jake, I need you to go to the police station and see if there's anything you can do for Liam. I'm not going to be released from here until this afternoon, so I can't go," I instructed, squeezing his hand.

He nodded, looking concerned. "You sure you don't need me to stay with you for a bit? Are you alright?"

I nodded and smiled weakly. "I just need Liam to be OK. So if you could do that for me, Jake," I requested, nodding towards the door.

He hugged me again. "OK. I'll call you if I hear anything." He kissed the top of my head and put a bag of my clothes onto the floor next to my bed. "If they let you out, call me and I'll come and get you and take you home," he said sternly.

I nodded and pulled him into another hug so I wouldn't have to lie to his face. "OK. Please go see if you can do anything," I pleaded.

"Right. See you in a bit." He smiled reassuringly before turning and running from the room.

I gave him a minute to leave before I pressed the call button on the wall. A nurse came in within a minute. "Hi, how are you feeling today? You need some more painkillers?" she asked, smiling kindly.

I shook my head. "No, I want to discharge myself. My brother's gone to get the car. My mom's had an accident. I need to go," I lied, swinging my legs off of the bed.

"Amber, you can't just leave, you had surgery yesterday," she scolded.

"The doctor said I could go home this afternoon. It's only a few hours early," I countered, grabbing the bag that Jake brought and starting to pull on my clothes, wincing as I moved.

"Amber, you shouldn't be out of your bed yet! Even when you get released this afternoon it will still be for bed rest for a couple of days," she explained, frowning at me.

"Look, I appreciate your concern, but I'm leaving this hospital right now. You can't keep me here against my will. I know my rights. I can discharge myself early as long as I sign a form to say I'm leaving against doctor's orders so that I can't sue you later," I said sternly. She was starting to piss me off; I didn't have time for this.

She looked at me a little shocked before she nodded. "I'll go find a doctor," she muttered, heading towards the door.

"Tell him to bring the forms with him, I don't have time to wait," I requested, biting my lip. I was anxious to get this done; I needed Liam out of trouble, now. I finished getting dressed and packing up my stuff and sat on the bed, impatiently watching the second hand on the clock tick round. Finally, after what felt like forever but was probably about three minutes, a doctor came in looking at me sternly.

"Amber, I don't recommend that you leave the hospital yet," he stated.

I shook my head. "My mom's had an accident; I need to get there with my brother. He's waiting in the car for me, I need to go now. Just show me where to sign." I nodded towards the clipboard in his hand.

He sighed and passed me the form pointing at the bottom. "This is basically a waiver, saying that I've recommended you stay in the hospital and you're leaving against my orders," he explained as I signed my name in the three places he pointed. I nodded and passed it back to him, grabbing my bag. "You need to take it easy, Amber. If you start to feel dizzy or weak, then come back in. If you start to bleed heavy or get any strong pains, stronger than normal menstrual cramps, then you need to come back immediately," he instructed, looking at me worriedly.

I nodded in confirmation. "I will. I need to go. Thanks for looking after me," I replied, already making my way to the door. I didn't stop to look back; I walked as fast as I could over to the taxi rank and jumped in the first available cab, giving them my father's address.

I grabbed my phone and checked the battery, setting up a new family group with Jake, Liam, Johnny, Ruby, and my mom's numbers in it.

I typed a message to Jake, ready to send it when I got there. I guessed it was about fifteen minutes of fast driving from the police station to my father's house - that would be plenty long enough to get my father to drop the charges and for Jake to get there before anything happened. At least, I hoped it was.

When the cab pulled up outside his house I was so nervous that my hands were shaking. "You OK there, sweetheart?" the driver asked, looking at me concerned.

"Yeah, I'm fine. Thanks," I mumbled, handing him the money, taking deep breaths to try and calm down.

I shut the door of the cab and sent Jake the message that I had pre-typed:

'I'm at Dad's. Please come and get me, right now. DON'T CALL ME BACK. Amber x'

Chapter 23

I knocked on the door and held my breath, waiting for him to answer. The door opened almost immediately. There he stood, the man that made me lose my baby, the man that's making my boyfriend stand against charges of GBH. His face was a mess. He was right; Liam certainly did a good job. His nose was strapped and swollen, almost every inch of his face was red and sore looking, and he had two wicked black eyes. I couldn't help but be a little proud of Liam, I knew I shouldn't be, but my boy was a badass.

He smiled. "Amber, come on in. How are you?" he asked politely.

Is he kidding me? How am I?

I walked past him and ignored his question. "Let's dispense with the pleasantries. What is it that you want so that you'll you drop the charges against Liam?" I asked, willing my voice not to betray how terrified I was.

He grinned and turned and walked into the lounge, obviously expecting me to follow. As soon as he was out of sight, I flicked the latch on the door so all Jake had to do was push it open. Then I followed him into the lounge.

Please let this work, please.

"Have a seat," he instructed, sitting on the sofa and patting the space next to him. I knew I needed to stay on his good side, I also knew I needed to stay as close to him as I could, so I made my way over and sat down, turning in the seat to face him and getting ready to run if I needed to.

"So, who's baby is it? Or don't you know?" he asked, sneering at me.

I could feel my anger and grief threatening to spill over because he was talking about my baby. "I lost it thanks to you. Why did you hit me?" I asked, trying not to cry.

He laughed, shaking his head as if I had said something stupid. "You fucking deserved it," he said angrily.

"You hit me and made me fall and lose my baby. That's why Liam hit you," I replied, matter-of-factly.

"That little fucker, he always was trouble," he growled, his hands clenching into fists.

I gulped. Oh God, this wasn't working! "It was your fault. You came around to our house wanting a fight, you wanted this to happen," I goaded.

He nodded; a sly smile crept on to his face. "Yeah, I was hoping to get your fucking brother in trouble, but that little punk from next door stopped him. Jake always was trouble, even when you were kids he used to get in my way," he barked, shaking his head annoyed.

"Jake used to stop you beating me. He stopped you trying to rape me. Is that what you're talking about?" I asked. Oh God, please answer the question!

He looked at me angrily. "Rape? Screw that, it's not rape. You're my daughter; you owed me for all the shit I had to put up with. You were fucking ripe for the picking," he stated, looking me over slowly, making my skin crawl.

My hand tightened around my cellphone in my pocket. "You think you can beat the crap out of your wife and two children for years, sexually abuse your own daughter and try to rape me, and that's OK?" I asked, my voice breaking.

"You lot made my fucking life a misery! You needed a good slap to keep you in line. I was disciplining you, that's all," he spat, getting up from the sofa gripping his hands into his hair.

"Discipline? One time you punched Jake so hard in the stomach that he couldn't eat for a days. You broke his arm, and ribs. You made us all scared to do anything in case we made you angry!" I shouted, trying to provoke him.

He rounded on me and I stood up quickly, needing to be on my feet in case I needed to run. "Jake deserved all of that! I should have fucking drowned that kid at birth!" he shouted, slamming his hand down on the coffee table, making me yelp.

"What about Johnny, Matt and Ruby? Do they need discipline too?" I asked.

He nodded. "Yeah, they all need to learn some respect. Where is Ruby anyway?" he asked, his eyes trying to bore holes into mine.

"She's gone back to Mersey," I lied.

237

He made an angry growling noise and gripped hold of the coffee table, tipping it over roughly. I jerked back as it almost crashed into my feet.

Come on, Amber, you can do this!

"I want you to drop the charges against Liam, and leave town," I stated matter-of-factly.

He laughed and rolled his eyes. "Right, that's not going to happen. I tell you what, I'll drop the charges against that little punk, if you come and live with me," he bargained, looking me over again slowly. I cringed back, feeling sick and slightly dizzy, then I realised it was because I wasn't breathing so I drew in a ragged breath.

"No. You're going to drop the charges and leave town and never bother me or my family again. And when I say my family, I mean Ruby, Johnny and Matt too," I said sternly.

Oh God, this was going to work! I couldn't help but smile; I brought my phone from my pocket and pressed send. I laughed quietly before putting my poker face back on.

He was looking at me like I had lost my mind, making it seem even funnier to me. "And why would I do that?" he asked, his voice coloured with amusement.

"Because if you don't, I'm going to go to the police and tell them everything about what happened when we were kids. Trust me; the time you'll spend in jail will be a lot longer than the time Liam will get. And, you'll be in a much worse part of the jail too, where they put the rapists and paedophiles," I shrugged.

He burst out laughing. "And who's going to believe a dirty little tramp like you? Knocked up at sixteen. I'm a respected professional. I can afford the top lawyers to rip your case to shreds, and besides, you have no proof. This happened so long ago, it's your word against mine," he growled, stepping closer to me.

I felt the bile rise in my throat and I prayed that Jake was close. How long had it been since I sent that text?

"Actually, that's where you're wrong. I have your word too," I corrected, smirking at him as I pulled out my cellphone. He looked at me like I was stupid again. "Clever things phones nowadays, they have all sorts of gadgets in them; cameras, music players, calculators........ voice recorders," I chirped, raising my eyebrows at the last one.

I flicked through the menu and played back our conversation that I had just recorded on my phone. I watched his face with a satisfied smile.

"So, who's baby is it? Or don't you know?"

"I lost it thanks to you. Why did you hit me?"

"You fucking deserved it!"

"You hit me and made me fall and lose my baby. That's why Liam hit you."

"That little fucker, he always was trouble."

I stopped the recording. "Heard enough, or do you want to hear what else is on here? Can you remember what you said? What you admitted to? Abuse, attempted rape," I said, grinning like an idiot. He grabbed my phone and dropped it on the floor, smashing his foot down on it, hard. I fought hard against the urge to laugh. "Oh, Daddy, that phone cost me a lot of money. Do you know how much a brand new iPhone costs nowadays?" I asked sarcastically.

He grinned, obviously thinking he had won. "You've got nothing now." He grabbed my wrist and pulled me closer to him.

I laughed and nodded in confirmation. "You're right. *I* don't, but my family do. I sent it to them just now. Five other people have that recording, and if you don't take your dirty pervert hands off of me right now, that will be going to the police," I stated smugly.

He slapped me hard across the face, making me yelp as his hand crashed into my already sore skin. I held my face and looked at him; I hated him more than I had ever hated anything in my life.

"You drop the charges right now and leave town and never contact us again! Otherwise, I'll make sure that all five of those recordings make it to the police. I'm serious, you drop the charges and leave and I'll let it go. I just want Liam free," I instructed.

I didn't care about anything else. We would always have the recordings; if he ever came near us again I had no problem with pressing charges and get him sent away for good. But I couldn't do that now, Liam would still be facing jail and I couldn't take the risk of him being found guilty and sent to jail for defending me.

My father was looking at me hatefully as he thought about it. I could tell by his angry expression that he knew there was no other option. If he didn't want to be charged with attempted rape, child abuse and a couple of accounts of assault then he needed to go along with what I was saying.

"You're just like your fucking brother," he shouted venomously, as he shook me by the arm.

I smiled. "I'll take that as a compliment. Jake's the best brother in the world."

"You little bitch," he hissed.

I yanked my arm out of his grasp. "Call them now, drop the charges and I want to speak to them after to make sure it's done," I ordered. Oh my God, it's working! It was really going to work.

I heard a car screech up outside and seconds later Jake burst through the door. He looked murderously angry as he bounded towards us with his fists clenched.

"Jake, everything's fine. We were just talking. He's decided to drop the charges and leave town. Right, Stephen?" I explained, sneering on his name. Jake looked at me, shock clear across his face. He grabbed my arm and pulled me behind him, as he glared at my father. Wow, if looks could kill! I gripped his arm, squeezing gently to get his attention. "Everything's fine, Jake, just calm down. I've sorted everything," I stated, fighting the urge to just let him kill him, but I couldn't let Jake get into trouble too.

"Sorted everything?" he asked, his eyes not leaving my father's face who actually looked scared of Jake right now. To be honest, I wasn't surprised he was scared. Jake could be damn scary when he wanted to be.

"Call them and drop the charges," I ordered. My father sneered at us both and turned to grab his phone.

While his back was turned, Jake looked at me. "What's happened? What the hell are you doing here?" he asked quickly.

I smiled. "Check your phone."

He frowned at me, and pulled out his cellphone. "One voice message," he read, opening it and playing it. I watched his face as he listened to it; it went from anger, to shock, to happiness. He looked at me proudly and slipped his phone back in his pocket, wrapping his arm around my shoulders, holding me tightly to his side.

I started to feel a little weak on my feet, I needed to sit down and rest. All I wanted to do was go back to sleep. "Jake, stay calm and finish this, OK? He's going to leave town. I sent that message to Mom, Liam, Johnny and Ruby too, so you just need to make sure he does what he says. I just need Liam free," I said, as I sat down in the armchair behind him.

"You alright?" he asked, concern colouring his voice.

I nodded, smiling. "I'm totally fine. I just need to sit down. You can take it from here, just stay calm," I replied, feeling my body relax knowing that I didn't have to talk to him again. Jake would sort everything out, he always did.

I watched as my father called the police and dropped the charges. Jake called them from his phone and they confirmed that the charges had been dropped and that no further action would be taken against Liam. He was hovering protectively in front of me the whole time, staying in-between my father and me. He really was the best brother anyone ever had.

After about ten minutes, Jake turned to me. "We're ready to go, Ambs." He took my hand and pulled me up from the sofa. He pushed me towards the door in front of him, his eyes not leaving my father the whole time. "You better not come back, old man. Next time I see you, either I'll kill you or we'll be headed to the police station to press charges, all of us. I'm not sure which option I prefer, personally, I'd love to stand there and watch you burn," he stated, with a small smile, as if he was imagining it. He wasn't joking, I had no doubt in my mind that Jake would kill him, and if Jake didn't, I was pretty sure that Liam would. "Leave town today!" Jake growled as he slammed the door, pushing me towards his car. He made sure I was in before heading around to his side and speeding off down the road without saying a word.

After about two minutes of driving he pulled over and cut the engine. His hands gripped the steering wheel so tightly that his knuckles went white. His jaw was clenched so tightly I was surprised his teeth hadn't crumbled under the pressure. OK, I knew he'd be pissed with me! He took a few deep breaths, obviously trying to calm down.

"What the fuck was that?" he growled.

I winced and looked at him apologetically. "Jake, it worked."

"Do you have any idea how freaking stupid that was, Amber? Think about it, what if it didn't work? What if I didn't get your message? What if he had decided to hurt you? Or worse!" he shouted, slamming his hand on the steering wheel angrily.

I flinched. He'd shouted so loud and it echoed in the car making it even louder. "Jake, I'm sorry. I needed to do it; it was the only way I could think of to get Liam free. Now we've always got that recording so he won't come near us again," I explained, pleading with him to understand my reasons. He didn't say anything, he was still really angry. "You should be proud of me," I whispered, giving him my puppy dog face.

He sighed. "I am proud of your idea, Ambs, but that was freaking idiotic. Just because it worked, doesn't mean that what you did was right. You're supposed to be in the hospital for goodness sake. How the hell did you get out? Oh crap, please tell me you didn't sneak out or something and they're looking for you," he said, grimacing.

I laughed and shook my head. "I discharged myself. I'm fine, I just need bed rest, which I'll get plenty of once my boyfriend is out of custody," I said, smiling at the thought.

Jake laughed wickedly. "You know what? I'm not going to shout at you anymore. Liam is seriously going to be pissed with you for doing this too. I'll let him deal with it," he said, laughing as he started the car back up again. Oh crap, he was right; Liam was going to be really angry that I put myself in danger like that. Jake looked at me and laughed again. "Well, I'm glad I don't have to be the one to rein you in all the time now. Liam can take over." He smirked at me and I couldn't help but laugh, he actually looked a little relieved. "Do you need to go back to the hospital?" he asked.

I shook my head. I felt fine, I was just tired and needed to sit down, my body felt like I'd ran a marathon but I wasn't in pain or anything. "I'm fine, honestly. We can go pick up Liam and then go home," I suggested, resting my head back on the headrest. I just needed Liam to hold me.

"They told me on the phone that he'll be another hour at least. They need to process him out or something. I'll take you home and you can wait for him there." He smiled at me reassuringly and headed in the direction of our house.

When we pulled into our drive, Ruby and Johnny came running out of the house, looking at me concerned. "Oh, Amber, are you OK, honey?" Ruby asked, fussing over me as we walked to the house.

"I'm fine. I'm just tired." I nodded.

"What was that message? Did you go and see Stephen?" Ruby asked, frowning.

I nodded and looked at Jake pleadingly; I just wanted to go to bed. "I'll tell you in a bit, Ruby. Ambs needs to rest," Jake interjected, steering me towards the back hallway. I smiled at him gratefully. I couldn't deal with anymore; the reality of what I had just done was sinking in. I'd really been stupid. I tried not to imagine all of the things he could have done to me. I shuddered lightly and pushed the thoughts away, it was over now, nothing happened. I was lucky. Jake followed me into my room putting my bag down for me; I kicked off my shoes and got in the bed fully clothed. He sat on the edge of my bed, looking at me sadly.

"Ambs, I'm really sorry you lost your baby, you know that, right?" he asked quietly.

I nodded. "Yeah, I know. You would have been a kickass uncle," I teased, smiling weakly.

He laughed. "Yeah, I would have spoilt that kid rotten, just to spite you and Liam."

I smiled. "I bet you would have done too."

He bent down and hugged me, kissing my cheek. "You were really brave, and I'm proud of you, but don't you ever do anything like that ever again," he said fiercely.

I nodded and yawned. "I won't. Are you going to go pick up Liam?"

He shook his head. "No, I'll ask Johnny to go and pick him up. I don't want to leave you here until I know that asshole out of town," he replied. I nodded and closed my eyes, needing to go to sleep; I was physically and emotionally exhausted.

I woke up as I felt someone get on the bed. I opened my eyes groggily and looked over to see Liam getting in the bed with me. I burst into tears and threw my arms around him. I'd never been so happy to see anyone in my life. He hugged me back tightly, stroking my hair, rocking me gently as he pressed his lips to my neck, the same as he always does when I'm upset. I tangled my hands in his hair and didn't ever want to let go. I never wanted him away from me again.

"It's OK now, Angel. Everything's fine. How are you feeling?" he asked softly as he pulled back to look at me. His gorgeous eyes blue were looking at me concerned. I smiled and kissed him, pressing myself to him tightly. He smiled against my lips and I pulled back.

"I'm fine. I'm pleased to see you," I promised, tracing my hands down his beautiful face. He ran his hand through my hair, just looking at me tenderly for a couple of minutes.

"Jake told me what you did," he said, his face turning stern.

I gulped and grimaced. "I'm sorry, I had to," I mumbled apologetically.

He buried his face in the side of my neck. "I'm not going to shout at you, if that's what you're thinking," he replied, chuckling against my skin. I let out the breath I didn't realise I was holding and relaxed. He pulled back to look at me. "I am seriously pissed at you though. I hate that you did that, but I don't need to put any more pressure on you than you're already under. You've been through so much already," he said sadly, his hand trailing down to rest on my now empty stomach. "I'm just going to say this; you don't *ever* put yourself in a situation like that again. You *never* put yourself in danger again. I don't care what the reason is; it's not a good enough reason for you to get hurt. Do you understand me?" he growled.

I nodded, I could see he meant it; he was crazy mad, he wanted to say a lot more than that too, but he wasn't because of the

243

baby. "I understand." I nodded, smiling guiltily. "I love you, Liam, so much." He was the most important thing to me. This whole situation just proved to me how much I loved him, I would do anything for him, even face my worst nightmare.

"I love you too, Angel," he whispered, bending his head and kissing me gently. By the time he pulled away we were both slightly breathless.

"Liam, can I ask you something?" I mumbled as he settled down on the bed next to me. He nodded, taking my hand and weaving his fingers through mine. "Do you still want to be with me? Answer me honestly. After I lost the baby and everything, do you still want me?" I asked, biting my lip, terrified he would say no.

He looked at me like I was crazy. "Angel, I've always wanted you. I will always want you. Always," he said fiercely.

I smiled, happiness bubbling up inside me. OK, ask him, come on Amber you can do it. "You said when we found out that I was pregnant that you were thinking about asking me to move to Boston with you," I started nervously.

He nodded. "Yeah." He looked a little confused as to where this conversation was going.

"Boston is an awesome opportunity for you, isn't it? And if you could do anything you would go there, right?" I asked, needing confirmation before I asked him.

He looked even more confused. "Yeah, but it's fine, I want to stay here with you. You're the most important thing in the world to me," he replied, kissing my temple gently.

I shook my head, that wasn't the answer I wanted. "Liam, answer this honestly, don't think about me. The best thing for your career is Boston, is that right?"

He nodded. "Yeah but-" he started. I put my hand over his mouth to stop his answer.

"I want to come with you, if you still want me to. You said before that you wanted to ask me to come with you. Do you still want that?" I asked, looking at his shocked face, he wasn't expecting that at all. He didn't answer; he was still looking at me, his mouth hanging open. "Liam, do you want me to come with you?" I repeated, squeezing his hand gently.

"You would do that for me?" he asked, looking at me so lovingly that it made my heart melt.

I nodded. "Yeah, I'd follow you anywhere if you asked me to."

"But you'd be leaving so much behind, Angel. Your school. Your friends. Jake. Your home," he whispered, cupping my sore cheek gently.

I nodded. "Yeah, but I'd get to be with you, so that makes everything worth it." I shrugged.

"How the hell did I get a girl like you?" he asked, rubbing his thumb over my cheek softly.

"Maybe you were a murderer in a previous life," I teased, making him laugh.

He nodded. "Serial killer," he joked, making us both laugh again. He bent forward and kissed me so softly and tenderly that it made me feel like the most special and luckiest girl in the world.

He pulled out of the kiss way too soon for my liking. "Will you move to Boston with me, Angel?" he asked.

I grinned and hugged him tight. "I'd love to, Liam."

I needed a fresh start. So much had happened here that I just needed to go and start over. I needed to forget everything and look to the future - my future with Liam.

Epilogue

~ 5 Years later ~

~ Liam ~

I glanced down at my watch and gasped. Crap, it was almost two thirty. "Pete, I need to go! Is this gonna be finished or not?" I shouted through to the other room.

"Yeah, boss. Go. It'll be done, don't worry. Call me as you leave and I'll do the last bits, OK? And good luck!" he shouted back.

"Right. Bye, and thanks for doing this," I called as I ran out of the building and jumped into my car.

Oh crap, please don't let me be late!

I sped to the college, panicked, and ran as fast as I could around the back to the field. It was ten to three now and it was due to start in ten minutes. I slid through the crowd, looking for them. I spotted Matt straight away; he was standing up on his chair scanning the crowd. He waved like an idiot when he spotted me and I couldn't help but grin.

I started making my way to them, when a guy stepped in front of me. "Wow, you're Liam James! Can I get your autograph? Seriously, wow, I'm like your biggest fan," he enthused, as the woman he was with fumbled through her purse for paper and a pen.

I laughed. They were all my biggest fans; seriously, I heard that like fifty times a day. "Sure." I smiled politely, holding out my hand for the pen. I scribbled my name and slapped him on the shoulder. "I gotta go get my seat."

"Yeah, of course. Thanks!" he chirped, grinning wildly and looking lovingly at my name on a scrap of paper.

I knew I would never get used to that, people got so excited just because I signed a scrap of paper. I mean, yeah I know that I play for one of the best teams in America, but I'm still just a person at the end of the day. I'm no one special. I'm just Liam, and I'm lucky enough to get paid a lot of money for doing something that I love - not many people can say that.

I made my way through the crowd and sat down at the end of their row. Matt immediately dived for my lap. "Hey, kiddo. Being good?" I asked, tickling him, making him laugh and squirm around.

"Get everything set up?" Jake asked, grinning.

I grimaced and nodded. "Yeah. Christ, man, I'm so nervous." My hands just hadn't stopped sweating all day.

He laughed and shook his head. His girlfriend, Charlotte, leaned over. "You'll be fine. Just calm down," she stated, rolling her eyes. Charlotte was awesome, her and Jake had been together for about six months and he was really into her. She was his first ever real girlfriend, and I could really see it lasting.

I waved to my parents who were grinning proudly, chatting to the random stranger next to them as usual. I smiled; my mom seriously could start a conversation with a mute.

"Hey, Liam," Margaret greeted as she squeezed down the aisle to hug me.

"Hey, Margaret. How are you?" I asked, hugging her back tightly. I hadn't seen her for about four months because she'd been travelling with her new husband, Greg.

"I'm great. Greg couldn't come though; he's stuck in Thailand for some promotion. He's so upset that he's missing it," she replied, frowning.

I smiled. "Well, just make sure you take a load of photos for him then."

Matt jumped off of my lap and ran back to his mom. I smiled at Ruby. Her, Johnny and Matt still lived in Timberfield, but we got to see them quite a bit - they came to stay with us in the holidays and stuff. We had more than enough room, and we also went back there whenever we could.

Johnny and Kate didn't last. They managed to date for a year before they just drifted apart; they're still great friends though. Kate hadn't settled down in the slightest. She's still a flirt and is currently 'playing the field' as she liked to put it, but she's always been a great friend to Amber so she comes to stay with us too. I just have to keep her away from all of my team mates; she would seriously eat them alive.

A lot had happened in the last five years. Stephen Walker,

Jake and Amber's father, got arrested about a year after we left for Boston because he'd apparently been scamming money from his clients. He was currently serving six years for fraud and embezzlement. He never did get in contact with any of them, and they all still have the recording that Amber made of him admitting to the abuse, so if he ever did come back they've agreed they would all file charges against him.

Suddenly, everyone started clapping and my heart took off in overdrive as I scanned the crowd for her. I spotted her standing off to the left of the stage, chatting with Samantha, one of her friends. She looked smokin' hot in her blue and grey ceremonial robes. I hadn't seen her all day. I'd left her just after breakfast. She thought I was at practice today, I wasn't, I was setting up a surprise for her as a graduation present.

Amber was graduating college today with a full degree in dance choreography. I was incredibly proud of her; she'd worked so damn hard for the last few years at college and was graduating with honours. I tried to listen as the little man gave his speech about the graduating class, and then started going through the list of names of the graduates, while they walked on and shook his hand getting a certificate. I couldn't concentrate; I was so freaking nervous that I actually felt sick. I couldn't take my eyes off of her, she was so beautiful. She honestly still took my breath away every time I saw her.

The paparazzi loved her too. They were always following us around, wanting photos and interviews. They loved the story of us being together for five years. They just loved Amber, full stop. She would always be in magazines and newspapers, little pictures of her out shopping with her friends or something. They always thought she was adorable and people would come and ask for her autograph just as much as they did mine. Amber just found the whole thing amusing and would tease the crap out of me when we got stopped in the street or something.

People often ask me how it is that I stay grounded, with the fame and the money, and I always say the same thing. None of that was important to me; the only thing that mattered to me is my Angel. She was the only thing I needed. If everything else went away tomorrow, the big house, all the cars, the money, I wouldn't care. As long as I still got to hold her every night, I would still be the luckiest guy in the world.

I heard the Dean shout her name and I grinned, clapping like crazy. She was beaming as she scanned the crowd; she spotted me and waved her little certificate at me, proudly. I winked at her and watched her skip off of the stage happily. I was shifting in my seat nervously because it was almost over, it was almost time. I rubbed my hands on my jeans, trying to dry them. I'd honestly never been so nervous in my life.

After another few minutes the last certificate was handed out, and I saw her slinking her way through the crowd towards us. As she got to me, she threw her arms around my neck and kissed me. I lifted her off of her feet spinning her in a small circle as I relished the feel of her lips against mine. She pulled back and laughed, she was so happy that it made my heart beat faster.

"Congratulations," I cooed, grinning. She kissed me again and I held her tighter. Damn, five years and I still couldn't get enough of her. I pulled out of the kiss, very aware that her little brother was sitting there making loud kissing noises and singing *'Amber and Liam, sitting in a tree'.*

"Thanks. I was worried when I didn't see you; I thought you couldn't make it." She smiled as I set her back down on her feet.

I smiled and brushed her hair behind her ear. "I wouldn't have missed this for the world," I replied.

She was pulled into hugs by all of her family. Matt, as usual, was clinging to her legs so she couldn't move. He adored his big sister, not that I blamed him, I mean, who wouldn't adore my Angel? You'd have to be crazy. I bent down and pulled him off of her, tipping him upside down by his legs, making him laugh.

"So, what are you guys doing now? Shall we go have a drink or something?" Amber suggested.

Oh crap!

Everyone looked at me. OK, wow, add more pressure, I'm already freaking terrified! "Um…. actually, Angel, I was wondering if I could take you somewhere after. I've got something to show you," I answered, trying not to give anything away.

She looked at me curiously, she hated surprises. "Yeah? What?" she asked, wrapping her arms around me.

I bent and kissed her nose. "You'll have to wait and see," I replied, smirking at her, knowing this was probably killing her. She frowned and narrowed her eyes at me, making me laugh; I grabbed her hands, unwrapping them from my waist. "You ready to go now?" I asked, hopefully.

She nodded and looked back at her family who were grinning like mad people; my mom was crying happy tears. OK guys, tone it down! She looked at them all a little confused, obviously wondering what they were all acting like this for. "I'll see you at ours later then. One of you has a key, right?" she asked.

Jake jiggled his keys at her. "Go. We'll see you later," he instructed, nodding towards the exit.

I wrapped my arm around her waist and we walked towards the front. "So, how did practice go?" she asked.

"Um, yeah good," I lied as I opened the car door for her.

She kissed me again as she got in. She was grinning, obviously proud of herself for graduating. I phoned Pete on the way round to the driver's side to tell him we were now leaving.

~ Amber ~

Something was definitely going on. I glanced over to him again, he looked nervous about something; he was sitting really straight in his seat. This wasn't the normal, relaxed Liam, that I loved to death. After about twenty minutes of driving and making small talk about the weather and my graduation ceremony, we pulled up. He grinned and got out.

OK, where the hell are we? I thought he'd be taking me to dinner or something. I got out and held his hand as he led me forward, stopping outside a building with glass doors. I think it used to be a gym or something, but it looked like it had been done up recently, the outside had been painted a nice cream colour and the windows had been replaced.

"What do you think?" he asked, wrapping his arms around me from behind.

Think about what? What am I missing? "Um, it's great?" I shrugged, confused.

He laughed. "OK, you have no idea what I'm talking about do you?" he teased.

"No. Sorry, lover boy, should I have?" I asked, smiling apologetically.

"Well, see that building in front of you, with the glass doors?" he asked. I nodded, still a little bemused as to what this was all about. "It's yours."

Mine? What the hell is that about?

I turned around to face him. "Liam, I don't understand, babe. I'm sorry," I said apologetically. Damn it, I was ruining his surprise.

He smiled and brushed his fingers across my cheek lightly. "I bought it for you. I've had it all done out inside.... it's a dance studio," he explained.

Oh my freaking God, he didn't! I gasped, looking at him to see if he was joking. He grinned at me. No, he really wasn't joking, he was totally serious.

"Oh God, Liam, you're kidding me!" I squealed as I threw myself at him, wrapping my arms around his neck. We'd talked about me setting up my own studio but he had convinced me to wait a year after my graduation, I bet that's because he was planning this! Jeez, I have the perfect boyfriend! "Thank you, thank you, thank you!" I cried excitedly.

He kissed me gently. "You're welcome. Come on, let's go look." He turned me towards the doors, smiling happily.

I could barely contain my excitement as he handed me the keys. My hands were shaking so badly that I couldn't even get the key in the lock, so he had to do it for me. As we walked through the doors, I was already crying. There was a little reception area that led on to two huge dance studios that had mirrors on the whole of one wall and gorgeous hard wood floors, perfect for dancing on.

"Oh, Liam, this is perfect!" I cried.

He smiled. "I had someone come in and design it all. But if there's anything you don't like, we can change it, OK?" he stated, taking my hand and pulling me out of the door. "Let's look upstairs," he suggested, motioning towards the back.

I nodded and skipped along excitedly at his side. He was always so freaking thoughtful and sweet. He had been the best boyfriend anyone could ever ask for in the last five years, better than I could have ever dreamed.

Upstairs, there was a little recreation room with a pool table and air hockey table, a juice and snack bar with tables. There were even changing rooms with showers and everything. He took my hand and pulled me towards the last door. He looked really nervous again. He wasn't smiling now.

"OK?" I asked, squeezing my arm around his waist tighter. I couldn't keep the smile off of my face. I loved him so much that it was almost painful.

He gulped and nodded, pushing open the door. I looked in to see the room was in semi darkness. There were hundreds of little candles all scattered around, making the room flicker and look beautiful, the candles were reflected in the wall of mirrors. There were red and pink balloons floating along every single inch of the ceiling and some tied to the backs of chairs. There were bunches of red roses everywhere, red and pink rose petals scattered all over the wooden floor. It was beautiful.

I looked at him, shocked; he smiled and pulled me into the room, closing the door behind me. As he pulled me into the middle of the room I could feel my heart trying to burst out of my chest. This whole situation was so romantic that it made my stomach flutter and my skin prickle.

He kissed me softly before bending down on one knee in front of me. I felt my eyes filling with tears and I resisted the urge to shout yes before he even asked me.

He pulled out a little black ring box, lifting the lid to reveal a gorgeous diamond ring that must have cost him a fortune. "Angel, I've loved you since the first time I laid eyes on you. It's only ever been you. It will *always* be you. Will you marry me?" he asked, looking really nervous. Did he really think I would say no?

I swallowed noisily. God, could I even speak? "Yes," I whispered. He smiled a heart stopping smile and pulled the ring from the box, taking my hand and slipping it on my finger, where it fitted perfectly.

He jumped up and grabbed me, kissing me fiercely. I smiled happily against his lips and he pulled back to put his forehead to mine. "I love you so much," he whispered.

"I love you too." Those words just never seemed enough to me. Three little words, how could they possibly cover everything that I felt for this amazing boy?

"Please can I have the first dance in your dance studio, future Mrs James?" he asked, his eyes dancing with excitement.

I grinned, oh God I loved the sound of that name! "Absolutely, future husband," I answered. My heart was beating way too fast. Liam still had the power to set my body on fire with one of his smiles, even after all this time.

He pulled a little remote from his pocket and pushed a couple of buttons, making the music start up. I gasped as the song started. It was our song. Amazed, by Boyz II Men, started and he pulled me closer to his chest, wrapping his arms tightly around me.

Could this boy be any more perfect? I couldn't take my eyes from his as we danced. He held me tightly, one hand moving up to the back of my neck, his fingers weaving into the hair there. My breathing was coming out in small gasps as I took in every inch of his gorgeous face, my fiancé's face. I pressed myself closer to him, feeling his gorgeous body pressed tightly against mine.

Everything about this moment was beautiful and I never wanted it to end. "Liam, could you get any more romantic?" I breathed, rubbing my hand over his chest lightly as we swayed slowly to the song.

He smiled. "I'll try. Ask me again in fifty years," he whispered and he bent his head and kissed me softly, stealing my breath and making my heart crash in my chest.

Surely no one had ever been happier than me in this moment. I had the perfect family, a new dance studio which had been my dream since I was little, and the man of my dreams had just asked me to be his wife. Life couldn't get any better than this; I honestly felt like the luckiest girl in the world.

Made in the USA
Lexington, KY
12 September 2012